A HUGE, ENTHRALLING NOVEL OF CHINA IN THE 1920'S

The Bonnards—young Lucien, beautiful Anne Marie, and Albert, the French consul. Their lives were swept along on the treacherous tides of China's turbulent history.

The French consul lived in a world of deals within deals controlled by the French power-brcker Dumont; by the seductive Corsican police chief of the French Concession in Shanghai; by Johnson, the British millionaire, whose opium and arms empire had suddenly begun to crumble; and ultimately, by the all-powerful Tu Yu-seng, Grand Master of the Blue Band, who, on an hour's notice, could call up an army of 40,000, extort a fortune in protection money from rich or poor, command—from any number of "brothers" sworn to silent obedience—the performance of the bloodiest tasks.

"Sensually rich, intellectually resonant . . . dramatically reveals the patterns of China's network of power . . . Lays bare labyrinthine intrigues."

—*St. Louis Globe-Democrat*

THE FRENCH CONSUL

by Lucien Bodard

A DELL BOOK

Published by
DELL PUBLISHING CO., INC.
1 Dag Hammarskjold Plaza
New York, N.Y. 10017

Dell ® TM 681510, Dell Publishing Co., Inc.

ISBN: 0-440-12527-8

Reprinted by arrangement with
Alfred A. Knopf, Inc.

Printed in Canada

First Dell printing—September 1978

To Marie

PART
ONE

China
1930

The young woman, a mass of black hair over her oval forehead, an enigmatic smile on her face, looked at the entrance to the gorges: a kind of hole. Her husband stood beside her, prudent, dignified, dapper, scrubbed, his mustache well brushed and his part straight, saying the correct words: "Don't be frightened, Mimi." The junk creaked. The Chinese helmsman clung to the bar as if he were being crucified. All around, the waters swirled.

A year ago, in her Anjou village, Anne Marie had been married. And now for more than three weeks she had been sailing up the Yangtze Kiang. Shanghai, metropolis of the white man, the rich man, the gentleman of the tropics, was already only a bubble swept away by time. Afterward there had been a rusty steamer commanded by a drunken English captain with bloodshot eyes. He didn't care a damn for anything, especially the human deposit of Chinese piled up on the deck among their bundles. After that, ports, docks, loading and unloading, receptions in the clubs of the foreign Concessions, banquets, speeches: the exacting rites of colonialism triumphant, a ceremonial mixture of French chatter and British jokes. Whiskey. Red faces over dinner jackets. Chinese servants trained not to hear anything. Eternal conversations about business and the dirty tricks of those yellow bastards. A whole protocol which Anne Marie was learning to observe discreetly under the approving eye of her husband. He would encourage her: "Good, very good. You managed very well." His satisfied smile. Her indifference.

Then came another steamer, older, more decrepit, more overloaded, whose "skipper" was a fat, pale fellow of indeterminate race, what was called an "old China hand." He addressed nothing but insults to his Chinese crew, who wriggled their ribs and shoulder blades and cheeks to express obedience. Everything on board was rotten. A yellow fog hung over a watery universe, an endless, shoreless, muddy, lapping expanse. Rusty waters swallowed up by China, by all sorts of swarming things, by an invisible humanity crowding on planks, rafts, sampans. A floating people. Sometimes Anne Marie glimpsed a scrap of sail, a bit of mast, but these visions slid away and disappeared. One evening there was a bump, a smashed boat, bodies sinking. The steamer didn't stop. The captain was drinking straight from the bottle. The faces of the native passengers were a wall of passivity: unstirring eyes and wrinkles. Anne Marie started and pulled at her husband's arm. "Shh. People don't do that." He was teaching her China.

At last the landscape ceased to be just a void, and there rose before Anne Marie the barbaric magnificence and strange shapes of ancient China. Temples full of monsters, roofs ending in dragons' tails, statues with turned-up eyes, ringed towers like caterpillars standing upright, vibrant with bells. In a creek, on wooden hulls, eyes stared—the eyes of the junks that braved the snares of the water spirits in the gorges of the Yangtze Kiang. The steamers stopped here. To go any farther you had to hire one of the wooden boats.

It was on a Sunday, at noon, that Anne Marie on her junk entered into the nightmare. One of those terrible dreams where you are in a prison both deep and narrow, a dungeon of mysteries. No real daylight, only a gray gleam falling down the smooth bare walls nearly two miles high, parallel, oppressive. At the bottom, the shadowy water. The giant corridor cut by the river through the mountains writhed like entrails. The sheer sides looked flayed alive, the ruddy rock like beef on a butcher's block. Sometimes the gorge grew darker still, murky and funereal.

Anne Marie was afraid. Her husband squeezed her hand. He had come up through the gorges before, in the middle of the monsoon, when the level of the pent-up waters rose by forty or fifty yards and the river was a gleaming torrent. Then the currents were swords, clashing against one another in eddies and whirlpools which tossed boats about like tops until they fell apart. At high water, many junks, especially those going downstream, were smashed against the eroded cliffs, flung by the violence of the rapids, especially where the river, which held them as in a vise, twisted through sharp curves—celebrated and sinister stretches where everything that was destroyed, ships and men, vanished into the depths and was carried down to where the Yangtze spread out over the plains.

Anne Marie's husband acted the strong man. He told her this was the season of low water, when it was less dangerous. But what she saw was a graveyard of junks. Each little cove was full of wreckage. At low water the Yangtze no longer rushes; it scrapes and seethes. Everywhere there were white patches, wreaths of foam around sharp rocks which no one had ever thought of blasting away, and on which small boats impaled themselves.

For hours, for days, Anne Marie was shut in by this geographical cataclysm, this frenzy, these madly zig-zagging gorges. There was the endless thunder of the waves, the monotony. Nature was so terrifying it seemed to blot out the presence of man, reduce it to the tense, intent shapes of those on other junks as they swept along. The junk she herself was on advanced yard by yard beside a notch made in the sheer rocks, a notch that was a path. What dragged and hauled the boat along were lines of naked men roped together and whipped by overseers. These towpath coolies, the dregs of wretchedness, nearly all died by the age of twenty, from blows or exhaustion. Anne Marie could hear them panting.

She and her husband, both dressed in white, some-times looked up toward the tops of the overhanging rocks and wondered whether brigands might not come hurtling down from them. Brigands, the man knew from experience, one had to talk and argue and negotiate with, in a fierce kind of comedy that could easily turn to murder, blood, execution. Her husband's uneasiness gradually infected Anne Marie. It grew a little lighter where she was, as if the gorge were widening out. And indeed, on a cliff face that was less sheer, she could see a kind of wound in the earth, an excavation, a hollow containing a temple towered over by two weathered statues of Buddha.

A bell rang. Prayer or signal? On the coolies' path stood a respectable-looking robed Chinaman, an oily, affable, knowing, jesting smile spread over his yellow face. But behind that smile what threat lurked? What flattery, what enticement, what extortion? The junk stopped, the coolies flopped down gratefully on their

haunches, and the man came on board. He was indeed what the Frenchman with the little mustache
had feared: an emissary of the bandits who had set up
their headquarters in the pagoda. Anne Marie stood
stiff and motionless, as if insensible, and listened to
the harsh gutturals of the dialogue in Chinese between the man and her husband. It began with polite
exchanges and bowing and scraping. Then the visitor's
face grew set, his words conveyed an obstinate demand punctuated by flashes of anger and ending in
what amounted to an ultimatum. Anne Marie realized
that, like everything in China, this was a gamble, with
her head, other people's heads, everyone's head, as the
stake.

Her husband, white as a sheet, murmured to her
in French, "The pirates are demanding two thousand
taels. It's an enormous amount. And if I give them
that they'll certainly ask for more." She could see men
pouring down from the pagoda, with turbans on their
heads and cartridge belts around their waists. "Don't
be stingy," she said to her husband, who had started
quibbling again in Chinese.

An arrow of silver shone out on the Yangtze—boat-
swains' pipes, propellers churning up the water, a
bugle, a tricolor at a masthead, then shells plowing
up the mountainside. It was a French gunboat. The
emissary disappeared, likewise the bandits. With some
difficulty the ship maneuvered up alongside the junk,
and Anne Marie, still oblivious, climbed up the ac-
commodation ladder. Her husband followed. Then a
formal welcome by the naval officers, and it was on
the gunboat that the couple arrived in Chungking.

Chungking is where I was born soon afterward, for
Anne Marie was carrying me when she made the journey up the Yangtze. I may have been the first Euro-

pean child to come into the world in that distant city. The midwife was a navy doctor, a military brute little versed in that sort of operation, and to my infant eyes he applied drops that turned them into rounds of white, like poached eggs. For several weeks I was blind. Anne Marie watched over me calmly; my father was agitated. While I was still in that state I was baptized by Monseigneur de Guébriant, the most famous missionary in South China, a saint with a great hairy face like a wolf. And after I was christened I began to be able to see.

The years went by, and I saw Chungking: a town on a rock thrusting up out of the meeting place of formidable waters, the waters of the Yangtze and of its tributary the Kialing. The city is a sort of scab or patch of mange climbing over the mountain. Above, the palace; below, hovels clinging to the precipice. On the steep slope are giant stairways, stone steps worn away by wave after wave of men in their incessant quest for a scrap to eat or a moment of pleasure.

A ladder town. I took my first steps on those giant stairs, under the protection of Anne Marie, and it was then that my mind was engraved with my first images of China: dung and dead bodies.

Every day on the lowest steps there was held the biggest market in the world for human manure. I used to wander among the fetid tubs, the jars of stuff bought, sold, and picked over so as to arrive at the right consistency, the perfect mixture. There were special brands, special secret recipes. It was the most venerable of trades, but it had its frauds and forgeries. My father stopped his nose, but Anne Marie had learned not to notice the smell, as if nothing could touch her. As for me, from my earliest years I smelled absolutely nothing.

Then I went down the steps to the foreshore of foulness and mud left behind by the Yangtze when it withdrew at low water. There, on poles of bamboo, straw huts clustered like so many pustules, in the seething proximity typical of China. When the water rose during the monsoon, it attacked in waves laden with debris torn from upstream, from the magic mountains of Tibet and the Himalayas. Decaying carcasses became entangled in the pilings of the floating dwellings, themselves disintegrating. It was by the number of corpses washed up that the Chungking officials calculated how high the floods were likely to be. One day I saw a little girl lying on the bank, her naked belly swollen like a leather bottle.

From the heights of Chungking you could see the "gunboats of civilization" lying at anchor on the other side of the Yangtze. A reassuring sight. But when I was three my parents moved farther away, to the city of Chengtu in the province of Szechwan, the most marvelous and the most backward province in China, cut off from the world by a ring of huge mountains. Inside them, as in a natural cage, sixty million men and women still lived as in the days of Confucius. The only signs of modernity were a few tools, and guns. It was the China forbidden to foreigners: no more Concessions, no more extraterritorial rights, no more banks or blocks of apartments and offices. Just beauty and adventure.

I have only dim memories of the long journey. We had to leave the Yangtze behind and strike endlessly into the interior. No roads, just the embankments of the paddy fields and the tracks across the mountains; the power of nature, the blaze of the flowers, the terraced fields, the leapfrogging mountains, and the peaceful villages. The jesting yellow faces. My father had gotten together a caravan of horses and coolies to carry the supplies necessary for us to live in European style. A whole grocer's shop advanced on packs and on shoulders. My father rode horseback, my mother and I traveled in a litter. No holdups. In the evening we put up at inns that were caravanserais.

Chengtu, in the middle of the garden of the Flowery Kingdom, among the red foothills, was still buried in a past that had left behind it, one after the other, a Tartar, an Imperial, and a Chinese city. Feudalism still reigned. There were a score of Europeans, just tolerated by the Chinese.

The town was surrounded by great crenelated ramparts, with four huge gates that were shut at night. There, hung on chains or stuck on spikes, was the day's harvest of lopped-off heads, with bloody gashes, hair matted with sweat and the fluids of death, dirty skin strangely darkened by entry into the Realm of the Eternal Shades, and either eyes upturned and showing only the whites, or, if they had been gouged out, just the empty sockets. These were the heads of bandits, defaulters, troublemakers, people who had displeased the war lord. An order from his lips, his finger raised to point between his plumes and the big curved sword hanging from his belt, and the soldiers seized the prisoners and decapitated or impaled them. In the latter case they writhed like worms on a hook.

But I was happy. I began my city life on men's backs, in a chair carried by bearers. Eight coolies in uniform made up two shifts of four, and they let out great pants and grunts as if I were a crushing burden. This was only to do me honor, to make me think I was majestically weighty. From up on my perch, looking down from my small height, I learned indifference. I dominated the world, the labyrinth of alleys oozing with urine and spit and excrement, with things so obscene and disgusting that even men who were themselves the refuse of society could scarcely eat them. A stinking maze where gloom concealed the unnamable. People in rags, and rags hung out on bamboos to dry. My bearers shoved away beggars, lepers, flesh that was only wounds, scabs, and flies. Unkempt hair fell over sexless faces that had become only agony. But in China these human specters, these creatures eaten alive by hunger from within and by disease from without, possessed a peculiar vigor. That which was not already dead had a ferocious will to survive, a formidable technique for snatching a few more moments of life. Their tactics consisted in gathering together for the attack, in encircling, in returning to the charge, with heartrending cries and piteous litanies, but also with dark and muttered threats, and derisive laughter underscored by mutilated stumps. They went about in horrific gangs—the horror was carefully, crazily calculated. In Chengtu they had their own quarter and their own king, and these tatters of men threw themselves on the wealthy as they passed, not to move their immovably hard hearts but because the privileged were fastidious and would throw them a few coins to keep off the stench. Unless, of course, the beggars picked the wrong person, someone who was really powerful, with henchmen who drew their swords and laid about them to clear the way. My own coolies whacked them aside.

Seated in my chair, I often passed over bodies that were dead or in the process of dying. Starved beggars, concubines who had committed suicide, the putrefied flesh of baby girls abandoned in the gutter, the ruined flesh of coolies who had collapsed in harness, the wretched flesh of peasants who had sought refuge in the city after some famine. As long as he thought he could still go on living, a Chinese would go on struggling and fighting fiercely; but then came the moment of resignation, when he stopped groaning and simply accepted. Before too harsh, too crushing a fate, before the inevitable, he would summon up a last smile, the pride to outface defeat. In the land of the Sons of Heaven, fate was implacable toward losers. But at least a dying man died in peace, alone, in a complete isolation where his last "face" was to accept death. People, bustle, crowds at last drew aside. It was both dangerous and sacrilegious to intervene in anyone's death agony. A gesture of pity toward a man giving up the ghost was an affront to nature, gods, and man that cost dear. It might anger the spirits hovering around the dying man to seize their prey—his last breath. A corpse was a dangerous thing, surrounded by emanations, phantoms, and an aura of hell. The bodies of these unfortunates were not even buried, but thrown into filthy corners, under the crumbling ramparts, or into the river. Mangy dogs were often to be seen devouring human shins or hands.

There was even greater inequality in death than in life. The poor were not buried, while for the rich, death was a celebration. Often, during my excursions, I met wonderful processions of people dressed in white, men and women like walking shrouds. White was the color of mourning. The street would be full of carts and palanquins, halberds, sticks of incense, a world of ceremony. Firecrackers alternated with rattles, gongs, the transports of professional mourners, and the deep singsong of the priests, a kind of plainchant woven around the Buddhist "om," which signifies the universality of the world. A racket to drive away demons. Bright funeral fires consumed paper representations of the departed's possessions, so that they would go with him into the Realm of the Yellow Fountains. For if the rites were properly carried out in this world, he would lead the same affluent exis-

tence in the other. The important thing was piety,
duty, the tablets of one's ancestors, splendid ceremonies to give "face" to the deceased and his descendants. His sons stood grave and rigid behind the
sumptuous coffin, which had been kept for years, like
some object of joy and consolation, in the bedroom
of the now departed. All was decorum. No grief. It
was as if they were incapable of feeling. Anyway, men
in themselves did not count. All that really mattered
was the infinite succession of generations, the stream
of time in which, from father to son, the rich made
sure of having the best of everything in this world
and the next.

Sometimes I was taken to the gates of the city, on
to the grassy sepulchral mounds stretching away into
the distance over the plain. Just mounds, without any
signs or marks. The race of the respectable dead was
there, in those thousands of hillocks. It wasn't a cemetery—only nature taking back men's mortal remains.
But these majestic dead ate up the living poor by
occupying land that might have produced crops.

I liked those peaceful hummocks. I used to walk in
the wind and the dust past human caravans, long lines
of coolies all jerking in a rhythm meant to lessen the
burden of sacks of rice or blocks of rock salt weighing
fifty or a hundred kilos.

How thrilled I was when I was six, and the horse
dealers came to my parents' house to sell them a horse
for me, and how endless the celestial bargaining while
I seethed with impatience! I remember a horse with a
fiery coat, but the colt they selected for me was a bay.
He was lively and graceful, though, like the steeds in
Chinese frescoes. For me, amid the fabulous and
wretched existence of everyday China, horses have
always, ever since my childhood, represented beauty.

In a land where man was a beast of burden, horses, even beneath their packs, even skinny and rawboned and beaten till they bled, were the incarnation of intelligence. The little Chinese horse with its slender muzzle, its quivering nostrils, and its round belly balancing all, trotted on forever, more surefooted than man, more inexhaustible, better at scenting danger, better at climbing up and down the breakers of chaotic nature, the ten thousand steps of the Chinese mountains whence men and things ebbed and flowed. And the horse was as proud and determined as man, too, never dying until all was over. Then in vain did the caravaneer turn his pointed stick in the wound he had made behind the horse's ear to urge it forward. The animal just lay down and shut its eyes, a hunk of meat to be hacked up.

My horse was my title of nobility. From now on I was a lord. Great care was taken to find a suitable mafu for me. At first I was put off by his taciturn mien, heavy features, and half-shut eyes, but he could run behind my horse for hours in his blue groom's uniform. He was to be my first companion.

Riding about, I gradually discovered the peculiar gifts of China: infinite horror, infinite preciosity. They were complementary, interdependent. And it was because of this that Chengtu, a sewer and a prison like all Chinese cities in those days, was also a jewel and a permanent joy.

It contained the extremes of luxury and filth. It was one vast theater of gorging and prostitution. Counterpointing the agonies of the dying were the intellectual pleasures of sharks' fins, sentiment, and singsong girls. The harsh yet fascinating voices of girls calling out the winning numbers in the animal game. Above the shouting of shrews, a background clatter of mah-jongg pieces, showing that life is a game. Girls singing, men painted to look like women, virginities bought, slaves sold, the red chests of wedding processions, the incense and images of Buddha, the prayers of the priests, the beauty of porcelain towers eighteen stories high, the tilted roofs of the pagodas. There were the popular districts, whole quarters of brothels, opium dens, theaters. There were craftsmen's guilds working in full view of passers-by, and the merchants' quarters with their banners and counting frames and forest of written characters. From the hubbub of the street you passed suddenly into a bare and cloistered shop, where all was fastidious silence and a unique marvel was offered for a customer's single glance. The quietness was really a calculated violence, designed to break the client's nerve and make him yield to temptation.

I often used to go into the wood belonging to the great pagoda and gallop about among the venerable mulberry trees beneath the great ramparts—a picture landscape. I was in a dream of lakes and hills, bamboos and rhododendrons, a universe of great peace bathed in mossy light. Sometimes I would catch a glimpse through the shadows of the curved outlines of some nobleman's house, the painted roofs glittering like a rainbow of greens and ochers. The atmosphere was of supreme tranquility. The sentries guarding the lord's yamen did not even have the smooth nervousness of policemen. Peace reigned, and also mystery. For life was hidden away behind the high walls with a large round hole for a door, a perfect circle signifying happiness. Through it I saw concubines and servants bustling to and fro among miniature rock gardens and small but rich pagodas. Birds sang all around—a rare and luxurious sound, for in Chengtu the birds shunned the turmoil of the crowd and kept to the woods of the gentry. Another sound was the ringing of bells. A tall priest in saffron robe went by, his shaven head gleaming in the sun, his hands moving in the automatic gestures of the mendicant.

But soon I would be back again among the hovels and the mob. "Make way for the foreign lord!" my mafu would cry, and I galloped along, my horse whinnying, his hoofs clattering on the road. Urging him on with my stick, I felt that I was crushing my way through the crowd. They scattered before me, falling down with their burdens. I remember one girl striding along to the human dung market carrying a yoke with a reeking bucket at each end, but she fell and spilled it all, losing at once the produce of her family's innards and its bowl of rice for the next day. It was thus I came to understand the great difference between those who carried and those who were carried. Being carried allowed the privileged to cross without inconvenience over the sewer where the rest lived and died as best they could. My horse was my dragon. I toured on until sunset, when the chain-clad doors in the city walls were shut, and the night watchmen started to go around beating the ground with their long sticks and crying out to the people to sleep. But China never slept. Always, in the darkness, there was the same seething murmur.

My way home led me along an alley in the shade of a crumbling wall, an old wall of the Manchu quarter with holes in it where stones were missing. I could hear behind me the heavy breathing of my mafu, exhausted at last. I pulled on the reins, for my horse pranced as it scented the stable, and its shoes made a clatter on the uneven cobbles. Then suddenly I was under the protection of two enormous tutelary gods, red-spotted, solemn, with beards as heavy as hewn stone. These deities flanked the entrance to the house, to guard it against evil. In the first courtyard, with its smooth flagstones, large and somber, the tricolor floated above me on its white pole. For this was the French consulate. My father was the French consul.

My mount pawed nervously at the ground and bared his great teeth, and I jumped off. The mafu crouched down on his haunches in the classic Chinese attitude of repose, that intense and avid science. Sometimes I arrived just as they were striking the colors, and my father, standing at attention among his staff— two white men and the rest yellow—would call out to me to stay where I was. My mother would signal to me from a doorway to come quietly over to her so as not to annoy the French consul. She kissed me but asked no questions. She wanted me to be a gentleman.

The consulate was a large yamen with a series of courtyards, gardens, ponds, humpbacked bridges, lotuses, jasmine bushes, and pomegranate trees where white egrets huddled among the ruddy fruit. There was a whole multitude of turbaned servants. In this enchanted labyrinth stood Chinese pavilions with great lacquered beams, black columns, and fretted woodwork. The tiles on the roofs were like frozen waves, each row of troughs followed by a row of crests, and on the ridge stood china animals to bring good fortune. The windows were of oiled paper on dark frames joined together in weird angles forming Chinese characters. Cardboard lanterns swung to and fro in the dim rooms. Sometimes there was a glimpse of a Buddha through the gloom, for my parents were great connoisseurs of "curios."

But there was in my world one place that in theory I was not supposed to go near. This was my father's office, a huge, solemn place in which he appeared every morning at eleven o'clock. It contained a large desk with sets of drawers; on it were bundles of documents, a bust of Marianne, and a little bouquet of French flags. Two big photographs hung on the wall, one of himself and the other, the same size, of the current war lord, who had appended a flowery dedication. There were greetings from the vice-consul and the head of chancery, two scared and eager little white fellows. But according to my father, one of these was a scatterbrain and the other a bore. Much ceremonial. The French consul frowned as he sat alone contemplating a city seething with plots, executions, true or false wars, and endless bargaining. Nothing was evident—you had to guess, you had to be able to understand. My father applied himself to this task daily in the conviction that he alone knew China well enough to be capable of doing it.

He didn't look Sinicized. He was slim, with a small, dark face in which bushy eyebrows and a prominent nose contrasted with an elegant little mustache and other features that were delicate and attractive. He was very French, in the solemn 1900-picture-postcard style. Lots of charm. Not only was he "the consul," but no one had ever been more the consul than he. Women, including my mother, had to accord him precedence at official receptions. He wore his sword and his braided uniform on every possible occasion. His especial pride were the decorations—all the white elephants in the world, dozens of the kind of medal handed out by exotic kings, on the advice of their French counselors, to all the good servants of France. How splendid my father looked when he was getting himself up, and all the household—including my mother, very reserved—was mustered to help him dress!

My father always started his day in a stiff collar and bow tie. Toward noon he would sigh and tug at his mustache, pick up his goose quill, and begin to draw up a report for the Ministry of Foreign Affairs. He wrote with great care, poring over every comma; nothing must be allowed to disturb him. When he thought he could see daylight through the mass of Chinese confusions in which everything has a meaning but a meaning that is devious and inaccessible, he would call my mother and read out what he had written. She, with her great pure brow and periwinkle eyes turned toward the door, found it tedious, and would go away again, murmuring, "Poor fellow, you do make things difficult for yourself. It won't do you any good." Then my father would start lamenting, a doleful expression on his face. Sometimes, before my mother made off, he said, "You don't take any interest in me and in what I do for France and for you as well. Do you think you'd be a great lady if it wasn't for me? All the trouble I've taken! I've ruined my health." And on days when my mother seemed particularly lacking in enthusiasm, he would collapse; his face would go green. At first he would bravely say nothing was wrong, then he would suddenly gasp, "My amoebas!" A dreadful word that struck terror into Europeans: all white men's intestines were eaten up with them. The lives of all Western ladies and gentlemen were divided between leaden pains and frightful diarrhea; they writhed all through official ceremonies and banquets. My father was much too conscientious to protect his own innards by refusing to partake of fish guts when he sat down to a spread with some war lord.

When he felt well and pleased with life, my father could talk about his amoebas for hours, not shrinking from total clinical detail. His large intestine was his war wound. My mother didn't approve of this sort of joke. "If he wants to be a hero," she would murmur, "why doesn't he go and fight at Verdun?" But she liked it even less when my father talked about his amoebas in the midst of pangs and groans and lamentations. That revolted her—scatological matters were too "Chinese" for her, and by a curious exception she never suffered from them.

On other occasions my father, when he was really pleased with what he had written, would go to any lengths in search of approval. Scorning the vice-consul, a flabby and insipid fellow with fair hair, he would resort to his Chinese interpreters—for though he spoke the language of the province perfectly well, dignity required that he use translators. The priests provided these from among their best catechumens. Every time the interpreters duly produced an admiring chorus of "Yes, Monsieur le Consul"'s. All the long yellow gargoyle faces were bent in the utmost respect, the respect of former choirboys before the monstrance. Lanky bodies cased in narrow robes. Sickly smiles. Perched on the nose of one of them was a pair of spectacles, a recognized instrument of command in China. This interpreter was my father's favorite—he always needed a favorite, someone whose virtues he had discovered and to whom he could unbosom himself. This fellow served as a sort of minor spy. My mother, who loathed him, called him "Fishbone": he was all spine, and the eyes behind the steel-framed glasses were cold as a cod's. One day she came into the office with the chief cook, who was scratching his round hairless face with his dirty hand. All the gossip of the house and of the city eventually came around to his stove, and one day this loyal servant had told Anne Marie: "Monsieur le Consul's secretary is rich. He sells consulate secrets to anyone who'll buy them." The chef repeated this assertion to my father, who had put on his pince-nez to make himself look more severe. He even went into detail about the information sold—the negotiations conducted by my father, who, in the name of France, bought opium for the government trade in Indochina and sold arms to the war lords. Apparently it was the talk of the town. My father was very angry, and sacked his pet despite an impassioned plea by the priests.

The latter were always hanging about the consulate. They were bursting with news and my father often fell back on them for conversation. They were stout fellows and thorough patriots, but sometimes my father would burst out against his ecclesiastical friends, crying, "They're insatiable. Always asking, always harping, always causing trouble between me and the Chinese! What more do they want? They've got a finger in everything, they control the dung trade, they even run the houses of pleasure. And by that, I need hardly say, I don't mean their churches." Father's rage would end with knowing smiles at his own jest.

The person who impressed me most in my father's office was a stunted, wizened old scholar. He had horny twisted nails like claws, five or six inches long and protected by chased silver covers, all that remained of the wealth he had enjoyed as a mandarin, a jade-buttoned imperial subprefect. It was he who undid the beribboned scrolls, magnificently sealed, brought by the emissaries of war lords or great merchants. For nothing could be transacted without countless messages in the form of flowered tubes containing floods of poetry, which eventually came modestly, almost secretly around to the matter under debate—for example, a delivery of arms from the factory at Saint-Étienne. When my father, after a period of intense concentration and fixed expression, had finally concocted his answer, he would smile gaily, and the scribe, his brush forming an additional talon even longer than the others, would set down majestic characters in which my father expressed torrents of humility and stuck to his price. There was magic in that monstrous thin, almost atrophied yellow hand forming the ideograms. Last came the rite of the sealing—a sputter of melting wax, a smell of burning, and the imprinting of the blessed stigmata, the mark of eternal France affixed to the rice paper.

If I went uninvited into my father's office I would get a box on the ears. But sometimes he would send for me to make a fuss over me. Whereas my mother's affection was always something distant, a sort of mirage, my father's was warm, sticky, and sentimental. Sometimes he would exhort me like a schoolmaster. Sometimes he would say almost tearfully, "One day, my son, if you've very good, you'll become a great consul of France—even greater than I am."

My mother often told him he'd lost all sense of the ridiculous. "Yes," he'd answer, "but I've acquired the sense of 'face.' And that's what matters here. Listen, I've got an idea. . . ."

I remember one of his ideas, which was a long time taking shape. For days he stayed in his office, deep in meditation and in a foul temper. If he'd been disturbed by the slightest sound it would have been a disaster. The whole yamen was turned upside down to prevent any noise; everyone went about on tiptoe.

His immediate colleagues trembled. The servants huddled in corners, trying to be as quiet as possible. Whether in work or in pleasure, it is difficult for the Chinese not to accompany their activity with a series of little personal or professional sounds, sputters, splutters, chortles, and expectorations that start deep in the belly and end in a gob ejected like a cannonball. Only fear can silence the Celestial People. So on these occasions they did their best, and my mother used to go the rounds to check the soundproofing. She couldn't bear my father's scenes, and tried to prevent them if she could. She would go through all the courtyards, ironically signing to everyone not to open their lips.

The only one she had trouble with was the laundryman. He was a gnomelike creature, slightly hunchbacked and with a bit of a goiter, a typical mulish and narrow-minded Chinaman, the very personification of obstinacy. He was a conscientious workman, with a mouth like a maelstrom: he damped the linen with a spray of water directed through his stumps of teeth, using his tongue simultaneously as suction and force pump, both very loud. It was an age-old technique, and the poor fellow was astounded when my mother told him to stop it.

So the consulate was a palace of supreme quiet, until there came to my father's ears the distant echo of an argument between a grumpy old amah and a young amah who didn't show sufficient respect. It was enough to split my father's eardrums, and he summoned the head boy, who came in with a smooth cool face, ready to ride out any storm. The sovereign over the other servants expressed a million regrets for his unworthiness, but how was one to impose silence on such stupid creatures as women?

My father, his face still furrowed, had no answer for this. But he remembered that he'd found a hair in his soup the previous evening, a thing he couldn't abide. For the Chinese, a hair in the soup was a matter of no importance, but in spite of his Sinification my father still had some of the white man's peculiarities. The head houseboy had been trained to put up with foreigners' funny ways. It was his job. But that day my father reviled the chief of the domestic staff more than was fitting. The man put up with the insults without showing any sign, but a certain pink, a tea-rose pink, began to show in the yellow of his cheeks. This was a sign that his Ch'i might overwhelm him at any moment. Ch'i was the spirit of violence shut up inside every man, and my father knew only too well that any Chinese in the grip of it, war lord or houseboy, turned into a wild beast. So he cut his harangue short.

It was at this point that I came on the scene, only to receive a clip on the ear. My father started to limp, complaining that I'd stepped on his foot. It was a well-known fact that he had extremely sensitive extremities. But this time I felt I was being unjustly accused, and began to cry. My mother came in, shrugged her shoulders, took me by the hand, and led me away.

My father was stricken with remorse and prowled round and round his office. My mother didn't speak to him. She put me to bed, and next morning when I woke up my father was there beside me.

"A few weeks from now you're going to be proud of me," he said. "I'll take you with me in a marvelous procession. It's an idea I've had."

The silence was over, and the consulate came to life again. My father's meditations had borne fruit, and wreathed in smiles he explained to Anne Marie. Chengtu had just fallen into the hands of a new war lord, who had to be won over by some wonderful present. Why not a white enamel bath, the first ever to be seen in Szechwan, to be handed over with great pomp and ceremony?

Anne Marie hadn't much confidence in the ceremonies dreamed up by her husband.

"Why don't you give the bath to me instead of presenting it to that ruffian?" she said. "Besides, you only risk being humiliated."

But the consul stuck to his guns, and one day the diplomatic bag from Shanghai contained an especially large packing case. It was lugged onto steamers and junks, and borne along by porters. No one was at all surprised. My father was famous for the size of the bag he had sent to him every month. It always contained tons of packages marked "Secret," as if they held state documents, but in fact the contents were mostly the goods necessary to my father's type of diplomacy; wine and spirits were his primary arguments in negotiating with the war lords. A few months before, some coolies crushed beneath their burdens had slipped into a reeking but valuable tank containing dung for the rice fields, so that through the feces rose the bubbles of champagne designed for toasts to Franco-Chinese friendship.

At last the bathtub arrived in Chengtu, though apart from my parents, no one knew what it was. My father recruited hundreds of vagabonds and put them into the livery of the consulate servants and got up a great procession with drums, dragon dances, banners, firecrackers, censers, perfume braziers, and litanies by the Buddhist priests, who had settled their fee beforehand. Father rode on horseback in the middle of the column in his best braided uniform with cocked hat and sword, followed by the bath borne carefully along by the sturdiest of the recruits. I was beside him, and we rode amid banners proclaiming in giant characters that my father was humbly bringing the great general a present in token of eternal alliance. The general, in the form of a huge photograph, already hovered over the gift that was on its way to him.

Through the medieval alleys we went, among a crowd of onlookers. Anything out of the way in Chengtu produced an immediate flood of humanity, which submerged everything and surrounded it all with jests. For the ordinary Chinese, anything unusual that was not a catastrophe was regarded as a joke, and that day the only catastrophe was a thump or two from a truncheon, delivered by soldiers hastening up to clear the way. The effect was miraculous; the crowd parted. The Chinese, pleased and laughing, considered the affair an excellent idea, full of "face." My father was delighted with himself.

The procession passed by gates, bridges, and the sentries guarding the general's palace, and arrived before the war lord himself in the flesh, at once surprised and stately in the main courtyard. The object was handed over; there were speeches and an unleashing of gongs. There was even a review of troops in front of the bath—the general didn't know it was a bath. It was impossible to explain, for fear of making him lose "face." The ceremony was lengthy, with all present starchily serious, their faces simultaneously solemn and wreathed in typical Chinese smiles which only added to their gravity. It all went off very well. The great war lord had his present carried to his gynaeceum by his guard of honor, for the concubines were curious to see this mysterious object. My father and his procession took their leave. In the course of the days that followed he learned that no dignitary had yet had the courage to tell the war lord that the thing was for washing in. The war lord himself decided it must be a kind of large saucepan. And so the bath perished in flames.

However, because of the bath the war lord found himself in my father's debt, and could not refuse his next request. And so it happened that a few days later, because the national prestige of France had been insulted in my small person, I was the cause of two men's being tortured to death.

One day I came in from my ride with my cap grazed by a bullet, probably some stray shot. The French consul, who had a great sense of the dignity of his homeland, at once put on his famous uniform and went and demanded justice and reparation from the general. The latter expressed his own indignation and promised to make resounding amends. He didn't go into detail, but made an appointment for the following morning at ten o'clock on some waste ground outside the north gate of the city that was used for military maneuvers. My father wasn't an early riser, and he and I arrived late at the appointed place, an enclosure surrounded by barbed wire and without any spectators. In the middle were two posts, and two executioners were addressing themselves very professionally to the two men tied to the stakes. They were in the process of dismembering them alive. By the time we came on the scene they already had practically no arms, shoulder blades, or ribs. They were just lumps of meat and shrieks, which were exhibited to us to the sound of bugles, the degree of our gratification being carefully observed. My father declared the honor of France amply satisfied. He was careful not to say it was more than he'd asked for: that would have been a grave insult to the war lord, who showed the degree of importance he attached to the French consul and his honorable scion by the degree of torture he imposed. We left, but the execution continued.

My father, somewhat shamefaced and horrified, couldn't help saying pompously to my mother when we got back:

"So that's all right. But if the general wanted to show us his generosity, why didn't he have the execution in the city with the whole population looking on? That would have been a greater act of reparation, with some political meaning. But I suppose that would have meant admitting he was partly responsible for the offense, and he would have lost 'face.' Such are the subtleties, my dear Anne Marie, that are the soul of Asia."

Anne Marie looked away. "So you're proud of your exploit, are you?"

I, at any rate, felt like a hero, for the amahs congratulated me and the servants all crowded round. It was my initiation into cruelty.

Would I have been struck with remorse if I'd been told the poor victims hadn't done anything? That obviously they hadn't fired at me—they were just coolies picked up in the street, or more likely prisoners in some jail, for the war lord wouldn't have gone to the trouble of trying to find the real culprits, who, more likely than not, were some of his own soldiers.

I lived in happiness, as did both my father and my mother. All three of us shared in the felicity of China. When I was still quite young I realized that in China all was joy, and that life was stronger than death.

But already I had a vague feeling that my father's

attempt to be Chinese was a bit forced. In actual fact
he was a grind, with the whims and vanities of a
despot together with a sort of "poor white" vulgarity
in which sentimentality and imperialistic cynicism
mingled. It was my mother I admired. All the servants
in the consulate loved her. There must have been fifty
or a hundred of them, all wearing white robes and
blue turbans: houseboys, laundrymen, cooks, messengers, watchmen, bearers, mafus. They were very well
off, as you could see if you watched them crouching,
a dozen at a time, around piles of steaming rice, silently savoring the delight of swallowing, putting food in
their mouths with a smooth and incredibly rapid
rhythm of chopsticks. These servants were great lords
themselves, with their own servants who cooked huge
meals for them in caldrons and were allowed to eat
what was left over. They all rose and bowed when my
mother appeared.

My mother knew instinctively that it was no use
lecturing the Chinese, shouting at or rebuking them,
giving them orders and making scenes when they
didn't or wouldn't understand; when after saying "yes"
they went and did something that ordinary nagging
European women considered completely ridiculous.

Anne Marie never lost her temper. To begin with,
she was aware that she was a woman, and therefore
an inferior being even in the eyes of a manservant. So
she was never cross, and never raised her voice. The
most she ever said to the servants—in Chinese, for
she'd learned the language of the province—was:
"Your way of doing it is good, but try mine—it may
not be a bad method either." This technique produced marvelous results. For example, the cook
stopped blowing his nose with his fingers, and the
gardener no longer used dung from the lavatories to

manure the vegetables in our kitchen garden. True, this was partly because he realized it was in his own interests to depart from this age-old and sacred principle, and sell the products of the consular innards in the town.

My mother was always tranquil and relaxed. She could guess things. She guessed the gardener shared his profits with the other principal servants in accordance with a strict internal hierarchy—not the official hierarchy, but a secret and purely Chinese one. She ruled through the happy medium. She never asked for her share of small household profits, as a Chinese number-one lady certainly would have done. And unlike the European ladies who wasted their time checking unverifiable accounts, she never quibbled. In China nothing was clear, figures had no meaning, you had to trust people.

I never heard my mother say to a servant who'd filched something, "This time you've gone too far." My father had explained that you mustn't catch a Chinaman red-handed unless you have it in your power to have his hand cut off. To accuse a man is to humiliate him, he said: to defend his honor he is obliged to pile up such a complicated structure of lies and denials and stratagems that the accuser is left bemused, with the feeling it is he who has committed a wrong. But despite what he preached, in practice my father often let himself get carried away, and then he would see the object of his invective turn on him in the Chinese manner, with innocent wide eyes, indignant protests, haggard looks, and all the other features proper to the victim of a miscarriage of justice.

Anne Marie never made this kind of mistake. She knew how to let herself be stolen from: not too little, which would have been unworthy of her position, and not too much, which would have made everyone take her for a fool. If anyone went too far she didn't say anything, but just wore a special expression. The fact was that the servants as a whole had established their own just rate of theft, and they kept to it, whereas in badly run houses they had to invent tricks in order to obtain what was regarded as their rightful due. Everyone had his pride in our yamen. Everything went smoothly: for the servants, who were left in peace, and for my mother, who didn't have to exercise much more than an amused vigilance. The reason was that while China was a terrifying place for many people, for her it provided constant entertainment. The labyrinthine workings of the Chinese brain produced results which never failed to delight her. For instance, when she met the gardener, an old man with wrinkled terra-cotta cheeks, enriched with his ill-gotten gains, she would ask: "Most honorable ancestor and grandfather, is the market price a good one today?" This was considered a subtle allusion, showing both my mother's perspicacity and her sense of propriety.

Everything about Chengtu seemed quite natural to her, even finding a cobra in her bedroom, seeing a basketful of heads left lying near the porch of the consulate, or having a machine gun leveled against her window. Though she was usually the only lady present, she was perfectly at ease in her lace tucker and flounced skirt at the ceremonial blowouts with the war lord. It was with a benevolent Gioconda smile, a curve of the lips, that she listened to the bragging of the missionaries and the jeremiads of the nuns. Nothing surprised her, not even finding herself in a junk swept away in the floods or among the living dead of a famine. Every morning she coiled up her hair and made the rounds of the yamen, inquiring about the events and misfortunes of the day with an easy simplicity that gave her "face" without the least effort. Even the successive war lords had a respect for her which went beyond mere politeness, and showed her special consideration. They didn't make her the showy presents they gave to the women of barbarians, but sent her delicate finery symbolizing a homage that came from the heart. The fact was that they had a sense of dignity, and they honored the dignity of my lady mother.

What really counted in Chengtu, however, was not the opinion of the war lords but that of the servants, who had a sort of propaganda about her among the people that protected her like a shield. I loved going with her through the narrow streets of the town. Often we went into the old city, with me riding on horseback behind her sedan chair. Whereas the Chinese ladies with their bound feet were hermetically sealed up in litters, the curtains drawn so that they should not be sullied by the eyes of the mob, my mother was carried along openly, in broad daylight. And she never had any trouble. There was never any jostling designed to topple her from her heights, nor any of those obscenities that are the most terrible in the world, nor any crowds of soldiers or beggars obstructing the way. And yet, showing herself like that to everyone was, for the Chinese, unseemly.

So she floated along above what was seething below. She didn't see the prostitutes or the lepers or anything else that was too macabre. It wasn't that she averted her gaze; it was just a decent ignoring. And it led us to beauty. Generally we went to the shops of the rich merchants in the streets of silk, of bronze, or of lacquer—the district of precious things made for the delight of the rich.

The chair would be lowered, a rhythmic movement of the coolies which allowed my mother to alight and walk along on her unbound feet, leading me by the hand. We would go toward a cavernlike shop protected by fences and rows of posts, which could be closed whenever necessary with huge clumsy padlocks. After going along by bare walls and corridors, I would follow her into a big empty room. Semidarkness reigned, relieved by the red tips of burning incense sticks, and we were greeted by the voice of a woman scarcely visible because her silver-gray robe was the same color as the half-light. In one corner, above a red glow which was a lacquer chair, there gradually arose what looked like the head of a tortoise. It was the head of an old man so ancient it took him almost a minute to heave up first his head and then the rest of him. The slow unfolding revealed that the venerable old gentleman wore an antique robe embroidered with animals symbolizing good fortune. Everything was distant, muted, belonging to another world: the world of treasures. For my mother great hidden chests would be opened, object after object brought out, ancient statues, old porcelain, fretted ivories, draperies on which warriors in red masks did battle. There were jades in every shade of green, Tibetan tapestries full of black devils, Buddhas with flowery navels, Indian statuettes of gods embracing. The slowness of old age accorded well with the ancient's task of lifting each marvel out of its ebony or sandalwood case and offering it up for contemplation, admiration, and lust. I already sensed that in China trade was a kind of delicious torture: there was an immemorial technique for arousing desire in the purchaser and for sizing up the strength of it. The price was determined by the amount of desire. Gesticulation and playacting in bargaining were purely conventional, good enough for the common people. What really mattered was for the voice and what it said to be neutral, for hidden passions to vie with one another in apparent disinterestedness. My mother spoke Chinese with an Angevin accent, and her quietness acted in her favor. She used to come home with the choicest of pieces, and when she showed them to my father he would be vexed at not having found them himself, and say they were probably fakes. But in China fakes can be four thousand years old.

Every so often a few stout fellows would come to the consulate carrying enormous bundles on their backs, from which they produced gods, vases, perfume braziers, and other things that they sold very cheaply.

This used to happen after some great disaster, a flood or drought, when the survivors bartered such articles for rice. Usually the war lord's troops had seized some small town, as I learned from my mafu, who had once been a soldier. He used to tell me about his former profession:

"It's very difficult to make anything out of looting. As soon as the people hear any troops are on the way they bury all their possessions. The peasants have ancestral hiding places for their rice and salt and cabbage stumps. In the cities the leading citizens have long ago set aside secret rooms to hold their bars of silver and gold, and they go and hide there themselves with their sons and their favorite concubines. You have to work like a mole and look out for the least gleam of light, the least chink that might lead to a corridor or a hole. When you find someone with possibilities, you often have to roast the soles of their feet or slit their bellies open to make them talk. You promise a servant or a child slave his life on condition that he betray his master. And you have to examine every square inch of a town or village before you set it on fire. The best thing is a nice fat pagoda. The priests curse you, but what do you care?

"It's a tough business, because what you grab, other people grab from you. They kill you like a dog. The officers insist on having their share. I never got rich myself. I marched, I carried heavy loads, but everything I ever got was stolen from me. And the things that were pinched from me always ended up in Chengtu, with the rich. The rich people here get richer on what's stripped from others who used to be rich in the provinces."

My mafu recounted his misfortunes gaily, and his laughter was one of the permanent lessons I learned from Chengtu. I saw the same teaching everywhere—on the face of the old scholar in the consulate, on the faces of the servants. For a Chinese, misfortune, whether his or another's, was always a subject of jovial, positive, cynical, pitiless amusement. The reason was pride. One must show one was unmoved, immune, superior to fate. Above all one must not admit to being a victim, and must laugh at all who were. I, too, learned to feel nothing and just to laugh when my father scolded me.

My mafu was unusually stony-faced—he had a thick, square, almost featureless countenance with eyelids just revealing dull slits of eyes in which you sensed slyness and brutality, but where vague gleams proved he had feelings. He used to run behind me like some great strong beast, a beast I guessed to be dangerous, but one that became completely devoted to me and began to talk to me. His life had consisted of wars and massacres, and while he told me about them his face lit up with pleasure. He looked after me like the apple of his eye, his hand always resting on a big cudgel as he guided me through the dangerous alleys of Chengtu. He was my friend.

In the yamen I was coddled and pampered by my amahs, nurses, and maids. They loved me first and foremost as a young male, contemplating, praising, and gloating over my virility. It was a great source of pleasure to them. They laughed to see that white men were different from Chinese, but that just the same they were quite normal. For among the common people the tale went that white men had monstrous, diabolical sexual organs, with torturous barbs and thongs that ripped women to death. Thanks to me my amahs knew this was not so.

My chief amah, the one who was my second mother, was called Li. She had a big snub-nosed face that was always hovering over me, a face like a bowl or a lamp. She was a young peasant, and her feet had never been bound. She used to rock me to and fro in a hammock hung between two pomegranate trees, and to send me to sleep she would lavish on me, in accordance with the custom of the country, what people in the West might find somewhat extraordinary caresses. Fortunately Anne Marie never suspected. She did forbid my attending magic ceremonies for driving away evil spirits. She knew that every so often the servants used to meet in the garden in the presence of a sorcerer, a cripple in a dirty robe, with a wart on his forehead like some revolting third eye. To me in my room, it seemed that my hyperactive senses actually experienced the sounds, the lights, the perfumes of the ceremony. I knew Li was out there throbbing with excitement in the front row. I knew that once he had been paid, the officiant was piercing himself through with a sword and driving great twisted nails into his flesh. Then I went to sleep.

Because of my amahs, the first language I spoke was that of the Celestial People. I was a little white Chinaman brought up on legends. Li often told me terrifying stories full of monsters, winged serpents, demon kings, and man-eating dragons. But she said I would triumph over these horrors, these emanations, wraiths, dreams and nightmares, though they seemed like real creatures and real threats. I bore the signs of good fortune, she said, and one day I would be a king of heaven. Meanwhile, during the day, I went bare-assed, according to the local fashion. In Chengtu rich people's children, muffled up in thick silk, their cheeks painted, had a sort of flap let into their trousers, leaving their precious bottoms bare to do their delicate little businesses, which were carefully collected. Mine, to Li's great regret, were not used to nourish the asparagus and artichokes that were the pride of my mother's kitchen garden—she was the first to introduce Western vegetables into Szechwan. My mother spent her time disinfecting everything, but I, with my amahs, stuffed myself with Chinese soups, rotten eggs, pickled beans, and palm worms. But just the same, I found it humiliating to have my behind exposed, and it was this that caused my first anti-Chinese rebellion. I won, and they dressed me as a sailor boy. I led a delightful life. My friends were the sons of the consulate coolies, naked urchins with big bellies and little dangling penises. Following after each boy was a dog specially trained to lick his bottom clean with its long tongue when required.

In the monsoon season, when the clouds hung over the earth like sticky, dripping giants, when the rivers overflowed and the water dragon came, the amahs gave me a young female panther as a present. I played with this living bundle all day, and at night it was shut up in a little tower with a barred window. But one stormy night when the sky was like the fire snorted out by demons, the panther, terrified, broke down the bars and jumped out the window. The rope she was tied to held her in midair and strangled her. It was my first sorrow. I was so grieved my amahs put on their mourning clothes and we had a real funeral, with all the servants taking part in the procession. I, too, was dressed in a white robe, and my mother gave permission for us to send for a very pious Buddhist priest. So there were gongs and litanies, and my panther was laid to rest under a mound in the garden.

Then my amahs gave me tall marsh birds—flamingos, cranes, and herons—which would stand stockstill on one leg for ages in a little pond down in the garden. Their eyelids had been sewn up to prevent their flying away, but my mother found out and gave orders for them to be unsewn. They lost no time then in flapping off toward the distant marshes. I was furious with my mother.

I grew in wisdom and experience. Much more than my parents, I inhabited the real China, among my amahs, my mafus, and the servants who gave me chopsticks so I could eat with them, like them, and among their children scuttling about like rats. In the street I was friendly with the sellers of soup and cakes, and with the old scholars who had set up shop as public scribes. Through my mafu I got to know carters, muleteers, water carriers, and even soldiers. But the most important thing was that my amahs got into the habit of taking me into town with them. My mother was told we were going to see the nuns, but we always hung about the Buddhist monasteries and the soothsayers who consulted strange herbs and scraps of flesh. The auspices were good. But I didn't tell Anne Marie.

When I went with Li we rode in her sedan chair, a wretched rented affair carried by only two coolies. Inside, she would take me on her knees and rub her nose against mine. Her long black pigtail swung about behind her back, and I would pull it and make her jump and laugh. One day she said she was going to introduce me to some princesses. We stopped outside a sort of dirty temple. It was a theater where they showed the age-old grand operas of *The Three Warring Kingdoms*. A great crowd, shouting, hawking, spitting. The floor was covered with refuse, including the results of people with colds blowing their nose by stopping up one nostril at a time. Firecrackers were exploding everywhere, the empty cases littering the ground like great red petals. Beggars in the last extremity ate bones and scraps as they fell from the mouths of the audience, who never stopped chewing. Waitresses in blue served tea to spectators who brandished coins, the jet of hot liquid falling accurately into the cup. All was confusion, with people fighting and yelling. Grunts of satisfaction came from the crowd: the Chinese masses loved excitement.

There was plenty of excitement on the stage. An emperor of the Han dynasty stood there wearing a terrifying red mask, the mask of majesty. He rolled enormous eyes through the slits of his mask; his brows were coal-black thickets, his beard an inky river. He wore a three-cornered hat with curling plumes, a bunch of flags hung on his back, his robe was inhabited by dragons. His voice was like thunder, thunder that shrieked, that sang, that fell into silences, unleashing drums, gongs, tambourines, and flutes. There were bangs, rustlings, acrobatic trills—music like some wild and cloying enchantment, slow yet frenzied. Everything built up toward the climax. The emperor had finished with tirades, arguments, deductions, and was pronouncing sentence. In hoarse roars he ordered his henchmen, who were hopping around him like fleas, to put his daughter to death: she had been lacking in filial respect. When the father's voice died away, the prisoner appeared to play out the classic scene of fruitless supplication. Feminine tears only gave the emperor the chance to show even more severity, the pleasure of cruel duty, the great Chinese virtue.

The princess, her hair scintillating with a thousand jewels, came forward on her mutilated feet, spreading out her arms to keep her balance. She moaned like a dove, rolling up her eyes, faintly rippling her hips. Within her silk sleeves her hands implored, the fingers holding a gauze scarf to hide her face and conceal her emotion when the fatal verdict was uttered. The Chinese audience, who never cried in real life, wept. The executioners seized the princess and led her off to death, the sound of their instruments rending the air like steel. The princess was slain. But I knew she was still alive, and that I was moved by her.

I wanted to share my theatrical experience with my parents, and I showed some emotion as I told my father about the princess. He laughed and twirled his mustache.

"Your princess is a man. All theater princesses are men."

And he turned to my mother with a mixture of pedantry and ribaldry, of scandal and delight, and whispered something I was not supposed to hear:

"These actresses are all catamites who are neither one sex nor the other. They're great favorites with the rich men here. Even the general's quite a connoisseur."

My mother was shocked, not by what he said but by

the way he said it, by the act he put on, the combination of prudery and coarseness. A twitch of annoyance passed over her face.

As for me, without knowing why, I didn't feel like going to the theater any more. But dear Li introduced me to other pleasures on our excursions in the sedan chair—pleasures bestowed by the new war lord, anxious to entertain and instruct his people at the same time.

The new war lord of Chengtu was "modern." He assumed the title of marshal. He was no ex-vagabond or former monk who had got to the top through cunning, belligerency, a bloodthirsty sense of humor, and a genius for stealing, impaling, and forming brigands into an army. The marshal of Chengtu was a person who had been educated in a military academy and had even studied the modern sciences. And to please the population of Chengtu he added to the refinements of the past the refinements of progress. He had an orchestra in frogged uniforms, with brass and trumpets, the army band, which had learned tonic sol-fa. He'd sent for a bandstand from Shanghai, and it was installed with great ceremony in the main square of the city, which was also the place of execution. Sometimes the two orders of activity were combined. On holidays the band would play Beethoven or pseudo-Beethoven, and the elite of the town would gather for the show: the celestial gentlemen in their robes and the celestial ladies with their bound feet, stumps that contrived to be at the same time a sort of excrescence—all were there with their families and children. They listened to Western symphonies mingled with drums and firecrackers. And they listened also to screams. For a naked man was tied to a post on the rostrum, and

between each musical selection the executioner cut
off another piece of his body. He flung the bits into
the crowd, who jostled one another gaily so as not to
be hit or splashed with blood. Meanwhile the victim
was still alive, becoming armless, legless, a bleeding,
shrieking trunk. Everyone was agreeably entertained.
Li laughed in her enjoyment, looking younger and
more charming than ever. She lifted me up over her
head to get a good view. The whole gathering was delighted and expressed its satisfaction. All around us
people were saying how good the marshal was, a great
man who'd brought such peace that order could be
maintained with just a few tortures and executions.

This seemed to me so patriotic and virtuous an occasion that I mentioned it to my parents. My father as
usual made a few scholarly and didactic comments.

"My boy, what you've just seen is mere butchery, a
sign of the decadence of the times. The fellow was cut
to pieces and bled like a pig, and he was dead in a few
minutes. In my time I've been present at a genuine
death by inches, a real anatomical dissection. First
they removed just the muscles, from the chest, the
arms, and the legs. No vital organ was touched, and
the dying lasted days and days. The skeleton was undressed of its flesh, and when nothing was left but the
bones, they were first dislocated and then broken.
Finally they cut off the head."

Again a nervous shadow crossed my mother's face.
"Stop it," she said. She sent me to bed, and began to
rebuke Li severely. Li was astonished and didn't know
what she'd done wrong: wasn't it a good thing for a
child to see crime punished?

In 1918 and thereabouts, Chengtu was full of the
blessings bestowed by the new war lord, who wanted
to promote the arts and sciences of the West.

This made my father all the more ardent in the service of France.

"Think of all the deals it means! I must see that they go to the French companies in Shanghai. If the English think I'm going to let them hog it all . . ."

The people of Chengtu were not so happy: they knew it was they who would have to pay. They looked uneasy when the marshal announced that he was going to show himself to his people in a machine that went along by itself. A proclamation ordered them to gather and admire the motorcar.

A triumphal way became urgently necessary. The maze of overhung, refuse strewn, twisting alleys provided no suitable route for the motorized marshal. The order was given for the rich merchants in the street where silk was sold to raze their shops to the ground in a twelve-foot swath, and that within twenty-four hours. My mafu took me to see. Nothing seemed to be happening. An elderly public scribe explained.

"The merchants have been putting their heads together," he said. "They collected a large sum of money and offered it to the war lord, and he graciously consented to hear their plea."

In was another, slightly less wealthy street that was then in danger. But there, too, the people managed to get around the marshal's whims. The same thing happened in all the narrow streets of the city. Finally soldiers appeared with machine guns, axes, and firebrands, and knocked down the hovels in a reeking alley where no one had enough money to conciliate the war lord. All the inhabitants were driven out; those who resisted were killed. And so a path was cleared that was wide enough for the tun-kyong, the war lord, to make his appearance on wheels.

When the great day came, a crowd was gathered around the square—the troops had seen to that in no uncertain manner. The Chinese who had been driven there wore no expression other than the grimace of compulsory enthusiasm. There were trumpets and fanfares and a battalion marching along beside a long metal bonnet. With a primitive spluttering and under the protection of his army, the war lord, standing, rode by in the first car ever seen in Chengtu.

"And not even a French one," lamented my father to Anne Marie at the consulate.

That was the only time the car was ever taken out. After that it must have rusted away somewhere in the tun-kyong's palace. Whenever I met the war lord in the city he was going about in his ordinary fashion, the usual mixture of the old China and the new— gongs and salvos, banners and standards, robed dignitaries and men in military uniform. There were always bayonets, but also the traditional whips and chains of the executioners who accompanied the marshal everywhere. The marshal himself rode on a horse beneath a large parasol. And before he appeared, the streets would always grow mysteriously empty. There was not a face to be seen, and the silence of fear reigned, for if anyone showed himself, the eye of the war lord might light upon him and give the marshal an idea.

I wasn't afraid of the war lord. He came frequently to be entertained at the consulate. Li would tell me about his visits in advance. I often used to find her holding little fingers—a sign of love—with the bald chef. I was jealous, but it was because of him that Li was in the know.

The servants in the consulate would become solemnity itself, their expressions reflecting the utmost zeal, together with the "face" that the marshal's visit imparted to the whole yamen. You could have cut their earnestness with a knife. Only my mother showed no trace of emotion, explaining things to the chief servants, who scornfully replied that they knew, especially when they didn't know at all. She got them to make dishes from her native Loire valley, using mandarin fish instead of pike. The cooks were proud to penetrate the secrets of the West, but once they knew them they insisted on improving them in the Chinese manner. The trouble my mother went to to stop them cutting everything up into bits!

My father was the personification of forethought, especially in his treasure chamber, entered with much fumbling of locks and bolts. It was there that the marvels from Shanghai were kept, ranging from packets of cotton wool and balls of string to tins of cassoulet and truffles. As my father said, "The bills were pretty stiff, but it was a question of France's future on the Upper Yangtze." What a thrill it was for me, every two or three months, to watch them opening the iron-bound packing cases full of tins. Tins meant more to me than jades and Buddhas—they were a glimpse of an unknown world. And I would stand there for hours as my father counted the tins and told the head houseboy there were so many of this and so many of that. The head boy just nodded impassively, but he knew he was really being warned to keep his hands off.

What a delight it was when my father went down there to draw up his plan or campaign for the great dinner party.

"So many bottles of champagne. So many of Bordeaux. So many of Muscadet—that's in your honor, Anne Marie. And so many of . . ."

"That's far too many. You'll get drunk, and so will the marshal. It'll be disgusting."

"I'm not doing this for my own pleasure, you know,

Anne Marie. I must just sacrifice my own wishes. What about a few tins of pâté de foi gras?"

"So that the guests can throw that up at the same time as the wine? What's more, the marshal may think he's been poisoned. He doesn't even know what it is."

"He'll pretend he does—out of respect for me."

My father was in tails, my mother in evening dress, and the hour approached. Both parents were ready, but my father made all kinds of fuss—his collar was too tight, his shoes hurt his corns. He walked with an ostentatious limp, he cursed the houseboys, castigating his valet especially for his clumsiness. Then my mother appeared, a tulip in lace with a jade pendant on her bosom, and at the sight of her the consul calmed down. Assiduous, affectionate, hierarchical, at once husband and officer in charge, he said:

"That dress cost a lot of money but it suits you. Don't forget I'm relying on you not to talk too much tonight. Women should be seen and not heard."

He tried to kiss her, but she moved away.

There was a noise in the courtyard—whinnying, the sound of hoofs, coolies shouting at each other, all the sounds of a caravanserai. Riders dressed to the nines dismounted, throwing the reins to the grooms. Great Chinese merchants weighed down with fat and silk eased themselves greasily out of their litters. Here and there in the courtyard, gleams of light fell on the faces of coolies, bodyguards, a whole crowd of faces picked out from the darkness, stuck on crouching bodies, covered with rice powder. Then came the great military to-do of the marshal arriving, with his guard of honor on the alert, ready to kill in the event of the surprise attack that was always possible. There were flashes of steel and glimpses of guns being pointed as the marshal approached my father, who was bent double in a bow, and my mother, who had the un-heard-of-privilege of remaining upright, with just her head slightly inclined.

Once inside the house, all was cordiality and jollity, a meal consisting of a hundred dishes, and no end of damask and crystal and silver. The maids had let me hide in the pantry, and through the serving hatch I could see into the banqueting hall. The war lord was installed on a sort of throne covered with tiger skins. An aide-de-camp tasted all the wine and food before he touched it. The guard of honor was still out in the courtyard, fingers on the trigger.

I watched the rites of friendship build to a crescendo. At first all faces were stiff with politeness. But my father was in his element on occasions like this, which called for speeches, compliments, and jokes. It was splendid, sparkling. I could hear the words and the laughter. There were flowery discourses, pleasantries bringing forth applause. My mother was not in the least put out by all these ruffians trying to eat in the European manner. It was a farcical battle between the guests and their spoons and forks. The problem was solved with the help of hands and belches, and the spitting out of bones. When the servants brought in the roast mutton, it was a massacre.

The French consul went all out, pouring forth pomposities about France, about China, with accesses of mirth that were duly taken up by the whole assembly. He was a worse pontificator than the Celestial People themselves, a jesting pontificator who dispensed "jokes"—they were referred to by the English word—that were indexed, classified, and familiar, a sort of diplomatic fun book for use in the China of the war lords. Automatic jokes, and automatic laughter: my father knew that in China truth was sacrilege, and any allusion to reality unseemly. I realized that the ideal evening was one that was entirely unreal.

Unreality included license. My father began his first kampé, or round of toasts. He stood up, and drained his glass once, ten times, fifty times, holding it out each time both in homage and in challenge toward the guest who was being honored. Finally he came to the war lord, who also stood up, and the Frenchman and the Chinaman drained their glasses simultaneously in the time-honored manner. The consul and the potentate faced one another in a duel of fraternity, with glasses as weapons. The atmosphere was tense, electric, aggressive. Little cries and laughs came from the guests, urging my father on. Far from steady on his feet by now, he proposed a general toast. There was a clatter of voices, clinking, gulping. Someone—the first—threw up. My mother kept sitting there beside the marshal.

Outside, two or three shots were accidentally loosed by the soldiers, but no one paid any attention. The coolies slept in the courtyard, and inside, on the besmirched table, the poker began. My father seemed fragile, almost vague, among the Chinamen, now solid and impassive as rocks. They raised the bidding tersely, without expression; their yellow fingers threw down the cards and heaped up the notes. The Chinese were imperturbable when in the grip of genuine passion. The air was full of cruelty. The consul was losing. Then more laughter, more kampés, belching, bodies rolling under the table onto the filthy floor. The yellow faces were green and distorted, their owners displayed the national talent for making noises with their intestines, membranes, and mouths. My father was pleased—this was the way a banquet ought to end. He was determined to last out, to stay on his feet for the honor of France. He observed the war lord closely, watching the way he smiled, trying to interpret his slanting eyes. The war lord was still as good as new, and in a culminating gesture he sent for two enormous jars full of cognac and challenged my father to a great kampé. It was a draw, and they had to start again. The marshal drank, my father drank, the marshal fell off his throne. The victory was my father's, but it was an awkward one, and he wondered afterward whether he oughtn't to have been the first to collapse. Such were the insoluble problems of "face."

Then came the mopping-up operations. Soldiers took the marshal away, coolies and bodyguards dragged the others from under the table, each servant taking his own master home. Then, when the room was finally empty, my father threw up. He'd been a hero, he'd done his duty splendidly. And now he, too, was carried away.

When everyone had gone I went into the now squalid room, and made myself one big kampé out of all the wine left in the bottoms of the glasses. At that moment my mother appeared.

"Do you take yourself for a consul, too?" she said.

The next day there had to be absolute silence in the consulate until six in the evening. My father then reappeared in his pajamas, a wet towel around his head and looking to be on his last legs.

"You were rather cool yesterday evening," he said to Anne Marie.

"I stayed beside your friend the marshal to the bitter end," she answered. "It was lucky he didn't drag me down with him when he fell. But the dress you said was so expensive is ruined."

"Don't forget you are the wife of the consul."

"I know—you're always telling me."

"You behaved very well. It was a splendid evening.
I calculated that the marshal smiled twenty times,
laughed twelve times, and proposed fourteen kampés.
When my English opposite number finds out, he'll be
livid! Thanks to me, I may say, French influence pre-
dominates in Szechwan. It'll be a great help to me in
my more important plans."

He cleared his throat to get his complexion back to
normal.

"I shall immediately inform the Quai d'Orsay that
my relations with the marshal have never been so
good."

He went and got properly dressed, then summoned
his senior staff—i.e., the vice-consul, the head of chancery, the old scholar, the interpreters, and Anne
Marie. Under the affectedly enthusiastic gaze of his
entourage, he began his report: " 'Yesterday evening,
the marshal, to demonstrate his love for France, came
to dine in state at the consulate. . . .' What do you
think of that for a beginning, Anne Marie?"

"Very good. But don't forget it's nearly dinnertime."

"Don't be so exasperating."

My father went on working, delightedly covering
sheet after sheet, forgetting all about dinner. My
mother waited, but her eyes lit up when a messenger
arrived from the marshal, bringing her a little black
wooden case. When she broke the seals and slid back
the cover, she found two glittering rings and two
bracelets of dark green jade.

But a fortnight later the consulate was hemmed in
by a circle of men and steel, a forest of bayonets, and
soldiers tense with the apparent indifference of lurking beasts. Officers shouted orders, and groups of uniformed men trained one machine gun on my father's
office and another on the drawing room in which he'd
entertained the marshal so sumptuously.

One furious little monkey of a man with copious plumes strode toward the door of the house, yelling in a rasping voice that he was going to destroy the consulate—it was a lair of thieves and bandits, enemies of China.

It was ten o'clock in the morning, and my father was alone in his office with my mother and me. The Chinese staff were cowering in the back courtyard, watching what was going on with eager curiosity, but doing nothing. My father beat his brow.

"Of course it's only blackmail. But why?"

"Perhaps it's a present from the marshal," my mother suggested ironically.

"Let me think. Perhaps it's because of those guns my agent ordered for the marshal in Shanghai—apparently they were waylaid by some other war lord."

The fellow with the plumes was still bawling away, and shouting and bawling was always a serious matter in China. It meant that the mask was off, that compulsory politeness had given way to action. But what action? The man was brandishing his sword, but the soldiers hadn't stirred. Nothing seemed to be happening.

"What sort of guns are they?" asked my mother.

"Old 75's. The seller I recommended, Monsieur Dumont, isn't really a crook. He acts for one of the most famous and respectable firms in Shanghai."

"You always bow and scrape to businessmen, and those Shanghai bankers have already caused you no end of trouble with their tricks."

"But these are specialists in selling arms to war lords. They know what they're about. No, I think this is some skulduggery among the Chinese themselves that I'm having to bear the brunt of."

In fact, the consul was yet again caught up in one of those Chinese imbroglios he knew so well, the result of inertia and ferocity combined, in which you could struggle vainly for days and days, with words having no meaning or effect, before a Great Wall of caviling that had nothing to do with the subject in question. You even forgot what it was you were arguing about, such was the power of Chinese misunderstanding. In this case the misunderstanding was deliberate playacting, with a few hundred armed troops as actors. The marshal's own guard, in fact.

The consul wore the expression he put on for deep cogitation.

"Don't be frightened, Anne Marie. It's nothing serious. The servants haven't run away, and the marshal hasn't roused the rabble against us. The soldiers are just a way of opening negotiations. All we have to do is wait for a message from the marshal."

It was a long wait, and a vain one. My father decided to go out into the courtyard, and was encircled by bayonets. There was an interminable argument with an officer, who explained they were going to kill him—it lasted an hour, with the officer alternately working himself up and calming himself down. Then my father came back into the office as if nothing had happened. My mother kissed him on the cheek.

At last there came the sound of galloping hoofs—an emissary from the marshal at last, bearing a scroll. The old scholar reappeared just in time to read it to my father. It said: "It is to protect you that I have sent one of my unworthy regiments to surround your yamen. The city is threatened by hordes of bandits."

For two days messengers galloped back and forth, fetching and carrying scrolls bearing the seals of the war lord or of the French Republic. Compliments were exchanged. My father said he was overwhelmed by such solicitude, and felt it was a signal honor to be looked after by such a wonderful body of men. He offered the marshal ten thousand thanks for his goodness. However, because the war lord's genius, generosity, and love of the people had caused peace to reign throughout the city, he felt he had no need of this protection. But these arguments left the marshal's modesty unmoved. He replied that the spirit of evil was abroad everywhere, and that his own unworthy talents had been unable to keep at bay the dangers threatening Chengtu and the French consulate. His esteem for my father and our family obliged him to ensure our safety—it was his sacred duty. He would cut his own throat rather than allow the consulate of France to be in peril.

In the days that followed, the army element was still there, but with the shine off, sagging, sprawling on the ground, with women. Their heads were not firm on their shoulders, they looked both lost and horrified, as if crushed by despondency or fatigue. Some of them were shaven-headed children of twelve or thirteen. They'd thrown their cartridge belts down, and the slings of the machine guns drooped miserably. The officers had vanished. It was one of those states of inertia in which troops are even more dangerous than when they are hysterical, because they tend to start acting on their own. As the marshal wasn't paying his men a penny, my father decided to pay them himself. The servants distributed small coins and food. A fine blowout was had by all.

My father paced up and down. When and how would the marshal show his hand? It might take any one of a number of forms. At this point there arrived in a sedan chair a merchant of the old school, a pot-bellied individual with his hands hidden in his sleeves, his eyes hidden in his flesh, and his thoughts

hidden in his skull—a round ball that rolled to
Monsieur le Consul's office between lines of soldiers
who drew respectfully aside to let him pass.

He was a little yellow millionaire, such a small one
he declared himself unworthy to speak to my father.
But on the other hand, Mr. Lu, the head of the silk
guild, might be able to give my father some useful
advice. Unfortunately Mr. Lu couldn't come to the
consulate himself because of his advanced age. Would
His Excellency deign to go with him, Mr. Lu's servant,
to see Mr. Lu?

So off went my father to one of the dark and distant
caverns hidden behind reeking walls, with great bolts,
peepholes, invisible observers, and passwords, where
the yellow millionaires slept on their wooden platforms. Off he went to see the powerful Mr. Lu.

Back at the consulate, we waited. The staff were
very intrigued. The cook was astounded that Mr. Lu,
whom no one had ever set eyes on, should have been
willing to appear before my father. His considered
opinion was: "I think it will bring good luck to
Monsieur le Consul."

My father came back after two hours, very pleased
with what had happened. As we sat at table he told
us how he'd been taken to a deserted, dilapidated
place without a soul to be seen, not even the furtive
shadow of servants or doorkeepers. Within all this
was a room full of darkness where an opium lamp
threw gleams on the hips of goddesses and the bellies
of stone Buddhas. The dim light, which came almost
from ground level, from near a mahogany floor, also
encountered a sliver of face and a recumbent scrap of
body—a transparent skeleton that was all that was
left of Mr. Lu, without flesh or muscle, just a little
blood and shrunken bones. Yet he was one of the
masters of Chengtu.

Mr. Lu had followed the way of ancient Chinese wisdom. In his day, no doubt, he had been one of those who delighted in naked bellies, belching, and guzzling, with women about him to serve his every need. But as the years went by and carnal pleasures lost their power, all that was left him was the opium dream, the crackle of the burning pellets, the life of inertia in which the brain was queen. For while opium paralyzed the body and did away with vulgar desires, it imparted supreme acuity to the mind, mind as a game, as war, as cold ferocity, the most refined voluptuousness, the seat of power. No more feelings, no more good or evil, only intelligence, only the arguments that annex even more power and money.

My father made the most of his story.

"What could Mr. Lu want with me? He gazed at me with his dried-up, intense, petrified eyes, inclining a noble face in which the wrinkles were like pillars, like an icy yet burning framework supporting a dead skin. He was a ghost with the terrifying brutality of the other world. What did I know about him? That if he rose from his couch, he who was only a breath, a wisp of smoke, he could murmur any order he liked and be obeyed. People do not disobey Mr. Lu, who does his counting on an abacus but is richer than a marble-fronted bank in Shanghai.

"Who is Lu? He is cupidity itself, a combination of all the trades of the Middle Ages and all the rackets of the twentieth century. He knows all the secrets of a China full of foreigners obsessed with profits and machines, dollars and factories. Even there in his lair in Chengtu, he knows what 'business' means. He's in with all the merchants and compradors of Hankow and Shanghai. And at the same time he's still in the Chinese tradition, the tradition of 'squeeze,' where you manage to make something out of everything—civil

war, famine, massacre. He knows about everything.
What is there he doesn't finance? Revolutions, kidnappings, looting. He's in cahoots with the war
lord and the rich bourgeoisie, but also with gangsters, secret societies, pirates, every kind of underworld. In China everything intermingles in one yellow
fog. But men like Lu know their way around in it!"

"Did you smoke opium with Mr. Lu?" my mother
asked.

"After taking a good look at me, he stuck a skinny
finger out of one of his wide sleeves and beckoned to
me to lie down beside him. He handed me a pipe with
a jade mouthpiece, then prepared a pellet for me himself, grinding it up, heating it, and putting it on the
hand-shaped burner. We smoked almost ritually, in
silence, the object probably being to make me as disincarnate a being as himself. There was not a woman,
not a concubine, about—just an ageless man to assist
us."

I was sitting beside my mother, and the consul was
opposite, eating as he spoke. It was a typical family
scene, with the heat of the monsoon and my father
flapping the unusually energetic flies away from his
face with his napkin. The boys brought in the courses,
and night was coming down on us, and the knives and
forks, the "barbarians'" instruments for eating. "Don't
use your fingers like the natives," Anne Marie said to
me. Then she turned to my father, interrupting what
he was saying.

"How many pipes did you smoke? Have you got a
headache?"

"You haven't been listening, Anne Marie. What Lu
told me is of the utmost importance both for me and
for France."

"What was it?"

"I'll tell you. After half an hour, Lu emerged from his nirvana and said in a low voice: 'I met you at a very interesting time, a long while ago in Canton. Dr. Sun Yat-sen was preparing to bring the empire down with bombs. I was his secretary. One day I was asked to go to the International Concession at Shameen and find a French gentleman, a secret emissary sent by the authorities in Indochina. It was you. You were dressed as a Chinaman. I brought you to Dr. Sun Yat-sen, and in the name of your chiefs you offered him your country's aid. It was because of this that Dr. Sun Yat-sen was able to go to Saigon to foster urban insurrections in Yunnan and Kwangtung, and to prepare the way for the revolution of 1911, as you are well aware. Meanwhile the French found no difficulties put in their way in the building of their railway from Hanoi to Yunnanfu. It's because of these memories that I asked you to come here now, so that once again I could ask you for France's help. Our marshal in Chengtu is a follower of Sun Yat-sen. Just after our Republic had been founded and was in danger, it was the armies of Yunnan province, French Indochina's neighbor, that saved us. The marshal was one of the Yunnan heroes who crossed hills and mountains to come and help defend the Chengtu revolution. But now the ungrateful people of Szechwan, bought by the feudal overlords in the North and the British businessmen in Shanghai, want to throw him and his army out. Some of them who call themselves generals are raising troops and having arms supplies brought up the Yangtze. But the modest amount of arms our marshal buys in Shanghai somehow never gets through to him. So when the French 75's he'd paid for disappeared, he thought you must be one of his enemies, too.'

"I need hardly tell you, my dear, that I was taken aback by this accusation. I thought to myself: that swine Dumont's played one of his dirty tricks without giving a damn about the consequences for me. But what surprised me even more was Lu's attitude and the way he spoke. There was none of the usual Chinese sort of conversation where the person you're talking to looks perfectly polite but denies everything and is completely impervious to argument. Lu put his cards on the table right away.

" 'Monsieur le Consul, the marshal has heeded my humble prayers. In his wisdom he has seen that it's the English who are out to destroy him. They've spent a hundred years acquiring control over the route along the Yangtze, and now that they have power over the river up to its sources they want to extend their influence first to Szechwan and then to Tibet. As you know, Monsieur le Consul, English troops from India have already occupied the Roof of the World in the past. They have agents all over the place, they lord it everywhere. The great idea of the Colonial Office and the War Office and the gentlemen of business is to command a route from Shanghai to Calcutta through the Himalayas. The English only have time for dogs that fawn, and that's why they hate the marshal of Chengtu, a great patriot and revolutionary and the biggest obstacle to their baneful ambitions.' "

By this time we had reached dessert. I watched my father as he went on imitating Mr. Lu's mandarin manner.

" 'But the marshal knows France is generous, Monsieur le Consul. Did she not bring peace to Indochina and build a railroad from Tonkin to Yunnan, the poor primitive province where the marshal was born and whose mountain ranges act as shield and protection to the magnificent province of Szechwan? Yunnan is a friendly step in the direction of China for the French friends of the revolution. French arms can reach Chengtu from Hanoi in a few weeks, by train to Yunnanfu and then on by caravan. But wouldn't it be a good thing for France as well as China if you extended the railroad as far as Szechwan?'

"He returned to his opium and shut his eyes. You'd have thought he was dead and embalmed, but then he suddenly sat up and flapped his sleeves at me silently by way of farewell. So I came away."

My father had got such rhetorical relish out of telling his lengthy tale that he had hardly touched his dinner. When he talked he was always totally absorbed in what he said, choosing his words and effects with great earnestness but kindly taking care not to go over his audience's head. But the audience was often my mother, and she was blasé and skeptical.

"In short," she said now, "the old rascal deliberately set fire to your imagination."

"Don't exaggerate, Anne Marie—this Szechwan railroad idea is not a new one. I used to take a lot of interest in it a while ago. My first bosses in Hanoi before the war—little gents with goatees and huge pith helmets coming down over their ears—never thought about anything else. But the Chinese just didn't want to know."

"All the marshal's after is machine guns from Indochina. The rest is just bait, and you swallow it."

"Maybe, maybe. But suppose I did manage to bring off the railroad? They'd make me consul general. It would be marvelous. France would be established right in the heart of China, of all Asia even. And all the resources of the upper Yangtze, and of Tibet, would find outlet through Hanoi or Haiphong instead of Shanghai."

"Castles in the air."

"Not at all. But the English aren't the only ones who wouldn't like it. The big fellows in the French concession in Shanghai would be furious, too. And some of them are bankers and businessmen with a devil of a lot of influence in Paris. It needs careful thinking out."

"But are you going to take up the cudgels for Yunnan here in Chengtu?"

"What do you take me for, Anne Marie? There's a civil war just around the corner, and I don't want to get all three of us massacred. No, I must outsmart them."

The consul beamed with self-satisfaction, quite confident of his own powers of duplicity. My mother wasn't so sure.

Dinner was over.

At any rate, the marshal's troops cleared out of the consulate. The servants were all smiles again, as if nothing had happened. But the head boy reported the theft of a mandarin's jade scepter, the apple of my father's eye. Sometimes he would put on a dragon-patterned robe and brandish the scepter as if he himself were a dignitary of the Celestial Empire. He'd even had himself photographed in this getup. When he was told his treasure had disappeared he of course concluded, since soldiers can always be blamed for anything, that the servant had taken the opportunity to steal the scepter himself. But it would have been unseemly to doubt his good faith.

Li was restored to her usual good humor, and so was the mafu, who told me, grinning cheerfully:

"There's an army outside the city."

But was it the war lord's ally or his enemy? The mafu gave a smile of blissful ignorance. In the narrow streets the people went about their usual business. The gates of the city weren't shut, but merely guarded by a handful of troops, fanning themselves and eating their meals impassively.

I went out by the great south gate and after a few hundred yards found myself in the burial ground, where a dirty, ragged crowd was lolling about among the mounds. This was the army. There were cooking pots, musicians, the most miserable wretches, camp followers, peddlers, people who had nothing to lose. But there were plenty of bayonets, too, and even a few guns trained on Chengtu. At the sound of a bugle, the men made some kind of effort to pull themselves together. Apparently a general was about to inspect the troops.

"This is the Szechwan army," said the mafu, laughing. "They're going to throw out the Yunnanese."

Tattered and torn as they were, the men seemed to be preparing to do battle. Some were concocting the various magic potions that impart courage. There was a long queue waiting for a great mangy tigress, tied to a stake, to relieve itself, so that they could buy the urine and drink it.

"That's the best way to get the strength of a tiger," explained the mafu, with his army experience. "At least, if you can't get hold of a bit of human liver."

In the days that followed, all remained quiet. The battle mysteriously foreseen by the good people of Chengtu did not materialize. The consulate servants said the Yunnan marshal had treated with the Szechwan army, and the latter was to occupy the southern part of the city and collaborate with the marshal in maintaining peace and harmony in Chengtu.

But to save "face" the marshal organized a great celebration, just as if he had really won a victory.

Fifty prisoners were produced for the purpose—what sort of prisoners no one could say, since Szechwan and Yunnan were now supposed to be friends. As usual they were poor vagabonds picked at random. A great crowd assembled, with music, and the prisoners were brought forth in bamboo cages, chained and with their hands tied behind their backs. Already they were no more than skeletons with just a scrap of flesh and life left, bloodstained wrecks, beasts that had endured long tortures. When they were turned out of their cages they were so weak they fell down in the mud, and the executioners had to haul them to their knees and use all their strength to keep them from collapsing again. A group of assistants arrived with long heavy knives, which they held with two hands, poised behind the necks of the victims. A shove placed each of these in the most convenient position, and a thump with the blade did the rest. It was all over in a few minutes. The pile of heads was taken away in a tumbrel. The next day my father would have to go and offer his congratulations to the war lord. Rather a tricky situation. Ought he to hail him as a conqueror or as the keeper of the peace?

I had been growing in wisdom and experience, and was now quite grown up in some ways. I knew every corner of Chengtu, with its couple of million inhabitants. When they saw me go by on my bay, followed by my mafu, the populace—the coolies, the beggars, the respectable merchants—would have an amused look in their eye, and on their lips the words "There goes the white boy." I had become a person of note.

The war lord himself now marked me out as an object of his esteem. One day he sent me a horse as a present, a fiery steed with steaming nostrils, always pawing the ground and champing at the bit, when he wasn't kicking out with heels like lightning. A great scroll, with red characters inscribed on rice paper and addressed by the marshal to me, hoped I would enjoy "the two thousand felicities on this ignoble animal." Anne Marie didn't want me to mount the horse, which was still being held by the two soldiers who had brought him, but my father thought this would be insulting to the war lord. The mafu, with his inane air, went up to the horse and calmed it down and helped me into the saddle. And I pranced proudly through the city on my marvelous steed.

I had a bad fall but didn't hurt myself. Then I ran over a man. The mafu told me not to stop. But that evening a howling crowd covered in rags and sores clustered around the gate of the consulate cursing the foreign devils. A hollow-voiced dwarf conducted the chorus of imprecations, and my father came out of his office into the courtyard to see what was the matter. The head boy explained.

"These people say they're the relatives of the person who was knocked down by His Excellency your son. They say he's dead and they want compensation."

It was probably a trick, but the crowd was getting larger. My father thought it best to hand over the price of a death—a few strings of coins. The hideous faces disappeared. Custom had been observed. Everyone was satisfied.

My amahs had got fat, but they went on eating more than ever. What they liked best, the delicacy that really lent the finishing touch to their rice, was fish bladders. Before they were cooked they looked like a heap of airy, gory soap bubbles, soft, liquid, light. One day outside the ramparts, on the handsomely paved north road, I came upon a shapeless,

viscous, gleaming mass which reminded me of the
delicious fish bladders. But these were something different: human. Not a heap of eyes, though, or of ears,
common as it was to remove such appurtenances and
pile them up in times of trouble. But this, though I
didn't realize it until later, was a heap of human sex
organs. All I saw at the time was an oozing mass, and
my mafu told me there'd been some little battle or
other the day before, and the winners had castrated
the losers. The bodies themselves lay in an indistin-
guishable mass in a pit some distance away. But the
putrefying phalluses were left as a sort of triumphal
arch on the road, rotting bits of meat at which no one
batted an eye. For on the road where I stood, life
was going on again as before, the eternal, pulsating,
unceasing, wondrous life of China, the life which
moved the peasants and the carts and the buckets of
dung and the burdens, and which nothing but enormous catastrophes could stop or slow down for an instant.

But things looked bad in Chengtu. The town buzzed
with threatening rumors, and the consulate servants
glided about like ghosts again. Li, my smiling Li,
looked out at me from a countenance I didn't know. It
was as if a veil had blotted out the features and left
only a shapeless and expressionless mask. It was the
shapelessness of fear.

As she eventually told me, in horror, it was because
the Stone of Supreme Death had reappeared. In vain
had the people sealed it up in a temple, buried it
beneath layer upon layer of stuff that defied time, destroyed all records and reminders of its hiding place,
in an attempt to ward off fate. For anyone who set
eyes on the stone was bound to slay his fellow men,
and a few days before, the wall behind which it was

hidden had collapsed, and the stone stood revealed, together with its inscription:

"Heaven has created ten thousand things to help man. But man has not done one thing to help Heaven."

For the people of Chengtu this was a presage of blood. Blood had been the mystical passion of the terrible being who caused the stone to be set up—the man who had made himself king in Szechwan, King of the Grand Orient. He seized the throne after the tragic and long-drawn-out decline of the Ming dynasty in the seventeenth century. There amid the ruins he tried to avenge the rightful emperors, and the scepter he wielded was from hell. His dream was to bring about the end of the world, and no day was complete for him without its heap of corpses. Impelled by an accursed mixture of madness and pride, he slew out of sheer hatred for life. In his view the human race had betrayed heaven, and all men were traitors and deserved to die. He exterminated thirty million people, leaving Szechwan an empty desert, an overcrowded graveyard. To make a mockery of wisdom he subjected the sagest to the most exquisite refinements of torture. He was backed by an army that believed only in death. To test his officers' loyalty he had their wives' feet cut off, had them piled up in a heap, and gloated over them. His favorite concubine, to show her love, cut off her own right foot and threw it onto the heap. The King of the Grand Orient rejoiced, then killed himself. It took more than a century of immigration from the neighboring provinces to repopulate Szechwan.

And now was the mask of mighty death going to come down over the face of Chengtu once more? As the days went by, Li grew more and more terrified. She dreamed she saw a junk swept away by a black wind and sinking in a river of blood. All the sooth-sayers in the city had apparently seen fiery signs in the heavens—the tracks of the dragon of war.

My father sat in his office, knowing it all, unruffled, reassuring his staff, who stood at attention. Anne Marie waited by the door ready to make her escape, but held back by her husband's stern gaze.

"The Stone of Supreme Death? Well, one can easily see why the good people of Szechwan are terrified. They know very well this China of theirs is stricken every so often with nervous convulsions that may last a couple of centuries. It's irresistibly drawn toward annihilation. The China of the emperors, the China of the prophets, the China of the rebels—all fell into the abyss. And it wasn't such a long time ago, either. When I first came out here as a young man the older white men still used to talk about the Taipings. That business had properly put the wind up them. The white men themselves were spared, but there were forty or fifty million corpses scattered along the Yangtze valley. And the worst of it was the job they had afterward, trying to reestablish European trade and find some customers who were still alive."

The Taipings—a dream of justice, a belief that happiness is possible in this world. At the summons of Hung, the Holy One, the poor rose in revolt, beg-gars in red caps, hordes miles and miles long, exter-minating the oppressor, exterminating all. For virtue always leads to death. The rebels put the imperial garrisons to the sword—fifty thousand headless bodies were floating in the Blue River when Nanking fell. Any inhabitants who survived were forced to bring out their wealth—gold, silver, jewels—and made to worship Hung, who proclaimed himself emperor.

The junketings in Nanking lasted ten years. Hung made his closest friends kings, and himself sat enthroned beneath a forest of flags and banners. At noon all the dignitaries fell on their knees before him, chanting eulogies like those in use at the court in Peking. "Ten thousand years, ten times a thousand years for Hung."

Every king or chief had his own court and harem and favorites. Every petty ruler led a life of debauchery behind altars laden with flowers and incense. Officials in yellow robes, their long hair bound up in a net, would sit at a table bearing a box that contained tablets inscribed with various sentences. People would be brought in for judgment, and the official would select a tablet at random. Whichever he chose, the sentence was always death. Only the method of execution varied. The victims were led off by rascals in red caps, and the faithful knelt and prayed amid a reek of garlic and unbelievable filth.

"I was present," said my father, "at the funeral of the Empress Tsu Hsi in Peking in 1908. To think that fifty years before, that old girl had saved the empire from the Taipings. A genius she was, that woman. She served the virtue of heaven and earth through murder, because in terms of the wisdom of the Celestial Kingdom, murder is a good thing in itself, and in particular a cure for the evil of the revolt of the hundred names—in other words, popular uprisings."

The protocol of respect continued to surround my father as he spoke, but the vice-consul had the misfortune to sneeze. The consul gave him a withering glance, and went on.

"But I must admit poor Tsu Hsi made a mistake at the end of her life, when the unfortunate woman took it into her head to slaughter the Europeans as well. For this purpose she entered into association with the same secret societies and magicians and other crude fellows she'd so brilliantly suppressed when they called themselves the Taipings. In 1900 she allied herself with the Boxers, with the result that not only did she forfeit the Temple of Heaven, but the whole of the civilized world took the opportunity to teach her a lesson. I believe the Chinese have realized ever since then that they mustn't lay hands on Europeans."

"Sometimes you say quite interesting things," said Anne Marie, who all this time had been leaning against the door.

"You're too kind."

"But what I'd like to know is what's going to happen here and now?"

"Things have changed. The heavenly cosmic order no longer exists. The underground mystical passions that sometimes used to inflame the masses have decayed. In big cities like Shanghai the chiefs of the secret societies have become organized gangsters who maintain law and order in connivance with the police of the Foreign Concessions. Where China is still medieval, as in Chengtu, they've become war lords. There are middlemen and merchants everywhere, and over them the white men, and all of them thinking of nothing but money. We've given these people a sense of the dollar they didn't have before—that's our victory, the victory of modernism, the victory of the Chinese revolution of 1911."

"And don't you think about money, too?"

"No. I think of France. I'm only an outpost. But it all fits. The famines, the war lords, the fine foreign concessions on the coast and the lower Yangtze, the Sikhs and the marines, the famous clubs in Shanghai with notices saying 'No admittance to Chinese or dogs,' the yellow millionaires, the banks, and also the consuls, the clergymen, the Catholic missions, the converts, and the priests. They all form a huge system of common interests battening on the corpse of the Celestial Empire, with top hats rivaled only by surplices and nuns' caps. In fact, at the moment, surplices and nuns' caps are the chief manifestation of France in Szechwan—the place is swarming with them. But France's situation here will change if I get my railroad."

"Do you really believe in that old choo-choo of yours?"

"Yes, but I must wait for Lu to raise the matter again. The war lord is going to need arms. The Yunnanese position in Chengtu is deteriorating."

"Will there be trouble here?"

"Without any doubt. Not massacres, as there were in Tsu Hsi's day. There's not enough virtue about now, only self-interest, with all these upstart generals positively eaten up with greed. What will happen is a sort of Chinese comedy played out among them, naturally a comedy full of hate and horrors, murky treachery, incredible atrocities, and elaborate compromises. There'll be troops everywhere. The ordinary people will get it in the neck, but they don't matter. Very probably the whole province will be in chaos.

"But as you know, Anne Marie, disorder is in the white man's interest. And in Chengtu we consuls—my English and Japanese opposite numbers and I—are in on it all. We're necessary to all these ruffians in robes or uniform: for their deals, to act as go-betweens and arbitrators when it happens to suit them, perhaps to shelter those that get the worst of it. They make use of us; we make use of them. Though of course every consul, despite all the handshaking and the bridge parties, is the enemy of every other consul, and as you know, we all try to outsmart each other. But although the Chinamen who are now masters of Chengtu tend to take us for fools, this doesn't mean that out of self-interest or dislike they mightn't play us some dirty tricks.

"There'll be bloodshed in Chengtu, yes. Just a bit of slaughter here and there—death is one of the bargaining counters. But I think we consuls will be sacrosanct, in theory, in all this. They need us.

"The danger lies in the mob. There's a tradition by which the population works itself up into paroxysms of rage over the most absurd tale or rumor, and then thousands of hands and knives are ready to tear the white men to shreds. It's an ancient instinct; it's been slumbering, but it could wake up. To kill and torture the 'long-nosed dogs' is still the constant dream concealed behind the rigmarole of politeness. But fortunately I can assure you that the war lords are 'civilized'—we are on a business footing with them, and they know how to quiet the mob."

Anne Marie had gone slightly pale.

"Don't worry," her husband told her gaily. "You might be killed, but your honor isn't in much danger. The mob can't really bring itself to rape European ladies—not even beggars, or soldiers otherwise capable of anything. Cutting them to pieces, slitting open their stomachs, juggling with their innards like balls of string—yes, they're all for that. But they don't fancy the other. It would have to be made a patriotic duty, and the Chinese don't carry patriotism that far yet."

Anne Marie remained calm. She wouldn't have let her consul of a husband upset her for anything in the world.

"But it won't happen, my dear. And in any case, they'd kill me first, and you'd have a few moments to mourn me."

For as far back as I can remember, the day my father shone was the Fourteenth of July, Bastille Day, a real fête and no mistake. The gate of the consulate was thrown open and a special path laid down across the paved courtyards. It was made of rare Chinese carpets with potted plants spaced out along the edge. Its route passed under a triumphal arch created by a small pagoda, with huge crossed flags, one French and one Chinese, over a red lacquer panel on which the characters signifying "Eternal Friendship" were inscribed in black. All around were perfume burners, vases, hanging lamps, and above all banners and festoons of flags of every shape and size—the colors of all the countries who were China's allies, a profusion in which naturally Marianne predominated. Some of these standards were stuck in vases like bunches of flowers; some climbed up the walls like vines; some interarched on the ceiling like palms. Three steps led up to the main drawing room, thick with hangings on which red-masked warriors symbolized the might of France. At noon Monsieur le Consul took up his position behind a kind of altar—partly in honor of country, partly in honor of ancestors—to make his speech, a piece of eloquence he had spent days polishing and repolishing in his office, on the subject of France's zealous and sensitive devotion to noble causes and great ideas. Loud applause.

The Tout-Chengtu was always there, consisting of

some fifty people, white and yellow. The war lord and
his chief generals came in uniforms that grew stricter
every year: flat caps with peaks coming right down
over their eyes, huge tall leather boots, stiff jackets
buttoned up at the neck, and a multitude of belts,
swords, straps, badges, and also lanyards, the latest
sign of military progress in Szechwan. There were no
more baubles—just khaki and the symbols of valor
and virtue. The marshal, even stuck away there in
Szechwan, had realized the threat and power implicit
in the sort of simplicity every great army in the world
had adopted since the battles of Verdun and the
Marne. The marshal and his assistants and aides were
as formidably stiff and courteous as if they'd been on
Foch or Hindenburg's general staff. But it was all too
new: the details were wrong, and they all looked tied
up like sacks of potatoes. Here the trousers were baggy,
there a mouth gaped, a mustache was ragged, an eye
was watering, or a hand flapped at a fly—and their
military salute was a farce. But still they were doing
their best, and they didn't spit. The marshal and his
men stood nobly still throughout my father's speech,
and when it was over the marshal opened his lips just
long enough to tell the French consul he loved France.

At some distance from the warrior caste stood the
"important yellow men" of the city, mostly officials,
magistrates, and district governors, for modern Chengtu had adopted a European form of administration.
The sole preoccupation of those who held office was
to avoid having their heads cut off by the war lord,
and to feather their nests by taking what little was
left to the population by the soldiers and the bandits.
This was a difficult, thankless, and even dangerous
task, but an inevitable one because such officials were
never paid. These supers stood about starchily, look-

ing partly like mandarins and partly like experts imported from Shanghai. They wore traditional robes, as did the millionaires and the masters of the guilds and corporations. There were about twenty of these in all, much less stiff than the officers, like big cats with their claws sheathed, their faces shining with sly or jovial affability. They had both money and power. But which were the war lord's accomplices, which his future victims, which his enemies?

The other white men present were the other consuls and their nationals. Only two consuls, the Japanese and the English—there was no longer a German, and not yet an American consul.

The Japanese consul was a little monkey of a man got up like a popinjay, formal as an undertaker's mute, bowing so low at every phrase that his sword hit the ground, then jerking smilingly upright. But it wasn't an Oriental smile—it was a smile that tried to be white. As a matter of fact, the Japanese consul was regarded as a white of the highest quality and importance. Though they didn't admit it to themselves, the real whites were relying on him should matters go badly in Chengtu. For it was a well-known fact that the Japanese could deal with the "natives." They always kept cool, and knew when to use words and when to resort to blows. And they also had the necessary means, for was it not officers from the Land of the Rising Sun who ran the Chengtu military academy, which had turned out the marshal and his troops so nattily?

Despite the current Entente Cordiale, my father had no liking at all for the English consul, for he too wanted to get his hooks into Szechwan. Strangely enough, he was a sort of Anglo-Saxon version of my father, in the same turn-of-the-century style. Like my father, he appeared smaller than he was, very much

the middle-class embassy type, well-made and attractive, a combination of benevolent vanity as regards
society and fanatical meticulousness toward his work.
He looked rather like a baby, with his chubby face,
blue eyes, and little fair mustache. But a baby son of
Albion, and tough. My father was jealous because this
"unimportant character" had a finer yamen, a bigger
staff, and more money than he. And my father sensed
that this man had behind him all the weight of John
Bull, and that of the famous services which had been
nibbling away at Asia for centuries, not to mention
the big British companies in Shanghai, the masters of
the golden calf. The English consul in Chengtu had
many distant and formidable gentlemen behind him,
whereas the people at the Quai d'Orsay were only
poets, the French were only small fry.

My father believed that his English opposite number was a rival full of evil designs. The feeling was
mutual, and each man kept the other under permanent observation in a perfectly reciprocal obsession.
They bribed their Chinese interpreters, their houseboys, and their cooks for information. They made polite accusations against one another to the war lords
and the local dignitaries. But this did not stop them
from falling on one another's neck when they met, and
at the end of every Fourteenth of July, after the last
handshake, the Englishman would say to the Frenchman, "Well, it all went off splendidly." My father
congratulated the British consul just as warmly every
year on the King's birthday, when a ceremony of the
same kind took place in the Britisher's yamen. Moreover, company was so hard to come by that the two
families often had dinner together. And nearly every
day Anne Marie dropped around at the end of the
afternoon for an ordinary little colonial visit to the

British diplomat's wife, a charming woman like a delicious clear English fruit drop. I used to play with the children, who had an English nanny and were on no account allowed to mix with the "natives."

But even more than His Britannic Majesty's consul, my father hated the English vicar with his black suit and dog collar. He was a gray eminence, a power behind the throne in Chengtu, a man who enjoyed the good things of life and had a face like an eruptive pudding. On the Fourteenth of July along he came, flushed and taciturn—the morning after the night before—but with his little eyes sparkling. Then he suddenly clapped my father on the back and asked, "Is the champagne going to be as good this year as it was last? Vive la France!" His wife, a good-natured elephant with flesh like pink porridge, said, "Behave yourself!" My father was convinced that this corpulent, red-faced, grog-blossomed gentleman was really the chief agent of the Secret Service in Szechwan, the master spy, who was also in the pay of the English trusts. My mother liked both him and his wife.

Sometimes, after the party, my father would say, "Thank goodness there isn't a German consul here since China declared war on them! The whole thing's a farce, but at least it got that terrible Prussian off my back. When I first came to Chengtu as a young man he bought up the subject of Sedan every time he saw me!"

After the victory in 1918, French prestige rose high in Szechwan, and the Fourteenth of July was the climax of the international season in Chengtu. Everything went smoothly. After the ritual speeches and congratulations came a flood of petits-fours and sandwiches, a sea of glasses, and an endless popping of

champagne corks. The marshal, having drunk a toast
to France, left, followed by the other representatives
of the Celestial People, and by the Japanese consul.
Now it was the turn of the "French colony." In other
words, the priests, the nuns, and the three doctors. In
short, the family.

After the consul's stirring speech, you should have
seen the amount of champagne the holy fathers managed to tuck away through the holes in their beards!
There was a full circle of jolly old faces, gaily emaciated beneath their grizzled hair. And could they talk!
Every Catholic missionary priest had a cascade of
whiskers down to the ground, a cascade infinitely more
powerful than the few thin hairs of the great native
scholars. It was a cascade that swept its way through
China, where some of the oldest priests had lived for
forty or fifty years without ever leaving their little
islands of Christianity. The monks were my father's
eyes and ears, his best informers—but he had to pay
for it!

As for the nuns, in their big white caps, they stood in
a group apart, shy and silent. Of course they scarcely
touched the champagne. But the amount they ate!
Earnestly, noiselessly, without stopping. Unlike the
monks, who lived well, the sisters fasted every day and
were half dead with hunger. While the priests were
still blustering away, the nuns tiptoed off replete,
humbly thanking my mother for having invited them.

As for the doctors, they were gay dogs who ran a
French institute outside the city for the making of
serums. What was the idea of having a place like that,
so typical of the good old colonial France of the Third
Republic, in an out-of-the-way place like Szechwan? I
suppose someone must have thought that in Chengtu,
in one of the most far away and densely populated

parts of China, there would be a lot of epidemics. It was one way of doing good works until they could build the railroad. So they sent out "scientists" who were in fact army or navy doctors. French logic. And when there was an outbreak of cholera or smallpox and the abandoned corpses got to be a nuisance, my father would go and put the services of the institute at the war lord's disposal. And every time the marshal would shake his head and decline: "People need to die—there are too many of them." Chinese logic. And my father agreed with him.

"It would just produce terror and revolt if the Chinese were forced to let the foreign devils give them injections. They'd think it was witchcraft—they might even kill the doctors. And if they did that we'd have no one left to play bridge with."

The doctors were not overburdened with work, nor with family responsibilities, since they all had to be bachelors. So they were the ornaments of Chengtu's social life. If, for me, the missionaries were synonymous with whiskers, the doctors were synonymous with boots. They always wore leather boots that seemed to spread out and envelop them completely, like a second skin. They were all peremptory little chaps with mustaches, lively, gallant, attentive, with a sort of garrison sociability. Szechwan did not impress them. They'd all more or less spent their lives in the colonial service, and this was nothing new. They lived in the institute as if it were just some little provincial town in France, not because they were stupid but because they were blasé. As there weren't any clubs, they frequented the consulates, where they became permanent guests, helpful, cheerful, always ready to entertain or play a game of cards, downing Bordeaux with my father and whiskey with the English. My father's Chi-

nese prosings bored them, although they were very
fond of my mother. But they preferred the British
consulate as a place to go. This was regarded as treason
by my father, who would occasionally cold-shoulder
them. As if they cared! Anyway, there would soon be a
reconciliation. The conversation consisted of rumors
from Shanghai and Hankow, and discussion of dances,
races, adulteries, elections, and investments. When you
really got down to it, China in all its immensity was
just a little out-of-the-way hole where you knew everything except what the Chinese were up to. The good
doctors were friendly with a few yellow millionaires
who supplied them with some little entertainments
from time to time, but they never spoke of these in
front of Anne Marie. They drank altar wine with the
priests, and got drunk with the Protestant parson. My
father thought they were lacking in patriotism, but
they always showed up on July 14 and January 20.

January 20 was my father's birthday, and perhaps
an even grander occasion than the Fourteenth of July
in the political and social life of Szechwan. It was as if
whatever concerned France's representative were as
important as France itself; or rather as if my father
were France incarnate, the living embodiment of
France from head to foot, with his black frock coat
and his sooty eyes and brows.

The Tout-Chengtu was there again. The big drawing room was turned into a sort of benevolent throne
room; the banners and flags were the same as on the
Fourteenth of July, but the drapes were different, and
instead of the red warriors of might there were the
dragons of prosperity, decked with flowers and ears of
corn. In the midst of these auspicious omens was a
banner about ten yards long bearing, in letters of gold,
the words: "Happy birthday to Monsieur Albert Bon-

nard." My father's name 'shone out like some sacred inscription. But on this occasion the marshal, the generals, and the consuls, instead of wearing uniforms and bearing swords, were in mufti—though evening dress in broad daylight was as informal as you could get in Szechwan. For today was simply in honor of friendship. On one occasion the marshal even came in a blue robe, a refinement that showed the delicacy of his feelings since it signified that he attended from inclination and not obligation. As my father pointed out afterward to my mother, this only added to the political significance.

The birthday greetings entailed the marshal's screwing up his face to augur the consul a long life. The word "longevity" occurred in every Chinaman's greetings—not the hope, but the certainty of longevity, for a mere hope would have been considered inadequate, dangerous, and coarse. There was no question of the Chinese wishing my father good health, for that would have been to admit that he might be ill. It was left to the English consul to murmur the phrase, mischievously, and as he did so the French doctors smiled to themselves, for Albert Bonnard was their best patient. He went to the institute regularly to have himself x-rayed, for he took a close interest in the state of his interior fluids. And he'd gotten the doctors to draw him up countless certificates about his various infirmities, from nervous intestine to myocardial fatigue, which he sent to the Quai d'Orsay as proof of zeal. My father vaguely sensed this Anglo-French joke, which made my mother smile. Fortunately, at this moment the monks and nuns came, bringing up the rear, and they were serious people. They lavished God's favors on my father, the more so as they suspected he was a Freemason.

But on January 20 my father was always in excellent form, and his earnest features beamed with good will. He thanked all his guests one by one, with praise and hyberbole and allusion all laid on with a trowel. Everything was idyllic. What greater happiness could he wish the marshal, who had already made Szechwan the land of felicity? While remaining faithful to the great wisdom of his own race, he was bringing progress to the province by a judicious choice of the greatest benefits of the West. Electricity, the telegraph, and the telephone would make Chengtu into a model city. Let the marshal be assured that the aid France was ready to lend was absolutely disinterested.

Having chalked up this point against his English colleague, my father set about making a hearty apologia for the Britisher. "You're a jolly good fellow," he said in English. "And I am happy to see the Entente Cordiale between our two governments bearing such rich fruit here." When he got to the Japanese consul, my father cautiously limited himself to saluting him and his Mikado over and over again in flowery phrases. Then he rapidly dealt with the "French colony," the doctors risking their lives struggling heroically against epidemics, and the monks and nuns bringing their faith and charity to a land that welcomed every kind of truth.

Such a celebration of friendship was not complete without endless photographs. People had to be arranged in groups in such a way that Eastern and Western protocol did not clash. It was no easy matter to assemble the Tout-Chengtu without causing someone to lose "face" but of such arts my father was a master. He stood beside the war lord. Then came the other consuls, then a row of generals, a row of rich merchants, a row containing the doctors and the bishop, with the other priests and the nuns forming a background. As January 20 was not really an official occasion, my mother was admitted into the noble group, as was I, in my straw hat and sailor suit. Then everyone stood at attention in their top hats, dinner jackets, Chinese robes, and stiff collars, waiting for the click. Then again. Ten or twenty clicks, with the whole august assembly smiling affably toward the big tripod covered with a black cloth, the lens, the bulb, the pleated box, behind all of which crouched the photographer, a little green creature from Shanghai, without nationality or official protection. He claimed to be a Cantonese. But he was so indispensable to public life in Chengtu that he and his paraphernalia had nothing to fear.

When everyone had gone my father went and stood under the banner saying "Happy birthday to Monsieur Albert Bonnard," and posed there on his own for a few minutes so that the wretched photographer could round off his humble efforts.

Two or three days later the consul sent out the photographs by special messengers. They were almost as good as paintings, stuck on thick cardboard and framed, with captions both in Chinese characters and copperplate denoting the great event and specifying the day and year. Every friend got his, plus a photograph of my father alone, and one of his visiting cards. Visiting cards and photographs were the two great novelties in Szechwan, and my father's consumption of both was enormous.

The new civilization was making its way in Chengtu. It had been a long while since the French consul had given the war lord a bath as a present. Now he gave him a big generator on behalf of the President of the French Republic. Chinese mechanics brought

up in a mission school came from Shanghai to unpack
the cases as they were unloaded from the coolies'
backs, and to mount the machinery. The consul, who
didn't know anything about science, watched warily
as they fitted the gears and wires and bolts together.
Then came the inauguration. The marshal pressed a
switch, and there was light. It was a marvelous moment, when electricity burst forth in Szechwan under
the auspices of the consul of France.

The net result was a few naked, dirty light bulbs,
which were always going out, in the yamens of the
marshal, the consuls, and a few local dignitaries. In
the streets, people saw bare tree trunks set up with
wires draped from one to the other. Beggars and
soldiers used the posts to lean against.

1922. The consul was going to be a year older, for tomorrow would be January 20 again. The usual preparations were being made at the consulate, but my
mother was introducing a new specialty, a gentleman's sandwich, made according to the recipe supplied by the Protestant parson's fat lady. Anne Marie
worked away at the head of her band of cooks and
houseboys, all of them silent and earnest. With her
hair twisted into a kind of scepter, she was heaping up
mountains of geometrical rounds and slices of food,
with the chutneys and condiments dear to the Indian
Empire and the highly spiced sauces found in the
clubs in Shanghai. There were copious layers of toma-
to—a triumph on the part of my mother, for ours was
the only garden that grew them. She took great pleasure in sending a basket of them every week to the
wives of the English consul and parson.

That day my father was shut up in his office, wearing the expression reserved for grave situations. He

didn't even come out to cast an eye over the arrangements. Monsieur le Consul was preparing for any emergency, his face composed to convey deep reflection. For once again Chengtu was threatened with destruction.

All the morning there had been a stream of visitors. First, as happened every time there was a calamity in the offing—it was a sign in itself that catastrophe was imminent—came the bishop of Chengtu. He was a gaunt rough-hewn giant with a suspicious glance, prominent cheekbones, and skinny hands. His cassock was so worn and patched that its original purple dignity had turned to a sort of pee color, an earthy brown, a dusty yellow, like the robes of mendicant Buddhist monks. But his pectoral cross sparkled, and every time he saw me he gave me his ring to kiss, spluttering out a blessing through teeth yellowed by the tobacco he chewed.

But this time the holy man didn't even notice me, either coming in or going out. He stayed more than an hour with my father, and left him very worried, sweeping out of the office like a whirlwind and leaping straight onto his old horse, as bucktoothed as himself. Then he galloped off scowling, upright on his clumsy Chinese wooden saddle as if by a miracle.

After him came a group of smarmy rich Chinese merchants, suave as ever. These were the leaders of the Chinese chamber of commerce in Chengtu, the millionaires who always attended the great ceremonies at the consulate but never entered my father's office. But this time they were deposited outside in three or four chairs, having suddenly felt it necessary to "intrude upon Monsieur le Consul."

At about one o'clock there appeared a yellow gentleman much younger than the others, who often came to see my father, but very discreetly. He used to slink along on foot, which was highly incongruous, for he, too, was a rich merchant. He had a sharp, chiseled face, pointed at the top and the bottom and with a slight widening in the middle. His appearance presented a strange juxtaposition of East and West. The body was clad in the traditional manner, a black silk tunic falling down over a long white skirt, but his egg-shaped skull wore a trilby hat dented in the approved fashion. He had a thin European mustache and of course spectacles, though with their thin gold frames they were almost invisible. In short, the height of modern elegance, judiciously modified.

This gentleman-cum-merchant was something of a mystery to me. He spoke French very well, though with a dictionary vocabulary and a slight nasal twang. His pronunciation of "Monsieur le Consul" was perfect, but what struck me particularly was that instead of just gazing at me in dignified silence like the other important Chinamen, or perhaps just complimenting my father on his offspring, this person always found some agreeable little thing to say to me, such as, "Well, are you having a good time, son? Would you like me to get you a pedal car from Shanghai?" And he would give a jolly laugh. And when he spoke to the consul, instead of preserving the impassiveness that was considered seemly, he would become animated and utter little nervous exclamations, and his thin face would twitch as if with the gesticulations of his thought.

I'd received the pedal car, and even used it. In front of my parents I'd thanked him for it, and he'd said, "So you liked it, eh?" But I didn't like him. For one thing, I couldn't make him out—he was so different from the marshal, the respectable millionaires,

Li, my mafu, the servants, and the mandarin calligrapher. And the monks had told me not to trust him. He was a Christian, but one of the kind produced by the Jesuits at their university in Shanghai. The priests in Szechwan were afraid of the Jesuits, who didn't mind what they did, and who a long time ago, several centuries, had worshipped the Emperor as the Son of Heaven just as if he were the Lord Jesus himself. In those days the Jesuits had gone about as scholars and been accepted as the "learned men of the West"; they had taught mathematics, and made strange objects such as watches and compasses and even guns. But they were opportunists who practiced ancestor worship and revered dead rulers as if they were saints. In order to convert the Chinese they had turned the Holy Roman Catholic religion into a system of ethics serving both heaven and earth, like Confucianism. Theirs was an abominable error which had been condemned by the Pope.

The missionaries in Szechwan had told me this over and over again. They were all for the Sacred Heart and the Immaculate Conception, but they distrusted the Jesuits in Shanghai, who had now begun to turn out intelligent Christians who were educated and had read Voltaire and Galileo and were even trained to discuss dogma. This could only produce scoundrels, schemers, perverts, and traitors, worse than out-and-out heathens. They were always mixed up in every dubious transaction, serving as go-betweens, intermediaries, middlemen, concerned only with their own interests instead of God's. How different from the simple pious Christians of Szechwan, whose knowledge was limited to taking communion and obeying the priest!

But this Chinese gentleman in Chengtu was not a

middleman, for in Chengtu not only were European firms banned, but any of their representatives, white or yellow, was liable to terrible penalties. He was just an important tea merchant who perhaps dealt in opium, too. But secretly he acted in the interests of the big French company in Shanghai that specialized in arms, and had sold the famous guns to the marshal that time. This was why, taking suitable precautions, he occasionally turned up at the consulate. His tales often annoyed the missionaries, those saintly men who were not always merely plaster saints.

At two in the afternoon my father finally emerged for lunch. As always, he had to tell my mother everything, and this time she listened intently. He began by bursting out:

"I must say that bishop's got a nerve! He tells me that the marshal, who's already collected taxes five or six times this year, is now demanding that the city hand over another million taels. So his grace wants his Christians to be excused. And that's not all. Apparently the war lord's allowed it to filter through to the well-to-do that if the money isn't forthcoming in three days it might so happen that part of the city is destroyed by fire, preferably the merchant quarter. And the bishop is worried about the church of Notre Dame nearby, which would go up like a box of matches, so he wants me to go to the war lord and protest, and do all I can to get him to send some other part of the town up in smoke, somewhere where there's no chapel and no converts. He talks as if misfortune doesn't matter so long as it only afflicts pagans. But as soon as one of his flock is touched, that's another matter."

"What did you tell him?"

"I told him I had no intention whatever of intruding on the marshal, especially not for the purpose of accusing him of arson. For while he may use the threat to coerce the merchants, he'll make sure he comes out of the matter with clean hands. It won't be his soldiers that start the fire—it'll be brigands gotten up like coolies that he'll recruit from among the hundreds that hang around the camp of the Yunnanese army. The people know they're there, and already live in fear and trembling.

"The bishop left in a rage, hinting that he would complain to his superiors and to the government in Paris. My head was absolutely splitting by the time he went! But I'll fix him in my report to the Quai d'Orsay. I'm not going to jeopardize my whole policy for him, including the railroad, which may well materialize out of all this."

"What!"

"Let me tell it in the proper order. My next visitors were the leading merchants, all bows and smiles and groans about their inability to raise the enormous amount the marshal's asking for—but not a word about the fire that's supposed to make them cough up. What did they want? For a long time they went on beating about the bush, the whole gamut of polite procrastination. Then finally their leader, one of those survivors from the old days who haven't learned to be a little bit less filthy when dealing with white men, all hawking and spitting amongst his flowery speeches, started grunting and yapping in earnest and kept it up for a good ten minutes. At the end of each squeal he stopped to excogitate the next, salivating away as if he'd suddenly fallen asleep, while his companions nodded their heads approvingly at what he'd just said. Then he'd wake up again and mumble out a few more words. A typical Chinese speech of the old days, in short.

"He started by saying how happy he was, how happy

all the merchants in Chengtu were, to contribute toward the strengthening of the excellent armies of
Yunnan and Szechwan, united for the protection of
Chengtu in these uncertain times. They were all ready
to sacrifice themselves, their families, their children,
even their ancestors, to this noble end. But unfortunately they were already so poor . . . Business was
so bad . . . They were humble men overwhelmed by
their patriotic burden. But could not their foreign
friends, especially their French friends, the protectors
of beautiful Indochina, help the Chengtu forces by
supplying them with equipment? Such help would
merit a thousand blessings.

"More throat-clearing and coughing. They all stared
at their slippers so as not to appear to be awaiting
my answer—which only meant they were awaiting it
very eagerly. I was flabbergasted. I realized they
wanted me to get arms from Indochina for the Yunnanese. Just like Mr. Lu. But Mr. Lu is the gray
eminence behind the Yunnanese, whereas these people were citizens of Chengtu, traditional Szechwanese
who really hate the marshal and his 'foreign' troops,
ruthless ruffians on the point of burning them and
their precious shops to bits. They must certainly, in
fact, support the Szechwan army, which is swelling
enormously and getting recruits from all sides. So why
had they come to me to ask me to help their enemies
in their now dangerous plight? What traps, what
awful pitfalls, lay behind their strange proposal? I
put on my best smile and told them they were quite
right to have faith in France's love for China: it had
often been proved, and France was ready to show it
even more clearly in the future. But, by reason of this
very friendship, France must respect the great wisdom
of the Chinese, who were quite capable of weathering

temporary difficulties and emerging into the happiness
which lay belond.

"I heaved a sigh of relief when the old humbugs
left. They're always incomprehensible, these Chinks—
and what did they want of me now? I started to think."

And when the consul thought, that was really something! I can imagine him now, the old South China
hand, pacing around his office not understanding a
thing, reduced to anguished sighs. For sometimes Albert Bonnard, France's consul in China, a very good
consul, a consul in every fiber of his body and every
hour of his life, whose job was riveted to his very
soul, whose knowledge of the country was extraordinary—sometimes he was overcome with weariness and
repugnance. And his consular face, fearing pitfalls,
would grow dejected.

In these periods of depression my father would be
haunted by yellow faces, friendly-looking countenances reflected back and forth within his brain as in
a hall of mirrors, motionless countenances concealing
twisted, elaborate, crazy designs which would be put
into cruel execution. What deviousness had to be gone
through before the clever ones, by the law that seemed
to favor intelligence and guile, crushed their enemies
like so many ants! No such thing as pity or sentiment,
just implacable calculation, dark intrigue, pent-up
energy, deception, with great banquets that were really
traps, followed by the pleasure of exploiting, humiliating, and torturing the losers or those who were
merely the underdogs. China was permanent revolution, endless war, not just between armies but also
between individuals, within families and guilds, everywhere. It was kill or be killed, be bloated with wealth
or die of want. Everything was slow, yet at the same
time extraordinarily swift. Anything was possible, any-

thing went. Virtue consisted of such useful vices as
brought profit and pleasure, and pleasure was the more
keenly felt when counterpointed by catastrophe afflict-
ing others, whether the others were vanquished enemies
or the ordinary mass of mankind. But nothing was
ever settled once and for all; nothing was ever finished. For everyone the game was one that never
ended. Life was a wager, a conflict of human wills
which lent fate a thousand changing and contradictory masks. The threat of death, actual torture,
dreadful suffering could be metamorphosed into opu-
lence, pride, and pleasure. And vice versa, with the
drop into misfortune and death. The peaceful-looking
Chinese really seethed all the time with hidden fury,
ready at any moment to explode. And all without loss
of "face," with proper decorum, with skillful avoid-
ance of seeming to inflict or suffer humiliation. Everything had the appearance of calm; the lid was kept
on tight. When treachery and cruelty did not serve,
there was always the possibility of arrangement, a network of compromise and reversal, intricate webs, delicate balances that could last for quite a long while.
And then at last one day the thunderbolt, the revela-
tion, the kill. The victor would go through ritual
gestures of affront and insult and revenge, as if the
very act of resisting him had been a crime beyond
description. Woe to the losers, who before they were
chastised must confess and express remorse and sue
for pardon. It was only right that the losers implore,
and the winners refuse with howls of wrath, protract-
ing their hatred and enjoyment up to the moment of
execution, when torture must be as long-drawn-out as
possible, for the greater satisfaction and triumph of
the victor. Woe to the poor, woe to the unfortunate!
China the proud was rent by terrible scenes of slavery

and slaughter, by millions of corpses withered with want or drifting through the water while the rich gorged. Such was Buddhist China, where the symbol of life was a wheel on which men were whirled round by passion, and where that headlong flight could only be arrested, and nirvana and salvation attained, by a complete and absolute renunciation of the illusions of happiness. But sages detached from reality were rare —apparently even the priests were scoundrels.

China. Of that mysterious, murky China my father, despite his brightness and his earnestness, was, deep down, afraid. Like all the white men, all the Westerners, who with their own kind of fury went on trampling the country down, conquering and debasing it, loading it with chains and treaties and obligations. They were haunted with dread even in the midst of their Concessions, of their blocks of flats and their wealth. In spite of their Bible, their dollars, their warships, their police and informers and colonial regiments. It was a dread that never completely left them, and that made them rejoice at the extermination practiced by the Chinese themselves, though they hid their true feeling beneath scorn and condescension and expressions of pity. The English papers in Shanghai gave five lines to five million Chinese dead of starvation in Shantung, a couple of hundred miles away. But would the Celestial People's astonishing ability to bear anything last forever? For the Chinese, even though they were docile and destroyed one another and regressed to primitive savagery, could inspire terror.

My father's secret fear was all the greater because there in Chengtu, in forbidden China, he was alone, just tolerated among the war lords and the masses of Chinese. He was at China's mercy, playing China's game in the Chinese manner in order to survive and win, in order that France might win. He was surrounded by danger or the illusion of danger—for sometimes his wild cogitations would lead him to invent trouble where none existed, to conjure up imaginary dangers out of ordinary events and Chinese apathy. On such occasions he would look drawn and preoccupied, and my mother would say, "Aren't you feeling well, Albert?" At such times it was not the doctors, but rather the priests, the only white men who weren't at all afraid, who set him to rights again.

On that particular day, however, the day before his birthday, my father only grew more and more dejected and depressed. But he straightened up in his chair and, beneath his specs, composed his face in two great creases of resolution. It was a stand he was taking, at once full of pity for himself and yet fiercely and meticulously mulish—the expression of a hero overcome by his own heroism, of one sacrificing himself to duty. For despite his various kinds of weakness and cowardice, his sighs and his valetudinarianism, the consul, once he had shaken off his affectations, was a man absolutely devoted to his always perilous purpose. Real fear was replaced by fear of another kind, bold, sly, and devious, and shrouded in self-satisfaction and self-admiration. But he liked others, and in particular my mother, to share this admiration, and this gave rise to all sorts of devices designed to demonstrate his bravery.

As he needed to screw up his courage on such occasions, he used to work himself up beforehand in the privacy of his office. This time he must have told himself: "War is about to break out in Chengtu. If I keep quiet the Quai d'Orsay can't blame me, but they will notice. I'm not an archbishop's son, like all those other consuls that don't do a thing and then boast about their deeds afterward. They came up the easy way, and the dimmer they are, the quicker they rise. But I did it the hard way, taking on all the rotten jobs no one else would touch. Well, now I'm going to make my presence felt at last in this devil's caldron here. It's starting to boil—it must be, or those old boys wouldn't have lowered themselves to come and see me. But what are they hiding up those silk sleeves of theirs? Whom can I consult? I can't ask the bishop to come here again after our set-to this morning. I'll send for Mr. Cheng."

So that was how Mr. Cheng came and went, furtive but gay, a merry little bird of prey. And that was how my father, having worked his way through lunch on the bishop and the merchants, and having told the head boy off because the salt didn't pour properly, came to the dessert: the strange Mr. Cheng.

"You know him by reputation, Anne Marie," he said. "Monsieur Dumont recommended him to me at the terrible dinner we went to in that huge great bungalow of his, with the grand piano and chandeliers and rare paintings, ha ha, and the Chinese servants got up as footmen. What a show-off Dumont is, with his red face and his loud mouth, banging on the table and telling tall stories. We've talked about him before, with his diamond cuff links and his tails, and his head sticking out of the top like a pumpkin. And to think his father was just a Marseilles layabout who worked as a deckhand on English clippers, smuggling cases of opium from Bengal to the red rocky coves of Kwangtung. And the son's a millionaire and put on patronizing airs with me. You remember, I had to protest because he almost failed to show you the proper respect, and one of the other guests had to pacify him—a policeman from the French Concession in Shanghai, a nasty little bit of work with gimlet eyes and a curly mustache. And Dumont's wife, a Vietnamese half-caste he'd picked up in Saigon, roared with laughter. I wasn't even given the place of honor. It was given to Tu Yu-seng, one of the three biggest gangsters in Shanghai."

"Yes, I remember. Dumont fleeced you afterward at poker."

"He was drunk! He kept throwing down handfuls of dollars and yelling, 'I'll raise you!' It was most ill-mannered! He was trying to show me that I was a nobody next to him. And then, you may recall, he took me aside to talk business. Tried to tell me what was what, to dazzle me with famous names—bankers, ministers, important people in Paris—his associates, according to him. Not to mention how friendly he was with the big businessmen like Jardine and Matheson, Butterfield and Swire, and the Hong Kong and Shanghai Bank, and all the English firms that have the Asian trade in their pockets. 'And I know all the war lords,' he said. 'Great friends of mine. I know how to look after myself with the Chinese. They're clever enough, but I'm smarter. They've only got one idea—to make more money so as to get more soldiers, and to get more soldiers so as to make more money. They want any toy they can lay hands on so long as it will kill. China's a fantastic market for arms. The English work through their financial power, the Japanese use armies of spies and the threat of the sword. I use my common sense. Wangling's the French method, as you know.' "

"He sent me a huge bunch of flowers the next day, I remember."

"And to think that Dumont's one of the most eminent members of the French colony, admitted into the best English clubs, and always at the races with a carnation in his buttonhole. And a prominent member of the French Club, lording it in front of the biggest bar in the world. And a friend of the French consul general, the head of the French Concession!"

"You wouldn't mind being in his shoes!"

"I should think not! He employs a million men, a thousand of them white! The city council, the French administration, the French police and legal system, the French forces—they're all at his beck and call. He's even got a battalion from Indochina. He's a king!"

"And the Concession is such a beautiful place. I'd like to live in one of those shady streets, especially the Avenue Foch or the Avenue Joffre, with all those flowers and fine houses."

"All full of war lords who've come unstuck in their own provinces and are waiting there, safely out of the way, for better days, smoking opium and surrounded by their concubines, their kids, and their treasures. I personally would rather be actually on the job with them in Chengtu."

"And anyway, Albert, in Shanghai you'd always be having upsets with the Europeans—you're so touchy. If you took precedence over the ladies, as you do here, you'd split the French colony down the middle for months, and be an endless subject of conversation for the gentlemen as they drank their apéritifs."

"No risk of anything like that with the present consul there, anyway. He's an artful one—a human tapeworm, as thin as a match with the wood scraped off, who winds everyone up in the coils of his charm. Slav origin, you know. That gives him the right to be in-

dulgent to the point of cynicism, and contemplate
vice and crime with mere amusement. He's quite a
home in that super-Chicago. He's picked up the typi
cal tone of the French Concession—gossip, snobbish
ness, and vulgarity. He just laughed in my face when
I complained about Dumont. 'He's a very good fellow
Not exactly distinguished, of course. It's a funny thing
—when the English get rich they become gentlemen
even if they're only gentlemen sharks. But the French
—our handful of Shanghai millionaires stay as vulga
as ever."

Then my father went on at length about his fellow
countrymen in Shanghai, all upstarts according to
him, boors who stuck out like sore thumbs among the
formal British. Albert, though not very distinguished
himself, was amazed that the Eengleesh, the Breeteesh
who were dignity itself (not that he liked them, for
all that), accepted that Gallic bear garden, and wa
almost shocked that the British, who would scarcel
touch the Chinese with a ten-foot pole, didn't mind
their colleagues in the French Concession rubbing
shoulders just as they liked with the Chinks.

But Albert made the necessary distinctions among
the French in Shanghai. Among the leading light
there were some stiff gentlemen in stiff collars, with
handles to their names, and given to the hand-kissing
flowery speeches and other eccentricities of elderl
philanderers. They were all bad lots. The others, th
coastal fraternity who had knocked about all the Chi
nese dives, strong enough characters to have survive
and come out on top, these seemed to be quite goo
sorts—crazy when it came to making or squanderin
money, but that was a disease that was general i
Shanghai. Avid for life, they'd been sent right aroun
the bend by China. They pretended to be as toug

as the Celestial People themselves, and, mixing with
them, suffered the natural consequences. Under their
air of toughness they were half crazy, with their brazen
vivacity, gaiety, and self-indulgence; they were at one
and the same time Sinified, Anglicized, and yet more
French than the French in the Concession. They
didn't pretend butter wouldn't melt in their mouths,
of course. But most of them, one day when they were
tipsy, had committed the irremediable mistake of
breaking some promise made to a Chinese merchant.
Few of them realized that once an agreement was made
it had to be kept to, all the more so when you were
all gangsters. And this was what distinguished the real
tough guys from the false ones.

And now even Dumont has gone and played a
dirty trick," sighed Albert. "He thinks too damn much
of himself. But I shall have to support him and his
beastly Mr. Cheng."

He rolled his eyes upward in despair.

"I've had about enough of him. But I'm keeping
an eye on him. I didn't tell Mr. Lu, of course, but our
priests kept me in the picture about the business of
the 75's right from the beginning. After that I began
to have my doubts, but at the time Cheng swore he
was innocent. And I was fool enough to believe him
and his boss Dumont—Dumont was vouched for by
the French consul in Shanghai. Then came the day
when the missionaries told me Cheng had cleared off,
and everything was plain, if that's the word."

"Why didn't you tell me?" said Anne Marie with
a shrug. "I'd have been less puzzled to see the marshal's troops around the consulate. I think you made
rather a muddle, my dear."

"I was afraid you might be worried. . . . Well, sure
enough, Cheng, who turned up again in Chengtu not
cut up in pieces but actually smiling, let the cat out

of the bag to me a week ago. It was Dumont who had arranged it all, to please the English, who are against Yunnan and the Southerners. Cheng wasn't even let in on it, and only had time to get as far away as possible from Chengtu. He went to Ichang, where he managed to get the local war lord to hand over a large sum of money for the guns the Yunnanese had already paid for. He sent half to Dumont and brought the rest back to Chengtu, where he did a deal with Mr. Lu. He said to him, 'I'm paying you back part of the money, but for the other part I've got a good idea that won't cost you anything and will get you much better weapons than the ones that went astray.' The idea was that the war lord of Chengtu should pretend to be angry with me and besiege the consulate, while Lu offered to get me out of it by asking for machine guns from Indochina in return for a promise to let the railroad be extended to Szechwan."

"And after all that you still trust Cheng?"

"Yes—his telling me all about the guns was an extraordinary thing for a Chinese to do. Only a very sophisticated, Jesuit-model Chink would be capable of such a move. He was quite straightforward, quite open—as if he was making a bid at poker. He's come to see that the truth can pay, too, in certain circumstances. And that's something really degenerate in a Chinese."

"He'll betray you."

"Not now—our interests are the same. With his French arms merchant supplying the Szechwanese, he needs me to cover up for him with the Yunnanese. What's more, as it was he who got me mixed up with Lu in the first place, I've insisted that Cheng keep me fully informed of what's going on if he wants me to help him keep a head on his shoulders. One good turn deserves another."

"Cheng looks like a ferret or a fox, with those deceitful eyes."

This only made my father all the more pleased with himself.

"You've got it quite wrong, Anne Marie. Cheng was quite marvelous this morning. He arrived almost as soon as I sent for him, and when I'd told him—with some anxiety, I admit—about the merchants' having been to see me, he gave a long, quiet, nervous cough, which for him no doubt signifies the utmost hilarity, irony, and amusement, then cleared his throat and told me I had absolutely nothing to worry about. 'On the contrary, Monsieur le Consul, it's very amusing. The honorable Chengtu merchants are like lambs being torn apart by eagles. They're longing for a savior, and they think it might be you.'

"He went on to explain, my dear, that they're desperate to find some way out, for if the present situation continues they'll be crushed and flattened till not even blood and bones are left—mulcted of their last sou, after all the methods of making them disgorge have been applied, from arson and murder to the kidnapping and abduction of their concubines and the mutilation of their sons, and many other well-known practices. There are three armies battening on Chengtu: the Yunnanese; the army of Kweichow province, their ally; and the Szechwanese army, which is getting larger every day. And they've all got their tongues hanging out. So the merchants, who are well aware of the fate in store for them, are desperate.

The poor Chengtu merchants crowded in the consul's office were the victims of their own naïveté. They had welcomed the Yunnanese at first, when they appeared from the tropical land beyond the clouds to drive out the mercenary armies of the formidable Yüan Shih-kai, trying to proclaim himself emperor in Peking. The tough and haughty Yunnanese warriors, still scarcely more than savages, were known as "the tigers." But the richness of fertile Szechwan unleased their greed.

For years Chengtu had been full of sentry boxes, toll gates, customs posts—a great web in which the Yunnanese officers sat like spiders stuffing themselves with goods and money. Suddenly, instead of the smiles of the old corrupt officials, you got a thump with the butt of a revolver. The marshal was always demanding taxes for the upkeep of his army. The local dignitaries would go and see him, oozing politeness and fear, each having attempted to conciliate the marshal beforehand by sending expensive gifts, banners wishing him prosperity, their favorite concubines or minions, and scrolls containing not only greetings but also bank notes. But it was not enough. Nothing was ever enough. So the peace-loving Chengtu merchants shut themselves up at home. Little good that did them. Either they would receive an official summons from the general, or he would send wily emissaries to propose a deal. And the deal always cost far too much. So the merchants of Chengtu got together. They had been patient for a long time, but now their patience was exhausted, and in a sudden access of courage they hired some Szechwan veterans to get together an army to drive out the Yunnanese. For at that time all that was left in the province were a few quiet old militia regiments with the traditional sunshades and opium pipes, the usual immemorial roughs and scoundrels. But after the mysterious confabulations of the merchants the town started to swarm with generals, men of letters, monks, and exmandarins. A mysterious set-up run by mysterious money—in fact, the money came from the chambers of commerce.

After a few months this stir produced concrete results, and a number of Szechwanese army groups formed around the city. The soldiers assumed attitudes calculated to inspire both terror and confidence in their resolution. Just like actors on the stage. The army grew larger and larger, moving out of the Middle Ages into modern times, the men adopting rigid drill instead of the old easygoing ways that had been half kindly and only half bloodthirsty. And then of course there were all the arms—the bayonets and machine guns and artillery.

The merchants unwittingly brought about their own undoing, for these Szechwan generals of theirs only meant to feather their own nests and weren't in any hurry at all to fight. The merchants kept on at them in vain; the answer was always a reference to military strategy: "The time is not yet ripe. We must wait and increase our strength enough to wipe out all the Yunnanese at a blow."

The millionaires of Chengtu were worried, and not at all eager to undo their purse strings any further; they preferred to pay out after the victory. So the Szechwan generals encouraged their generosity by means of discreet examples—disappearances, and bodies discovered with their heads cut off. But these annoyances might also have been due to the Yunnanese, who, angry at the competition they were encountering, were even more brutal and exacting than before. It was as if all the ever-increasing armies, while hating or pretending to hate each other at the same time as they exchanged formal salutations, were in league to strip the population to the bone before joining battle.

The merchants racked their brains to try to find a way of forcing "their" Szechwan generals to fight and be done with it. Wise heads were put together in long confabulations. Amid the universal despondency the solution came in an innocent remark by a gentleman resembling a cocoon of silk: "They say the Yunnanese are awaiting the arrival of powerful machine guns given them by the French in Indochina, and then they'll take a bloody revenge on the Szechwanese." That was a marvelous thought. The next thing was to bring this rumor to the ears of the wily and reluctant Szechwanese, so they should see themselves already slashed to death by the Yunnanese, who though few in numbers would be hellbent on extermination as soon as they had arms. The merchants carried out their plan of making the Szechwan army believe the French arms were on the point of arriving, so that the fear in their innards would drive them to take the initiative and crush the Yunnanese beneath the weight and flood of numbers. The merchants' visit to the consulate was the key point in their strategy.

The consul, swallowing his last mouthful of strawberries from the garden, was pleased with himself. He had duly shown Anne Marie that he had understood everything, got it all under control. Before leaving the table he let fall a typically brilliant remark designed to put the crowning touch to his wife's admiration.

"You know how careful I am. If I'd uttered one compromising word in front of the merchants, if I'd shown the slightest knowledge about the arms from Indochina, I'd have triggered off the battle of Chengtu. As soon as they'd left me they'd have gone and told the Szechwan generals: 'Now it's certain. You'll be massacred if you don't attack the Yunnanese at once!' You see the responsibility of my position."

"Good," said Anne Marie. "So there won't be any trouble in Chengtu, thanks to you. At least not much. But what about the delights of the immediate future —what about the famous fire due tomorrow or the day after?"

"I put the question to Cheng, as you may well imagine. He smiled sweetly. Taken against the background of current events, it won't amount to very much. Of course there will be a fire, otherwise the marshal would lose face. But after all, it will only be a poor quarter that's burned down."

My father's face was all lit up as he went to take his customary siesta. As if he thought he'd been very clever. As if he held in his mind all the threads of all the plots in Chengtu. As for my mother, she went to see how the preparations for Albert Bonnard's birthday were getting on. They had been proceeding smoothly in the peace of the consulate, apparently undisturbed by that morning's diplomatic storm. But there is no doubt that my father's interminable comments over lunch had percolated to the kitchens and courtyards, and that behind the diligent masks of the servants preparing for the party, their minds were equally busy.

It was half-light under the avenue of pomegranates in the garden of the consulate. The earth was warm beneath the jagged scrolls of the leaves and the curves of the crackleware fruit. A stele with a worn lion's face, a stone unicorn, reflections from the shining paint of the roofs mingled with the dark foliage in an unreal iridescence of shapes and shadows. Symbols. Not far off, the lilies in the pool were living hearts. It was a world of deep peace, and where the dark was densest and most golden under the thick flowering bushes, a woman in a white tunic crouched on a wooden bench. It was Li. She was making a strange little noise, at the same time a gasp and a trickle. Moisture filled her eyes, flowed down her flat cheeks, made them a watery plane. I was taken aback. Tears, damp sorrow, real suffering were unknown to me. Chinese men and women did not weep. They screamed and yelped in a mad whirl of words and gestures, terrible expressions, using their hands like rakes to curse with, their lips like spouts for insults. Such scenes and hysterics were completely conventional, a mere technique for expressing anger, pain, or hatred, all kinds of feelings whose sincerity one never could be sure of. The shrill plaints of professional mourning women, the croaking of professional beggars—all these exaggerated cries and noises were either playacting for reward or magic intended to impress. But that a human being, someone like Li, might, all by herself, without profit or audience or calculation of effect, give way to sorrow, struck me as embarrassing. I felt rather ashamed for her.

Her usually calm and placid face was touching in its distress. She went on sobbing:

"The Yunnanese will kill us all. They'll kill me just as they did my parents, who were wretchedly burned to death. But this time the whole city will be reduced to ashes."

How many times had Li told me the story of the destruction of her father and mother and an indeterminate number of younger brothers and sisters, some years ago! The family had sold bits of fried fish in a little street near the great south gate. It was an itinerant trade, right among the crowd, the only equipmen a cart, some cleavers, and a fire under a pot of all kinds of fats. Into the seething mixture were flung scraps of carp, bladders, fins. The flames lit up the customers' delighted faces, pleasantly drying up the sweat; mouths munched; coins were threaded on strings. It reeked to high heaven, but it was a marvelous life.

One evening another flame, a huge one, the tongue of the fire dragon, licked at the little alley where these poor folks lived. In a few hours the human mass was consumed in the red brazier. The "firemen," instead of throwing water, beat on drums and gongs to frighten away evil spirits. But the wind dropped, and the fiery furnace, instead of swallowing up fresh prey and other streets, stopped where it was and consumed itself, turning from red to black, gradually dying alongside its victims—tens of thousands of anonymous creatures of whom nothing remained, not even their names.

Li ran toward the great swirl of flames and smoke. She saw a few people, like singed ants, escaping from the blaze. She waited for hours, and found herself standing before a funereal layer of debris three feet deep. Over it all hung a stifling heat, which gradually lessened until at last Li could walk over the macabre expanse purified by the fire. Around the edge were a few corpses that hadn't been burned; hordes of stray dogs were digging them out. Within the burned area itself, everything was uniformly reduced to cinders. There were no men to be seen but thieves, and a patrol in which one soldier was also an executioner and carried a machete slung over his shoulder. Then other human shadows appeared. They were relatives, and instead of looting they were searching the debris in the hope of finding bones belonging to those they had lost in the fire. The dogs were better at this than the people, but whenever a cur uncovered a burnt shoulder blade or humerus there was always a man or woman there to snatch it away, declaring: "That belongs to my honorable grandfather." Such discoveries made it possible to perform the rites, to put up stones, to build an altar to one's ancestors. It was a consolation. But Li went away with nothing. She could not do honor to her vanished parents. Shame was added to misfortune. All that was left to her was a sister who worked in a teahouse.

And now, in the consulate garden, was this creature of desolation really my Li, with her joy of living, of eating, of caressing her young master? My Li, living so placidly beside me, fearing nothing but the evil spirits that she drove away with amulets? Under my clothes she had once hidden a little bag full of strange things—elephant dung, poison from a cobra, blood of a man executed at full moon. But my mother found this talisman and threw it away.

I didn't recognize Li. When she had told me about the spontaneous combustion of her parents she had spoken about it with indifference, as if it were a bit of bad luck, an everyday incident, part of the common routine. I wondered if some malevolent being, some devil, had taken possession of her. My father, who for some time had thought that Li was rather strange, had another explanation.

"She's a fool," he would say to my mother. "If she keeps on like this we'll have to replace her with someone older and more sensible. We can't have her frightening the boy. She's got a mad hatred for the Yunnanese, as if they burned her family deliberately. But once or twice every year there's a fire in Chengtu that destroys one quarter or another. Either it's an accident, or the most convenient way for some rich property owner to rid his land of human vermin. It may well be that the Yunnanese officers, the marshal even, have been kind enough in the past not to take offense at these somewhat peremptory methods—it's possible they may have looked the other way in return for money. Just ordinary commission, the usual custom in these parts. The mandarins used to do the same."

"But this time it's the marshal himself who's going to start the fire, isn't it?"

"That is a little different, I agree. But it's a matter of high politics, my dear. There's no danger in the consulate. They're not going to roast us. Li is making too much fuss."

And certainly, there in the garden Li was gradually overcome with rage. I tried in vain to calm her down by rubbing my nose against hers. Instead of weeping quietly she started to rasp like a corn crake; she started up all disheveled, her face distorted. The Ch'i, the black humors from inside the body, had gone to her head.

"A soothsayer told me," she shrieked. "In a few weeks, thousands of conquered Yunnanese will be buried alive outside the walls, with their heads above ground. And I'll go and tear their eyes out with my fingers!"

Despite the preparations for the party, all the servants were by now crowded around us. They seemed embarrassed. Among them was the cook, Li's protector, with his skull round as a rice bowl and his ogling eyes surrounded by tiny crow's-feet, like the navel of a Buddha. His paunch bore witness to his prosperity and wisdom. It was he who was the real head of the staff, not the official head boy, the thin ungainly fellow who flattered my father. The cook spoke little, never departing from the almost sacerdotal dignity proper to a man who filled bellies. In a few words,

but as if he were not speaking at all, his features unmoving, he could always give my mother good advice.
I never saw him make a sudden gesture, at least until
I saw him catch hold of Li and give her a drubbing
with his big fists. Immediately, as though awakening
from a nightmare, she turned back into my own Li
again, charming and gentle. But I heard the chef
whisper to her:

"What are you doing, cursing the Yunnanese in
front of Monsieur le Consul's son, when you know he's
on their side!"

I was a taciturn, rather haughty youngster, and this
sort of hullabaloo no longer amused me. I was already
blasé. So I went off, leaving behind me the consulate
and its agitations, its whims, and its earnest preparations for the party.

My escape was to go into Chengtu with my mafu.
He, his thick head full of gaiety, the veteran, the ex-
brigand, the hardened old trooper who'd served so
many sides and so many war lords impartially, poverty's mercenary who'd impaled and disemboweled and
beheaded with supreme indifference—little he cared
about the Yunnanese or the Szechwanese. He was
happy at the thought of war approaching, gradually
settling in, promising Chengtu its horrors.

A sticky weight hung over the town, a Chengtu de-
void of meaning, dumb and deserted. All was consumed in a cloud of uncertainty. The thin, unstirring
crowd was torpid, idle, apathetic. No shouting, no
shrieks, no haggling, no ferocity, no joy. It was a
China of shadows, of inert faces, people approaching
one another cautiously, just for a few words and gestures. And in what was almost a void, in those mazes
bereft of their swarming denizens, the dirt caught you
by the throat even more than usual. The stench, left

to itself, without the enlivening intensity of the people, without the heightening effect of lights, noises, nerves, and voices, was sickly as it emerged from heaps of rubbish. Tatterdemalions' sores, lepers, flies, dogs covered with mange—all that was usually borne along by the torrent of life, a bewitching and voluptutous immersion in good and evil—was now mere ordinary putrefaction drying in the sun. Even the dung, instead of being lovingly gathered up, was just left where it was. The beggars no longer attacked with their stumps, but crouched in corners like sick animals. Not to mention the seemingly dead: boatmen sleeping open-mouthed, their skeleton limbs bent under them.

Finally I came to the river, a tributary of the Yangtze, a kind of ditch full of almost solid liquid, which dried up at low water into an expanse of mud, and at high water became a silt-laden flood. But this was January, and the stream flowed with difficulty between the banks of refuse. Kites wheeled overhead, on the lookout for carrion. In the floating city of junks, usually seething like a swarm of crabs with coolies, whores, sailors, small-time thieves, murderers, soothsayers, sorcerers, men, women, and brats, all was quiet with a special kind of anticipation. These dregs of humanity, lower than the professional beggars who were organized in castes, were hoping for Chengtu to be put to fire and sword, so that when the soldiers had finished they could emerge to scavenge.

In the midst of this void of hope and fear, one form of activity still went on—that of the human beasts of burden who under the foreman's lash loaded onto galled shoulders sacks of rice weighing over two hundred pounds and rising up behind their skulls like monstrous humps. Each gaunt naked body scurried along under its cope or cangue, head crushed down, ribs jutting out, in one rough dash, almost a blind rush, so as to throw off as soon as possible the almost unbearable weight. They had to run up narrow, uneven, rickety planks suspended over the half-solid, half-liquid riverbank onto the big square-sterned wooden boat which took the grain into its round belly. Then, with scarcely time for the panting to stop or the muscles to unflex, they ran down again. An endless shuttle, a round, a stream of creatures scuttling and hustling one another so as not to break the rhythm of their wretched assault, each man seeming enormous with his burden, then almost a skeleton as he descended to become huge again under another load.

Their round was the round of prosperity, for their work meant life, the movement of supplies, trade. But everywhere else in Chengtu, especially the wealthy part, the part for which these coolies were still toiling, a watchful apathy reigned. In the main streets, with the massive towers of the pawnshops and the high observation posts of the night watchmen rising above them, the merchants' banners dangled sadly over the smooth pavement. No more sounds of mah-jongg, no more gentlemen amusing themselves flying kites or showing off exotically beautiful birds, the most prized being kingfishers with feathers like the azure surface of a lake. No dream ladies, ladies of pleasure, slim sheaths surmounted by tiaras, faces like chased metal, emerging from sedan chairs to disappear, tottering and fluttering like wounded butterflies, into dark corridors. The teahouses were deserted. The shops were only half open, the padlocks all ready to be fastened. Everywhere, behind the partitions and walls and ramparts, you sensed invisible Chinamen in consultation. Outside, men with well-worn armbands trotted along the streets, the incarnation of those calculations, the agents of the important people who were shaping destiny. The humble messengers went to and fro with propositions and counterpropositions. Chengtu was in incubation.

There were soldiers everywhere. You came on them in every temple, their little black horses carelessly tethered to some Buddha. Groups of them lay sprawling in houses, courtyards, and streets. Most of them only ate and slept, others cordoned off alleys or patrolled the streets in squads. There wasn't even any looting. They too, were in a state of anticipation, looking forward to bloodthirsty pleasures and good profits.

The faces of the Kweichow men, dogsbodies of the Yunnanese, were impassive. Although they were bristling with weapons, they did not brandish them, and they presented a pitiful spectacle: barefoot in straw sandals, what had once been uniforms reduced to khaki tatters. The only thing about them that was almost as it should be and lent them the dignity of dignitaries was their peaked caps with badges. My mafu pointed to them.

"They're occupying the center of Chengtu, probably getting ready to betray the Yunnanese. Their general's negotiating with the Szechwanese. He's even ordered his men not to molest the population. He's a fool—even if the Yunnanese are beaten the Szechwanese will lose no time cutting off his head."

Elsewhere the impassiveness was more terrifying still, as I found when I went through a gate in an old brick wall inside the city ramparts. I was now in what had been the imperial city, where the viceroy used to live. In the last few years I had often galloped among those splendors falling into ruin: woods, meadows, pools, palaces, the hill of the tortoise with all its pagodas, its statues of Buddha given a patina by the centuries, and its effigies of emperors with candles burning before them. I'd been told the Tartar warriors had once gone about here among cages full of raging wild beasts, held in only by sliding panels. They collected insects with chopsticks. Otherwise, they did nothing. Their wives, who had camellias in their hair and unbound feet, just sat about smoking pipes or cigars. The viceroy's train would pass with a flash of the eunuchs' sabers, the clash of cymbals, genuflections. But I never met all these proud Manchus—they were slain in the 1911 revolution. Since then the imperial city had become a wilderness: splitting, cracking ruins, with some still beautiful remains. Then hard-working Chinamen, peasants, had cultivated the soil and grown fields of vegetables everywhere—cabbages and turnips surrounded by pits of dung. What I was used to seeing here were the backs of the indefatigable farmers, digging, hoeing, or spreading excrement.

But for some time now the Yunnanese army had installed itself in the imperial city as in a fort, the last bastion should there be a general assault. And that day I saw soldiers by the thousand. Behind each lookout hole a man knelt with his weapon trained on Chengtu. Every enclosure contained piles of guns and rows of troops, sitting or lying down. Strict discipline. No disturbance. Nothing but soldiers, stiff and very clean, with hair either shaved off or cut very short. Everything was cool, the gestures automatic: raising one's gun, cocking it, aiming, expressing aggressiveness and the desire to kill. They were thin, as if sculpted in hard wood. Smooth, their skin like a uniform, their uniforms themselves no more than fatigue dress. All their heads were bound up in red turbans the color of blood and fire, and around each flat stomach was a belt of cartridges. Though seemingly inert, they were solid blocks of cruelty, scorn, superiority. Some very young ones had combs in their breast pockets, a compulsory comb, sign of hygiene, modernism, and revolution.

No one stood in our way, and my mafu and I came up to a former Buddhist monastery converted into a command post. We went into a chamber decorated with glowing lacquerwork, in which a guardroom was rigged up in the presence of the gods. Suddenly there was a raucous cry, a concentrated yell, a guttural explosion. It was a challenge. There was the sound of breeches being loaded. All around us, eyes that seemed to be taking aim, bayonets, and the mafu waved his arms and shouted, "It's the French consul's little boy —the French consul—your marshal's great friend. If you hurt him your heads are as good as cut off." The soldiers' faces looked set and obstinate, as if they hadn't heard, hadn't understood. Then an officer turned up and at once gave the sign for us to be let go.

We went back across the imperial city, my mafu conducting me carefully, leading my horse by the bridle. He was in jovial spirits. Along we went past sentries who watched us go by without the least gleam in their eye, as if we did not exist. They were stationed along our path in a dangerous attitude combining arrogant stiffness with nonchalant pride. Everything was as usual. A little way off, the soldiers' wives crouched down cooking rice. They were strapping, full-cheeked creatures with wrinkled leathery faces, weatherbeaten from following their menfolk across country, through battles, sieges, and blood. They scarcely looked like women at all—chunky, bustling

objects only comparatively human. And almost all of
them carried in a sort of bag on their backs, without
ever allowing it to interrupt their work, their last-
born infant. Naked children were laughing all around.

There was the sound of orders sharply given. In a
field, well-disciplined soldiers were drilling, sticking
bayonets into straw dummies with meticulous, precisely repeated movements, the steel penetrating what
was supposed to be a heart, a chest, a belly. But my
mafu, when he saw them, spat with disapproval. The
old brigand's sense of decorum was offended. For these
front-line troops were girls in uniform.

"These Yunnanese have no respect for anything,"
he said, scowling. "They've even got the cheek to have
women in their army, whole battalions of them."

For him as for all the Szechwanese, the women soldiers were sacrilege, both an insult and a mockery.
The people of Chengtu always spoke of them with indignation, licking their lips over the prospect of tearing out their innards at the first opportunity.

We were approaching the exit from the imperial
city. Here a flock of lower-class Szechwanese bustled
about—whores, scribes, itinerant merchants, jugglers,
sellers of scraps of meat, all the people necessary to
soldiers' needs, even if they are enemies. A typical
caravanserai with its noise, its haggling over a cabbage stump, its twitter of voices, its professional singsong. Suddenly everything went rigid and silent. A
trumpet sounded. From the shade of the gateway, a
deep passage, emerged a spanking Yunnanese regiment.
The standard gleamed, a general saluted with drawn
sword. Behind him was a flood of bayonets, borne by
soldiers marching with a stride, at once leisurely and
swift, that enabled them to cover incredible distances
and obstacles. This was their glorious return from an
expedition into the suburbs.

They were heavily laden with bags and bundles. Groaning carts carried the general's share. It really was a triumphal entry, as you could see from the men bent beneath their spoils and the general swaggeringly announcing his victory. He exhibited prisoners reduced to nothing, already almost beaten to death. They were said to be brigands, but obviously they were not—Yunnanese were friends of the knights of the greenwood, and even bestowed ranks on some of them as protectors of the people.

At the rear, encircled with bayonets, came five or six hundred ragged wretches who still seemed to have bodies. They were bound to one another with long chains and advanced in little jerks like a caterpillar, while the soldiers pricked them or pretended to prick them with bayonets. Some of them had carcanets or wooden collars around their necks. The regiment disappeared into the imperial city, and we emerged from it. The mafu explained that what I'd seen was just routine, the usual way of finding conscripts, simply a recruiting drive. The Yunnanese must have appeared before some carefully selected township unencumbered by any garrison belonging to either side. After encircling and sacking the place, they then captured every member of the male population who looked reasonably sturdy. The operation must have been carried out in collaboration with the bandits, who infiltrated the town beforehand disguised as coolies and helped them find both men and treasure. That was how it usually happened, according to my mafu—a minor affair compared to the operation known as a "brigand hunt," a much more profitable type of foray but much more complicated, which required preparations and negotiations and might perhaps not work out. There might even be shooting.

My mafu had gotten over his disgust at the Yunnanese girls in uniform and been restored to good humor by what he had just witnessed, a scene eminently pleasing to a veteran.

"That was what it was like in the good old days," he said happily. "But now things are going to go badly. A lot of soldiers are going to be killed. I don't know when, but it'll be real war, the kind that doesn't do anyone any good."

According to him it was the fault of the Yunnanese. They seemed to be everywhere, but Szechwan was so big they were lost in it. The vastness, the amorphousness of the country, the force of numbers, all were against them. They struck like steel fists, but more and more as into a flock mattress, a mattress of hatred. In their pride and cruelty they would not relinquish their prey. But they were beginning to fear the Szechwanese, who though they were not warlike were driven by a desire for revenge.

"For several months the Yunnanese, not wanting to be on their own, have been trying to get hold of the Szechwanese and make soldiers of them," said the mafu, with a grimace of distaste. "Every week they bring thousands into their camps, especially in the imperial city. Those who won't come they shoot on the spot. They shoot others during training, to put the fear of God into the survivors. Blows with rifle butts, brutality, executions, spitting people on bayonets— those are the war lord's normal methods of military training. But despite this harshness, the Yunnanese see only the vagabonds and coolies and peasants whom they collect and give a uniform and a trade to decamp at the first opportunity. It's no good making mincemeat of them. They just clear off. The ones that are left the Yunnanese don't dare trust with guns. So they're on their own. Only the brigands are still loyal, and not all of them. Which doesn't prevent the marshal from issuing proclamations saying he's going to exterminate them."

We crossed a Chengtu as drowsy as before and went over to where the Szechwanese were. Complete inactivity reigned. On the great south gate spitted heads were drying amid clusters of flies; there weren't even any fresh heads. A few dirty, bored-looking officers and men stood about by the huge doors, still open. The chains that were supposed to be used to close it lay in heaps on the ground. A dark tunnel led out under the ramparts, but no one went through it any more. Utter quiet. I left my horse and went up some worn steps to a guardhouse shaped like a pagoda, just above the big tunnel. Soldiers were sleeping flat on the bare floor. They were old Szechwanese, wily little fellows from local militias that had abandoned the art of war to the Yunnanese.

My mafu joined me, having left my horse in the charge of a child who'd beaten the other rickety specimens in the rush to get hold of the reins. He started to talk to one of the ancient militiamen, who was smoking a water pipe with suitable scrapings and raspings and a happy air of being above all contingencies, including the mosquitoes clinging around one eye, almost closed by a wart.

"So, honorable grandfather, you'll soon be killing lots of Yunnanese?"

"Yes, my son. I'll cut them up so neatly each one will supply a whole butcher's shop. But for that they'll have to bring them to me alive and properly tied up."

"Who's going to fight them then, grandpa, and bring them to you and your knife?"

"Look out over the battlements, and all round Chengtu you'll see Szechwan's young armies, more plentiful than tigers' teeth. You know how ants attack a big animal, smothering it, paralyzing it, then carrying it away and destroying it. That's what our soldiers will do with the Yunnanese."

The ramparts surrounded Chengtu in an irregular circle with many bulges and indentations. It was a fine wall, more than thirty feet high, ancient stones enclosing a seething, tangled retreat of human beings. At the foot of the ramparts lay bare expanses, rusty patches in the midst of the magnificent landscape—the parade grounds of the Szechwanese.

From where I stood I gazed at the distant horizon. Peace, beauty. The rice fields stretched out in layers, stairways of young shoots reaching right up to the tops of the hills. The river Min twisted and turned through the red earth, rich and undulating and covered with a lush vegetation of woods and shrubs. Flowers too, including the hibiscus, symbol of Szechwan. And everywhere against this luxuriant background there was human activity, endless desperately hard work, life in the form of winding paths, a checkerboard of dikes and canals, a mosaic of mud villages, groves shading a temple or a yamen, the crouching bodies of peasants in the fields. Backs bent century after century, day after day, just to eat, to survive. Beyond, among the clouds, were the mountains, long crests, ordered chaos, range upon range going up like steps to the nearby Himalayas. The advance guard of the Roof of the World was the holy mountain of Ho Mi Chang, a heap of rocks where fifty-six pagodas succeeded one another up the slopes, amid precipices and the blessing of Buddha.

But just below Chengtu, what a frenzy of warlike activity! Unlike the Yunnanese in the imperial city, somber, silent, icy-eyed, the Szechwanese were all hustle and bustle. Wave after wave of men crawled, charged, jumped, leaped ditches, put their guns in firing position, and let them off amid wild cries and clouds of dust. There was the sound of detonations. Where did the missiles fall? No one cared. It was like a carnival, a sort of nervous excitement and abandon, with an indeterminate element of playacting and showing off. A mounted escort, flag flying, surrounded a man with a skull like a gorilla's, his face so snub and flat it seemed to have no openings, not even eyes and ears. This was the Szechwanese's principal general.

I and my mafu went down again and through the gate, a damp darkness leading out onto barbed wire and machine guns. We went along a road among grinning soldiers—instead of the chill fury of the Yunnanese, Szechwanese grimaces of which it was impossible to say whether they were friendly or not. Here, too, but much larger, there was a crowd carrying out various kinds of minor trades with the troops, but unmoved by the arrival of a string of conscripts, this time for the Szechwanese army.

The mafu commented on how few guards there were.

"It's much easier for the Szechwanese to recruit people. They use the same method as the Yunnanese, but more gently. When they've surrounded a town and gathered all the male population together, the senior officer makes a little speech appealing to their better nature to help save Szechwan. Those who can give a tael are left, and those who are too poor are tied together with ropes. A few executions, but not very often."

Just in front of us, about a thousand men had been

carrying out a practice attack. They still wore the typical Szechwanese grin—cheerfulness or rage. A group barred our way and became threatening. Fingers pointed me out. A hand leveled a revolver at my head. The mafu let out a volley of insults against these "louts," a torrent of imprecations. There was a chorus of yells in reply, but the mafu shouted the loudest, and the soldiers moved off, muttering. In China, in certain circumstances, mere verbal superiority ensures victory. The mafu pulled on my horse's bridle and turned him about as fast as he could. We rode off back into the deep tunnel of the city gate.

When I got back to the consulate I told my parents of my exploits, but instead of congratulating me they were very cross. They sent for the mafu, but he was obstinate and would only say:

"There was no danger. It was only exercises. . . ."

He took himself off, and after some thought my father said to my mother:

"Perhaps the boy ought to have a military escort?"

"What?" she said. "Use soldiers to guard him from other soldiers? Wouldn't they be tempted to kidnap him?"

"Not if I pay them well. But it would be expensive —they always ask more if you make them promise to be loyal."

He sighed.

"I could talk to the marshal about it. He'd give me some Yunnanese who could be relied on, but the Szechwanese generals would be furious and quite capable of plotting against me. And if I did the opposite and used Szechwanese soldiers, it would cause even more bother."

"In short," said Anne Marie, in an expressionless voice conveying her contempt, "you're thinking about your little diplomatic maneuvers, and not about the child at all."

This was too much for my father. He put on his martyred expression, raising his eyes to heaven—not ostentatiously; just enough to show what he had to suffer.

The outcome was that I was forbidden to go near the army camps. My father assumed his deepest voice —his official voice, issuing from his mustache—to promise me a good cuffing if I disobeyed.

My mother shrugged.

"You don't know how to deal with the child. Why don't you speak to him nicely instead of acting the consul even with him?"

In spite of this the consul was very chirpy the next morning. That is to say, for the great day a modest little expression of satisfaction shone out from between his well-brushed hair, his pince-nez, and his frock coat. All was ready for the reception in his honor—in particular, the huge banner saying: "Happy Birthday to Monsieur Albert Bonnard."

That day amity flourished as never before. Never had the august assembly of guests been so jovial: felicity was on all the good yellow faces, cordiality in all the handshakes of the whites. There was the usual human décor, with a suitable touch of severity throwing the politenesses of the marshal and the generals into relief. There was the veiled frankness of the millionaires, with their smiles that came and went and their little cramped gestures. There was English dignity, somewhat stiff in the case of His Majesty's consul and gaily unbridled in the case of the parson and his jokes; the Japanese consul and his automatic bows; the bushy whiskers of the missionaries; the nuns

with their caps like worn-out sails over their wizened
faces; the gay bachelordom of the three doctors and
two male nurses, rather tired because of a slight epidemic of bubonic plague, which had led a few Szechwanese to try out the efficacy of Western science.
There was even a sign of modern times in the person of
a very insipid gentleman belonging to the French post
office. Though there were no public services in Szechwan and nothing worked, the post was highly efficient.
This was a major contribution from France to China.
While the English gentlemen were masters of the
customs, it was the dry little Frenchmen with their
goatees who, even in this province still buried in the
darkness of the ages, had organized a postal service
of almost exemplary regularity. Even when for some
reason or other, people were dying all around by the
thousand, letters still arrived with their seals and
stamps, and the postman called with his little book
for the addressee to sign for registered packages. These
might sometimes contain strange objects, such as ear-
lobes or a whole ear, a fingertip or a whole finger.
Little organs removed from a kidnap victim to soften
the heart of his miserly family, who were taking too
long to pay up. A conventional language, an ultimatum telling the relatives: "Hurry up, you're making
your honorable protége suffer. If you don't make up
your minds to be more generous, there soon won't be
much left of him. It's not our fault—it's yours, for
being so tight with your money."

But the insipid little gentleman was not concerned
with the contents of registered letters, only with their
delivery. He was one of those moronic-looking, insignificant Frenchmen who work like slaves for whatever public service they happen to be in. He could
hold his own against anyone. But because he didn't

brag, my father had little respect for him. Moreover, as he was almost always traveling about on a mule through places infested with bandits and troops, he wasn't often present to pay his respects on the great festive occasion at the consulate.

My father, for his part, was more apprehensive about what was inside the letters. Especially with all those priests in every nook and cranny in Szechwan, up to all kinds of captiousness and squabbling. Sometimes, putting on a grieved expression, he would tell of some misadventure that had befallen one of his colleagues, another French consul, who had been sent a missionary's finger, or two, or a missionary's heart. Then he would add: "No fear of that happening here—the priests are too involved in all the schemes."

Yet on this day of birthday rejoicings at the consulate, who would think of those manifold horrors— the wars, the slaughter, the kidnappings, the epidemics, the tortures, all the different scourges of heaven and earth? Looking at those charming society pusses, who would think of corpses past and to come? And yet these Chinamen, and even these Europeans, as they congratulated one another, were incubating strange and mysterious things. At the same time as they offered my father their felicitations, the assembly were all getting ready for the Chengtu wars. It was a drama of which the outcome was still unknown. All kinds of combinations and permutations were possible. The only thing certain was that this was a meeting of death.

In fact, war was already present. The marshal, the war lord of the Yunnanese, was surrounded by his enemies. He stood there slim in his uniform, with his ascetic features, his gaunt sharp visage, rather like a heron with his haughtily vague glance, its vacuity dictated by "face," as if he declined to see any danger. And yet he was surrounded by dangers in the highly actual form of the generals who were exchanging greetings and knocking back champagne with him. Beside him was a general commanding the army of Kweichow, province of a hundred thousand mountains, low limestone heights split and overgrown with jungle. He was a huge boor of a fellow, with a head like a kind of jar pouring out flesh: a big pink growth hung down one cheek, the other was completely flat, and the whole adorned with a curly mustache and buckteeth. And yet there was a certain nobility in this ponderousness and bestiality. He seemed to be a faithful follower of the marshal, but the marshal knew he was in communication with the Szechwanese.

These latter positively skipped about with affability. There were seven or eight of them, greeting the marshal, the consuls, the whole assembly, including the priests, always with the typical little Szechwanese snicker, which on this occasion meant good will. Today was the first time these officers had been entertained socially in Chengtu, where they strutted about with a sort of arrogant humility. In their musical-comedy uniforms, they were obviously scoundrels who had risen through crime from the dregs of society, and now they were the leaders of fine armies supposed to bring about the liberation of Szechwan. The gorilla-like creature I'd glimpsed the day before among his troops outside the ramparts was a former Buddhist priest. One of his amusements had been to put poisonous snakes in the trousers of village women and then provoke the reptiles with sticks. The other Szechwanese were the scourings of the cities, with little impudent, gnarled, rheumy-eyed faces. One flashed gold teeth, another had mere hairy holes for nostrils. In short, the amateurs among them were a pretty sinister lot. The Szechwanese professionals presented a somewhat better appearance. They were men dating from the empire, who had gone back into uniform out of greed: there was the spectral military mandarin, long-faced and completely unbending, and two professional old sweats, one fat and one thin, both full of spite but sanctimonious, both with swift shifty eyes that seemed to be watching for the chance to pull a fast one.

And then, always slightly apart from the military worthies, the gentlemen of the robe, the millionaires with their air of grave benevolence, the "sages," differing only in physical detail—some round as pots, some thin as ninepins, some with skin so smooth it looked hairless, some with a complexion like a nutmeg grater. Some were almost young. Some, the "ancestors," were like broken down old women. What dark mysteries hung about them! Some were known to be the evil geniuses of the war lords who were present. Every general, if he and his sword were to do good business, needed a commercial adviser, someone of quick wit and bold imagination who was always up to the neatest tricks, and the most devious. These experts in the art of extortion were even more formidable than their uniformed patrons. Among them was Mr. Lu, crony of the Yunnanese marshal, who for once had emerged from his lair and arisen from his cot to appear at the consulate. He was thus conferring a great honor on my father, but after having congratulated him, a puff of smoke that has suddenly materialized, he retired into the background. His eyes were almost shut, but the merchants eagerly sought him out to bow to him, and he returned their salutes with mechanical precision. From his position there in the background he dominated the scene.

There was also a little squirt waddling about like

a duck, with sarcastic blubber lips and huge eyes in a face no bigger than a man's hand, who was the terror of Chengtu. He was a distinguished silk merchant, the brain behind the Szechwanese, especially the huge ex-monk. There was nothing he wasn't capable of. It was he with his fiery words who had gotten the great millionaires of Chengtu to help with the financing of the Szechwanese armies. And now he came back and laughed in their faces, saying, "Fork out some more, or else. . . ."

So all the notables of Chengtu had gathered together at the consulate as brothers. In addition to the struggle through which each millionaire did his best to fleece others and not be fleeced himself, there were also outside influences: the consuls stationed in Chengtu, the political representatives of the great powers, the interests of big business whether white or yellow in Shanghai, the representatives of the other great war lords: the "revolutionary" war lords of the South, and the terrifying Confucian war lords of the North, who had succeeded Yüan Shih-kai in the regions of bare plains and yellow loess—all despots with vast armies.

That particular day the whole gathering at the consulate showed special consideration for a little Chinaman in a top hat who occupied the place of honor, a shrimp huddled into his dress coat who was exerting himself to amuse my father. He gibbered like a marmoset, but in the European fashion and even in French, with bursts of laughter, winks, a whole set of gymnastics with his arms and a mobile mouth that was a sort of elastic oven. This gay dog addressed the consul of France in the manner of a Paris urchin.

"Ah, Your Excellency! France, France . . . ! I spent my youth in the Latin Quarter. The beers in the brasseries, the larks with pals, the lectures of the aged professors at the Sorbonne, at which I used to doze so respectfully. The times I've walked up and down the Boulevard Saint-Michel. They used to call me 'the Chink'! Not that I was grim or enigmatic—I was having a wonderful time in your lovely city. And the painters and the little models in Montmarte! Do you know, Monsieur le Consul, I married one of them and brought her back with me to China—that will show you, Monsieur le Consul, that I love France from my heart. And while I'm a good Chinese, I also consider myself a good Frenchman. So you see you can count on me and my humble powers."

The consul mistrusted this character extremely— he was the envoy extraordinary in Chengtu of the President of the Republic in Peking. This Republic was of course a mockery: to all intents and purposes it didn't exist. But it was highly sought after by the Northern war lords, for whoever got hold of it appropriated its legend, and exploited its self-styled legitimacy to justify unlimited ambitions everywhere, even over Szechwan. That was why this card, this former denizen of the Latin Quarter, had been sent to Szechwan to sow discord, to stir up the Szechwanese against the Yunnanese, to prepare the ground.

Albert Bonnard was for the Southern party, for an "advance" area stretching from Canton to Chengtu. This was the old idea of a South China confederation, free of Shanghai and Peking, which would naturally come under the influence of France acting from Indochina by means of the railroad—the railroad my father was so anxious to have extended as far as Chengtu. How often did I hear my mother say to him:

"In Indochina the French are the advocates of law

and order. How is it that we support revolution—or rather what's called revolution—in China?"

And my father would reply:

"You wouldn't understand, Anne Marie. Politics is a very subtle matter."

For some time my father had noticed that inscrutable gentlemen kept arriving in Chengtu from the North, their words full of honey, their hands full of gold, and especially promises of gold. They came from Peking—Peking magnificent and ramshackle, a wilderness where foreigners strutted in the district specially allotted to the legations. It was only a shadow of the real Peking, a tragic void where now no emperor ever visited the Temple of Heaven to perform the ceremonies that would make the earth fruitful and bring forth the harvests. The dethroned scion of the last dynasty collected pornographic pictures, was ruled with a rod of iron by a dubious white tutor, and lived on an official pension which was never paid. Foreign gentlemen in dinner jackets and ladies in evening dress came and went in the big hotels, dancing to the strains of "The Blue Danube." War lords came and went within the ramparts of the august, dead city, after grotesque and not even bloody wars which nevertheless brought about the death of masses of people. Hundreds of thousands of troops confronted one another without really fighting, for battles were decided at the level of marshals and generals, who were bought and sold in a whirlpool of treachery, a cascade of dollars. But all these innumerable soldiers, poor fierce wretches preoccupied with survival, themselves formed a mass of want living off the vast general destitution. All Northern China had been reduced to scorched earth traversed by armies endlessly changing sides. Year after year—arson, murder, looting. And above all, dirt. Empty, abandoned landscapes where there was no more loot to be found. The haughty negligence by which nothing was kept up, nothing mattered any more, neither lives nor things nor the modern equipment that was the war lords' pride, was more terrible than actual brutality. The great railways built by the international banking consortium were now only intermittent stretches of old iron carrying dawdling troop trains. Trucks full of dejecta and masses of bored faces. Trains groping around insofar as wars permitted. Trains of fear. Trains formed on the order of some war lord who happened to have gotten hold of a line and some stations and trucks. And sometimes, amid universal awe, a luxury express would go by bristling with soldiers, their guns trained outward, a spick-and-span Iron Guard, for inside, in his special saloon car, a war lord was cavorting with his concubine.

Among these war lords of the North there were some who were terrifically powerful, superlords of dread repute. Each potentate lived constantly inside a protective ring, a circle of armed soldiers when he was stationary, an escort of armored vehicles when he was moving about. They had their own technique of security. Of pomp, too, with a general staff, a court, chamberlains, a head of protocol, private secretaries, a keeper of the seals, ministers, and executioners. A world of terror. And the most terrifying of all these characters was Chang Tso-lin, a former pirate transformed into a fanatic of wisdom, order, and virtue. He held Manchuria. This old satrap, with a body like a little sparrow hawk's, had all the intellectuals killed, as well as anyone else with modern ideas or whom he mistrusted. He had a gentle air and wore a little skullcap, yet led a life of blood. Always more and more blood, "to protect society." At a word from him, thousands of heads rolled. Hecatombs, banditry, and a pretense to saintliness. Another of these war lords was a Christian general who sported Chinese robes and a fan, and who ever since his conversion was always quoting the Bible. His troops, baptized with a hose, used to enter the towns they overran singing a Chinese version of "Nearer my God to Thee." His origins were obscure and he, too, had made his way by crime. He was an arch-hypocrite and an archtraitor, so treacherous he astonished even the Chinese. He would cry his eyes out when ordering the rich to be tortured to make them disgorge their wealth. Millions of dollars, cases of bullion, the imperial treasures—all these he stole in the name of the sorrows of Christ and Christian charity.

In short, on the bare and icy plains of North China, beastliness had become banal, commonplace, boring. Nevertheless, in the middle of all these horrors and these monsters of war lords, there was one "gentleman." At least that was the unanimous opinion among the enlightened in business, finance, diplomacy, and the British Navy. At the smartest dinner parties in Shanghai, those of the British and their equivalents or where everyone at least was white except the servants, the guests constantly analyzed, with satisfaction, optimism, and superiority, all the incredible defects of the Chinese: the same conversations, arguments, anecdotes, assertions, and proofs, over and over. But for some time now there had always been some Britisher, some old China hand, some minor John Bull of trade, who would bark out point-blank almost as if it were a challenge, or at any rate a surprising admission: "But General Wu is a decent fellow. A very good chap. Hard to believe he's Chinese, really Chinese."

Wu was the ruffian then in possession of Peking, till the time came for him to be driven out by another ruffian. An old brute, an old war hound, who had a face perhaps a little less sinister and habits slightly less atrocious than his rivals', but caused just as much slaughter and destruction. He ruined everything except Britain's interests. He was as vigilant as Cerberus about anything belonging to British subjects or companies and their vast mechanisms of exploitation. While Chang Tso-lin was in the pay of the Japanese and the Christian general in cahoots with everyone, Wu was the pawn of England and the greatness of Albion. Albion's man, and therefore one my father was not at all fond of. The more so as it was he who in aid of some skulduggery or other had sent the top-hatted joker from the Latin Quarter to Chengtu.

My father was gloomy. He was sure England wanted to hand over the whole of China to Wu, starting with Szechwan, that garden of the Hesperides, that golden apple, the bit of China guarded by the oldest mountain masses in the world, on which through all the ages armies had been unleased from icy North and tropical South. It so happened that for the past few years the Yunnanese had been protecting Szechwan, and my father was perfectly happy with this arrangement. But he wouldn't like it at all if through some sinister machinations the English succeeded in throwing out the Yunnanese and handing the province over to Wu, and all they'd have to do would be to get the Szechwanese to wipe out the Yunnanese.

So the French consul was in a bad temper. He had a peculiar skill in differentiating the degrees of his displeasure. Usually, with people of no importance, it took the form of a pouting peevishness, a kind of rigid contraction of the face accompanied by suitable home truths. The sulkiness was modified when he had to deal with people of more consequence, unless he was really annoyed and his sensibility as a consul offended. It sometimes happened that he sulked and was gloomy, silent, and scowling throughout the whole of some social evening, just answering "Nothing" when Anne Marie asked "What's wrong, Albert?" But on this special day, his birthday, there could be no question of his being grumpy. He was playing the great pontiff of universal love to Chinamen of all kinds who were partaking in fraternal communion under French auspices before they went away and slaughtered each other somewhere else. He had to restrain himself, and did so with an artificial smile. But inwardly he raged.

Albion's perfidy and collusion were there before his eyes, under his very nose, in his own consulate, being flaunted at his own birthday party. Only a few yards away from him the hypocritical little ape from the Boulevard Saint-Michel was soft-soaping a middle-aged English Apollo who'd been brought by the English consul—a gentleman from Shanghai, just arrived in faraway Szechwan for a short and mysterious visit allegedly on "business." But it must have been very special business, for the person concerned was no less than the eldest son of the famous Johnson family, a dynasty that worshipped the golden calf, respectability, and loot no matter how it was acquired.

Amid the sickly sociability which demonstrated that the party was a success, my father was pierced, as he would say, by "thoughts like daggers."

"I knew it! A stab in the back. If a Britisher like that comes to Chengtu it can only mean the worst. And the fact that he's here at the same time as Wu's nasty little weasel can't be an accident. It all goes to

show that the Yunnanese and I have got it coming
to us."

And yet nothing could have been more innocent,
at least in appearance, than the conversation between
the tiny Chinese and the handsome Englishman. The
little face of the man from Peking—muzzle poked
forward at the Englishman, teeth, lips, and chin all
oozing giggling affability—came up against the blank
wall of British good breeding. The gentleman hovered
there, inaccesible, his heavy but trim body wrapped
in the cellophane of correctness. His social demeanor
was perfect—all distance, all courtesy. He was the
very model of a scion of a quasi-imperialist firm. He
had none of the John Bull aggressiveness or blatant
duplicity of the young colonial tradesmen representing minor companies. Nor was there any of the aristocratic airiness of the Oxford types who loafed around
the Far East on the off chance of pleasure or excitement. This fellow, who'd been brought to the consulate as a surprise, was solid English, with an invisible "and Co." trailing him like a "de" or "von"
on his name. He belonged to the nobility of trade,
the "merchant adventurers" who in the thoroughly
exploited tropics had become the Establishment. He
belonged to the third or fourth generation of big
business, the business born in the scum of Shanghai
in the city's early days. Those days were not really
long past, but now they had vanished, now all was
solid. Power, resources, and vast amounts of money—
the visitor carried the aura of all these with lofty
certitude. But his assurance, from which pride was
not far distant, had the appearance of decorous modesty, a careful, detailed protocol binding both on him
and on his interlocutors.

In any case, he was an absolutely charming person:

the right age, regular features like a Greek statue, on the heavy side, but nice and pink as a beefsteak, hair a mass of blonde curls, light eyes inexpressively grave, and a suggestion of mustache so faint and airy it was like a wisp of straw. He was dressed with sober elegance, a carnation in his buttonhole. He had a certain bearing, a certain manner of being present at the same time actively and passively, of being tall but not fat, of saying nothing but commonplaces in a hesitant voice. A clubman, a sportsman, an administrator, and man of the world. And all this with an optimistic punctiliousness and the discreet certainty, about his voice and attire, that everything was "as it should be," and a half-smile that ranged from approval to impenetrable reserve. When he arrived he kissed Anne Marie's hand, shook hands firmly with my father and then with the rest of the guests, then scarcely ruffling his calm, did a few little skips and jumps to show his good will and spoke a few words here and there—the sort that were expected. When the little man from Peking got hold of him he answered slowly, with half-shut eyes, that he had had a good journey and was very happy to visit the beautiful city of Chengtu.

My father knew this type of Englishman very well —these taipans as they were called in Shanghai, who had a peculiarly British gift for concealing their intelligence, and who were really monsters capable of anything, especially getting the better of a smart French consul if he didn't watch out!

So the consul was consumed with suspicion, his heart was wrung with mistrust. He must have been muttering to himself:

"They're all a lot of boors, the English, especially these taipans and their millions. That courtesy Anne Marie likes so much is really a load of rubbish. And this latest nonentity, so dim you can't tell whether he's awake or asleep, this playboy they do me the honor of lugging in to see me, must be a real out-and-outer. The more angelic this sort of Englishman seems, the more of a devil he is. I'm going to ask Cheng what he's up to."

For Cheng was there, the upper part of him, the part he usually Westernized with his felt hat and spectacles, re-Sinified in a silken skullcap. His main concern was clearly to remain as inconspicuous as possible in this august assembly. He gave a little twitch of vexation when my father went up to him and said, "I'll want to see you tomorrow." Cheng, his face averted, muttered, "I have to go away this evening for a few days. I'm extremely sorry, Mōnsieur le Consul." And off he slithered.

This added to my father's annoyance. And all these English people, pretending to be so innocent! His Majesty's consul, all sweetness and light, his wife beaming at his side, was thanking Anne Marie for the last lot of tomatoes she'd sent them. The parson, his bloated purple face seeming to burst out of his dog collar, uttering barks like explosions, was knocking it back as fast as he could, with a bunch of warily chummy missionaries. As for the taipan from Shanghai, he was flitting about from one war lord to another, from those who looked like weasels to those with the air of gallows birds. It was a ballet of airy but reserved affability. He was taken around by an interpreter who told him the titles and offices of these honorable persons, and at every introduction, to each new face, he said "Delighted to meet you." Just as if he knew nothing, as if he couldn't tell the difference between Chinks from Yunnan and those from Szechwan or Kweichow. Just a round of introductions—innocence itself.

And God knows they're not innocent, these Englishmen, my father must have been thinking to himself. I bet the Yangtze's full of seedy-looking British freighters with their holds stuffed with guns and ammunition for the Szechwanese armies. And Cheng slipping off like that. But I'll show them I'm no fool.

Whatever he was thinking, it caused his face to harden, making him look like a beetle with glasses. It was a heroic impulse: the poor little French consul in Szechwan had made up his mind to outface Shanghai and its English traders conspiring with the war lords, Marshal Wu and the rest of them. He, Albert, would pull a few strings, too. And they would see what they would see in Chengtu.

It was time for the consul to dismiss his guests. There they all were, everybody who was anybody in Chengtu, as smug as ever, all the Chinese silky with suppressed effusions and expressing themselves only by a nodding of heads, a rustling of sleeves, a glimmer of the eyes, and, spread over the faces, the creases symbolizing affability. My father began to speak, but with severity, almost annoyance. Well-turned phrases came forth in his crispest tones, curtly, punctuated with pauses.

"I thank ten times ten thousand times all the august persons who have honored my birthday. Today, when with one more year I draw closer to the wisdom of age, I offer up countless good wishes for the happiness of China and of Szechwan. The greatest of all blessings is peace, and I see that all the friends of Chengtu devote their efforts toward it. But perhaps we should beware of fishers in troubled waters, people come from afar to sow discord in our hearts and provoke us into damaging conflict. France, I can assure you, will always work for understanding between the Chinese and for the development of China."

How shocking! Insofar as anything could be said to be shocking to China. All the war lords, all the millionaires, all the yellow people present, acted as if they hadn't heard. Perhaps their smiles were a shade too wide, too forced. Then all the Celestial People of every kind, in groups, made their last little bows, uttered their last millions of good wishes, and decamped. The only Chinaman left was Wu's little envoy, who was splitting his sides. He'd had plenty to drink, it must be added, and was tipsy.

He clutched hold of my father and wrung his hand enthusiastically.

"Jolly good, Monsieur le Consul—that's the stuff to give 'em! But if you were alluding to me you're wrong, way off base. The heart of my august master, Marshal Wu, is pure, and even more to the point, his purse is empty. So if you think he sent me here to hand out gold, that just makes me laugh, Monsieur le Consul. He keeps his gold to himself. So let's drink to France, Monsieur le Consul, and to the generosity which may persuade her to give some arms to her good friends for nothing. The French are an easy touch, Monsieur le Consul. Not like the English; they always insist on being paid. Vive la France!"

And the little monkey, fidgeting about and pulling all sorts of faces, his top hat awry, let go of the consul and grabbed a priest.

"Drink with me, Father—to the glory of Catholicism. You might be taken for a Chinaman, Father, but a Chinaman of the people. You don't sell your God except to the poor. But instead of stirring up the common people with far-fetched stories about crucifixions and so on, why didn't you become sages and philosophers, as our emperors once suggested to your predecessors? We true Chinese, the really educated ones, don't take religion seriously—it's just superstition for the masses. And I am an educated man, you know. Don't think I'm still just on the spree in Paris. I've already passed the triennial examinations. I tell you, Father, you made a mistake. What are you doing in China, with that wretched clientele you live off? Hand out communion wafers, that's all. At least the parsons, especially the American ones, have plenty of money to give the Chinese."

And then the little man threw up. His honorable entourage carried him out to his chair. And now the only people left were white men, one of them scarlet with rage. The English consul was bristling, a fighting cock spoiling for battle. He drew my father aside, and soon there were raised voices, shouts, storms of abuse; they almost came to blows.

"What about the fire?" yelled the little Englishman. He'd well and truly lost his composure. "The fire the Yunnanese promised to start? You supply them with all those arms, and you won't intervene to stop them committing this horrible crime!"

My father, white as a sheet, started to invoke the honor of France.

"What influence have I got with the Yunnanese? I assure you we haven't supplied them with a single gun. But can *you* deny you've sent the Szechwanese the wherewithal to put the whole province to fire and sword? It's you who are provoking war in Szechwan. What's that young taipan from Shanghai here for? Or the envoy from Wu, your ally—the little wretch who's just behaved so disgustingly?"

"It's not true. England hasn't been arming the Szechwanese. But England can't interfere with the business that, unless I'm much mistaken, some of your compatriots in Shanghai are mixed up in."

Two consuls yapping like mongrels and calling each other liars. The English taipan from Shanghai stood by with his eyes popping out of his head, astounded at such an exhibition of bad taste. He was so flabbergasted he could do nothing, so the clergyman with his brawny arm grabbed hold of his consul and said, as if to a naughty schoolboy, "Come along now and behave yourself."

No one remained but the French colony and my father faced them, the crestfallen victor. He felt no waves of admiration wafting toward him. In fact, the French doctors, stifling their mirth, were tiptoeing out, and once outside they burst into peals of laughter, all good clubmen amazed at the seriousness of people in general. One of them tapped his head and said knowingly, "Old Albert surpassed himself today. He sees himself as the Talleyrand of the Yangtze Kiang. His poor wife. . . ."

As for God's people, they had camouflaged themselves, the nuns behind their coifs, the priests behind their beards, their wrinkles, and the folds of their eyes. They had formed a square, and finally the bishop, the key man, came over to my father and flung at him his whiskers and his stentorian tones.

"As I told you yesterday, I think you should have remonstrated with the Yunnanese marshal."

"But, Monseigneur, I'm sure you yourself have taken all necessary steps to protect the property of the missions. . . ."

There remained Anne Marie, upright and slim, but turned aside. Her long lashes covered her eyes, her lips were closed in a slight grimace, there was a disturbing half-smile on her averted face. This was her expression of scorn—nothing dramatic or violent, just repugnance and serene disdain. She was about to go away when my father called out to try to wring some approval from her.

"Don't you think I was right?"

"You were ridiculous, my dear."

"But I had grave reasons. . . ."

"Perhaps. But so often you just imagine things. . . . And in any case, there was no need to make a spectacle of yourself."

Hence an official state of vexation between husband and wife. At table not a word passed between them. Anne Marie, though silent, acted as if the tension did not bother her in the least: she ate heartily, and gave the servants their orders in a perfectly easy and natural manner. But Albert sat with his head bent over his plate, chewing the same mouthful over and over again without zest and never swallowing anything, his face wearing an expression of stiff attention that combined grief and fury.

"What's the matter, Albert?" she asked him at dessert, pretending to be puzzled.

"Anne Marie . . ." he said, and subsided again into silence. A long sulk ensued, culminating later in raised voices and a scene in their bedroom.

"You don't really love me, Anne Marie."

"What do you expect? You seem to forget that you bought me. But I remember very well the way you looked me over on the platform that day at Ancenis when I'd just come back from Nantes. Like a horse trader. And you didn't waste any time. The next day you came to our house all dressed up. And you brought your brother the mustachioed captain, who was garrisoned in the town. And without more ado you asked my mother if you could marry me. The whole family got together—all the old aunts and cousins—and dinned into me that you were a very pre-

sentable young man, a diplomat in the Far East with
a brilliant future. I was against it. But my father had
just died a ruined man—he'd drunk up all his money,
and no one in those parts would want to marry me.
I didn't have a dowry—that ruled me out completely.
I was surrounded by all those petty squires and old
maids and uncles, all more or less ga-ga but well off,
repeating, 'It's your duty, Anne Marie.' Only my
mother, already a widow twice, said a little more
kindly, 'You know I only want what's best for you,
Anne Marie. But Albert adores you and he's extremely courteous.' And indeed you did have the lawyer
put an imaginary dowry into the marriage contract.
But I cried on my wedding day."

"But, Anne Marie, we've been happy since."

"I carried out my part of the bargain, that's all.
But I never liked you. You're too petty-bourgeois. I
used to love the Loire and its hills and vineyards, the
sort of life where gentlemen didn't work, but owned
farms full of old royalists. I admired my father because he led a gay life, he was one of the gilded youth
of lower Brittany. He used to sail in the regattas at
Vannes, he had his own boat, he went to all the clubs.
He sold his farms one after the other and died insane.
But he was a man of the world, even if he left us
destitute.

"You, Albert, you can't understand that sort of
nobility and disinterestedness. When you took me to
La Rochelle to meet your family, I was horrified. That
old house that was the pride of the Bonnards, a four-
story heap of stones looking out on a street that was all
walls, just like a prison. And it was damp and dirty
and full of horrible smells, sinister corners, sour shadows, worn flights of stairs. And as dried up and worn
out as the house, and more bent and mummified than

an old Chinese woman of a hundred, there was your
old mother, also a widow, wrinkled and yellow and so
skinny her head was like a skull. All that was alive
in it were the eyes, which could hardly see any more,
and the lips, soft like yours. She'd been your father's
servant—he'd married her just in time. She was a
kindly old woman and I was afraid she was going to
kiss me. She kept saying, 'Make Albert happy, he's a
good son.' What horrified me the most were your
mannish elder sister and her husband, already chubby
faced, with those fat little arms and legs. They ran
the family furniture store and there in the back room
I listened to their endless conversations about money
and careers and illness. They passed judgment on all
their relatives—one who'd gone wrong, another who'd
been promoted to chief clerk. And everything was
calculated, whether virtues or expenses. Your brother-
in-law, waving his hands about like bunches of sau-
sages, with a flood of common sense, ferociousness,
and stupidity, laid down the law about some little
cousin who'd tried to tap him for money, and similar
misguided relatives. And you were the phoenix in the
middle of it all. Virtue, yes—you and all your family
have got plenty of that. But it's a laborious kind of
virtue."

"You're a snob, Anne Marie. You even blame me
for the trouble I took to succeed, though you don't
mind enjoying the advantages of it."

"Yes, let's talk about that. I know how you got to
be a consul. It was by one of those tricks that are crazy
and shrewd at the same time—typical of you, and
shameless. I found out about it from your other sister,
that tough little item, all shreds and patches, who still
has to earn a living for herself and all her children;
she told me when you took me to Saigon to show me

off to her. She told me all about it. She was a teacher there, a respectable schoolmistress for the nice little natives, while her husband, who was also a teacher, treated her badly and ran after the local girls. It was this poor woman who sent you the money to try your luck in Asia when you weren't getting anywhere in France, and the only chance of success left to you was in the colonies. And it wasn't a very brilliant start either—all kinds of undistinguished little jobs. And then your chance came and you didn't hesitate to seize it."

"What's all this tittle-tattle, Anne Marie? You don't know what you're saying."

"I know perfectly well. Chance offered itself in the form of a plump little blonde—a well-rounded nymph that once worked as a model for a few rich painters who saw themselves as Renaissance patriarchs. I know —I've seen her photograph. At the time she was with a very important person from the ministry for Foreign Affairs who was making a big tour of Asia. The last word, the *ne plus ultra*. The republic of enlightenment, the age of positivism, humanism, science—all culminated in this noble brow, this playboy who'd fabricated his own romantic legend. You know who I mean? He had a handsome, well-bred face, sensitive, haughty, smiling, charming, superior—a typical bourgeois pretending to be a lord. A face like an archangel acquainted with life. A man who wanted to experience everything."

"I may be undistinguished, but I can recognize people of quality when I see them—as I did the man you are referring to, and as I did when I saw you later."

"Let's leave out the flattery, Albert. You know how to look after your own interests. You know how to set about things. The pair of them were due to arrive at some place in Indochina where you happened to be. You realized the scarlet lady wouldn't be invited to the official parties and receptions, so you offered yourself as her companion and guide—with the most honorable intentions, of course. Every morning you turned up all charm, with your best suit, your best smile, every attention, and a delightful program for the day. Each morning you brought a huge bunch of flowers, and you hadn't a penny to your name. But that time you were clever. For the lady in question was delighted, and the gentleman, before resuming his Asian pilgrimage, put on his air of influential benevolence and said, 'I'd be glad to do something for you. Is there anything you'd like?' And you answered straight out, 'To be a consul.' And you became one a few months later."

"Well, what is there to be ashamed of in all that? He didn't single me out just because of that little favor I'd done him. He saw I had something. He still treats me as his protégé, as he does other consuls in China who are becoming famous as writers."

"Stop, Albert—don't make me laugh. You know very well you'll never be a member of the Academy."

"Don't try to make me angry. You've seen the trouble I take . . . the risks. You've seen—"

"You're still a climber. You used to be servile, now you're vain. You're always trying to put yourself forward. And clumsily, without any subtlety, like this afternoon. People don't like you."

"But, Anne Marie, you're the one who's out of her mind with pride, with that air like a queen, as if butter wouldn't melt in your mouth, and your way of acting as if you were a living reproach to me. And you're the one who's clever. You never complain in public. You ostentatiously refrain from looking unhappy. So people say—I know they do—'What a brave woman, with a husband like that.' I don't know what you want—a nabob, I suppose, or a lord."

"To tell you the truth, I was upset at your picking a quarrel with the English. They're the only bearable people in Chengtu, the only ones with any manners."

"And I forbid you to see them any more, my dear. That would be the last straw."

"I shall go and see them tomorrow. I can't quarrel with everyone because of you. Get that through your head once and for all."

The consul sighed like a furnace, the sighs of a man trying to restrain himself. I, in the adjoining room, though I'd understood nothing of their quarrel, could imagine my mother's defiant face. Then silence, darkness.

The sky was a sponge filled with the spittle of evil spirits dropping onto the earth. A cataract of water like solid walls saturated everything, so that the filth became liquid and the flood rose like an overflowing sewer. My father went and inspected those walls of the imperial city that overhung the consulate, afraid they might collapse on top of us. For with the disintegration of the heavens the splendors of the past were further reduced to ruin and decay, to fallen porches and steles overthrown.

My father did discover a crack in the ramparts, a moss-grown black zigzag broadening downward into a mass of debris. As he went toward the hole, a soldier yelled down at him from above and told him to go away. So he came home, observing:

"It's on the point of collapsing. If war breaks out, a few shells will bring the whole thing down on our heads.

But for the time being the deluge was not regarded as a disaster, at least in Chinese terms. Chengtu just put up with it, even though in quarters where the houses were built of mud whole masses of shanties fell down, burying men and beasts in a sort of liquid manure. People and things were not destroyed by the fury of the rain, but dissolved in corrosive fluid. Wherever the shacks were washed away their inhabitants fled, and the thieves and the soldiers came on the scene, the former to loot, the others to offer to salvage (if they were rewarded for it) what could be rescued. This entailed lengthy bargaining, because every life and every article saved had to be paid for.

At the consulate, Li told me with satisfaction of one incidental consequence of all this.

"Everything's so soaking wet the Yunnanese won't be able to start their fire for the time being."

Life went on. Even though the heavens sent down not only rain but also horrible germs—germs that made the blood disintegrate or black liquids issue from the orifices of the body, hollowed it or made it swell, transformed the skin into a chaotic geography of sores and ulcers, made the victims hot and cold with the sweats and icy shudders of nightmare-ridden fevers; germs that killed.

Lightning flashes, apocalyptic clouds, the air thick with miasmas—and kings of it all, the rats. They crept out from everywhere and roamed the town in enormous hordes, armed with little eyes and teeth and black pelts. It was a capering band that swarmed over everything. They were bearers of infection, and many of them, after their caperings, collapsed and died. Thousands of little heaps of seething flesh lay radiating death among men. It was a time of cholera, of plague, of all kinds of affliction. Inside their mansions the wealthy Chinese, in the already suffocating heat, lit huge fires in every room to purify the air and drive away pestilence. Anyone in his death agony was shut up in a room and left to struggle alone with his illness. A hole would be made in the wall and from time to time someone would pass a bowl of water through on a plank, until the sick man finally expired. Water was the only charity, for the thirst of the dying was terrible. When the thirst came to be like molten lead, death was at hand.

Li told me the epidemics that year were not particularly terrifying. It was an average year. But she could remember the city being decimated when she was a child: there were so many dead they were just put on hurdles in the sun and left on the sides of the neighboring hills. Hurried groups of survivors went and deposited their dead there, and the smell they gave off drifted back to the town and made it almost impossible to breathe.

But on the afternoon I am speaking of a breeze arose and blew away the clouds. Then there appeared a sky the color of blue glass; steam as from a Turkish bath rose up from the earth toward a porcelain heaven. The sun was like a tiara. My mother sent for me to go out with her. My father heard, gave her a curious look, but said nothing.

We went off in our usual procession. The coolies who carried the chair, their naked feet splashing about in a mixture of mud and filth, bore Anne Marie along with incredible steadiness high above the dirty ground. My horse raised me above all destitution. My mafu strode along happily; he almost wore a smile. We were not going to the British consulate, but to see the parson and his wife.

Their yamen stood in a clump of trees. As soon as

we entered the courtyard we heard their welcoming chorus: "How nice to see you." The parson's wife, very large and dignified and also very kind, opened her arms and took me to her bosom. She hadn't any children, and adored me. But I drew back when she kissed me because the face she put forward was like a bulldog's. Then she gave me a slice of pudding. It was she who gave me English lessons and taught me to be a gentleman in the midst of all those natives. Sometimes she used to say indignantly to my mother, "How can you leave your little boy to be brought up by amahs and servants? He'll learn bad habits—he'll turn into a horrible little Chinaman." My mother would laugh and not answer.

When I arrived, the parson himself would usually gaze at me in silence out of his little piggy eyes. Then he'd hold out his hand and call me a young rascal. On days when he'd been drinking he would tremble and even shout. He could even be quite spiteful. But when he was in good shape he would treat me as a young man, whereas to his wife I was still only a helpless infant. This meant that every quarter of an hour or so he would bring forth a joke or an aphorism for my benefit.

The couple had been living in Asia for ages, and they had a highly developed sense of colonial comfort. I was astounded by the little houseboy who created a draft by pulling on a string attached to a strip of canvas. "That's a punkah, like they have in India," the parson explained.

My father was always telling my mother, "He's a strange fellow—watch your step with him." The parson had installed a little chapel, but except for Sunday, when the British consul came for morning service, the Bible remained undisturbed on the lectern. The parson showed little interest in conversion, and there were never any natives under instruction or any poor Chinese to be found in his house. But often the presence in his courtyard of a platoon of soldiers or of coolies bearing a luxurious litter showed that some war lord or rich merchant was paying him a visit. This only increased my father's suspicions.

In the parson's view, the Chinese had no souls. But he admitted they had bodies, and in these, since he had some medical qualifications, he took an interest. He had even set up a little infirmary containing some medicines and disinfectants and a scalpel. He performed the operations himself: each one was for him a sort of cool jest, and a gleam of cruel delight would appear in his eyes—the fixed yet slightly blinking eyes of a gentleman parson drunk. The whole thing was done with the greatest solemnity.

The main thing was to find a suitable victim: a Chinaman with Western aspirations who had some little thing the matter with him. When the parson found someone like that in the town he would thunder immediately, "Come and see me—I'll soon set that right for you." And the Chinaman was then caught, for fear of losing face.

That day the parson made no reference to the row that had taken place at the French consulate. But when he happened to leave us for a moment, his wife said to my mother: "Albert's rather nervy at the moment. In Asia, my dear, one must never get excited. And it's up to the wives to look after their husbands when they get worked up about nothing—it's up to us to calm them down." This was just a piece of kindly advice from a matron to an inexperienced young wife; nothing more.

The parson was absent for quite a while, in fact. "Probably carving up some Chinaman," said his wife. And indeed four coolies had set down a litter in the courtyard, and an inert form had been carried from it to the "infirmary." The ladies, as they chatted over their cups of tea, could hear the metallic clicks, the little thumps, the breathing, the yell that proved the clergyman was "practicing." After half an hour the Chinaman, still not dead, was carried back to his litter and borne away by porters as impassive and indifferent as if their burden were a gutted pig. —

"They played me a dirty trick this time," said the parson when he finally rejoined the ladies in the drawing room. His large face was scarlet and covered with drops of sweat. He poured himself an enormous glass of whiskey and downed it in one gulp. Then he gave a short laugh. A perfect performance of a gentleman controlling his feelings.

"A nice trick," he went on, with a half-modest, half-amused look, as if he were laughing at himself. "A Chinaman went and took me at my word, but only to try and catch me out. It was the head of the Cheng-tu silk merchants' guild, a bigwig I've often invited to try out my medical skill. And now that he's at death's door he's just taken me up on it. He's got bubonic plague! His family, only too delighted to get rid of him in such an honorable way, lost no time in sending him to me. I can just see his offsprings' faces when they see him arrive back home! Ha ha! He may even survive!

"For I lanced the bubo. I found myself faced with a huge hard lump, a ridiculous and terrifying sort of excrescence—the bump of death. So I drove my scalpel into the tumor, and it resisted. Then I got to a softer area, an inner pocket that let out a liquid like scrambled eggs. Apparently if you manage to drain this off the victim sometimes survives. I've always made a mess of that kind of operation in the past— that's why I've been left in peace. But if this confounded merchant doesn't snuff it, they'll be bringing me dying people in droves."

My mother gave a slight shudder.

The parson laughed. "Don't be frightened, my pretty dear. I've disinfected myself thoroughly and taken every possible precaution."

The parson really felt the Chinese family had tricked him. He was furious. This time the joke was on him. It was his habit to nurse a grudge until he could get back at someone or other. That evening he picked on me.

My mother and I were in the courtyard about to leave, she just getting into her chair and I mounting my horse. The parson's wife stood in the doorway blowing me a last kiss, and the parson, leaving his whiskey behind for a moment, was calling a hoarse "Bye-bye." He gazed glumly at my mafu as he handed me the reins with the grimace that in a Chinaman expresses good humor. Then the parson gave a start, and started to scrutinize the mafu with eyes like lotto counters. Unsteadily but with determination, he walked over to him, a smile spreading across his face as if he'd just made some highly satisfactory discovery. He tapped me on the shoulder, laughing.

"Look, boy—your mafu's got leprosy."

He made me look at his swollen, leonine face and wasted fingers. Anne Marie, already in her chair, asked calmly, "Are you sure?"

He triumphantly repeated his demonstration. The mafu put on the typical Chinese expression of complete obtuseness in the face of disaster. When Anne Marie asked him, "Have you got leprosy?" he answered, "Yes—but not very badly."

At last we set off back to the consulate, in the same order as we had come.

My heart was heavy as I rode home. I didn't want

them to take my mafu away from me. To me his friendship was more important than his stigmata. I wasn't afraid of lepers.

There were so many of them in Chengtu, for one thing! First of all, there were those you mixed with without knowing it, respectable, anonymous, hiding their sores and trying to live a normal life. No one was alarmed by their proximity. Healthy Chinese mostly paid no attention to lepers, and were neither ashamed nor afraid of them.

But there were those in whom the disease was too visible, those too eaten away, whose bodies were gradually disintegrating. These the population drove outside the walls. Some left of their own accord, without having to be told. Theirs was the Plain of Tombs. Whenever I passed by there on my horse I glimpsed a phantom people who had dug holes among the graves, mingling their still living remains with those of the dead. They curled up in their holes like fetuses: in the uniformity of woe it was almost impossible to tell men from women. Sex and age no longer existed; filth hid festering. Sometimes, when some wealthy man came to do homage to the real dead, the false dead would extricate themselves from their hollows and beg for alms. Then soldiers would beat them and they would flee, only to wander back again. No one knew what they ate, but they reproduced. There were mothers among them with their babies slung on their backs. It was the republic of bloody stumps and absent eyes.

When I rode by their encampment these monstrosities would gather round me, cheerful, laughing. Laughs without lips or teeth. I'd take a little string of coins from around my neck and scatter them about, and then, beneath the very hoofs of my horse, there would ensue a spectral battle which lasted until my mafu went into action. With a bored expression on his face, he would lay about him with his stick, shouting, "Don't go near the young lord. Your pestilential stench upsets him. Clear off!" And they would retreat into their lairs, laughing amiably.

But now my mafu, who drove off the lepers, was himself a prey to the disease. On the way back to the consulate he followed me as usual, perhaps a few strides farther from me than was his wont. My mother turned around in her chair to look at his face: in the sunlight it was like a chipped stone. Her profile looked pensive and full of sudden melancholy. I brought my horse up close to her and cried, "I want to keep him!"

She didn't wish to cause me pain. She smiled kindly and said:

"W'll get the French doctors to examine him, son. They'll tell us if it's possible to. . . ."

My father was pacing up and down in the courtyard of the consulate, clearly waiting eagerly to make a scene. His expression was severe. In his most caustic voice he asked Anne Marie:

"So, despite my express instructions, you've been to see the English?"

"Yes, my dear," she said. "We paid a very pleasant call on the parson and his wife. Extremely useful, too. Do you know what? The good parson discovered that the boy's mafu is a leper."

My father's face fell. He recovered himself at once, but his expression of vexation was replaced with one of professional concern. He was probably not sorry, really, to have an excuse for abandoning the quarrel with his disobedient spouse, the outcome of which was by no means certain. Unfortunately his new expression, the look, at once pedantic and eager, of a connoisseur of China and the Chinese, instead of disarming Anne Marie only irritated her profoundly.

"Why are you prowling round and round the man like that?" she said. "You don't know anything about it. The first thing to do is send him to the doctors for a diagnosis."

"Not at all. No point in bothering them. It's obvious he's a leper, and he's got it very badly, too."

He put on a swaggering air, an attitude of solemn banter.

"I know all about it. Before we were married I used to have a Chinese valet here in Chengtu. He had a very light touch—a real treasure. He never cut me when he shaved me, and he used to help me on with my underwear and shirt with the utmost skill. He even tied my tie. And he was that miraculous object—an absolutely clean Chinaman. Well, one day when he was rubbing me down after my shower, I noticed that one of his fingers was eaten away. Leprosy! And in someone who was touching me all the time. So you see I know what I'm talking about."

"Poor thing. What you must have suffered. And you married me so you'd have someone safe to take care of you instead of the marvelous valet."

"What do you mean, Anne Marie? If I had to rely on you to help me dress and turn myself out decently . . . It's true I was upset for a while. But not for long. If you start letting yourself be upset in China . . . Did I ever tell you about the time I stayed in a Chinese inn in the provinces and slept for several nights on a mattress filled with maize leaves? One morning it started to move. I'd been incubating a nest of cobra eggs—the babies were already rearing up and swaying their heads quite dangerously. Fortunately the parents weren't there!"

"I've heard you tell that story at least a thousand

times. You tell it at every important banquet, during dessert. You've had great success with it. But how is it that till now you've spared me any stories about the servant who was a leper?"

"You think I'm a bore, but you're wrong. All the ladies before you used to admire me for my wit."

"I know, Albert. It seems you have a way with women that's so gallant and ardent it's irresistible."

"That's not what we're talking about. But believe me, I've been through all sorts of things in this blessed country."

"Yes, I know how brave you are, Albert. You're wonderful; you can bear anything; you have a solution for every problem. But I'm sure you bawled the valet out in no uncertain manner when he so annoyingly turned out to be a leper."

"What was I supposed . . ."

"Well, with the mafu you have to behave differently. You must be very nice. He's really devoted, and the boy adores him."

During this little altercation the whole household staff of the consulate had gathered in various corners of the courtyard and was gazing at our little group there in the middle. I was sniveling, Anne Marie was stroking my hair, and my father was clearing his throat preparatory to addressing the mafu, who stood there like a log a few yards away from us. For the sake of his wife the consul put on a magnanimous smile.

"Why did you conceal the fact that you had the disease?" he said, as if more in sorrow than in anger. "It might have infected your young master. But it seems you have been a good servant to him, that you would have given your life for him. So I'm not going to reproach you—I'll even give you some money. But you'll have to go. . . ."

When he'd finished his speech my father threw some silver coins in the direction of the mafu. They tinkled as they hit the ground. The mafu did not pick them up. He stood planted there, sunk in the silent dark surliness which among the Chinese sometimes explodes into a flash of rage or madness. My father prudently drew back. But a faint smile spread over the mafu's rugged face.

"I'll go," he said. "But in spite of my unworthiness I have a great favor to ask. Will you let my brother take my place? I guarantee his loyalty. He's an ex-soldier, the same as me, and very strong, but he suffers from no divine affliction. He'll look after the child well."

The French consul pretended to hesitate, and Anne Marie took the matter into her own hands.

"Fetch your brother," she said to the mafu, and a few moments later he reappeared, accompanied by a sturdy little fellow with a crooked face and a sly expression. My father examined him as if he were buying a horse, making him turn up his sleeves and his trouser legs. But there were no visible signs of disease, and the bargain was concluded.

I set off for town at once to try out the new mafu. He ran behind my horse just as well as his predecessor had, and was equally good at shouting and laying about him to clear a way for me through the crowd. He was just an ordinary man, and showed a dull but somewhat disturbing servility.

It hadn't rained for a week, and Chengtu was restored to its former beauty. The sky was clear, an azure bowl set with a sun that drank up the earth's miasmas. All kinds of pestilence, oozing, putrefaction, liquid, and mud vanished into the air—an almost arid air which dried out the soil. Chengtu had gotten back its old peaceable animation, as if the danger of war had disappeared.

I didn't go about in the town much now, but spent most of my time with Li, the only Chinese I was really fond of since the mafu who was a leper had gone. But as Chengtu came back to life, Li seemed to go to pieces. Full of distress, in the voice of a professional mourner, at once impersonal and squealing, she predicted:

"Now that Chengtu is able to burn again, the Yunnanese won't lose any time setting fire to it. Before long we shall see the flames like the ones that destroyed my family. Flames that will consume us all. . . ."

And indeed at dawn the next morning a red glow hovered over the city. It was ominous and unreal and yet like some magical sunset: there was a subtle play of light, an iridescent shimmer on painted roofs. A mile or so from the consulate, at the extreme southern end of the city, a crater belched forth clouds of black smoke streaked with red—heavy dark whorls shot through with flame, spreading out over the town like a marbled, fleecy ceiling, an extinguisher finally blotting out the last sparks. Chengtu choked in a soot that kept growing darker and darker. At the same time, on the ground, waves of flame had reached the city walls and leaped upon them. The ramparts vanished briefly in the fiery glow, then emerged slightly blackened but intact. The stone fortifications kept the fire from spreading, and below them lay the remains of the only district that had been destroyed. The spectacle of the conflagration had lasted four or five hours.

In the courtyard of the consulate the French consul, a pair of opera glasses glued to his eyes and an avid and satisfied expression on his face, had scrupulously followed the incident. And upon Anne Marie, standing beside him, Albert the consul poured forth his worthy consular reflections. She seemed not to hear, but I was listening.

"He's really very clever, the marshal. He's thought it all out. Mr. Cheng told me. . . . By the way, where can he have been since he ran out on my birthday party? . . . Only a few alleys where poor people live have gone up in flames. The wealthy districts and the shops and houses of the rich merchants, His Grace the bishop's Catholic church, the big pagodas and the teahouses and the best-known brothels escaped. The marshal's a very decent chap—he must have gotten a pretty penny for not burning the rich people and their houses to a crisp. It seems it was arranged that the fire should be big enough to do the marshal credit, but shouldn't spread in a way that would have been undesirable in the present situation. The Yunnanese carried out their little barbecue making full use of such data as topography and the direction of the wind. An efficient piece of work, no end of 'face' for the wily marshal, and all in return for a few hundred coolies getting a bit singed."

I'd have liked to go and get a closer look but I wasn't allowed to. So I wandered around the garden. I came on a woman crouched on the mossy bench—it was Li, weeping again. As I approached she sat up, her eyes wide and frightening.

"The fire!" she groaned. "The fire that destroyed my parents has now burned up my little sister Nanhg, the only family I had left. The fire was in the district where she and three thousand other girls entertained the sampan men. I must find out what has become of her, so I can mourn if she's dead and rejoice if she's still alive. I'm going to see. Come with me. Don't make any noise. Monsieur le Consul and Madame mustn't know. . . ."

A conspiracy. Li slipped out of the main gate, a tall, sure-footed figure in a white robe. Meanwhile my wry-mouthed mafu had very furtively brought me my horse. I mounted and followed Li, who led me with a sort of brutish inertia through the crowd to the other side of the city.

I can still remember that expedition into the partly destroyed town. How many calamities I have witnessed in China since! But as a child I saw things with different eyes. Everything looked so normal! I'd set out to view a disaster and I found myself in a sort of carnival. It seemed to me quite natural to see people rejoicing at their own escape. What did the dead bodies nearby matter? It was wisdom to laugh at the dead because one was still alive. The smell of burning almost choked me, every now and then sparks would fall on me, wreaths of smoke still writhed along the ground. But all that didn't alter the fact that life was real and intense.

Li strode along, and my mafu and I followed her to a wide, well-to-do street full of strange banners depicting monsters and aberrations supposed to bring good luck. It was here that the main quacks' market was to be found—the fantasmagorias of Chinese eroticism were the specialty. Wonderful shops, very expensive, stacked with pharmacopoeias to give potency to wealthy old men so aged they were no more than hollow dwarfs, ancient Buddhas whose hoary heads almost touched the ground. Such of those old men who were not wise enough to stick to opium, which abolished desire, stuffed themselves with magic remedies. There were stalls covered with goods both spendid and sordid—shriveled, stinking, grotesque, strange, or dazzling, heaps of rotted flesh and dung and dust—one couldn't be sure whether animal or vegetable—dark leaves, black liquids, scales, pelts, fangs, weird roots. Among the latter were ginseng roots from Manchuria or Korea, like little human dolls, instruments of sorcery, terrifying pygmies. I gazed at them. Each was like a tiny corpse, but a corpse that could bring an old man back to life and give him the power to deflower a child, a little girl or a little boy. Each virginity was extremely expensive, and it was said that some millionaires took one a month, partly for pleasure and partly as medicine, for it was well known that contact with young flesh had a rejuvenating effect.

But horror was not far away. In this street whose trade it was to revivify men, business was good despite the smell of singeing, despite hot gusts of stench, despite the fact that the normal chiaroscuro was darker than usual with lingering smoke. The people were absorbed in their pleasures. Only the snakes were displeased. Of course there were serpents in all the temples, but those were of paint or stone, writhing dragons with terrible scales. The snakes that fascinated me here were really alive. They were even angry, probably frightened by the proximity of the fire. Each of the little dispensaries had a covered tub of snakes, usually heaped together in a horrible slippery mass. But today they had untwisted themselves from one another and were banging their heads furiously against the sides of their baskets.

I stopped a moment to watch. A decrepit old customer had stopped at a stall to buy some snake venom. A sturdy assistant got hold of one of the reptiles and held it in a forked stick. Its neck swelled out even larger, it grew immense. It was a king cobra, hissing and twisting, mad with rage. Suddenly the assistant threw a piece of cloth at it, which it mistook for a man. There was a flash, an arch, a rasp, a hurtling body, a fang piercing the rag, a trickle of poison. All the merchant had to do was put the cheated snake away and sell a few drops of the venom at a very high price to his venerable client, who would drink it to acquire strength. Acquiring strength was an obsession with the Chinese.

This scene lasted no more than a few seconds, but when I turned away to go on I was confronted by a mask—a man whose face was almost entirely covered with bamboo paper, with just little slits for eyes. The man stood motionless and silent in front of my horse, which stopped of its own accord and began to lick him. A very strange apparition.

But when it began to speak I at once recognized the voice of my old mafu.

"Don't be afraid, young master. I don't want to leave you. I'll still serve you in Chengtu. I'll never come close to you, and as an extra precaution I've bound up my sores. Don't say anything to your parents. But whenever you leave the French consulate alone I'll manage to come with you. The new mafu I got for you will always let me know. I'll never be far away—I'll be with a cousin of mine who sells soup a hundred yards or so away from your yamen."

I smiled at the mafu, who couldn't smile back because of his cardboard face. The poor fellow looked quite horrible.

"You must always come with me, mafu," I said. "But first take off all those dressings—they make you look like a monster. You're better with the leprosy uncovered."

"No, master. I've consulted a very wise magician,

and it was he who ordered me to wear these plasters. They have very great virtue, for even if they don't cure me they'll prevent you from being infected."

Li had stopped. She showed no surprise; it was as if she had already known. Then we all set off again in procession, Li in front, the mafu who wasn't a leper in front of my horse, and the mafu who was a leper behind.

The real China—I and my entourage were entering into it. I was dazed with joy. Then suddenly I was shaken out of my dream: my horse was jerked aside, my mafus protested, and above all I heard the shrill shouts of a woman's voice coming from inside the drawn curtains of a palanquin. The lady cursed me, but especially she cursed her clumsy bearers, who had knocked into me and jolted their precious burden. The litter contained a beautiful young woman, as I saw when, a little farther on, the coolies stopped and set down the chair with a series of uniform movements like soldiers presenting arms. The person they deposited flailed about unsteadily before managing to stand upright, then made off toward a dark crevice in a wall—one of those thick walls that surrounded every Chinese house and made it a closed world as likely to contain a mansion as a house of ill fame. The little creature tottered along for a few yards on her mutilated feet, then vanished into a murky passage. What I had glimpsed seemed hardly a corporeal being at all, but some creation of art, with a face like a brush stroke; make-up and jewels turning the features into a chill mask painful in its beauty and deathly in its intensity. Her face was nothing but lines, lines so pure and sharp they had neither weight nor flesh, like an image complemented by shimmering broideries and every most subtle artifice. All life was concentrated in the almond eyes, which were of a harsh and pitiless intensity, embers at once glowing and dead presiding over all.

I was in ecstasy. But at the sight of her the mafu who was a leper spat with supreme disgust. Coming closer to express his scorn, he said:

"That was a 'little flower.' "

A poison flower, slowly brought to monstrous perfection for the delight of fat rich men in underwear, men who demanded every kind of pleasure. We had seen her arriving at the house of some customers who had sent for her. They had probably dispatched a little boy as a messenger to her procuress, some matron who had bought her as an infant from her starving parents. The old bawd had thus saved her from being married to the spirit of the waters—for if it hadn't been for her money the child would have been drowned at birth. So her benefactress had fed the little girl, housed and trained and educated her, turning her into a work of art who would bring in a thousand times, ten thousand times, the price she had paid for her. But a girl brought up like that had a heart harder, more unfeeling, more rapacious than a devil. This royal prostitute was death and ruin.

It struck the mafu that Li might have seen him spit with disgust. At once he tried to correct himself.

"It's not the same thing with Li's sister—she's a real whore. A peasant who sells her body to anyone in order to live. She has never done any harm. She's very respectable. I have a great deal of regard for her. And she's very much like Li, too."

"You know her then, mafu?"

"I often go to see her," the mafu who was a leper said, laughing. "So I'm very glad she's not dead. We'll find her all alive and kicking; the fire stopped about a hundred yards from her little brothel."

"How do you know?"

"I was watching all the time. I saw everything."

And he started to tell. . . . First of all, men dressed as coolies, brigands in the service of the Yunnanese, had sprinkled gasoline on houses and huts, thrown lighted torches on them, and calmly gone away. For who would have dared to lay hands on such formidable characters? Is a few seconds all the separate fires had joined to form one mass of flames sweeping forward at a terrifying speed, consuming the wooden hovels and shops and leaping across the narrow streets. It swallowed up everyone and everything. And yet there were men trying to flee, laden with the wretched objects that were their only worldly goods, women encumbered by their brats. The half-burned, the slightly burned, and those not burned at all mingled together in a pitiful stampede, shrieking and stumbling. Those who fell were overtaken by the wall of fire driven after them by the wind. Then came a moment when the blaze slackened, then stopped, turning in on itself, gradually dying away, passing from the scarlet flames of extermination to a baleful mass of embers that changed color as they cooled, like the remains of some enormous funeral pyre.

The mafu went an and on in Chinese.

"I was there when the fire, which was going toward Li's sister's brothel, died down and halted. So I was sure Nanhg hadn't been killed, and I wanted to let Li know right away. Besides, it would have been dangerous for me to stay there a moment longer."

"But what danger was there for you, mafu? The fire was over."

"The Yunnanese!"

And now the usually impassive mafu was laughing beneath his mask. His eyes, holes in the cardboard, were merry. Arms, legs, and tongue were animated

with delight. He was as pleased with the exploits of
the Yunnanese as if he'd taken part in them himself.
He'd witnessed them, he'd almost been their victim,
but he admired their skill.

A whole regiment had appeared on the scene and
spread in a steel circle around the charred remains.
When the machine guns were in place, trained on the
disaster area, the troops advanced into the circle in
small groups, searching the ruins with their bayonets.
They were strictly supervised by officers, revolvers in
hand. The sort of people usually attracted by that
kind of incident had already arrived at the still-smok-
ing charnel house and were going through the embers
in search of something of value or a souvenir. But at
the sight of the war lord's troops they all started to
run away in a headlong flight stopped short by the
bayonets. The Yunnanese said coldly to every man they
seized, "You're one of the criminals who started the
fire. The marshal is immensely angry. He will see that
justice is done immediately." Their faces were terrible, with their words of death and their death-deal-
ing impassiveness. Any poor captives who had a few
silver coins held them out to the soldiers and were allowed to escape. The others implored in vain. There
were about twenty of these, and they were trussed up
like pigs and thrown in a heap to await the arrival of
the marshal. For the war lord was to come and preside
over their execution to show the horror he felt at such
a heinous deed and his love for the people of Chengtu.

As the mafu had not ventured into the debris, he
hadn't been surrounded by the Yunnanese, and so he
was with us now in the street of the druggists in the
middle of a crowd of their wealthy clients. His voice
lost its zest and he was glum as he told the rest of his
story.

"So I came away, as I said, and went into the consulate through a little back door at the bottom of the garden near the pond, an entrance Monsieur le Consul doesn't know about. When I told Li what had happened and said her sister was safe, she started to whine. She didn't believe me. She said, 'Have you seen her?' I said no. She said, 'Fire is a curse on our family. The flames are bound to have caught up with my poor sister today. First it was my parents' turn, now hers. One day it'll be mine.' So then I suggested taking her there, for there's no danger of any kind now. The fire's out, and the manhunt's over, too. Li agreed to come. Then I said we must bring you with us, because I wanted to see you again, and I knew you'd like to see the splendid sight of Chengtu in its troubles. So that's how our little expedition came about."

We had a long way to go. After the wide, luxurious street where they sold the fortifying medicines, and the narrow alleys of a teahouse quarter, we came to the other end of the town, where a heap of shanties propped one another up, a layer of little excrescences leaning against the base of the ramparts, which threw a great peaceful shadow.

I could see no destruction. The air was like pitch, the light coal-black, and it felt like an oven. But even there, so close to the disaster, all was tranquility, ordinary life went on. Along the paved alleys flowed a crowd of poor, respectable people. It was as if the humble, in pursuit of their pleasures, were ruled by a kind of reserve, or rather of avid shyness. The human tide moved along past rows of huts made of bamboo and paper, all alike and each a brothel; past the faces and legs of women crouched beside the footpath. Be-

tween the establishments, sitting on stools, were girls
in country dress, tunics of unbleached linen and blue
trousers. Their attitude was strange: they sat upright
with one plump white leg tucked underneath them.
In this fleshy pose they would remain for hours, dignified, on offer, very cheerful, and showing nothing of
their body but their feet. This was the age-old position of prostitutes, designed to "excite" customers.
But these whores had none of the immodesty or insolence of their European counterparts. They were respectable daughters of the people.

On one of these stools I saw, surmounting a flat
chest, a rough snub-nosed face, not pretty, which I
recognized at once. It might have been Li's, but it was
that of her sister Nanhg. With no sign of emotion,
with no demonstrativeness, as if nothing had happened, the two women went through the rituals of
greeting. The younger sister, having unfolded herself
from her seat, made us some long speeches and then
ceremoniously led all of us—Li, me, and the mafus—
into her brothel.

It was a family dwelling. We found ourselves in a
very dark room with a dirt floor—the common room,
very respectably decorated. There were even tributes
to piety—an altar to the ancestors, wooden halberds,
a fat-bellied Buddha, the bronze tortoises of longevity,
and one or two kuanings, full-bodied goddesses of
fertility. Sticks of incense burned before bowls of
sacrificial flowers. Red lacquer panels bore the well-
known aphorisms of wisdom and virtue. All was peace.

Li, as a person of quality, was given a respectful
welcome. The woman in charge of the house bowed
to her with folded hands. She was so old her head had
been shaven, as was the custom, and her skull shone.
In a corner a wrinkled old fellow was smoking a

water pipe with rhythmic gurglings: the old lady's husband. There were children, too—grandsons and great-grandsons. All was happiness.

It was a happiness not to be disturbed, and I endangered it by a blunder typical of a white child, a little "barbarian." For when the woman squeezed me kindly with her bony hand, I said by way of compliment and congratulation, "I'm so glad your honorable house wasn't burned." Her fingers were withdrawn, her wizened face moved away, her eyes closed in distress. Li and the mafu who was a leper were embarrassed, ashamed on my account. For what I'd said was a horrible hypothesis suggesting that such a misfortune *might* have occurred. The first principle of politeness required that one should never, no matter how indirectly, not even by wishing the contrary, allude to the possibility of misfortune. To wish someone good health, even, was a solecism in Chengtu. How many times had Li told me all this! Because of her I knew that the mere reference to some mishap might cause it to occur, by stirring up fate, the forces of darkness and evil spirits.

The woman of the house lit a coil of incense to drive away the bad luck in what I had said. It was a piercing, bitter smell, and with it mingled the sweet and spicy scents of the dream that allows the unfortunate to forget the pitilessness of life.

In Chengtu the smell of opium overcame all the ancient smells of China—that of the fertilizing dung, of musk, of the essences burned in the temples, of the perfumes of the small-footed ladies, of mud, slime, rice fields, of all the puddles and stagnant pools and rivers choked with silt. The smell of opium hung about the yamens of the rich old men who sought the pleasures of the mind, and descended into alleys and slums, all the places where the poor huddled together. There were dens everywhere, ill concealed by bamboo fences. The whole population gave itself up to opium in a kind of joyous suicide. Instead of eating their bowl of rice, the coolies, the human beasts of burden, the porters and the sampan men—all spent their last farthings on opium. Their strength flagged, and they died off even faster than before, hauling on the ropes of junks or bearing the straps of palanquins. Craftsmen and peasants worked less, the harvests were poorer, there was less to eat.

In the peaceful room where we now were, the greetings of Li and the woman of the house did not prevent business from proceeding as usual in an atmosphere of familiarity at once charming and cruel. We were in a brothel-cum-opium-den, but the two activities were separate. The area devoted to drugs lay beyond the altar to the ancestors, with the red glow of its joss sticks. From where I stood I could just discern gleams and cracklings, gusts of sweetness, flickers, a world of silence, a void in full production. On rows of planks one above the other I could make out bodies: inside a wooden hutch with several levels were layers of naked men, naked skeletons. It was a kind of heartrending squalor. They were so thin, so gaunt; their ribs stuck out; the veins were swollen on the fleshless limbs. The atmosphere seemed one of eternal peace, ultimate renunciation, and only in their eyes did life survive. Yet what vigor and eagerness were mustered by these stunted shadows, each no more than a stick or a pencil stroke or a line, when it was their turn to sit up and inhale the smoke. Then they would fall back on their cot in ecstasy, awaiting the next time. The opium was prepared by two huge fellows standing solidly upright, their production line consisting of a tray of little tools, the lamp, and the jar containing the drug. As soon as one of these fateful figures had prepared a pipe he would offer it to a mouth, bending down if the man was on a cot near the ground, and stretching up if he was lying on an upper level.

A death trap. The more so because these poor wretches were consuming not the real thing, not pure opium, but dross, the black, almost solid, poisonously strong residue left in the pipes of the rich who smoked luxuriously in their own homes, and afterward sold on the market. Often it was even the dross of dross, the residue of residue, a frightful concentrate which was all that remained after the original opium had been used three, four, or five times. It might then be so hard that it could not be smoked, but had to be eaten. The poorest of the poor chewed and swallowed this ultimate dross in order to enter into the dream. Often one of them would collapse, in the street or perhaps in the brothel den.

For that reason, it was quite usual here for a man to fall off his plank, and indeed it happened not long after we arrived. A coolie who had been eating dross fell to the floor, stiff, pale, unbreathing, his eyes shut. At a sign from the manageress he was taken out and deposited in the street. Perhaps he would wake up. Perhaps not.

Anyhow, good humor was restored. Had this incident appeased the malign spirits and warded off bad luck? In any event, Li was radiant and the woman of the house still more decorous. Two or three of the girls came and chatted with us. They all had normal-sized feet, including Nangh, Li's sister, a sign that they were whores of such low class that no one had even bothered to mutilate their feet.

Now and then these beauties would leave us for

coolies whose clothes consisted almost entirely of patches of different colors. These men were sturdier than the opium smokers, who lay in their part of the room without any thought of the flesh. With the stout fellows who came for fornication, everything passed off cheerfully. The man, having selected his partner after a brief chat full of wry faces and jests, would draw forth from his rags, almost as if from his very body, a roll of coins threaded on a string. Then he went off with his companion behind a bamboo curtain, the area where transactions took place. Noises ensued—the sounds of love. No one was at all embarrassed, and the satisfied customer usually joined our group for a few minutes afterward and drank a cup of tea or spirits. All was quite comfortable and easy.

The youngest and prettiest inmate went off with a sampan man, massive as a rock. I gazed at the curtain behind which they had disappeared. Through a crack I could see the dirt floor, a spittoon, and a wooden cot on which shapes writhed. When the man emerged, my eye fell on the naked girl, standing there gracefully, all gentle curves, the peach blossom of all the Chinese poems. It was a wonderful sight, even if the person concerned was prosaically engaged in pouring a saucer of dirty water into the space between her thighs and rubbing herself with her fingers, without either soap or towel. Finally she used a scrap of paper, as one might use a bit of toilet tissue. She sensed my looking at her, and gave a friendly laugh.

My admiration, my amazement! They were the first breasts, it was the first body, that I had ever seen. For in the China of the middle classes and the war lords, even partial nakedness in a woman was considered something monstrous. "Don't show too much bosom," my father was always telling my mother. Yet the wealthy Chinese went through an enormous number of women: concubines, singing girls, and "little flowers." But they had to be covered up, monuments of fabrics and jewels, always hidden, always sealed in their beauty. It was through art and secrecy that they aroused desire and acquired noble protectors. Their bodies were disturbing enigmas. This hermeticism led to overrefinement and depravity.

Such feminine charms as I had encountered I had seen only in the beggar women, the female coolies in the street, whose torn rags might reveal sagging breasts, often with a half-dead infant sucking at them. But these were repulsive visions, and it wasn't until I came with Li to her sister's that I at last discovered flesh that could give pleasure. I was both glad and slightly ashamed, for I knew that in the eyes of "respectable" Chinamen these were only low carcasses fit for coolies. To such Chinese the populace did not exist, and what they did mattered even less. And I myself was slightly contaminated by the Chinese scorn for the lower classes, and this somewhat marred my pleasure at being where I was and seeing what I saw. This despite Li, despite my love for Li.

However, I went on delightedly watching this flower who, when she had finished her ablutions, put on her rough clothes and rejoined us, her figure hidden in thick swaths of cotton and on her face a foolish smile. The miracle was over. But Li, who had spotted what I was up to, began to dance up and down with joy. Once again she cooed over and lauded my virility: she would have liked to exhibit it to the honorable hostess, who showed great interest in seeing this little white object. But I refused, to the disappointment of the circle of yellow faces consumed with curiosity. They made a great fuss over me just the same. I was a king.

In China, land of contradictions, this was a privilege of childhood. For even in this low place, among these dregs of society, the mere presence of an adult barbarian would have been something worse than fire or plague, a calamity bringing ruin and dishonor. Even the coolies would stop coming once the barbarian had been there. No Chinese would eat there for fear of contamination. But I, a child, was innocent, and they stuffed me with melon seeds. The sister who was a whore was off duty in our honor, and she skinned the seeds for me with her teeth.

Hers was a common story. Before her parents died in the fire they had been made destitute by a flood, and they had auctioned their youngest daughter in the street, in Chengtu. A few farthings for a little girl of seven or eight. But she was too ordinary for any procuress of importance to buy her and make her into a "little flower," torturing her body as Chinese gardeners tortured trees to obtain exquisite little monstrosities. It was the madam of this poor brothel, this "teahouse," who had purchased her and swiftly recouped the price with the sale of her virginity. Since then the life of Li's little sister had been a simple one. The years went by. She ate, so she was almost happy. Her job had no stigma attached to it in China. Were not all women bought or sold one way or another?

But her fear was of the future, of the time when anything might happen. Even if there were no great natural disasters she was doomed. When no further use could be made of her, it would mean immediate death. If she should be consumed by the disease that made men break out in spots, if her skin should be marred by sores or pimples, if with wear and tear her face became covered with wrinkles, then the old woman would throw her out into the street with her own hands. No one would take pity on her, and she

would surely die. For a while she would still be alive,
but starving, disintegrating, and then she would be a
corpse. How many thousands of women who had out-
lived their usefulness perished like that, unnoticed,
in Chengtu? It was better for them to throw themselves in the river, the traditional solution for destitute
women. The rivers of China devoured women, bearing
away the bodies like white grubs—the bodies of baby
girls not yet exploitable, the bodies of old women
exploitable no more.

Drowning or beggary, then—if all went well. That
was a normal end to life, for a whore. But sudden
catastrophe was also a possibility, the sort of disaster
that at the same time it engulfed Nanhg would also
engulf the old woman, the brothel, the street, the district, perhaps the whole town. Then, instead of a solitary death by attrition, it would be a collective death.
Nanhg, like all the other poor denizens of the brothel,
was, despite a real or assumed cheerfulness, haunted
by fear. Fear of fire, which had just missed burning
them all to a cinder and which must not be mentioned. Fear of the war that had been hanging over
Chengtu for weeks and might bring death in so many
forms. Fear of everything. For any day, any hour,
could bring extermination.

Who could be sure of surviving? That very day,
before my eyes, in that lowly den, my mafu, the one
who was a leper, had a narrow escape from death.
While my amah was queening it, he just crouched on
the floor, silent. It wasn't that he was embarrassed by
his strange bandages—no one paid them any attention. He simply wasn't in the habit of talking to people. So he sat and listened. But he had just, very
lightly, linked little fingers with Nanhg—a great demonstration of love in China, where no one expressed

anything. Then two Yunnanese soldiers entered the brothel. They did so neither fiercely nor affably, but like automata, with the indifference of those claiming their rightful pleasure. One got hold of Nanhg, the other went up to Li in her long white robe. She cried out. The mafu had let his sweetheart go—for her there was nothing to be done. But when the Yunnanese dragged Li toward him by the hair, the mafu leaped up, shouting, "Leave her alone—she's not a whore!" The soldier calmly put his revolver to the mafu's belly.

"Shut up, moldy-face, or I'll shoot."

But the mafu went on shouting:

"Look! Look at the little white boy! He's the son of the French consul, the marshal's friend. This woman is his amah, and if you harm her you'll soon find yourself without a head."

Everyone fell silent. Li stood with parted lips, not uttering a sound. I was drinking it all in, quite calm. It was a scene already familiar to me—I'd seen the same thing a few days before in the imperial city, and the mafu had used the same words. But then, I knew, there had been no danger, and this time I could feel the imminence of death. In the soldier's eyes was the desire to kill: for endless seconds he kept his finger on the trigger. Would he pull it? His face trembled with rage—an almost imperceptible tremor all the more dangerous for being nearly invisible. It signified the cold, mad rage of a Chinaman and a soldier forced to give up what he had publicly demanded. It wasn't Li who mattered so much as the humiliation, the loss of "face." The mafu didn't move. Then the Yunnanese turned away from him and went out, signing to his companion to follow.

The mafu sat down and took Nanhg's hand again

as if nothing had happened. Then Li began her usual imprecations.

"I won't eat another mouthful of rice," she yelled, "until the Yunnanese have been cut to pieces!"

The old woman, who had plenty of experience and had been through many a dark day, shook her head doubtfully.

"You were lucky they were Yunnanese, daughter," she said. "At least they're disciplined. You only have to mention their marshal. Soldiers from some other army might have killed the lot of us."

Li suddenly calmed down and settled herself to listen with deference, as a chit of a girl should to the wisdom imparted by a venerable elder.

"I personally don't want war in Chengtu," went on the procuress. "Even if it meant the Szechwanese could get rid of the Yunnanese. I know too much about what happens when one army takes a town from another. One wave of bloodthirsty wretches after the other—the conquered, who loot and massacre to get whatever they can out of the place before fleeing, and the proud conquerors, whose war lord decrees a couple of days of carnage both to reward his soldiers and to inspire a healthy terror in the population. There have to be heads on pikes, bayonets dripping with blood, girls stabbed. Then law and order is restored, and you have to pay. What was paid out before to the last war lord doesn't count. Trade is ruined, especially little businesses like mine, whose owners have no protection. In my long life I've seen these terrible upheavals in so many towns. And every time the soldiers stripped me of everything. . . ."

Then the mafu who was a leper abandoned his silence and asked her, actually grinning because he was so amused:

"Including your virginity?"

The old woman split her sides, and there was general hilarity. At last she answered, her ancient chops twisted into a laugh:

"They weren't quite quick enough for that. My mother sold it when I was eight."

Delight on all sides. When silence fell again the voice of Nanhg was heard. Her tone was solemn, and she had adopted the attitude of a suppliant.

"Most reverend elder sister Li, might you, who know the secrets of the foreigners, use your great powers to enable me to take refuge in the French consulate if there is a war or some other misfortune?"

Li's face immediately shuttered itself with a kind of harshness. Refusal. She who had shed so many tears and made such a to-do about the younger sister supposedly burned to death was now like a stone when it really came to saving her should it become necessary.

"No. Monsieur le Consul would be angry. He's forbidden all the servants to take anyone in, even their families. If he let them, the consulate would be invaded by hundreds, thousands of Chinese. And that would create many problems for my honorable master. Whichever war lord won would certainly complain."

Li's sister accepted this decision with the proper alacrity. Everyone present agreed with Li's words of wisdom: in China, egoism was sacred. Only the mafu who was a leper laughed mockingly. He saw Li as she really was, a typical woman, not to be trusted, a worthy Chinese dame always ready with protests of kindness and commiseration and diatribes against the wicked, but reduced to cowardice and calculation as soon as her own safety or interests were involved.

But I liked Li, who was always spoiling me and

showing me off. Little did I care what she really was
and whether she acted out of affection or not. I had
too much "face" to ask myself such questions. I was
Chinese enough to take no interest in Li's heart so long
as she pretended to have one, especially so long as
she did as I wanted. She was excellent at that, though
I was sure she would abandon me in the face of danger. But the mafu who was a leper wouldn't desert
me. He was the one I trusted.

A bugle call made him start.

"We must hurry," he said. "The marshal's coming."

We hastily took our departure, making our way
through a ragged crowd which was running to see
what was to be seen. Suddenly, beyond the hovels,
we came on an empty space a few hundred meters
square. Scorched earth, a sort of disgusting black bald-
ness. The ground was insubstantial, a layer of dust
into which your feet sank. Its mostly level surface was
broken here and there by taller heaps of ashes and
bits of debris not entirely burned away that stuck up
like wreckage out of the sea. There was the smell of
death in the middle of this annihilation—but it was
not the moment to think of the corpses still buried in
the flat carpet of ruins. The void that had just been
created by the fire was now full of splendor, and
military glory paraded itself on the ground so judiciously prepared by the flames. A squadron of cavalry
swept by at the gallop, the horses' hoofs throwing up
burned-out torches. A regiment presented arms. Banners shone. Salvos saluted the marshal as, accompanied by his general staff, he reviewed his troops. I
recognized him from where I stood—ungainly, cold,
haughty. He stopped. A sword whirled in his hand,
and at one stroke, with sumptuous skill, he cut off the

head of a man kneeling before a block. He was the "leader" of "the criminal arsonists." Other culprits still remained to be chastised, a row of prostrate heaps already placed in position for execution. But the marshal, having once set the example of justice, left the rest to his soldiers. In a kind of ballet, one man stood behind each victim and held his sword in suspense over him for a few seconds, until the marshal called out: "Kill!" Then, all at once, the flashes of steel, the heads falling, the blood spurting out of the sprawling bodies. It was a marvel of precision, and a growl of admiration arose from the crowd gathered around under the supervision of sentries with guns at the ready. Then came laughter and grins of satisfaction. And yet the poor wretches recently caught and now beheaded were people of the district, neighbors and relatives of many of those who were laughing. But the pleasure of seeing blood shed so artistically was too much for them. Also, they couldn't help feeling a certain respect for the marshal's cleverness, the astuteness of his trick. First he started the fire and put all Chengtu in fear and terror of him, and then he managed to make a splendid display of his innocence, publicly and ceremonially lopping off the heads of men who really were innocent and known to be so by all the excited audience. So the marshal gained "face" in every respect, first as a terrible lord who would stop at nothing and then as an honorable avenger of the people.

That day all was honor for the marshal. For among the notables in his entourage were all the Chengtu war lords—the boor from Kweichow, and all the Szechwanese generals including the mad former monk and the bunch of scrapings and old veterans newly promoted. They were all beaming and happy, congratulating the Yunnanese marshal on the virtue and courage that had saved the city.

"Instead of fighting over the prey, the tigers prefer to eat it together," growled the mafu when he saw them.

"What prey?" I asked.

"Chengtu," said the mafu.

When we got to within a hundred yards of the consulate he vanished, and I returned home with Li and the other mafu, the one with the crooked mouth. My parents knew nothing of my escapade. But I needed to unburden myself to someone.

It was the ancient scholar, the twisted old man who acted as my father's calligrapher, whom I took as my confidant. He, too, was a friend of mine. He taught me about the old China, the noble China, the China of virtue. It was from him that I learned to scorn manual tasks and to respect the supremacy of thought. He had the greatest disdain for all those louts of war lords. But I liked to tease him.

"I've just seen the marshal cut off somebody's head," I told him. "He did it in one stroke. It was great."

His reply was a rebuke, a flood of indignation and disgust.

"You actually saw it! I know the marshal does sometimes flourish a knife and slit someone's throat with his own hands. It's revolting. It just shows what a low creature he is—probably used to be a coolie or a bandit. How could you enjoy watching such a thing?"

"I thought he managed the sword better than he managed his fork when he came to dine at the consulate."

And from his long sleeves the wrinkled old man brought forth his twisted fingernails, the famous gim-

lets proving that however low he might have fallen
now, he had never stooped to physical labor. Then,
his voice suddenly lofty and swelling, he launched
into his great speech about the splendors of the past,
when such ignominy would have been inconceivable.

"What darkness has closed in around the Celestial
Empire since the fall of the Son of Heaven! I used to
be one of the thirty thousand sages who passed the
great poetry examination held every three years and
then ruled China in the name of virtue. I helped
maintain the eternal order of the world, I fought
against evil and all that could corrupt the course of
time and the generations of men. I issued my edicts
in my court, with my insignia, my robes, my seals,
my banners, my scribes, and my executioners. Since
every offense against morality is an abomination disturbing the foundations of nature and the world, upsetting the cycle of seasons and the gathering in of
harvest, it was my business to remove all trace of it
by destroying the authors of the sacrilege. Having
meditated on the laws of wisdom, I would choose the
most suitable punishment for them. It was my executioners, stout fellows with short mustaches who succeeded one another from father to son, who meticulously put the sentence into effect, cutting up flesh
and muscle and bone as I had prescribed, in my
presence. I acted not out of caprice but out of duty,
the most sacred duty.

"But I would never have let my hand touch an instrument of torture, or any other instrument. The
hand of the sage is only for holding the brush that,
through the grace of beautiful signs and the majesty
of characters, proclaims thought, which governs all.
No matter what the situation, the minds of the
mandarins, specialists in supreme Harmony, always

found the sentence conducive to the greatest virtue. While they themselves were divorced from everything material, they ruled over matter with their judgments, verdicts, and decrees. They were equal to anything; they were the personification of absolute Good. Below them, part of their entourage, a sort of extension of themselves, they had 'satellites' with real hands, hands that executed justice, hands that might fall on ordinary men. That was supreme Concord, with its keystone in the Temple of Heaven in Peking. But now Heaven has fallen and all that remains is universal confusion, a chaos of woe in which mankind, having rebelled against supreme Wisdom, gives itself over to unbridled and bestial passions. And in this abyss wallow the war lords."

I didn't altogether understand the former mandarin's eloquence. Sometimes he would talk that way to me for hours, in a language so learned that words and phrases escaped me. What I did gather from his obscure teachings was that a young lord like me should never stoop to any irksome task; above all, should never use his hands except for some noble purpose like holding the reins of his horse, writing, or eating. The most distinguished Chinamen even had concubines or "little flowers" to feed them. As for me, my amahs used to put rice into my mouth with their chopsticks. I merely had to be able to use a knife and fork when I was allowed to eat with my parents. I found this difficult and disagreeable, and didn't make a much better job of it than the war lord when he was a guest. I knocked things over and spilled food on myself and everywhere else. No meal ever came to an end without my mother saying to me in disgust:

"You *are* a dirty child . . . just like a little pig."

Such reproaches meant nothing to me. For me, as

for all the Chinese people I knew, dirtiness was perfectly respectable: it was necessary to enjoyment and "face," and it served as a condiment to the gourmandizings of the rich, where the quantity and quality of the dishes were designed to show off their wealth.

I was very fond of the old mandarin because of his verbal magnificence. He taught me to be magnificent myself. And I felt sorry for him, too, because after his great flights he would once more become a poor whining old gnome who clung to my nobility as if I might do something to improve his fate. All his pretensions crumbled away. With his famous pointed hand he would miserably scratch his armpit, whereas for such a humble purpose a scholar ought to use an ivory hand on a long stick. His teeth were nothing but stumps, his breath was awful, he spat, he whimpered. My amahs chased him away from me with a hail of harsh mockery, but he always came back. He was no taller than I was, and would quaver into my ear that life for him had been a sea of calamities. His sons had been murdered one bloody night of revolt by the dregs of the people, who remembered the justice he had meted out in the old days. In order to escape, he himself had hidden for several days in a tub of dung, where the passers-by relieved themselves on him. He had had to sell his daughters to a procuress, but in accordance with the great tradition of filial piety they had sacrificed themselves nobly and shed only a few modest tears over their fate. And now he was alone, without memorial tablets or descendants, without a coffin to await him, so poor he couldn't even afford the opium that brings forgetfulness.

As soon as my father appeared he would leave me and fawn on him, bowing and scraping right down to the ground, until Monsieur le Consul shouted: "That'll do—you've respected me enough." Everyone treated the old boy badly. When Anne Marie reproached Albert for his harshness toward him, he defended himself vehemently:

"But he's disgusting, the old wreck. When he was a mandarin there wasn't another who was more bloodthirsty, two-faced, and extortionate in the whole of Szechwan. Anyone who didn't pay up he had killed. People used to say he could get money out of a stone. And he's just as much of a hypocrite now as he was then."

But nothing could discourage the old boy. He would take no end of trouble to get one or two extra strings of coins out of my father. Whenever he found Monsieur le Consul smiling to himself he leaped at the opportunity. That is, once again he treated him to his supplication scene, a masterpiece of decorum, culture, and good breeding: he never actually asked, never spoke directly, for that would be barbarous behavior, not to be descended to even with a barbarian. The scholar would throw himself at Albert's feet and put on a voice of woe to recount his troubles. But these time-honored laments, designed to soften my father's heart and make him dip into his purse, were lost on him. Albert's only concern was not to be "had." So he put on an absent-minded expression. He didn't understand. He didn't want to. He didn't say no. What was worse, he didn't say anything. And yet, indefatigably, the old man tried his luck at least once or twice a month, and always in the same manner. Albert used to grumble, "I'm fed up with the old castoff. I'd have shown him the door already if he weren't such a talented calligrapher."

The day after the fire the old man came along with

his face all crumpled up, obviously crushed by some new catastrophe. He didn't shed a tear; on the contrary, his wrinkled countenance was like a torrid expanse of parched rice fields crisscrossed with dried-up ditches. But his little eyes glittered like those of an old madam getting ready to snare a client. When I saw this intense and well-simulated distress, I guessed that during the night the old boy had at last been struck by an "idea" that would work.

Having trailed behind my father for some time without being noticed, the old man came out to me in the main courtyard. First he gave a groan, and then he said:

"According to the ancients, a man's dignity consisted in suffering in silence. But perhaps old age has undermined my courage. And you are a child, and with you I can't restrain myself."

This preamble was followed by a clearing of the throat.

"I haven't told the whole truth even to you. One of my daughters was a prostitute, and gave me little presents out of filial respect. But alas, yesterday evening when I got home I was told she had been consumed in the fire. In vain, at dawn this morning, did I seek her remains. Long, a poor weak old man, did I wander."

Pause. Then the mewing sounds resumed.

"What will become of me without my child's gifts? Where will my rice come from? Great is the generosity of the consul of France. But my feeble body is too demanding. I shall die."

"I'll go right away and tell my father to have pity on you."

"Don't do that, child. I am ashamed. . . ."

I rushed away before the delighted eyes of the old

man. I burst into the office, where under his pince-nez the consul wore his most glum expression. But his bad temper didn't deter me. I started to tell my tale, but hardly had I opened my mouth than Albert exploded.

"The old baboon! That's all moonshine! His imagination's run away with him. To think of him using the fire to try the one about his dead daughter! I've been wondering for some time what he was going to dream up. The old lecher wants to buy a new concubine, some little eight-year-old virgin! The classic rejuvenation treatment for doddering old men getting on toward a hundred. Fortunately the head boy tipped me off. But to think of him mixing my son up in it! Tell them to chuck the old swine out!"

Poor old mandarin. He stood there green in the face, fingernails fluttering, all dignity gone, a wilting figure weeping and howling in Monsieur le Consul's office. Albert, extremely cross and covering his ears, signed to the servants to throw the scholar out, which they did with great enjoyment, dragging him along, beating him, laughing, and shouting insults at him.

"They say your daughters are so big in the ass they could do it with a tiger."

"You're bent almost double—how do you think your little worm of a member would be able to rear up enough to penetrate a virgin? Monsieur le Consul is only saving you useless expense by firing you."

"May you strain till your eyes come out of your ass."

"Your eyes won't see another cent, your belly won't receive another grain of rice. And may your body be like a bat's wing when you die!"

"May the ten thousand sorrows slay you!"

"May hunger so clutch at your innards that you feel they're a thousand li long!"

My amah plucked furiously at the few precious hairs which made up the mandarin's beard, a meager wisp like a brush mockingly writing the character for agony. Meanwhile the long cold silhouette of Anne Marie, coming from the garden, appeared in the round opening giving on to the rear of the consulate. Her tapering shadow fell on the floor of the court-yard. She didn't say a word. Her face gave no sign. But when she appeared all the servants' rancor faded away. They pulled themselves together, embarrassed, and quickly resumed the impassiveness proper to good domestics. I went over to my mother.

"We mustn't turn the poor man out. It's as good as condemning him to death," I said.

Anne Marie turned away.

"There's nothing I can do," she said. "Your father's too worked up. And you know when he's like that he'll never change his mind."

The mandarin was resigned. He limped over to the door and disappeared. I never saw him again. No one ever knew what become of him.

How many times in Chengtu did I see the common people, kind and familiar, bustling about their small affairs, suddenly seized with a fit of malcious passion! Then everyone, including old men, women, and chil-dren, would all gleefully attack some unfortunate. I remember a madman tied to a stake with enormous chains—the Chinese way of treating insanity. The man was almost naked and his only remaining con-nections with the world were through his rolling eyes and his gaping mouth. Around him a crowd had clustered, a thousand faces creased in frenzied hilar-ity. The entertainment consisted in biting the mad-man, tearing off bits of skin with one's teeth and making him bleed. To dress his wounds and calm him down, a cascade of spittle. And indeed the madman had quieted down, and only gave forth groans, which were drowned in the delighted laughter of the onlookers.

In the case of the mandarin I hold my father guilty. And yet he wasn't cruel by nature. But that day he was all set to explode, in such a bad temper his skin was yellow and he kept gingerly prodding his liver. His bow tie jerked up and down over his Adam's apple like a banner of peevishness. When he was in that sort of temper it was not enough for Monsieur le Consul merely to vent his spleen. He had to have a victim to vent it on. And that day it happened to be the mandarin. That's fate.

The reason he was so angry was that he'd just heard about the demonstration of national unity that had been given by all the war lords, both friends and enemies, in the presence of the Yunnanese marshal and on the site of the fire. It was a good thing my father didn't realize he was certainly the last person in Chengtu to get to know about it—only a day after it happened. He was furious enough as it was. For once again he didn't understand, he was engulfed in perplexities, theories, and fears. As soon as his storming had reduced his vice-consul and his head of chancery, timid nonentities at the best of times, to a couple of writhing grubs, Albert, slightly appeased, growled to my mother:

"Fancy doing this to me! What's going to become of me in all this, and of my policy and my railway? If all the military are in cahoots, I've had it."

"Don't be disheartened, Albert."

"I give up or be shaken in my purpose? Never! You don't know me, Anne Marie. I shall fight to the end. I've still got some tricks up my sleeve."

"You see."

"Anne Marie, you're very intelligent, for a woman. Very intelligent—yes, I admit it, I proclaim it. But even so, all your feminine intuition is not enough for you to grasp the complexity of the situation. You don't see all the reefs that lie ahead of me. You still think I'm exaggerating, talking nonsense."

"But, Albert, it's you who misunderstand me. I know very well you're an excellent diplomat."

"You say that, but do you mean it?"

"Of course."

"I live with my mind constantly stretched taut. I never stop thinking. I have to take tablets to make me sleep, and you complain because it makes me snore."

"You often do snore, my dear. And very loudly. Sometimes I wonder if you're not going to wake up the boy, in the next room."

"That's enough, Anne Marie. I'm serious. I'm always worrying. Everything's so complicated, and I have so little room to maneuver! I must always steer a completely accurate course. And never any letup. Before, I used to worry lest my getting arms for the Yunnanese might make the Szechwanese fall upon them and wipe them out before my equipment arrived. Then my railroad would have been down the drain. But now that all the ruffians in Chengtu have gotten together in some mysterious racket, my railroad's still up in the air. You see the sort of problem that keeps me awake. . . . But what could have brought the Yunnanese and the Szechwanese together? They're so fiercely opposed to each other in their greed. For all the generals to be satisfied with their share of the swag, there must be some terrific spoils to divide up. But what?"

Anne Marie gave a slight smile, mocking but kind.

"You worry too much, Albert. You'll sort it all out. You're clever enough to pull all the chestnuts out of the fire."

"Easier said than done."

Anne Marie's irony was like an inner exhalation, at least when there weren't little vertical lines around her mouth, signs of open disdain. But that day no lines were visible.

"And, Albert, how many times have you, the expert on the Celestial Empire, told me the Chinese are never sincere, even among themselves? According to you they only enter into alliance with one another in order to betray one another the better. According to your usual argument, the Chengtu war lords, even if they profess friendship to one another now, will be daggers drawn in a few weeks or months. Have faith in your own arguments that I've heard so often, and stop fretting. You'll get your railroad."

"But when they all come to blows I don't want the Szechwanese, who are in the pay of the English, to wipe the floor with my Yunnanese."

"Well, see that they don't, my dear."

My mother, who had had enough, vanished. My father threw up his hands and cried:

"Women, women! Even the best of them!"

Then suddenly he made his usual decision—an appeal for help. But whom was he to turn to? "The bishop? No—too much of a liar. Mr. Cheng? He'll tell me who cooked all this up. It wasn't the British consul, nor the playboy he has staying with him— they're not sharp enough to win over my Yunnanese. But didn't that wretch of a Cheng have the cheek to tell me, on my birthday, that he wouldn't be available to see me for a few days? That's proof he's mixed up in it. That being so, will he come, and will he talk? Is he even in Chengtu?"

The bell rang, summoning the head boy.

"Ask Mr. Cheng to come and see me!"

An hour later Mr. Cheng entered the consulate with extravagant assurance, like a great man, omitting the various little precautions he had been in the habit of taking when he entered our yamen. He was magnificent. He showed the consul an affability even more marked than usual—his very glasses sparkled with it. It was one of the days when he was done up in the European style. He had even perched on his thin skull a bowler hat which hung there as if on a peg. When at last he had removed this remarkable adornment, he began to shake Albert's hand effusively, with little hiccups of politeness lasting a full minute. Albert put an end to this exhibition by assuming his most noncommittal air and saying with a stiff, accusing little smile:

"Where on earth have you been all this time, dear Mr. Cheng?"

"I had to go and attend to a small matter—a mere misunderstanding. Just think—a boat came into Suchow carrying arms sold by my honorable chief, Monsieur Dumont, and the second Szechwanese army thought they were for them, whereas in fact they were to be delivered to the first Szechwanese army. The two armies were about to come to blows over this regrettable mistake, when along came a Yunnanese division, which tried to grab the whole cargo. There were several arguments between the leaders of the various groups. Several soldiers were killed, the city of Suchow was slightly set on fire, and the ship in question slightly attacked. The captain, who was British, was probably somewhat alarmed, and used his wireless apparatus to telegraph for help. His message was received in Chengtu, and all the war lords here were in favor of peace. They decided to keep

this trifling affair secret—even your colleague the
British consul knew nothing about it. Then they sent
very vehement orders for peace and love to Suchow,
asking me to go with the generals bearing these
orders. Everything was settled most satisfactorily."

"So nothing could be better?"

"Till quite recently my chiefs and I were very dis-
illusioned and discouraged. The Szechwanese war
lords were too short of money to pay for what they
bought. It was to settle this bothersome question that
young Mr. Johnson came to Chengtu a little while ago.
He was sent both by his influential father and by
Monsieur Dumont—they're partners. But despite his
remarkable skill, Mr. Johnson did not at first succeed. The Szechwanese generals would only keep repeating that they hadn't a cent, that they couldn't
even pay their armies, which were on the point of
breaking up. The war lords found Mr. Johnson's demands very unseemly; they were so angry they threatened his life."

"But it must all have been settled. Otherwise you
wouldn't be looking so flourishing."

"Yes, Monsieur le Consul. It was all arranged magnificently. Thanks to Monsieur Dumont's extraordinary intelligence. In Shanghai his friend Tu Yu-seng,
the illustrious leader of the Blue Band, told him he'd
be glad to buy Szechwan's opium. Certain approaches
were made in Chengtu to the Yunnanese officials—
for the Yunnanese army controls the wild and distant
areas where the poppies grow. After cautious prelim-
inary contacts, these dignitaries were told: 'Instead of
sending what you produce to Yunnanfu, where it's
sold cheap to the Indochinese state monopoly, why
don't you come to an arrangement with Tu Yu-seng—
he'll offer you much higher prices. But if you do,

you'll have to share the profits with the Szechwanese generals.' Of course the Szechwanese were all for the chance of pocketing some money, but the Yunnanese hesitated. . . . And yet what a rich and magnificent future would lie ahead if they accepted our humble propositions! All the war lords would have mountains of taels to buy arms from us, which would enhance their prestige and multiply their 'face' and power, while the 'black mud' would flow peacefully and without any trouble or scandal to Shanghai, going down the Yangtze under the aegis of Mr. Tu Yu-seng, who is a very remarkable organizer. And in Szechwan, thanks to this marriage of arms and opium, there would be peace and prosperity for all."

My father cut a sorry figure. His pallor was that of baffled honesty about to become the thundering scarlet of anathema. But first, in a faint voice, he uttered a broken-hearted cry:

"What, is even my opium—I mean the opium that used to go to the state monopoly in Indochina—to be stolen and filched away from me like this? Let me tell you, Mr. Cheng, it's scandalous, a swindle, an abuse of confidence!"

"Don't worry, Monsieur le Consul. Monsieur Dumont is a good Frenchman, and he'll safeguard all France's interests. You'll get on very well with him. He's coming to Chengtu in a few days' time with his chief assistant and two or three very experienced old China hands from the associated British firm—they're to help young Mr. Johnson, who turned out to be a little too young. There will also be some very discreet Chinese gentlemen coming, with such excellent manners they won't attract attention: senior dignitaries from the Blue Band. All these august persons will be moved by one great and magnanimous resolve—to make a pact with the Yunnanese marshal and the Szechwanese generals—a pact worth several millions. A treaty of friendship. . . ."

The only recourse left my father, astounded and appalled and defeated as he was, was to hide his discomfiture. This he did with leaden irony, a sickly smile, and a shrill voice.

"Ah, now I see why you're so uppish, Mr. Cheng. You're really His Highness Cheng, lord of double dealing. And when I say double . . . You've been very busy, Mr. Cheng. You must have pulled quite a few tricks, Mr. Cheng. But now, Mr. Cheng, thanks to your humble propositions, as you put it, instead of fearing for your skin you're the good friend of all these fine war lords."

"And I'm still your friend, too, Monsieur le Consul. In all modesty at your service, Monsieur le Consul. Oh, yes, in my excitement I almost forgot—Monsieur Dumont asked me to give you his regards and to say he and his assistant would be staying at the consulate."

Having delivered this *coup de grâce,* Cheng departed, with professions of deep deference and a countenance more solemn and unctuous than usual— the face of inner jubilation and victory, though not going so far as open defiance, for the future was always uncertain and my father might still be useful. As for Albert, once he was left alone he must have propped his spinning head in his hands, his elbows on the very desk where so many official documents, neatly arranged, had been preparing the way for his triumph, the railroad. But where was the railroad now? The consul remained there a long while, weak, prostrate. His dapper façade disintegrated—the part in his hair looked as if it had been invaded by briers, the heavy eyebrows fluttered, even his bow tie grew twisted, like a propeller coming to a halt. Everything was coming apart, wilting, even his fine mustache, supreme symbol of his pride. At last, pulling himself together with an enormous effort, but still overwhelmed, he realized that the nightmare was real.

"What can I do against the gentlemen from Shanghai, the biggest sharks in Asia, and the whole world?" he wondered miserably. "Young Johnson may be of no importance, but the father is another kettle of fish, with his face like a fiddle and his mop of hair and his jutting red beard. And those hard little eyes like headlights. And speaking of fiddles, he's up to all the blarney!"

Finally a faint spark of life began to revive in him. In the depths of his woe he was struck by a saving detail, a stab of irritation about procedure.

"But how could that wretch of a Dumont be so loutish as not to let me know personally, by letter, that he's coming? What does he take me for? I won't have him here. I won't even see him."

Next morning a highly respectful missive arrived from Dumont, complete with compliments to Madame. And a few days later Dumont himself and all his unit were in Chengtu. He stayed at the consulate.

PART
TWO

What was this Shanghai which, in the form of arms dealers and opium, caused my father such uneasiness by appearing in Chengtu? It was the most immoral epic ever perpetrated by the white man in the name of morality.

Shanghai was born of opium, and forced foreign opium on China long before China sowed its own fields with poppies, as in Szechwan.

At the beginning of the nineteenth century, before Shanghai existed, the slim sailing ships of the English roved the coasts of Kwangtung—puritanism combined with smuggling, excellent business organized down to the last detail. East India Company opium was landed mysteriously by the cargoful. The chief costs were greasing the palms of the robed and parasoled mandarins to make sure they turned a blind eye. The white merchants, the bosses in Calcutta and elsewhere, formed a common fund of a hundred thousand dollars for purposes of bribery. But the patriotic viceroy of Canton decreed that trade in the "unclean mud" would be punishable by death. So Albion launched itself into the Opium War.

In 1842 the *Nemesis,* a craft such as had never been seen before, pride of the British Navy and the first steam battleship to sail around the Cape of Good

Hope, appeared off Canton. Its formidable guns battered the town itself, and then the British warships fired a salvo at the thousands of junks of the imperial armada, which covered the water like another city of wood. When the smoke cleared there was nothing left but wrecks on the sea and corpses on the land. The English fleet continued northward up the coast, shelling all the ports. Every time there was slaughter, with people burned alive or blown to pieces and towns reduced to rubble. At last Her Majesty's gunboats sailed up the Blue River, and for the first time the Chinese living inland saw shells, real shells, cleaving the celestial air of the Celestial Empire. Then and only then did the Emperor in Peking give in. The result was peace, the first opening up of China, the legalization of the opium trade, and the giving over of Shanghai to big business.

The British certainly showed an uncanny instinct for finding the ideal site to make money. During the war the *Nemesis*, trying to make its way through the dangers of the huge, choked-up estuary of the Yangtze, had discovered the Whangpoo, a branch that was narrow but deep, a little finger of the Yangtze and the only one that was convenient and navigable. The surrounding landscape was an expanse of mud. A couple of miles from the evil-smelling river was a largish but almost unknown Chinese town, without a noble origin or a great mandarin or a past, and bearing the undistinguished name of Shanghai, meaning "upstream from the sea." Ancient earth walls protected a stagnant population of tradesmen and artisans. Departing from his usual custom, the English admiral did not sack the town, but occupied it and even posted up a proclamation saying: "All men are brothers and subject to the one supreme Father in heaven. They should therefore live together in brotherly love."

Shanghai. Who could have guessed that this squalid hole was to become one of the world's great metropolises? Until then there had been nothing but filth and poverty. Even after the peace was signed, no white man lived there. The first was a British consul, who arrived in November 1843 aboard the steamer *Medusa*. It was evening, and ashore there wasn't a soul. The diplomat decided to stay aboard until the next morning, and in the flickering light of the oil lamps he drank to the great future of the port, which was still only a desolate and pestilential swamp. But as he pored over the Admiralty charts, George Balfour —the consul—carried away by the magnitude of the task to be done, cried, "Barbarism must yield to our superior civilization."

At dawn, barbarism presented itself in the form of a chair with bearers, sent by the taotai (or magistrate) of the town. The inhabitants of Shanghai—owners of multicolored stalls, peasants smelling of human manure—greeted Balfour's first steps on their soil with a mixture of amazement and politeness. No insults, no spitting. But there was nowhere for him to stay, until a Chinaman in a fur coat offered to lease him a caravanserai consisting of fifty-four rooms. The reason for his benevolence became clear when he announced that in exchange for his loyal services he wanted the monopoly on all foreign trade.

Such were the beginnings of Shanghai. Balfour, after great efforts, persuaded the taotai to allow him to acquire a piece of land outside the town where British subjects could live. He selected the strip of mud on the banks of the Whangpoo, and fifty years later this had become the Bund, where the finest apartments and offices and the biggest banks in the world now stood, and the biggest liners berthed.

But then there was nothing but weeds and wild animals. After a year Shanghai had only twenty-three residents, a handful of white men leading a dull existence in shacks amid the miasmas from the marshes. Would the miracle happen?

British determination finally won. Balfour built a consulate where a small watercourse joined the Whangpoo, and at last the important people began to appear, the taipans and their griffins, gentlemen of the first water carefully chosen by their employers in London or Calcutta. The qualifications required were respectability, good health, experience in India or somewhere similar, a will of iron, ambition to succeed, and an atavistic love of money. The taipans were all about forty. The griffins were youths of twenty, and it was hoped they would prove as spirited as their namesakes, the wild ponies used on the first racecourses in subject Asia.

So the conquerors of Shanghai, of China, and of Asia were mere employees. But their first rule was to live like white men, like white lords. They were there to exploit the yellow men, not to mix with them. Well away from the Chinese town, along the banks of the Whangpoo, each taipan built himself a Western-type bungalow: offices on the ground floor, living quarters above, with colonnades supporting verandas where they drank their whiskey. These pioneers didn't have wives. But they led an essentially English existence, the typical life of an important trader in the tropics, with white suits and pith helmets. In the evening, after observing very strict working hours, they would dress for dinner and gather together to amuse themselves. All was ceremony and etiquette: genuine civilization. There was food and drink in abundance and all those English countenances, fleshy or gaunt, sat stiffly smiling around a table covered with silver but lacking a hostess. Dinner began with soup laced with sherry, and then came entrées, main dishes, various kinds of meats, and dessert, champagne, and cigars. Hugely developed jaws, growing paunches, and jovial fair pink faces. One must never show that one was depressed, never show any weakness, but wear a conventional smile as a decent veil to conceal the unavowable sorrows of the soul. These men, with their hours of hard work and their evening parties, were all like pieces of solid English rock. But many of them, taipans and griffins, were nevertheless not solid enough, and died, worn out in body or soul, from some malignant fever caught from the Whangpoo or from the water, often from some epidemic of cholera or plague that would carry off a whole group of gentlemen at once. Then came the first graves, and the words of the minister saying all flesh is grass.

But the ones who died were quickly replaced. There was a constant flow of new taipans and new griffins, all exactly like their predecessors. After a few years there were several dozen bungalows along the Whangpoo, identical bungalows for identical inhabitants, a few hundred tough but choice tradesmen, very Victorian but skilled in social distractions. These distractions were enjoyed partly for their own sake, but they also formed part of a philosophy, a code of conduct. a dignified way of living which reinforced the superiority of the Anglo-Saxons over the Chinese —inferior beings, and unseen.

The white "colony" and the yellow town were twin cities, but might have been separated by hundreds of miles. What self-respecting taipan would propose going into the old city to be met with yellow faces and catch germs? And yet they were decent folks, these Chinamen of old Shanghai, not like the rascals in Canton. As in the old days, the city gates were shut at night and the watchmen made their rounds beating on the ground with their bamboo sticks. No soldiery anywhere, and the big fat taotai was very friendly. Everything was so peaceful that the priests, whose professional duties took them into the town to attempt to make converts, used to come back saying, "Except for the dogs, who are not used to foreigners yet, not a voice is raised against us."

The taipans themselves remained in their bungalows, known as hongs. The only Chinese there were their servants or "boys," beautifully trained and completely adapted to the strange habits of the barbarians—a valuable science which they handed down from father to son. They were the best and most intelligent servants in the world, always smiling and knowing exactly what a gentleman's requirements were. They were as well versed as their masters in the complicated rules and regulations of colonial life —the exact moment for the first whiskey of the evening, the sanctity of sherry. They could even arrange decorations on a uniform correctly.

But there was another class of Chinamen that was indispensable and much more important. Without them, trade would have been impossible. These were the compradors, and they were "modern" Chinese, even though some of them had old moon faces, traditional gestures, the ancient deviousness of speech, and old-fashioned clothes. But at least their throats were no longer passages for gargling and spitting: they were wily enough to make a concession to the

English in the matter of hygiene. Most of them dressed
themselves up as barbarians and wore ties and lounge
suits. These were the ones who had traveled the southern seas and been to Singapore and Hong Kong, where
the gentlemen's law and order prevailed. They had
gentlemanized themselves, while remaining Chinese
to the core. They spoke not only every native dialect,
but also the language of Shakespeare transposed to
the level of business.

Every firm had its comprador, each of whom had
access to the office. Sometimes he even had a permanent little room to himself in some corner. The Chinaman, unctuous if he was one of the old-fashioned
kind, curt if he was a member of the new school,
would go to the sturdy taipan sitting up straight in
his chair but always more or less sweating. The taipan
would say, "Get rid of that load of materials at such
and such a price," and it was sold. Or, "Buy me a
hundred tons of tea of such and such a quality and
such and such a price," and it was bought. And all
without any fuss.

It was up to the comprador to sort it out, and sort
it out he always did, to the general satisfaction. No
one asked him how. They trusted him. For it was because of him that the taipans could do business in
China without having anything to do with the Chinese.

How could white gentlemen ever deal with the
countless ordinary yellow merchants? A gulf yawned
between them. The Chinese merchants distrusted con-
tracts, stipulations, European law and economics,
and all the traps they concealed. In the real China,
where the only authentic guarantee was the word of
the people concerned, the white men's way of doing
things was considered unseemly, childish, and tor-

tuous. How ill bred to insist on having everything written down! And then what perfidiousness later on when because of some incomprehensible clause the foreigners made some incredible claim and appealed to consuls and gunboats to carry out what was often only a swindle, even if it was legal according to their system. Each side found the other completely incomprehensible. The whites were always exclaiming, "The wretched creatures don't even respect their own signatures!" And the Chinese, horrified by such practices, remained shut up in their guilds, fingering their abacuses, secretive and mysterious. There was a gap of centuries between the two concepts of trade. Hence exasperation on the part of the Europeans and resentment on the part of the Chinese, who were used to being fleeced by their mandarins but didn't wish to be pressured by other merchants, especially merchants with white skins.

So thank goodness for the compradors! They straightened out these confusions, they were marvelous intermediaries between the handful of taipans and the immensity of China. The taipans stayed in their offices and played the gentlemen, waiting for orders from London, seeing to their accounts, their records, their bills, their reports. Meanwhile their compradors coped with the real China, arranging everything with all sorts of Chinamen—mandarins, merchants, bandits, not to mention the hundreds of millions of ordinary people. Gradually these men, incorporated from above into the European system, came to pull the strings in China not only for the advantage of the taipans but also for their own. Hardly knowing any more whether they were yellow or white, belonging to both worlds at once, they became millionaires in their own right. And it was through and thanks to them that despite the stand-offishness of the British merchants, the old China gradually became Westernized, though in an impure and inconsistent fashion.

That was a happy period. On the banks of the Whangpoo the taipans still prospered thanks to the opium from India. There were no customs duties to pay, for the empress Tsu Hsi, though celebrated for few other virtues, declined to profit from the "vices and want" of her people. But for decency's sake the drug was landed at Wusung, a few miles downstream. Here a dozen or so old hulks were permanently anchored and served as floating wharves where the Calcutta clippers could unload. These were slender-stemmed thoroughbreds of the sea with immense sails, racing proudly back and forth through the waves. They were marvelously rigged ships with crack crews who scorned storms and monsoons. In a typhoon the captain, a real aristocrat of the ocean, would merely amuse himself by putting on more sail, as if he were taking part in a race. Every cargo was worth millions, and each ship had heavy artillery to defend itself against the pirate junks infesting the coast.

It was a period of prosperity. But the taipans wanted to live in a real town, with all the facilities necessary for business and pleasure. Millions of coolies drove millions and millions of piles into the mud. How many died in the process? But that was how firm ground was created, ground where grass could grow and you could have fine gardens and avenues and clubs. And with more coolies and more piles the horrid banks of the Whangpoo were transformed into a respectable quay where more and more boats could berth. A town was built out of nothing. The taipans, with their dinner parties, their gray silk toppers, and their stiff collars so high they nearly choked them, said things were going very well.

Too well. One fine day in 1853 the celestial dragon awoke and rattled its fatal coils. The taipans were besieged by China, by its immensity, by its hidden mystery and menace and madness. The whole weight of China fell upon one or two thousand white men gathered together on their Bund, an evil meteorite from another world, insolently planted in the ancient celestial soil.

There were years of blood and death, not in Shanghai itself but around the city. There was no concerted attack on the Bund, but a muddled, absurd, inextricable yet bloody tragedy which in its fits and starts constantly threatened to sweep away the tiny particle of the West that as yet had hardly taken root in the mud. The Chinese beat in hordes against the very border of the Bund. Then came the battle between the Taipings and the imperial forces. Before the very eyes of the white men there unfolded one baroque, savage, ridiculous episode after another. What saved Shanghai from the greed of the yellow men was the hatred all the countless Chinese had for one another—whirlwinds of hatred in which the warring camps wanted simultaneously to make use of the white men, have them as allies, and slay them. It was a kind of madness in which the complicated minds of the various parties of Chinese, forever seeking out the most profitable subtlety or deviousness, were finally outmaneuvered by the white men they all loathed. Deceit and inconsistency combined to create a disease of the intelligence which was China's downfall.

They were atrocious years, during which the taipans played calmly, as if it were a poker game, with their own lives and those of all the other white men as the stakes. One wrong move, one miscalculation, might unleash the yellow hordes against the "barbarians," might lead to massacre. In the midst of that chaos never had the nerves of the taipans been stronger, their determination and their immorality greater. Their immorality was even more effective than that of the Chinese. Incredible sights were to be seen, such as the taipans and the griffins quitting their ledgers and forming an armed militia to repel Chinese forces of all kinds. This was English courage. But above all it was a sense of where their interest lay. Survival was not enough. Where would that interest lie in the future? Cold calculation, feats of valor, throat-cutting, reversals—these were the taipans' deliberate policy. Who could give Shanghai the Yangtze valley? Not the Taipings, who had no understanding of trade, but Tsu Hsi. It was of no consequence to the gentlemen of Shanghai that an official war had just ended far away in the North, a war in which the French and British armies, in exasperation, had made a sacrilegious march on Peking and—scenes of horror —sacked Tsu Hsi's palaces and desecrated the Forbidden City. Meanwhile the taipans maintained an army of white mercenaries who, with Tsu Hsi's blessing, struck a fatal blow against the Taipings. The Empress's generals could slay to their hearts' content, and thereafter, all along the Blue River, corpses would be replaced by merchandise from Shanghai.

Shanghai's real greatness began around 1865.

What a mix-up! It all began quietly enough, then gradually got more and more complicated, in the Chinese manner, with obscure and troubling developments succeeded by developments even more menacing and obscure. At first the white men were amused. They had front-row seats to watch the strange goings-on of the natives, who murdered one another so politely outside the Bund.

In fact, the taipans had scarcely heard of the Taipings or of Hung, who had proclaimed the "Empire of Celestial Peace" in Nanking. It was such a long way away! So they were rather surprised to discover one fine morning that the Chinese town of Shanghai had changed hands, and been seized by the Triad, a secret society affiliated with the Taipings. The plot had worked perfectly. Sinister fellows armed with pikes and knives had emerged from filthy alleys and attacked middle-class houses, looting and murdering. To tell the truth, they behaved very well toward the taipans. Their leader, Liu, could speak English, and paid a formal round of calls on all the big firms along the Whangpoo, telling each taipan: "Our Heavenly Father Hung is our Christ. He loves your Christ, and you and your Christians have nothing to fear." The parsons and priests, who by now had been settled there for some time, were overcome by this, and went and celebrated mass in the town. There was a fervent scene in which peaceable converts were outprayed by the red-daubed men of the Triad.

But along the Whangpoo the forest of masts was thinning out. Business was bad. It became even worse when the imperial forces arrived on the scene to make war on the Triad. The white men on their verandas thought they were in the Chinese theater. Outside was hysteria, gongs and howls, streaming banners, the weirdest of costumes, the strangest of weapons. The most curious comings and goings. The Triad's men had built earthen forts, which the imperial army attacked with fireballs. As usual, it was all completely incomprehensible. Mostly the hullabaloo would end without a shot being fired. Sometimes the houseboys would tell their masters, "Watch—this is going to be interesting." They were always right: when the moment arrived there would be a massacre, a bloodbath.

The taipans behaved like honest businessmen and sold guns and shells to both sides. This was the Bund's neutrality. But the taipans sagely told each other that some day they would have trouble with one side or the other, if not both. Then Captain Tronson of the Second Bengal Fusiliers drilled the young griffins on the brand-new racecourse and turned them into soldiers, and when one day the imperial army yielded to temptation and entered the Bund to see what they could pick up, Captain Tronson's three hundred volunteers immediately attacked the imperial headquarters, charging it in the face of the very shells their own firms had sold to the enemy. They won. This was the battle of the "mudbank," which lasted two hours.

The men of the Triad had watched the proceedings calmly from the ramparts of the city. But their success had gone to their heads, and they, too, became aggressive. The priests saw their converts in the Chinese town persecuted, and concluded that the members of the secret societies really did not have the same Christ as the Christians. The French missionaries were highly incensed, and kept on at the French consul—for by now there was one—to take vigorous action as a true defender of the faith.

This consul was a little independent potentate. How did this come about? He was a Monsieur de Montigny. When he arrived in Shanghai in 1848, the

taipans' hongs were already elaborate palaces in the
Italian or Moorish style. Other reverend signors, also
real businessmen even if they were only Americans
or Germans, had by now joined the taipans, and when
the consul of France first set foot on the miry bank
of the Whangpoo he was a sort of pariah. He looked
for land for France outside the Bund, and found nothing but desolation. But he was a tough nut, a human
tapir, a knight, a condottiere, a fanatic for France.
He had spent a dangerous youth, seen something of
the blaze of the Napoleonic epic, crusaded with Byron
for Greek independence. And as a true Catholic this
proud ascetic brought all his family with him into the
squalor and danger of Shanghai—his mother, his wife,
and his two daughters. The English bachelors leading their lives of luxury were dumfounded. Montigny
must be mad. More or less abandoned by his far-off
government, he looked for Frenchmen and found only
a few priests, who let him have a dilapidated hovel
between the Whangpoo and the Chinese town. So the
first consulate was on wasteland, treeless, waterlogged,
with dank ditches everywhere, and strewn with graves
and low shacks of dried mud. Cold, famine, brigands,
and loneliness.

The consul maintained that with the Chinese "you
had to be bold to get anywhere." He forced the taotai
to recognize his swamp as the French concession. This
was a master stroke. But he was still alone, for no
Frenchmen came to settle in Shanghai. Months and
years went by in wretchedness, then at last his first
compatriots came to live in this damp wilderness at
the foot of the Chinese ramparts. There were just a
handful of them, living apart from the taipans and the
other white men. The respectable ones included many
missionaries and civil servants—two French specialties.
But there were also a lot of tramps—misfits, deserters,

salesmen selling no one knew what, real or bogus commercial travelers, adventurers in search of fortune or
pleasure. Despite God and cassocks and the church,
despite the piety of Monsieur le Consul, there was no
puritanism; on the contrary. The Latin system,
wangling, was the one that prevailed, combining the
useful with the agreeable, dough with bliss. They enjoyed fraternizing with the Chinese gentlemen muffled
up in their robes, especially the taotai; they enjoyed
winning them over and the fantastic thought of approaching Chinese women and even of going to bed
with them. There was the excitement of alcohol, eroticism, the exotic; buffalo steaks and sharks' fins; the
sensations peculiar to the East, and the chatter and
joking and scolding beloved by the French. Their
minds were overtaxed by wild combinations of op-
posites: some became completely down-and-out, others
got rich. In spite of difficulties and bickerings, the
French faculty for creating a little anarchical yet
bureaucratic "colony" prevailed, with mass on Sunday, the first streets and villas, and the first brothels.
There was also a tiny army, consisting of a few men.

So the French were not at all pleased when the
taotai and the good yellow citizens with whom they
were on such excellent terms were bumped off by the
Triad and their allies the Taipings. It was the Catholic missionaries who hated the latter most; the English clergymen were inclined to be more indulgent.
This was because Hung's Christ was rather Protestant:
Hung's minister of foreign affairs in the Empire of
Celestial Peace in Nanking was the Reverend I. P.
Roberts. Finally, after a two-year period of patience,
it was the French who wiped out the Triad, with the
tacit approval of the taipans, who didn't want to get
involved.

One day in the Chinese city a convert was killed.

On the insistence of the priests, the consul immediately lost patience at the "anti-Catholic" atrocities perpetrated in old Shanghai, and ordered out his army. The French troops shot a hole in the ramparts and entered the city with bayonets fixed. The men of the Triad fled in disorder, but in vain; for the French had communicated with the imperial forces, who followed them into the city. Then there was massacre. Tsu Hsi's soldiers cut down in the streets anybody a passer-by denounced as a rebel. There were heaps of chopped-off heads. Anyone who looked like Liu, the leader of the Triad, was shot. Liu himself escaped, but a dozen or so shopkeepers who were taken for him were less fortunate. In their excitement the imperial troops broke open coffins and cut skeletons in half.

This excellent carve-up between the English and the French resulted in victory all around. Prosperity returned. Four hundred ships a year called at the port to take on silk and tea. Along the Bund there were nearly a hundred hongs, and the flags of eight nations. But even more terrible storms were soon to threaten.

This time they came from the depths of China, all the Chinas slaying each other in an orgy of death, determined to exterminate all the white men. But the latter, in the shape of French and English fleets and expeditionary forces, meant to conquer China and subdue it once and for all. And wouldn't Shanghai be destroyed in all this?

Danger threatened the city from all sides. It came first and foremost from the Blue River valley, from the interior of China, where millions of Taipings were on the march. With them came a wild cacophony of sword strokes, the clash of spears, war drums. It was the voice of hatred, of the bitter longing of the poverty-stricken masses who had heard of the marvels of Shanghai. What hordes might not one day appear?

But ancient China, imperial and holy China, also hated Shanghai just as fiercely, and used every possible ruse to prevent white domination of the Celestial Empire. Then England for the sake of trade and France for the sake of Catholicism, both in the name of civilization, decided to strike. And twenty years after the Opium War, they were officially at war again.

1857. The guns of thirty-two warships shattered Canton once again. But the Son of Heaven would not surrender, so the forces of "civilization" had to try to take Peking. It was a dark night of folly. On the part of the whites, a sort of fear of China and of its treacherous soul. On the part of the Chinese, bloodthirsty madness. They were just as cruel to their own people, and took pleasure in killing them. It was a universe of extermination, torture, reciprocal fury, bestiality. The Chinese left nothing behind them but scorched earth, corpses, a pestilential void. And the soldiers of the West, advancing, only made the murder and destruction worse. It was a nightmare. In 1860 the first "barbarian" troops entered the Summer Palace in Peking, the first foreigners to penetrate the harsh and twisted universe of Supreme Harmony. They found a disturbing fairyland of fabrics rich and strange. But these marvels vanished in looting and arson, as if the attackers wished to destroy forever the grim spirits of China. Of a China which capitulated, which was now forced really to "open up" to foreigners and to give itself into the hands of Shanghai.

Meanwhile the ragged but ostentatious armies of

the Taipings marched on Shanghai, whose regular defenders had been sent to Peking. Terror reigned. The chief Taiping general was advancing on Shanghai with one or two hundred thousand men. Suchow fell, a town famous for its silk factories less than two hundred kilometers away. The night was filled with red flame. Black smoke from burned-out villages sullied the hongs of the taipans, who were afraid, but not too afraid to think.

Their reflections were more important than their fear, for the stakes were enormous. For several years the taipans had been practically supreme, building up a mercantile republic rather like Venice, where consuls were a mere front and the merchants really ran things through a town council elected by the richest of the white men. Money, plutocracy, the West —these were what created the international "Concession" in Shanghai. It was in fact a government in which the citizens of all the white nations were represented except the French, who still stood apart. But this Shanghai, a Shanghai of taipans of all nationalities, but where English influence predominated, a Shanghai that could look to the consulates for alarm signals, had as its chief ambition the conquest of the Yangtze valley, which would make it the great repository of all hopes.

So the thing had to be thought out. The taipans were surrounded on all sides by hatred, but also by propositions. The Taipings sent messengers to the white men, warning them that they intended to sweep away all that was unclean and annihilate all that was bad. "We shall conquer the city," they said, "and reduce everything to ashes. But if you Europeans fear our countless armies, set marks on your houses and they will be spared." Not only this, but the Taipings also suggested that they and the white men become allies and combine to destroy the empire which the French and English armies had attacked in Peking.

But the thing had to be thought out, for the taotai of Shanghai and its middle-class citizens besought the taipans to fight the Taipings. The Chinese city was completely deserted; terror reigned. Everything was closed, everyone gone to earth. And the mandarins appealed for help to the white barbarians who a few thousand miles away were attacking the Son of Heaven. Their appeal was refused.

Prudence required that no Chinese force be allowed to enter European Shanghai. In the mutual extermination with which all the Chinese threatened each other, the white men might very well be destroyed too. The thing was to remain on the defensive, for the taipans hadn't decided whether to treat with Hung or with the Son of Heaven. Meanwhile, let all the Chinamen wipe each other out!

The taipans decided to defend Shanghai with their militia. At the gates of the Concessions the Taipings hacked to death a missionary and the children in his orphanage. The city was surrounded by flames. The Taipings, using trees, funeral mounds, and the ruins of old Shanghai, held by the imperial army, as cover, attacked the ramparts. But the English and French brought them to a halt by well-directed cannon fire. There was a certain amount of looting in the Chinese city and one district was set on fire, but the Taipings withdrew.

But they withdrew only a short distance and regrouped in entrenched positions and in nearby towns they had already taken. The country was like one vast hornets' nest, armed and ready to attack. Shanghai was transformed into a caravanserai, flooded with Chinese fleeing the war, fire, and death. To Shanghai, too, came all the outlaws of the Pacific, all the gallows birds attracted by fabulous tales of fighting and looting and soldiers laden with the spoils of China. The brotherhood of the coast, especially the Americans, flung themselves into a gold rush of vice and crime. Whole quarters of brothels and smoking dens sprang up, sure in the knowledge that the taipans hadn't had time to organize proper policing.

There was war profiteering. The taipans smuggled thousands of guns to the Taipings. The brotherhood of the coast were ready to sell themselves to the first bidder. About a hundred of these adventurers joined the Taipings. Some were executed, others became advisers to the coolie-kings. But most agreed to be bought by the taotai of Shanghai with money supplied by the Chinese merchants. Thus a mercenary army was formed in which all kinds of white men mixed with bandits from Asia or the Philippines. The leader was a man called Ward, an American gangster who'd been a racketeer in South America. He claimed to have been all around the world and done every kind of job so long as it wasn't respectable. He appeared in Shanghai dressed in Chinese clothes and with a Chinese wife. He got together a band of thugs made up largely of sailors and stevedores who'd jumped their ships, and carried out a number of assignments around Shanghai, putting everyone to the sword and amassing a fortune. He was as brave as a lion, and though he met with an occasional setback he was on the whole so successful that the empress Tsu Hsi made him a general and gave his men the title "Ever-Victorious Army."

The taipans didn't interfere. In fact, they were still

in contact with Hung. For during this time Peking had been taken and the Son of Heaven had agreed to open the ports of the Blue River to foreigners. The Blue River was in the hands of the Taipings. So wouldn't the most convenient solution be to come to an agreement with them if they would permit trade there? The English admiral, Hope, with a flotilla of twelve steamships, sailed up the Yangtze to establish consulates. He had an interview with Hung in Nanking, and Hung declared that trade was evil. So much for the Taipings, then.

It was the English against the Taipings. The Taipings didn't mind using the white men in minor roles, for obtaining various services and advantages. But they didn't want the foreigners and their trade becoming masters in their "Celestial Kingdom." So it was war again, armies again. Shanghai was surrounded by more men in red turbans than before, led by the great Chou Wang. This time Chou Wang opted for a long-drawn-out investment of the city, which he cut off by means of formidable redoubts and a whole network of other siege works. There was famine in Shanghai. The English and French sent ships and troops, and the city became a sort of porcupine bristling with weapons, feverishly fortifying itself on all sides. A curfew was imposed, all suspect Chinese were arrested, native boats were kept away from the harbor, idlers and beggars forced to build earthworks. At last, on January 30, the first day of the Chinese New Year, the Taipings decided to attack. Their bugles sounded. It was the middle of winter, the sky was leaden, snow fell day and night, covering the earth in white, and the Whangpoo was full of ice floes. Was the terrible cold an ill omen? Were the Taipings even more afraid of the Europeans than the Europeans were of them?

Whatever the explanation, the Taipings withdrew. But not far.

The taipans made up their minds to finish the job, and it so happened that there were two admirals in Shanghai all ready and waiting. One was Hope, the English admiral; the other was a Frenchman called Protet. Leaving two thousand soldiers in Shanghai as garrison, the two admirals landed the crews of their battleships and gunboats, sending out two mobile columns into the desolate landscape. It was a gay but terrible fight. It took place through mists and drizzle, fires, ditches full of water, a whole countryside riddled with traps. Everywhere there were palisades, barriers of felled trees, rows of pointed stakes, and above all eight Taiping encampments, formidable concentrations made from the remains of sacked villages and forming part of the rough but redoubtable network enclosing Shanghai. A devastated plain riddled with all the snares of death.

Death was everywhere. No sooner had they left Shanghai than the two columns came to an area which had been occupied by the Taipings. Coffins lay all along the roadside. The sailors hacked them open, stripped the decomposing bodies of their jewels, and pinned them on their uniforms. Then they entered a town entirely destroyed, without a living soul.

Farther on they came to the first Taiping camp, covered with flags and bristling with pikes. Earth and sky mingled to form one melancholy gray expanse. Artillery preparation, attack, looting. Coolies piled up on requisitioned junks whatever furniture and other articles remained, including tablecloths, chairs, and stools. Two thousand prisoners were taken. But what was to be done with them? Give them to the imperial troops bringing up the rear, who would simply have killed them all? A missionary said that among them there might be a few decent men who ought to be saved, and he interrogated them one by one in Chinese. Those he vouched for were released. The rest, the majority, with their ghastly faces, were handed over to the imperial troops. Then the conquered camp was burned.

But there were still other redoubts, other Taipings. So they had to go on shelling, making breaches, charging in the mud, swarming up the fences and walls and ramparts to the howls of the Taipings, who sometimes had as their standard a white man's head on a pike. Other white men, still alive, fought on the side of the Taipings. It was a monotonous tale of mud, gutted towns, corpses. There were losses, too. Admiral Protet was killed outright by a bullet, and ceremonially buried in Shanghai.

Shanghai was still threatened—the Taipings were approaching once more. It was clear that the regular troops were not enough an irregular army would have to be raised. The French had the idea of forming a Franco-Chinese force with a naval sublieutenant as general, marines as officers, and Chinamen, often former Taipings, as troops. A handful of white men leading a crowd of dubious Chinese, and at their mercy. They were armed with old weapons intended for the rebels by European merchants but confiscated by customs. More expeditions. More sieges. All was going well.

Moreover, the English taipans decided to form a decisive shock force, a mercenary army. For this purpose they took over the "Ever-Victorious Army," now in a state of collapse and even a source of danger to the honest citizens of Shanghai. Ward had been killed, and his place taken by his friend Henry Burgevine, another American gangster. Though brave, Burgevine was not a good leader: he was irritable and fought with his unpaid troops over the division of spoils, and with the imperial officials because they withheld the subsidies promised him by the Empress Tsu Hsi. In a fit of rage he went off with his bodyguard to Shanghai, where he insulted the Chinese banker Ta Kee, accused him of keeping back the moneys due to him, and helped himself to forty thousand piasters. There was a scandal; Burgevine was declared an outlaw and tried to join the Taipings with his "Ever-Victorious Army." Finally he deserted with two hundred of his men, fought with the Taipings against the white men, and after many vicissitudes came to a wretched end, imprisoned in a bamboo cage and thrown into the river.

There was great alarm, for the "Ever-Victorious Army" with its white ruffians and its yellow soldiery had very nearly gone over completely to the rebels. The real dream of these bandits in uniform was to form a great independent force subject to no law and belonging to no side, just living proudly off murder and looting.

But the taipans had found a man of destiny: they made Charles George Gordon leader of the "Ever-Victorious Army." He was a British soldier, the very ideal of an officer, a paragon of virtue. He was thirty years old and sported a cane and a clipped mustache. A perfect gentleman—who would have guessed he had a genius for adventure?

Two hours after his appointment Gordon inspected his men. He insisted on the étiquette of the parade ground. It was a crucial moment. Would he, such a very regular officer of the regular army, be able to subdue this collection of rogues and vagabonds?

His gaze, his stature, his scarcely moving lips did the trick. He was to be "Chinese" Gordon, savior of Shanghai and conqueror of the Taipings. First he reorganized the "Ever-Victorious Army," reintroducing respect for officers, a sense of hierarchy, extensive engineering equipment, and light artillery. Gordon's secret was rapid and concentrated fire.

He went from victory to victory, committing no cruelties in a land of cruelty, no looting, no executions. He gave his own money to help relieve want. A demigod had come at last to besiege the great Taiping army in Suchow.

Suchow was dying of famine. The Taiping monarchs slew one another in the course of a banquet, and Gordon went to see the survivors inside the rebel city and offered them their lives if they surrendered. He was held prisoner and almost executed, but finally they let him go and accepted his conditions. Suchow surrendered with a hundred thousand men and immense booty.

Gordon's progress continued, but one day he learned that behind his back and despite all the promises that had been made, the imperial generals had put the Taiping kings to death. Mad with fury and disgust, he went atfer them with a pistol, ready to kill them. But they had hidden. He sent them a message, saying: "You have dishonored me," and he and his army went on strike. After a few months he resumed the struggle and won further victories.

Meanwhile the fall of Suchow had brought about the end of the Taipings in the course of a few months. The taipans of Shanghai soon forgot Gordon, whose scruples were beyond them, and who left the Celestial Empire to meet his ultimate fate at the hands of the dervishes in Khartoum.

With Gordon gone, the question was who was to profit from his victory. The Empress Tsu Hsi was overjoyed and lavished honor on her Chinese generals as if they alone were the conquerors. Not a word about the Europeans on the Yangtze who had enabled her to save her throne. She had been clever enough to make use of the barbarians, and now it was time to take up the struggle against them again and to stop them, not by war but by cunning, from dominating and exploiting China.

But the taipans of Shanghai had no intention whatever of being taken in. They handed over the Blue River, in the heart of the Celestial Empire, to Tsu Hsi, but only so as to get more out of it for themselves. For they had become very powerful, they and their city, as the result of the Taiping war, and they entered into an apparent peace under cover of which, step by step, profiting from one incident after another, they succeeded some forty years later, in 1911, in first undermining and then bringing down the dynasty.

For the Taiping war had created a boom, a mad pursuit of profit. There was prostitution and trafficking of all kinds: the town on the mudbank began to ooze with gold. Land speculation was so wild that building plots were sold and resold ten times over for astronomical prices. Even the most respectable taipans couldn't resist the temptation, and put such superfluous areas as their lawns and gardens of magnolias on the market. They even got rid of their hongs, which were in due course replaced with great apartment blocks. Did this all mean that Shanghai's respectability was becoming a thing of the past?

Not at all. Once peace was restored, the fever was followed by a salutary reaction which cleansed Shanghai and gave it back its honor. There was a grand mopping-up operation in big business. Rash companies went bankrupt, six banks out of eleven ceased payment. The brotherhood of the coast gradually disappeared, that white riffraff who had been engaged in arms smuggling, the conveying of mysterious cargoes, even piracy aboard their junks. Some set out on mysterious operations at sea or in the interior and never returned.

The real Shanghai continued to progress, even though with the influx of yellow refugees the Concessions of the Victorian era took on a somewhat Chinese aspect. The taipans, who had been so wise and farsighted, were more than ever the masters, the sources and repositories of all wealth. With their banks, their fine houses, their complex businesses, their guns, their receipts, they were prosperous, safe, and strong. Titans.

Right there in China they led the lives of English gentlefolk, lives regulated to the minute. At ten in the morning, the office. Then, for the gentlemen, cricket, tennis, yachting. Excursions on the river in houseboats, drives to the Sparkling Fountain with carriages filled with fair-haired ladies—the lawful wedded wives had joined their husbands some time before. There were public parks where English children played under the supervision of their amahs, but which were forbidden to the dog coolies, the servants who exercised the pets of the English old ladies. There was lots of sweet music—concerts in a gas-lit room with ladies dressed in their best listening to "Les Cloches de Corneville." There were balls, paper chases, invitations to dine—ladies and gentlemen taking their predinner cocktails separately. Especially there were the clubs. The Shanghai Club itself was rebuilt several times, each time larger, until at last it became a frightful, solemn, colonnaded cube with more than a hundred rooms—dining rooms, billiard rooms, reading rooms, and especially bars overflowing with respectable gentlemen having a good time. The great social event was the races—three days in the spring and three days in the fall. Offices were all closed and the ladies showed off their gowns. There was an enormous crowd of spectators. No professional jockeys took part, only the taipans themselves on their own ponies. The winner of the sweepstake stood to gain two or three thousand dollars. It was always a respectable European, never a Chinese, who was the lucky one.

Virtue reigned. The big business houses were shrines to moneymaking. Alcohol was allowed, even encouraged, in the evening: you might get drunk then so long as you were fit for the office next morning. Adultery was not allowed. What was permitted was a hostess, with a wink, giving a few minutes' rendezvous in her dressing room to a guest in the know. Their first year out, the young griffins were expected to give proof of good morals. A few escapades were permitted, but definitely no regular relations with a Chinese woman. Anyhow, the Chinese beauties, except for the low-class whores who called out on the Bund, "A dollar a go, but from in front, not behind," were not very forthcoming toward white men for fear of lowering themselves in the esteem of their Chinese customers. The problem of the ladies was not an easy one. Here again it was the French Concession which found the best solution: at the Sporting Club it was the thing to sit at a table for two with someone other than one's own husband or wife.

The white men were so lofty that although they

were there in Shanghai only to make money, they never carried a penny on them. One didn't pay for things—one signed "chits," scraps of paper that were totaled up at the end of the month. Woe to the improvident griffins who scribbled their name too often for any old sum. You had to be a strong man to live in Shanghai, to resist the attractions of poker, chits, and the flesh. Inadequate griffins were sent home by their firm, and this amounted to ostracism. Shanghai society was a closed circle of gentlefolk, people who never carried a cigarette lighter because there was always a houseboy ready with a match.

The white men were so far above the yellow men in Shanghai! They had nothing to fear. If one of them committed a misdemeanor he was judged by his own consul or by a consular court. No punishment would be inflicted but the disdain of other gentlemen, exclusion from the clubs, perhaps advice that he should leave Shanghai. As for a Chinaman belonging to the International Concession who was accused of anything, he went before a mixed court presided over by an English judge, with a Chinese magistrate present for the look of the thing. This court awarded harsh sentences—prison, flogging. There were formidable police forces. The French Concession had more than two thousand policemen of all kinds, French, Annamite, and Chinese, though they had started out much more modestly with a couple of dozen Corsicans recruited by one Galonni d'Istria, a cop who was also something of a gangster. The fire brigade was a large one because the Chinese would set fire to a house on the slightest pretext. The Chinese paid taxes but had no vote or means of expressing their opinion, and were kept under control by armies of white bureaucrats, technicians, and clerks.

For it was an understood thing that they were capable of anything if you weren't firm with them. And then there were hospitals, universities, and priests and ministers to do good. Law and order.

The white men were the superior race. It was out of the question that the worst good-for-nothing among them should come into the power of the Chinese authorities. There were plenty of poor whites in Shanghai—barkeepers, gamblers, cardsharpers, a whole bunch who had come to try their luck and failed, and who were either sent away or made policemen or customs officials. There were also plenty of white prostitutes, mostly Americans from the Kiang-si Road brothels, but they would only go to bed with white men. Anna Ballard, a capable woman who had set up a chain of brothels with French girls all over Asia, was famous for having been found, at a Bastille Day reception in Shanghai, sitting bareback astride a naked French consul and shouting, "Giddyup, pig!" Apparently Anna allowed her girls to entertain certain Chinamen.

As time went by a new race appeared, that of the white natives, the Shanghaians for life, the real men of Shanghai. At the beginning not only adventurers but the taipans themselves came only temporarily, obsessed with the idea of making a good pile as fast as possible and then going away to live in some more normal world. But fortunes had to be made in the jaws of death. China was full of white men's graves. New cemeteries began to be built, containing family vaults.

By about 1900 Shanghai had become the property of a lot of terrible old men. The pioneers, having survived all those years and overcome every kind of difficulty, had turned into typical English eccentrics, odd

old boys rolling in money. Some had had humble beginnings tasting tea or testing silk. Others had been
dispatched as clerks by firms in London or India.
Subsequently they had founded their own companies,
firms which sent out tentacles, so that their owners
were now the very ground Shanghai stood on, the
masters of Asia with London right behind them, all-
powerful with the government and the ministers and
able to call for gunboats and consuls just as it suited
them. They thought themselves masters of everything
forever, and were sure that Shanghai would never end.

A few names, a few faces, some bits of old gossip
about their past. And now they were surrounded by
deference, servility, terror. Not that they acted like
despots or went in for luxury or regal whims and
fancies. Most of them were Scots, and a bit close if
anything. They had their offices, their houses full of
servants, their clubs, their decorous pleasures. But
though they rubbed shoulders with everyone at the
Shanghai Club, each was surrounded by an invisible
aureole. They all obeyed the same code, they were all
the same type whether they happened to be fat or
skinny, round or hollow. They all held themselves as
straight as ramrods and were dangerously affable, their
most ordinary phrases full of deadly meanings. They
practiced what was called understatement. But sometimes there would be a curtness in their eye or in their
words that would flash like lightning. Some were
peculiar enough to like reading or classical music, to
play the violin or go in for acting. They had incredible confidence in themselves, their accomplishments,
their power, their city of Shanghai. Obstacles did not
exist. They drove through everything, calculated
everything: in them toughness was an art.

Cloying English waltzes, the trickle of whiskey, the

stubborn little beards, the evening dress, the habit of calling each other by their Christian names, the bowings and scrapings so desultory as to seem the opposite. The half-solemn, half-natural affectation of being a good sort, the British sprightliness, the jokes, the laughter like minutely calculated salvos, conversations on such interesting subjects as cricket. One never talked business much outside the office. No gesticulations, no quarrels, no pretense of quarreling, no endless talk, none of the self-important or condescending airs of the Frenchmen in Shanghai, more French than the French, always at table, always squabbling between themselves and with their consul. But the English admitted that the French were very good at business. They, too, were real Shanghaians.

What was the occupation, the obsession of all the white men in Shanghai? It was always to get the better of, always to get more money out of China and the Chinese. The Celestial People were really such rogues and so hostile they had to be civilized—made to swallow steamships, railroads, locomotives, the telegraph, factories, trolleys, gas and electricity. It was constant war against these mistrustful and superstitious people, who didn't want any industrial revolution because they only believed in earth and heaven and man, who ruled the elements through labor and virtue. It was war against the people who feared machines would destroy their Celestial Empire, their ancestral society, and their ancient wisdom. War against the yellow masses afraid of the foreign yoke, a yoke of iron and steel and textiles. War against the Empress Tsu Hsi, trying to defend the eternal order of things.

Shanghai at war for fifty years. The front facing China was the Bund, ever more grandiose, a great gush of buildings, a mass of cement and stone, a rampart of strength replacing the oddly shaped old hongs. There were twenty major companies, the most important being the Hong Kong and Shanghai Bank, founded by the taipans to serve as their heavy artillery. The bank was an advance guard in the conquest of China. The bank found ways of going on that suited the Chinese, winning them over with taipans like Macgraw and Cameron, the first as much at ease dealing with a bearded envoy from Tsu Hsi as with a yellow millionaire from Shansi. They knew how to waste time, how to talk apparent irrelevancies to a Chinese until the very last moment, which was the one that counted. They didn't mind making a slight concession to Chinese ways—these were the tricks of war. The only Englishman who became Sinified was Sir Robert Hart, head of Chinese customs, which the "unequal treaties" placed under the control of foreigners. He was a shy, puny little man, bald and with a squint. Yet in fact he was an extraordinary character who lived like a mandarin amid the marvels of Chinese art and a lot of little Chinese boys, taking voluptuous delight in all that was China, including ancient calligraphy and the flute music his private orchestra played during dinner. He was a kind of old gnome living comfortably in a Chinese universe. His headquarters on the Bund were in a building resembling an elegant Chinese temple. He had little to do with the other white men, and was the only white man intimate with and in the confidence of the Empress and Chinese scholars. He could solve any unpleasantness with a compromise which saved the "face" of the Chinese but in fact favored the Europeans. People might sometimes make fun of him, but everyone feared him as the mediator between the white men and the yellow, at once a member of the Order of St. Michael and St. George and decorated with the peacock's feather.

But apart from the useful arrangements made by Sir Robert Hart, the taipans believed in taking the offensive. Their policy was to be always striking new blows at China and then to yield to no kind of resistance, whether it was shillyshallying, incomprehension, or threats of massacre. It was dishonorable to turn back. The Shanghai French had covered themselves with shame on one occasion by giving in. They'd decided to improve the sanitary conditions of their Concession, which consisted largely of a swamp covered with funeral mounds, collections of coffins and jars of bones, ponds of slimy water, reeking cemeteries, and accumulations of corpses in transit to their native province. There was even a pestilential well into which the Chinese used to throw infants. All was cleared away except the cemetery belonging to Ning Po pagoda. When the French tried to build a road through that the Buddhist priests revolted, the population went wild, there were hysterics, attacks, arson. Immediately the alarm bell rang out from the belfry of the International Concession and all the other nationalities arrived to help the French, soldiers, sailors, and policemen gleefully joining in the repression. A few Chinese were killed and order was restored. It was then that the real scandal occurred. The French consul, a man with too much imagination, had misgivings about China's deepest feelings, and issued a solemn proclamation renouncing the sacrilegious road which disturbed the coffins and troubled the peace of the dead. By way of reaction, the English taipans entered into a holy rage. They all exploded with apoplectic indignation in their clubs, at their tables, before their drinks. What a fine chorus of fury from all those ladies and gentlemen! Usually so polite, they suddenly revealed the hidden bitterness in their hearts. The calm of normal social life became a flood of songs and epigrams. Of course the Shanghai English papers, which every day hammered China with words—in an Anglo-Saxon style combining gravity, austerity, and morality with a strange skill in sarcasm and threats— began to send forth broadsides against the French consul. His own compatriots joined in the assault. The Shanghai of the whites accused the poor man of cowardice, and said he was lost, distraught, stolen, strayed, hiding under the bed. Why all this malice against the poor fellow? Because he was a traitor to his race, because his humiliation—i.e., his withdrawal before the Chinese—constituted a dangerous precedent.

It lasted a long time, this inner tension of the whites, this calm arrogance and distant scorn, the frantic determination to impose their will and their products, the desire to calculate and profit from everything and at the same time live more and more comfortably, the super-foreigners in a China being tamed for its own good. It was a mercantile crusade, in which, however, the English did draw back once. They wanted to build a little railway through the suburbs of Shanghai. They had lied and said it was only to be a road, but the rails appeared and the people lamented that they were going to wound the dragon of the earth, and the mandarins themselves, oily beneath their lowered eyelids, did not try to get out of it this time by a lie which would have ruined them. They stood firm when the British consul said, "The officers of the gunboats will be asked to act." Finally the mandarins bought the trucks, the line, and the locomotives, with the sole intention of destroying the baneful things.

Fifty years to tame the Chinese. In the rest of China, beset on all sides, there were wars, massacres, hatred. But the taipans of Shanghai managed things so that these misfortunes, even when of their own making, occurred a long way from Shanghai. They even went so far as to employ those practical and energetic yellow men the Japanese to hold back from the heart of Asia the Russians, who would have liked to get their teeth into too large a part of China. Thus Albion retained the Yangtze valley as its private preserve.

So, frenzy in the Celestial Empire and peace in Shanghai: the peace of Albion, of John Bull, a system exploiting Asia, with Shanghai as its capital. Once the system was perfected the English ambassador began to work on Tsu Hsi in her Forbidden City of Peking. The British consuls everywhere persuaded sympathetic mandarins with the weighty argument of their braided uniforms and the silhouettes of their gunboats. Tsu Hsi and her mandarins were gradually letting themselves go and sinking into an atmosphere of corruption and disintegration. The taipans manipulated things from a Shanghai sick with giantism, from the great center of mercantilism, where the Chinese themselves gradually clustered under the shelter of the taipans.

In China all nations were at each other's throat, and the taipans exploited it. But in Shanghai it was as calm as a beehive: the only revolt was that of the pushcart men, in 1897. They pushed enormous carts carrying goods and passengers, even whole families, across the city and around its various obstacles. To heave along this creaking and overloaded box there was one coolie, a mere ghost of a man. When the tax on each cart was raised from four to six cents by the town council of the International Concession, thousands of coolies banded together in the streets to pro-

test against the injustice. They grew excited, dangerous. So the great taipans of the town council decided
not to increase the tax after all. But all the other taipans got together in a fury and formed a taxpayers'
committee, which forced the town council to resign!
The rich white men, the well-fed masters, flew into a
rage at the coolies with their jutting ribs, for whom
a raise wasn't deemed necessary. The gentlemen got
into uniform in order to apply the typically British
principle whereby good citizens voluntarily contribute
to the maintenance of law and order. The worthy volunteers, instead of shooting, threatened to go on strike
if the highest authorities of the white community gave
way to members of the yellow. So in the end they
didn't give way.

Everything was quiet. Shanghai was hardly affected
even by the Boxer Rebellion. On the contrary, this
period was a victory for the spirit of Shanghai, for during it, with their customary caution, the Chinese
learned to accept the white men's machines—the machines they had loathed but now became enamored of,
railroads included. The Chinese began by adopting
rickshaws, which were unpopular at first because they
were imported from Japan. Then they formed steam
navigation companies, with a dragon for their flag.
They founded factories and companies as fast as they
could. And Chinese banks with frosted glass windows
and the words "& Co." There was a crowd of Chinese
capitalists, of Chinese obsessed with making money
wholesale, a universal frenzy and desire, a disease
caught from the taipans. In Shanghai there were all
sorts of Chinese, at once exploiters and exploited, in-
delibly marked by the West even if they hated it.

What did the taipans care about the fate of the Chinese who got caught up in all this? What did it matter

if there were now yellow millionaires whose fortunes came from the stock exchange or from manufacturing? It only added to the total activity. What did it matter if along with the profiteers there were victims, millions of workers, men and women, coolies, little boys and girls—all machine fodder? In Shanghai everything could be bought and sold. That was the main thing.

The seething dynamism of China was added to the cool dynamism of the English in all their glory, with their gentlemen's civilization made to measure, sons succeeding fathers, and business becoming even better thanks to the so conveniently contaminated Chinese. The taipans of the big firms and the great clubs were interchangeable through the years, through the generations, and through events, towering over the yellow tide that lapped at their feet even on the Bund. The taipans were delighted that the Chinese, having become consumers and even producers, had taken from the West only its vices. Even those who went in for finance and machinery could only understand "squeeze." Squeeze was king. The Chinese were incapable of mastering the laws of science, production, and organization. In the midst of all the rackets the taipans felt more indispensable than ever.

The Chinese gradually came to feel that the old China had lost, and that a new China had to be born in Europe's image. The result was the 1911 revolution and the Chinese Republic. And all that emerged was a gangsterism in which the goods of the taipans circulated freely and where the white men were acknowledged as untouchable monarchs even by the Chinese themselves. More than ever the white men had the impression that they had always been right and that China was at their feet.

Shanghai—a city of brothels, kidnapping, immensity, a city where half China's trade was carried on. Where alongside the merchants there arose protection gangs, the Blue and the Red Bands, encompassing everyone and with a finger in every pie. The taipans, as dignified as ever, got used to this new atmosphere, disorder being even more profitable. It was a strange and absurd universe, symbolized by the "Big World," a jumble of lotteries, theaters, zoos, and dance halls, where the Chinese spat on a tiger in a cage and laughed at a side show exhibiting a girl of eight who was pregnant. They loved monstrosity.

Shanghai was a goldfish bowl, a safe for amassing gold, an office, a club, a headquarters sending out orders and receiving profits. An excrescence on China, through which China bled. The Yangtze brought to Shanghai all the spoils of the interior. It took a century to make it the imperial path for the fantastic trade that went on beneath the Union Jack. Shanghai threw out tentacles farther and farther up the Yangtze, which was improved in order to facilitate the flow of wealth. The main sucker on these tentacles was Hankow. Halfway up the river, where it spread out in a vast brackish expanse and the water was merely a limitless dirty surface merging with the sky, Hankow was the hub of all kinds of trade. It was a sort of entrepôt—all manufactured goods were sold there, all fine raw materials were brought there from the yellow crowds drawn into the "system." It was an unattractive site, but there were so many towns and people and streams all gathered together at one point, gripped by one fever. The masts of the junks rose in a forest, the rusty waters were surrounded by masses of humanity, and the vast shopping quarters were submerged in shoddy English goods and towered over by the blast furnaces, incandescent metal, factory chimneys. Sea-going ships, after coming thousands of miles inland up the Yangtze, lined up along the banks like strange but useful toys, emptying and being filled. There were no majestic quays or Bund as in Shanghai because of the foreshore of gray, stinking mud, a network of gullies at low tide, and a torrent of sewage when the water was high. The ships made fast to huge pontoons linked to the shore with planks. On this shore the foreigner was master. Five Concessions, one after another, five different civilizations, five different flags, five kinds of street names, five police forces, and five laws. But everywhere, inside the Concessions and out, throughout the city, trade was like a poison, cut-rate progress, whatever brought in most, gangrening the Chinese. Hankow the market, Hankow the giant depot, the huge curiosity shop, the modernized caravanserai where the Chinese lost his soul, where China became a bazaar. A conglomeration of objects, appetites, and customers, all methodically fabricated by England, ruler of the Yangtze Kiang.

England was always pushing up the river farther into Asia. But British freighters, old tubs ready for any trade and any adventure, were for many years halted at the gorges of the Blue River. There progress was powerless before the fury of the elements, the mirage, the seething waters protecting Szechwan like swords, the terror of the rocks, the rapids, the floods, the whirlpools. But as always in the history of Albion, there finally emerged a "Captain Courageous," a man of storms and lover of danger, who attempted what was thought to be impossible. He was a man called Plant, an old sailor who at the end of the last century, in a wheezy old crock of a paddle boat a hundred and eighty feet long, conquered the spirits of the swirling waters and reached Chungking. The Chinese crew sacrificèd a white cock.

This pioneer opened up the way for the modern world. There were gunboats on the upper reaches of the Yangtze; epic explorations on the borders of Tibet of unknown rivers terrifying with their imprisoning black rocks of sandstone or limestone— hemmed in between cliffs and the brows of mountains, with reefs like giants and foam frothing over stones for miles and miles. Nature seemed too strong, and animated by a soul at once intelligent and malevolent, inspiring a kind of sacred terror. All around, horns rung out, sounded by the wild inhabitants.

Around 1900, progress dropped anchor at Chungking, which became a small foreign base from which traders and priests gradually spread out over the rest of Szechwan. The white merchants dreamed of rare goods, gold and emeralds; the missionaries dreamed of souls. Szechwan still lived in the Middle Ages, but these Middle Ages were exploitable; every year more cargo boats went far up the Yangtze and did profitable business.

Individual white mèn seeking their fortunes were followed by emissaries of the taipans, drawn there by the war lords and their arms-hungry troops. Above all, drawn there by opium.

The opium that "made" Shanghai was opium from India. This respectable import was protected by the English consuls and lasted a century, until 1917, right into modern times.

The masses of Shanghai, the peoples of the great plains and rivers, fell ill with desire for opium after imports from Bengal stopped in 1914. The taipans of Shanghai, those who had made their fortunes shipping the drug and given the taste for the black mud to countless millions of Chinese, observed this intolerable craving. They had to take care of it, even if it meant getting still richer.

It was only a question of organization, since for years whole provinces of China, but distant provinces of mountain and jungle, had been covered with poppies. On the tops of hills that had had their exuberant natural vegetation lopped off, grew fields of white and mauve flowers, fragile as a breath of air. They were cultivated by primitive tribes of natives, who cleared the crests of the hills and burned down the forests in order to plant and bleed the delicate stems, making cuts through which they drew the sap they sold under the name of "jam." The war lords and big merchants of Szechwan forced this kind of cultivation on the inhabitants of the savage heights: the large-headed Meos, the Miaos, and the Lolos with their silver collars. These primitives had quickly caught on and insisted they be paid in taels.

So it was Szechwan, with its marshals eager to buy arms and sell opium, that now attracted the gentlemen of Shanghai. They left Shanghai in all its glory, at its very peak and height, for the big money that was to be made far away in a gay and grim medieval land seething with corpses and torture. The big firms came because death was profitable. They sold machine guns, which killed fast, and bought opium, which killed slowly. War lords, capitalists, consuls all battened on Szechwan, like crows on carrion. Good business could be done there, and as we have seen, my father was much concerned with the prospect. He, too, was thinking of arms and opium, but his motives were different from those of the taipans. His motives were patriotic, and French!

PART
THREE

The dining room was like a brightly lit temple in the center of a consulate enveloped in murmuring darkness and the creaks and cries of takos, little lizards like minute dragons. In the distance were the lights of Chengtu: paper lanterns swinging to and fro like round boats, torches, oil lamps. And all human sounds were muted. My mother, who disliked Dumont, had gone to bed when dessert was served, saying, "I'll leave you, gentlemen. You must have things to say to each other." She was taking advantage of the colonial custom, British in origin, by which the ladies left the gentlemen alone after dinner. She disappeared so swiftly that Dumont, who had stood up to kiss her hand, found she was already gone.

"Please forgive my wife," said the consul. "She has a headache."

So there were three of them around the still uncleared table. Once the hostess had left, they sat about making themselves comfortable, starting by taking off their jackets. They were a little merry, but there were ulterior motives behind their high spirits. Their joking was a duel, their digestive humor veiled a conflict. Albert Bonnard suppressed his repugnance and pretended to be a good fellow, a sport, in order to pick up what information he could. This was fortunate, for

Dumont asked nothing more than to unbutton, even though his assumed naïveté was a trap. He thundered with friendship for the Consul of France. His bloated red face wore a little black mustache like that of a butcher's assistant. His growing paunch hit the edge of the table. He was fat, but stocky and strong.

"Monsieur le Consul," he bawled, in his brazen, vulgar way, "you're too kind-hearted. You let these baboons of Chinks get to you. Take my word for it, there's only one way to deal with them, and that's a kick up the backside."

"But these are not Negroes," protested the consul. "They never forgive, they're vengeful, they might very well cut your throat."

Dumont was amused.

"Not if you're clever. I've always mucked along with them all right. My poor father—he was a sailor, died of opium—left me a few bob, and after I'd lost that playing poker at the French Club I started to take things seriously. Fifteen fortunes and as many bankruptcies. I've knocked about all over the place. I've been a diamond broker in Tientsin, I've sold curios in Peking, I've been a caravaneer in the Gobi, a gold prospector in Tibet, steward of a monastery in Lhasa, and a croupier in Macao. And I've always gotten the better of the Chinks."

Dumont's assistant, a man like a candle, with a red gristly nose for a wick, nodded; there were no flies on Dumont.

Dumont went on, in the grave tones of a philosopher:

"The Chinese trick is to try to tangle you up, to let you stew in their confounded trickery till you go off your rocker. Then you're done for. Well, what I do—before I let them get around me, I hit out. And hard. And it's the Chink who gets the surprise, it's the Chink who's K.O.'d. They don't understand a sudden straightforward kick; for them, victory always comes after endless scheming."

"You go in for straightforward dealing, then, Monsieur Dumont?"

"When I'm hitting out, yes. Unfortunately the Europeans are going to the dogs. They're just a lot of greenhorns nowadays. And the Chinks feel it. Once we used to keep them at a distance, but now they do as they like."

He sighed.

"Decadence. Even the English taipans are decadent. Once they were so proud, and now they're obsessed by the Chinese, they're afraid of them, bow and scrape to them. There's only one left with any spunk, and that's old Johnson, a veteran of the good old days. He bellyaches about everything—everything the club or the town council or the English consul decide. You can be sure he'll get up at every meeting of the taipans and make a speech full of Scottish oaths about what he thinks of all the good-for-nothings who are letting China and Shanghai go down the drain."

"I've heard people speak of Mr. Johnson with great respect," said my father suavely.

"The old devil! You ought to see him swaggering along the Bund, waving his arms. People new to Shanghai, the innocents, whisper respectfully, 'That's Mr. Johnson.' That's because he made his millions with his own hands. The slickest deal ever brought off in Shanghai. It was around 1915, when imported opium had become scarce. Johnson got hold of all that was left in Shanghai and set up a corporation which worked through a Chinese guild. Because he had the monopoly, he could hand over Bengal opium in bulk to the worthy Chinks, who greased all the necessary palms and then distributed it in the provinces."

"I'd heard that Mr. Johnson's astuteness at that time was the admiration of all the European businessmen in China."

"It was a pushover. But moan and groan as he may, times have changed since then. He's dealt in arms with all the war lords that have sprung up everywhere, but he's old now, and can't quite keep up with it all. And his son, the young man who's in Chengtu now—between you and me, he's not the man his father was. A milksop. It was a mistake to send him to Oxford; he's just not up to scratch, and the business has gone down."

"According to all I hear it's still very considerable."

"Yes, but the old boy balked in the end. He wouldn't just stand by and see everything go to the dogs. He turned things over in his mind and one day, three or four years ago, he sent for me to come and see him in his office—me, who'd just been ruined for the umpteenth time and was a Frenchman to boot. 'I've heard about you,' he growled. 'I'll give you two million dollars and I want you to put my company on its feet again.' And he held out the check."

"So you represent Johnson now? How strange!" said my father.

"Not strange really. The old boy knew I'd bring Tu Yu-seng in with me. There are some good Chinese, and he's damned good."

My father had no trouble remembering who Tu Yu-seng was. He'd sat next to him at Dumont's in Shanghai. He was an elderly Chinaman of inoffensive appearance, with a thin, shiny face and a dull, cold, ageless, sleepy expression. There was something unhealthy about him, something rotten, which revealed itself in his fits of coughing. It was not the sort of cough the Chinese used as jokes, as little interjections of approval. His were the coughs of a sick man, a consumptive, and they were his only form of utterance. Everything about him seemed to be running down. There was a film over his eyes, his gestures were limp, his handshake was a fumbling of the hand, and even vaguer fumblings served to raise food to his dead mouth, set in a face like parchment. To look at him, you'd take him for an idiot.

Dumont liked to drop names.

"It was the police chief of the French Concession who introduced me to Tu Yu-seng," he said.

"Oh, I know *him!*" cried my father. "He's that handsome Corsican with the profile like a cameo, the gleam in his eye, and plenty of gumption. A hero, too. He won a military Legion of Honor as an NCO in Morocco. He saved some Frenchmen upcountry when the Arabs were about to wipe them out. A real soldier of fortune. He's been everywhere, even in the white army in Siberia with Wrangel, fighting against the Reds over the icy plains. A nightmare, but he enjoyed it. It ended in blood though, and he was demobilized in Vladivostok and found himself in Shanghai without a penny."

Dumont didn't give a damn for these fine phrases, nor for the heroic and patriotic career of the police chief in Shanghai. What interested him was that the man was his colleague on the job. He explained this to my father.

"When he turned up in Shanghai I was down on my luck, too. We both stayed in the same boardinghouse, run down by two generations of poor white lodgers. Imagine how dilapidated and how depressing—a family lodging house for derelicts covered with Oriental filth, and where the head boy was proudly known as 'Number One.' The landlady was a defrocked nun, an old tart of fifty whose good advice and elderly charms were both an offer. The adjutant and I became pals, and one day he said, 'They've asked me to be chief of police and I can't make up my mind.' I said, 'Accept.' "

"Didn't I meet him at your house in Shanghai?"

Dumont brushed this remark aside with a wave of his huge paw.

"No. That was his right-hand man. Used to be in the Foreign Legion; some suggestion of desertion, apparently, but it was all put straight. A real weasel. But my friend's quite another matter. A true gentleman."

"Yes, I've heard he's done very well."

"I'll say! A few months after he was appointed, he still wore his old army cap and had a cigarette in his mouth during working hours, but at night he wore a monocle and had become the most sought-after man-about-Shanghai."

And my father, his Adam's apple bobbing with impatience, had to listen to a sketch of a "prince," a man surrounded by adulation. The consul's mouth was full of dust and ashes: he really despised the Corsican, and was jealous of him. He knew without Dumont's seedy description the heights to which the fellow had risen in Shanghai: the gentlemen invited him to dinner, the ladies wheedled him, he cut such a figure in society you'd have thought he'd worn a dress coat all his life. The women were at his feet for a glance, the men for a word of advice. He himself was always on the alert, registering every nuance, able to set his face into an impenetrable mask, but also able, from the heights of his virility, to put into a tone or gesture the condescension that showed that he was amiably disposed. He was capable of anything—of ruthless decisions, but above all of subtle intrigues. He could understand everything in Shanghai, the elite and the dregs, the white men and the yellow. To my father all this was a vast "underworld" in which the other, a typical Corsican, swam about like a fish in a pool—with a revolver always within reach. It was plain he had a finger in every pie, and everything he touched succeeded. By a strange chance he had won the sweepstakes two or three times; clearly this was thanks to the European colony. But it was primarily the Chinese who sought his favors.

To impress my father, Dumont laid it on with a trowel about what close friends they were.

"When I went to see him in his office one day, he smiled indulgently and said, 'A strange country, this. When I open my drawer in the morning I often find it full of dollars. I don't know who'd put them there— some Chinaman, I can safely assume. The unknown well-wisher would be offended if I didn't pocket his tribute. But the mystery never lasts long. Soon afterward some Chink always comes and asks, "Were my unworthy efforts sufficient to give you pleasure?" ' "

"Your friend sounds a strange sort of fellow to me."

"He knows the ropes—you have to in China. First, he's a good policeman who hates disorder. As you know very well the French Concession had plenty of that before he came. To have someone killed in Shanghai only cost five or ten dollars. The wealthy Chinese had turned their houses into fortresses, with thick metal grilles and even blockhouses. Each one lived night and day under the protection of armed bodyguards, who often turned traitor. Whenever a millionaire went out in his car, a metal barrier between him and his always suspect chauffeur was not enough—he'd also lock himself up in the back, so that no one could drag him out. But all these precautions were useless if one of the big gangs attacked. The most famous was the Blue Band."

"I know, I know!" said my father irritably. "But how did your understanding friend manage to get the better of all that chaos?"

"He thought about it and came to the conclusion that if he wanted to fight against crime he had to get the criminals on his side, and make them understand the language of reason and self-interest. He soon found people ready to talk. He found them in his own force, among his own subordinates. Imagine, the honorable chief Chinese inspector of the French police, Mr. Wang, was also supreme head of the Blue Band. And almost all the yellow policemen in the Concession belonged to it. In short, the gang had its headquarters right in the middle of the police. It had been like that for a long time.

"Mr. Wang had had a very worthy career. He'd begun life as a rickshaw boy, and by dint of great prudence had managed to get to the top of both the colonial police and the gang. A gang boss and a police boss at the same time! At the period I'm talking about, having risen as high as he could go, he was about to withdraw into virtuous retirement in a flower-girdled yamen near Shanghai, surrounded by a harmonious swarm of wives, daughters-in-laws, sons, and all his progeny.

"My friend sent for Mr. Wang, who bowed respectfully. Then my friend put on a regretful expression and said, 'I'm afraid I'm going to have to dismiss you, Mr. Wang. You have taken advantage of your position to commit quite deplorable crimes. . . .' This would be a terrible punishment for Mr. Wang, for it would make him lose 'face,' and he one of the great men of Shanghai, reputed for his exemplary life. He was a tall man with a wrinkled face and the honorable stoop of age. A person in his position could have flown into a rage and uttered threats—and he could indeed, if he'd wanted to, have put the concession to fire and sword, just by whispering a few words to the members of the grand lodge of the Blue Band. As he waited for Wang's answer, the Corsican wore a haughty smile— for on that answer depended his own career, his life, and even the fate of the French outpost in Shanghai. It was double or nothing. Mr. Wang also smiled, with modesty and deference, like an inferior who had done wrong. But he knew very well it was not a matter of his being dismissed—it was an offer to negotiate. He played dumb. 'Sir, have pity on me. I'm an old man. And I've done a lot of good through the humble charity to which, in my leisure, I have devoted my limited talents.'

"This meant he agreed to negotiate. My friend was delighted, but he kept the same severe paternal expression and took the opportunity to advance his own game.

" 'Mr. Wang,' he said, 'you haven't been reasonable. In Shanghai and many other cities your charity controls many useful and remunerative activities—prostitution, entertainment, gambling, and everything to do with opium. No Chinaman in the city ever concludes a bargain without giving a percentage to your salutary cause, which also earns a lot of money by very persuasively selling protection to the great and the small. I quite understand that your pious institution needs enormous amounts of dollars in order to do as much good as possible. But how can it let itself be drawn into such deplorable acts as armed attack, burglary, bank robbery, kidnapping, and murder? It's that which cannot be tolerated. Mr. Wang, you are also a valued and experienced policeman with a good record. You must see that I want order to prevail in the Concession—an order not at all incompatible with the smooth running of charity. On the contrary.'

"Mr. Wang hung his head.

"'Sir,' he said, 'I admit my unworthiness. I have been lacking in vigilance. I have been too indulgent when some younger members of our fraternity have let themselves be carried away by enthusiasm. It shall not happen again. In future the French Concession will be a model. If we can carry on with our good works, I and all the other members of my society will help you in your fight against crime. Not only shall we now have no temptations, but we shall act as your hands and eyes. We will even help you unmask those who do not belong to our organization, and see that justice is done.' "

Dumont was puffing like a grampus.

"The reason why I can repeat this conversation to you in detail, Monsieur le Consul, is that my friend the chief of police has, with understandable pride, told it to me so often. It was because of this interview that the French Concession—and the International Concession, too—was restored to peace and prosperity. My friend's idea of transforming the crooks into virtuous managers of vice worked magnificently. How could it be otherwise? In China you can't do away with vice altogether. Can you see the Chinese without gambling or opium? As you know, it's a very important industry, by far the most important in Shanghai. So while they're at it, the Europeans might as well get something out of it, both economically and politically.

You have to let the Chinese live in their own way. My friend's great achievement was to metamorphose the members of the Blue Band and turn them into serious businessmen, once and for all on the side of European authority and respectable society. There are no better defenders of law and order, and none more reliable, on condition that they're allowed to go about their business undisturbed. In fact, the survival of Shanghai as a civilized city is due mainly to well-disposed Chinese gangsters. And one day they may be the ones that save Shanghai from the crazy war lords and the bloodthirsty rabble. They're the only Chinks I'd trust, I can tell you. All the rest, a kick up the backside. . . ."

At this point Dumont's stooge's nose turned red, like a stoplight.

"I think you're tiring the consul with all your stories about Shanghai, Monsieur Dumont," he said. "Let's go to bed."

"Don't interrupt me. I know what I'm doing."

Dumont filled his glass with brandy and egged my father on to a toast in the Chinese manner.

"Your health, Monsieur le Consul. I like to deal plainly. If I show you the cards face up it's so that you can understand how an honorable arrangement in Chengtu about the Szechwanese opium, by pleasing our ally the Blue Band, would strengthen the position of the French Concession in Shanghai. No one else would dare tell you that, but I dare. I'm not asking you to help with the negotiations. I and my associates are in a strong enough position to manage alone. All I would ask is that you don't make things difficult by setting your Yunnanese friends against us."

My father leaned back solemnly in his chair.

"My dear Dumont, I couldn't possibly interfere in

such a delicate matter. Don't forget opium is utterly
forbidden by Chinese law, even if that law is hardly
ever applied. My position is quite simple: officially I
know nothing about your activities. But morally I'm
in favor of undertakings like yours, which contribute
to the expansion of French trade. In other words, I
shan't put any obstacles in your way. How could you
have thought that I would?"

"To tell you the truth, Monsieur le Consul, I was
afraid you might be a spoilsport."

The consul gave a few little puffs at his cigarette,
like a miniature Metternich.

"I'm good at games, too, my dear Dumont. But I
like to choose the people I play with. In your case, as
I've said, I'll wait on the sidelines and watch the fun."

"Well, you won't have to wait long."

"Good. By the way, you've hardly told me anything about Mr. Tu Yu-seng, who, from what I hear, is
actually the key man in the Blue Band. Is this important character going to come to Chengtu himself to
conclude the deal?"

Dumont gave a strangled laugh.

"No fear! He's much too careful. If he were here
the Yunnanese might not be able to resist the temptation of taking him hostage and holding him for ransom. Awkward fellows, your allies. . . . Mr. Tu has
sent a couple of important dignitaries in his place,
important but not eminent enough to deserve forced
hospitality from the Yunnanese."

"And you have no fears for yourself?"

"I am French, I am under your protection, Monsieur le Consul. Your Yunnanese friends wouldn't
play you such a dirty trick as to give me any real
trouble."

Monsieur Dumont's puffy face ran with beads of brandy and joy.

"But who is Mr. Tu-seng?" asked my father.

"My friend. And also one of the most powerful men in China. When the worthy Mr. Wang felt his powers declining, he retired peacefully, as he had long intended, to his country house. He leads a happy patriarchal life there, although he keeps the honorary title of chief of the Band.

"Mr. Tu, his successor, is another kettle of fish. It was he who really modernized the Blue Band and organized this perfect setup with the chief of police of the Concession. It runs like clockwork."

I heard the exemplary story of Mr. Tu much later.

He was an organizer, a brain. And yet he came out of nothing and nowhere, starting off as a mere petty thief and petty murderer. There was thousands, tens of thousands like him on the streets of Shanghai. What a personality he must have had to beat all the rest of them to the top! Mr. Wang recognized his talents and gave a great deal of help in his career, finally appointing him his successor.

The whole of Tu's past was wrapped in mystery. All sorts of sinister deeds were attributed to him, including inviting his rivals within the Blue Band to a banquet, where he gave them swallows' nests so subtly poisoned they didn't suspect anything until they actually died. When it was time for dessert there was nothing left but corpses—and Tu, still very much alive, having them cleared away. Perhaps the stories were legends. One was true, though: one day he cut one of his concubine's legs off with an axe and left her to bleed to death. But that was a mere trifle in China.

Now, however, Tu was all discretion. He hated ostentation, even in crime. The strength of the Blue Band lay in its invisibility, in the fact that it was everywhere without anyone knowing. It had started as a simple guild of boatmen who worked on the imperial Grand Canal, a mutual-aid society for the poor, the floating population of the junks. How, in just a few decades, had it become such a formidable monster with tentacles everywhere? Now it was an extremely closed society. To belong to it you had to be initiated by a ritual of blood. Among magical trappings, the new member had to make a solemn vow of obedience and absolute secrecy, and undertake to carry out any order he was given, even murder, without a word. The penalty, the only penalty, was death. A cruel death.

The Blue Band was a honeycomb of different lodges, each with its own master and all under the authority of the Grand Master. The rank and file were recruited from the rabble of the streets, a swarming army of vagabonds who saw everything, spied on everything, kept an eye on everything, and who at a sign could be ordered to follow a man or form a crowd that prevented anyone else from moving.

Above these regimented dregs was a regular army of petty hooligans, who, their ugly mugs hidden by felt caps, circulated in every district at night, collecting protection money. They went into the stinking alleys, into huts where oil lamps showed whores and coolies enjoying life, into brothels grown up on heaps of garbage, into hovels where cripples and beggars sat around roughly painted trestles gambling away the coins that should have bought their bowls of rice. Into opium dens like morgues, so dried up were the people in them. One-way streets, dead ends,

shacks built on the mud; all the vast districts of the
poor. Everyone paid up respectfully to the Blue Band.
More distinguished members went into the streets of
more expensive pleasure, where broad electric letters
cast multicolored lights on the people there. Into
taxi-girl dance halls, where against the walls half-
human, half-vegetable shapes seemed to embrace in a
forest of fiber and flesh. Millions of dance halls, opium
dens, Chinese hotels—a cacophony of pleasure. They
all paid. Finally, respectable gentlemen with leather
briefcases visited shopkeepers, merchants, bankers—
they all paid, too. Shanghai was divided like a grid
map by the Band's agents. Each one had a revolver,
so that if he wished, Mr. Tu could call forth thirty
or forty thousand armed men ready for anything.

Mr. Tu speculated on the passions, above all on the
passion for gambling. Gambling to the death, to decline, to starvation, gambling as destiny and divination, was the passion and disease of all Chinamen.
Mr. Tu provided for this need by supplying permanent and universal gambling, which met people
halfway, which went into their very houses, and which
never stopped. He gathered up the money of the
poor—an enormous amount—through the game of
the thirty-six animals, a perfect system for mopping up
the people's dough, a marvelous and ingenious setup.
Shanghai was partitioned into sectors, each with its
own accounts, its staff and its executives, and a flood
of touts and tempters in the streets and alleys, shouting and waving bits of yellow paper daubed with obscure drawings and characters referring to ancient
poetry and the great legends of the Middle Kingdom.
They depicted all sorts of animals, monsters, sphinxes,
unicorns, over which old amahs, pretty taxi girls, and
shop assistants would ponder, trying to guess which

would be the right animal, the winning one. All these people, most of them illiterate, pored over the incomprehensible clues on the bits of paper, for these were supposed to indicate which of the thirty-six animals was the right one this time. Then a crowd of folk, each one thinking he or she had found the answer, would gather around another member of the thirty-six animals organization—the itinerant ticket vendor. From a sea of lined faces a forest of arms would hold out coins with holes in them or dirty notes while a voice cried, "So much on that one!" The process was repeated all over Shanghai. Everything was correct. Everything was in order. Each person who placed a bet was given a receipt. But it so happened that the animal that won was never the one the people had thought it was going to be, the one that all the signs seemed to point to. There was always a subtle distinction through which another animal with some resemblance was proclaimed the winner—for example, a bat instead of a mouse. This meant Mr. Tu always won. The result was solemnly announced from platforms, with a frenzy of gongs and a stunning hullabaloo. The announcement produced despair every time. The crowd gave a groan of disappointment which spread by degrees all over Shanghai. Then learned and gowned scholars would get up on the platform and explain at great length why it had to be the animal it was, with many references and quotations. These old rogues were so impressive, no one would ever have thought they were in cahoots with the others. But their job was to make the poor people swallow the animal that had ruined them and profited Mr. Tu. There were never any protests—that would have been unseemly and dangerous. And it all happened every day, twice a day. And such was the nature of the people of Shanghai that they never tired of the thirty-six fatal animals. A truly inspired racket.

Mr. Tu also applied his intelligence to the profitability of drugs. In his opinion, opium smoked in the usual way, lying down on planks, was a waste of time and opportunity. So he launched morphine on the market, in the form of pink pills, the pink being just a reassuring layer enclosing deadly poison. The pills, too, were smoked, but instead of the long ritual with the pellet of opium, you had only to put one of them in the bowl of the pipe. Happiness in a few seconds. Yet another idea of Mr. Tu's was morphine by injection. Morphine in large quantities, hand-me-down morphine, for the poor, for submen and subwomen. The customers were squalid, repulsive creatures reduced to sores and rags, and they were injected in wretched hovels, in dens on the borders of darkness and want, with needles never sterilized: butchery. As they wallowed there in the filth, their limbs stiffening, their skin like frayed leather, only their bellies were still soft enough to receive the injection. In other places it was worse—less repugnant to look at, perhaps, but in reality even more disgusting. The customers here were still upright. They queued up by a wall with a hole in it, and when one of them got to the hole he threw some money in and put out his arm for the injection, by someone on the other side of the wall who didn't even see the people's faces; a production line.

Mr. Tu considered himself a public benefactor. In his view, when people were miserable what they needed was not virtue but consoling vice. What did it matter if the outcome was death? For people like that, death was always ready and waiting. It was better for them to leave this cruel world with comforting illusions.

The Chinese took Mr. Tu's claims to philanthropy quite seriously. Perfectly respectable people considered it an honor to belong to the Blue Band. In its upper ranks, in its obscure and unknown heights, were to be found nearly all the upper crust of China, influential people one would never dream belonged to such a strange fraternity. When a European met a senior member of the Kuomintang, or a Chinese millionaire, or a respectable university professor, or even a war lord, how should he guess that he was an official of the Band? And yet such was often the case. If anyone had said the President of the Chinese Republic was one of them, no one would have been surprised. And so, in secret, Mr. Tu had a thousand formidable connections to call on. Nothing happened in China without him.

In 1927, Tu was to slaughter the Reds, and be considered by the taipans as the savior of their capitalist Shanghai.

Albert Bonnard listened in affable anl rather blasé silence to Dumont's bluster, with a slight air of boredom, as if to show he didn't belong to the same world as Dumont and his Mr. Tu. Nevertheless, behind his pince-nez, the French consul was uneasy: he felt closed in by Dumont's words as though by a net. The fellow was obviously trying to trap him. What Dumont had been telling him, my father, an old China hand who'd been all over the place, knew already, apart from a few details. But of course Dumont was bringing out all these old chestnuts in order to get to something else, something which would contain more definite blackmail and lead to more difficult demands. By showing that he knew everything and that there were no limits to what he could do, Dumont was trying to get the French consul under his thumb.

So my father, to hide his apprehensions, affected an air of impassive detachment tinged with lofty irony.

"My dear Dumont, tell me just what sort of big business Mr. Tu is concerned with."

"There are all kinds. There's one right in front of you. The business that brings me here."

"So you're not just Mr. Johnson's man of all work—you're Mr. Tu's as well!"

"I'd put it that I'm his comprador. Up till now the compradors have been employed by the Europeans to deal on their behalf with other Chinamen. I'm one of the new ones—a European employed by a Chinaman, Mr. Tu in this case, to act as intermediary with other Europeans."

"If I understand you correctly, Mr. Tu is speaking through you. Mr. Tu and his organization."

"That's it, Monsieur le Consul."

"You've got a nerve, Monsieur Dumont. So I, the consul of France, am supposed to act as host and guarantee for a Frenchman who's the mouthpiece of a Chinese gangster, and who even goes so far as to threaten me?"

"Don't be touchy. I've been telling you the truth, which is a rare thing, exceptional. You ought to thank me. I'm not trying to force your hand; on the contrary, I'm trying to help you. To prevent you from making what might turn out to be regrettable mistakes."

After his little show of indignation, my father calmed down a bit. He still had to find out what Dumont was really after. He sat stiffly among wreaths of cigarette smoke and asked, aloofly:

"But how did you manage to get into such a posi-

tion with a man as suspicious and reserved as Mr.
Tu? Doesn't he realize you're an adventurer?"

"An adventurer of genius, and therefore respectable
—that's what I am, Monsieur le Consul. You pay me
a compliment. But long before you did, Mr. Tu discovered what I was worth, thanks to my friend the
French chief of police."

"I might have guessed!"

"One day I found my pal in his office looking highly amused, with his feet on his desk. 'Now we shall see
what you're really made of,' he said, laughing. 'I've
got a marvelous proposition for you if you've got any
spunk.' Then he explained that Mr. Tu was looking
for that rare bird, a white man who could work with
him in the European and the Chinese style at the
same time. Someone clever enough to see advantage
everywhere, but, in particular, clever enough to understand that if he displeased Mr. Tu by the slightest
mistake or inadequacy he would find himself with
his throat cut or his belly split open.

"After expounding the attractions of this situation,
the chief of police grinned and said, 'I thought you
might be the treasure he's looking for. Interested?'
'Yes,' I said. He went on. 'I won't even ask you for a
percentage of the profits you'll make if you don't get
yourself knifed.' 'Thanks, pal.' 'Don't mention me to
Tu. He knows I'm sending you and that's enough. I'll
send my Mr. Pang with you; as you know, he's Mr.
Tu's personal representative. Of course he knows all
about it, but don't say anything to him. Mum's the
word with Mr. Tu as well, at least until he broaches
the subject. That might take time. Be very formal. As
you'll find out, Tu may be very modern in his business methods, but there's a traditional Chinese side
to him, too. You'll be surprised. You won't be going

to one of those ultra-new places some Chinese have. It's a huge, dilapidated yamen in the old style.' "

Dumont was dying to tell my father that he'd been initiated into the Blue Band. But not only that—he wanted to astound him with all the details of his initiation.

For an hour the worthy Albert Bonnard sat flabbergasted, unable to get a word in edgewise.

It had all happened three years earlier. The very day after his conversation with the French police chief, at about four in the afternoon, the time when respectable people emerged from their siesta, Dumont, accompanied by Mr. Pang, got out of a car in a distant quarter of the city, a very poor and dirty district with shacks dotted about on bits of wasteland. They went along by straggling walls daubed here and there with lime. A few young men dressed like coolies were hanging about with a vague and insolent air—probably Mr. Tu's sentries. Someone scrutinized the newcomers through a peephole; a wooden gate opened and closed. Inside, everything was bare, cold, and dirty. There were crumbling porticoes, humpbacked bridges, old dragons with the paint peeling off, courtyards, flagstones, grass sprouting up between the cracks. Here and there lay the recumbent forms of thugs wearing clogs, some of them propped up on their elbows to play a languid game of mahjongg. There were a few men in long gowns, crouching down and doing nothing, except expectorate into spittoons. More rooms, courtyards, corridors, a labyrinth of them, with watching faces. An atmosphere of neglect and carelessness, but also a vigilance and menace, the typical menace of China. It was hot and smelly; the place was full of dirt and flies. At last

they came to a big room, with no furniture except a
few tattered chairs, some of them under dust covers.
The walls were hung with cheap modern prints of
chubby-cheeked infants together with ancient banners
inscribed with wise maxims. As if discomfort were
really comfort, genuine Chinamen considered European luxury full of useless and boring complications.
This seedy setting was guarded by armed men, all
strangely jumbled together. It was a sort of camp.
Some stood dangerously alert, others slouched in every
conceivable attitude of rest, flung down anyhow, anywhere. But in an instant they could have been galvanized into hulks of icy rage or screaming sinews.
There was a sense of menacing indifference which
was really a crude and crafty brutality on the lookout, an uproar that was merely in suspension and
could be let loose in a moment. Beneath the surface,
everything was keenness itself in this caravanserai
without doors and with gaping windows, where everything communicated with everything else in a confusion at once innocuous-seeming and secretly tense.
The communal life of the gang appeared indolent—
its mysteries and its cruelty lurked in abeyance.

After crossing the huge neglected room that served
as a sort of guardroom, Dumont entered a dark ante-
chamber that seemed to be a study or sanctuary. There
were Chinese chairs of black wood, each like a big
somber Chinese character, and a European whatnot
containing objects of seedy splendor. In the middle
was a huge round table covered with a slab of chipped
marble. On it lay packets of cigarettes, pyramids of
fruit, sticky sweetmeats, cups of tea—all the material ingredients necessary for a Chinese conversation. Dumont's arrival was greeted with silence. Yet
there were several Chinese gentlemen sitting there,

very respectably done up, some in long gowns and
some in ordinary suits; they inclined their heads as he
came in. Among them he recognized various distinguished members of the Chinese community in Shanghai—bankers, millionaires, the president of the Chinese chamber of commerce in the International Concession, a city councilor in the French Concession. The
upper crust of the Chinese business world.

All these wealthy men, usually so proud even in
their false modesty, now, with their wrinkled faces
and compressed lips, preserved the silence of humility. Many minutes passed, and then there came, almost imperceptible in the heavy air, the shuffle of felt
slippers. A man emerged from some remote corner
and moved toward them with a tread suggesting som-
nolence and opium: it was Tu, who'd just had his
afternoon rest, during which he smoked the pipes that
give inner peace. To look at, he was the most ordinary
of Chinamen: short, with shaven head and slanting
eyes, his features squashed together as if in the bottom
of a bowl. At that time he didn't yet have the ab-
stracted, unhealthy look he came to have later. He
was in his prime, a hulk giving the deceptive impression of inertia, a man advancing like a beast in slippers. His face gave nothing away. Those present rose
and greeted him with a series of bows. He seemed not
to see them. He sat down on a raised seat, with a
cigarette in a long jade holder and a spittoon on either
side of him. Then he widened his eyes and decided to
take cognizance of Dumont. First he spat, then he said
to him point-blank:

"I know you."

"I am too humble an insect for my name to have
come to your attention."

"Yes, I know you."

He spat again. Then there followed hours in which Dumont felt as if he'd ceased to exist. The others present embarked on long and complicated compliments to Tu in which they tried to insert some request. At each of these suggestions Tu withdrew into himself as if to meditate, then suddenly answered with a whisper of agreement or a bark of refusal. Dumont couldn't understand much of what he said, for Tu didn't speak mandarin, but a sort of low vernacular, some provincial dialect. He went on spitting and chain-smoking. From time to time he would bow or smile or make a condescending gesture. An enormously fat woman kept pouring out cups of tea, aiming the long jet of liquid with scrupulous accuracy.

All this time it was as if Tu had forgotten Dumont's existence. Then suddenly he noticed him again.

"We'll have some champagne," said Tu. "For you. To your prosperity. To your understanding."

The glasses were dirty, the drink warm, just dishwater with bubbles. Tu stood, and rising up enormous a few inches away from Dumont, brandished a glass and called out, "Kampé!"

They went through the usual ceremonial and salutations, standing facing one another, emptying their glasses at one draught and then turning them upside down.

"Kampé again!" yelled Tu at the now subdued Dumont. Although Tu was taking Dumont over, he showed nothing—just the usual polite grimaces and time-honored gestures. But when the ritual was finished, Tu told Dumont, and it was an order:

"Come back often. Be here tomorrow."

Dumont visited for several weeks, and one night, toward midnight, Tu took him to a room with thick walls, guarded by men with machine guns. He pressed a number of buttons and opened a safe. It contained millions of dollars. Tu waved airily at the money.

"I'm a very simple man," he said. "So I keep the firm's money with me. A whole army couldn't get it away from me. And then I had an idea—I thought perhaps there was a better solution."

Tu's face now wore the immobility which is the Chinese smile.

"I don't trust banks. But if I had one of my own it would be different. I thought you might help me to set one up. But first you'll need to know more. I propose to continue your instruction."

Dumont and Tu went together through courtyards where armed men appeared in the wavering electric light. Then a dark shed without any windows was unbolted. An old padlock opened like a dislocated jaw. Inside, the light from the naked bulbs was brighter. On the mud floor were three naked men chained to iron balls, and two others wearing heavy wooden yokes. The groans which Dumont had heard as they approached stopped when Tu entered. All was silent. Tidily arranged on one side of the room were all the traditional Chinese instruments of torture: old bits of wood and wheels and pulleys, hooks and blades, pots and caldrons, bellows, knives, awls and pincers, picks and axes, little objects and enormous ones, everything necessary for tearing, hanging, crushing, and burning, all marked by time and use. The older implements had taken on a brownish tinge, which might have been rust or dust or earth or dried blood. At the other end of the room, on a set of glass shelves, was an ultra-modern collection of surgical instruments—scalpels, lancets, forceps, scissors, specula, trocars, needles. These were all of stainless steel, bright and glistening and sharp.

Tu ostentatiously played the host.

"Take a look at my torture chamber. I have some old torturers to punish people according to our traditional methods. But I have also acquired the services of a brilliant Chinese surgeon qualified in the United States, to punish people with the instruments of modern science. In another part of the house I have some big cages where I often go to stroke a tiger and a python that I'm fond of and that are fond of me. Sometimes I have a man thrown to them."

Then he went on mildly:

"I brought you here on a quiet day when there's no work going on, out of respect for your feelings. But as you can see, I'm very well equipped. I've all that's necessary for doing away with traitors and rivals. All that's necessary for getting to know the intentions of people I don't trust. To find some way of making men's minds reveal themselves—that's what matters to me. Otherwise it would soon be all up with me."

Tu looked Dumont straight in the eye.

"I'm a kind man. I only get really angry when someone I've decided to trust betrays my confidence. Then I get very angry."

Tu started to laugh.

"If you ever deceived me after you'd become my friend, no one would be able to save you. Not even the chief of police in the French Concession. Your corpse would never be found. No one ever finds my corpses. For I keep the promise I gave to the honorable chief of the French police. I undertook never to cause any disorder, and to have a corpse discovered would break both the law and my word. My method is to have a certain kind of person disappear completely. I don't resort any more to kidnapping or running off with people or violence. But I have to make examples of people in order to maintain the fame and discipline of our society. Think about it, and come back and see me if you feel like it."

Of course Dumont thought more about the dollars than the tortures, and he continued to be Tu's guest. At last, after a couple of months, Tu said to him:

"Now you must become our brother. You will be initiated into our sacred society and swear the blood oath."

At night, in a room lit by torches, it was like some medieval scene of magic and sorcery. Men with turbans and bare torsos stood with their short swords suspended over Dumont, while gongs and cymbals and drums made frenzied and funereal music, a shrill oppressive din, a supernatural cavalry charge interspersed with somber beats on the percussion denoting death, execution, the rolling of heads. Around Dumont lay shadow, with gleams of light flashing on pikes, halberds, daggers, giant statues, vessels sputtering with incense, and most important of all, an altar decked with mysterious rectangles of figures and numbers. This algebraic motley contained the supreme meaning of the elements: the key of the universe, with yin and yang, the union of heaven and earth, the movement of clouds and rivers. These secret formulae had been revealed in the City of Willows by the five mad monks who founded the sacred society of the Blue Band—at least this was the legend basic to the Band's theology. A huge lamp gleamed like a bleeding heart, guarded by five red standards. Dumont, in nothing but his shirt, crouched in a posture of humility at the feet of the Grand Master—Tu, wearing a tiara and a long embroidered robe. In an impersonal, almost sepulchral voice, Tu asked the postulant the sacramental questions: "Who are you? . . . What do you want?" This was a test of sincerity, a sort of police interrogation, which Tu punctuated with brief roars of "No, you're not telling the truth—you're concealing what you feel deep down." Dumont endlessly returned the same answers to the same endless repeated questions, looking up at Tu's daunting countenance. Tu in his loftiness and Dumont in his abjection were surrounded by a forest of symbols, parchments being consumed in perfume braziers, ideograms looming like letters of fire, clouds of smoke assuming human form. They were enclosed by a nightmare circle of strange intense faces that looked like inflated balloons with petrified eyes.

Then a change. The scene became less oppressive. Tu, instead of battering away to discover Dumont's real state of mind, took him on the mystic journey to the City of Willows. Together they—or their shades —made the fantastic voyage through space beyond the four oceans and the three rivers. Dumont, bearing a scarlet parasol, crossed abysses full of fiery waters, sailed on the ghost ship with twenty-eight decks and a hundred and thirteen bolts, landed on the shores of Utmost Felicity, walked a plank resting on nothing, and went through three enclosures one after the other to reach the City of Willows. There he entered the Temple of the Supreme Secret, where he ate a magic peach and a magic plum. Tu made him describe this odyssey in detail, episode by episode, saying, "Prove that you have been to such and such a place and that you've really done such and such a thing." Dumont obeyed each time by reciting a ritual quatrain buried in metaphors and parables, obscure utterances which he had learned by heart. It was a strange ceremony—Dumont had to show the reality of his imaginary journey just as seriously as he had previously had to confess who he really was. What a curious country China was, where the fiercest realism was always mixed up with dream and mumbo-jumbo and theory, and with the rules of poetry and philosophy. Everything was intermingled, even for gangsters.

The ordeal ended, but not before Dumont had been beaten with sticks and had a knife held against his throat. He didn't flinch—therefore he was pure. Dumont, lying on the ground, declared that he had told the truth. Then Tu pronounced in a voice of steel: "You will be allowed to make the sacred vows. Swear that you have told the whole truth. And that you will be forever obedient. Never tell anyone what you have learned. Know that the only punishment is death." Dumont stood up. An amulet was put on his arm: its concentric circles meant that he was a link that couldn't be separated from other links. He was led before a table on which lay a knife and a bowl. The time for the blood oath had come. He cut his hand with the blade, and a few drops of blood ran into the bowl. Tu and the others present did likewise. When the bottom of the bowl was covered, Tu added some rose-scented spirit. He told Dumont to drink, and Dumost swallowed a mouthful. Then, one after the other, the rest drank, too.

"Now you are a member of our society," Tu said, smiling. "I give you this little book so that you can learn its rules."

At first glance nothing could have been more edifying than the catechism he handed Dumont; it provided for everything. All the "brothers" were bound to help one another, and above all not to do one another harm. There was a complete list of the ways one brother could act badly toward another, for despite the most sacred bonds the human heart was always subject to temptation. More than a hundred "crimes" were described: to envy a "brother's" possessions, to steal from him, to take him into a gambling house and win his money, to seduce his wife or daughter, not to come to his assistance in a quarrel, to draw him into a fight that might lead to his death, to bear false witness against him in court, to slander him or listen to slander against him. Every instance called down terrible vengeance on the guilty party: he should be bitten by a snake, eaten by a tiger, he should spit blood and die, be slain by the sword, felled by a thunderbolt, or cut into a thousand pieces. This sanctifying litany was one of virtue among thieves: a sanctioning of the virtue that serves vice. Virtue consisted in supporting a brother against an outsider, whatever the brother might do, even if it was a crime. The highest virtue was blind and total obedience, doglike obedience, when an older or more senior brother or a master of the society ordered one to kill. Obedience had to be mechanical, with no question about what deeds were to be done, even if they were murder, massacre, arson, torture, or kidnapping. Sanctity consisted in arriving at complete insensibility, in carrying out an order with supreme serenity. The initiate had always to be ready for anything. He was an infallible instrument, a human tool for carrying out orders. The latter might come from the lips of someone completely unknown, a rich man or a beggar, so long as by a sacred sign he had identified himself as an "elder brother." The Blue Band had its own language, consisting not of words but of tiny gestures by which initiates could make themselves known to one another in any circumstances among the crowd, the ordinary crowd of outsiders who ate and slept, slaved and caroused. A special way of filling a pipe or pouring a drink or passing the rice was enough. Then the dignitary would tell the younger brother to whom he had revealed himself what deed he was to perpetrate. There were numbers of these indications, a calculated code for all occasions, including an appeal for help. A brother who had committed a murder would cut the left side of his forelock short and rub his right eye. Then all the members of the society, wherever they were, including those completely unknown to the killer, would come to his aid and protection, even if the crime had not been ordered, even if it had been done just for pleasure, for a whim, or out of self-interest or passion. Such was the blood brotherhood to which Dumont had been admitted by his oath. It was a world so absolutely disciplined that a member told to commit some act which left him no chance of survival, no escape, which was to all intents and purposes a suicide mission, didn't hesitate, didn't protest, had no regrets, smiled. He did the deed which would bring about his own death with cold meticulousness, showing nothing but indifference to the fate awaiting him. It was an extraordinary thing, that Asian ability to accept anything and hope for nothing if a man belonged to a powerful organization which might say to him, "You have been chosen on your merits for this great deed." Often he wasn't even told that he would die: it was superfluous, obvious, the official who gave the order knew, the man himself knew, silence showed a sort of pride and modesty and mutual respect. The rules of the Blue Band were very precise. Everything was spelled out, including the behavior due from a brother who was a policeman or an official or a judge or a soldier. And yet there was some liberty within the organization: the liberty that al-

lowed everyone to carry on his own small affairs of
vice and profit so long as they didn't interfere with
the grand designs and big rackets of Mr. Tu. So long
as a brother did not break the law of the gang, he
enjoyed its formidable protection. When it was real,
and not mere "squeeze" or a means of extortion, protection was China's most sought-after commodity. In
China everything ramified and got tangled up and
confused in all directions. Mr. Tu fiercely protected
his own initiates, but at the same time he bled the
noninitiates with his paid protection. The Blue
Band was a machine at once precise and nebulous. It
had its own rites, phraseology, courtesies, implacability; sometimes even kindness, but mostly cold-hearted
cruelty. Order and disorder contrasted with one another, and made it possible to win on all fronts. And
business always came first.

Secrecy weighed like a mountain on all the brothers.
Silence was obligatory. The initiate must not reveal
that he belonged to the Blue Band, not even to his
wife or his aged father or his eldest son. His lips were
sealed, if he talked he had them unsealed, or more
precisely, "had his mouth washed out." In other
words, his cheeks and ears and even his brain were
split with a blade. The steel was so sharp it went right
on through the lips and teeth and horizontally through
the bones until it left the head in two halves—the top
was simply sliced off, leaving the lower jaw resting on
the neck. The victim shrieked, and the audience
mocked him, saying, "Now you've got some reason to
squeal. Your mouth's getting so big it'll swallow up
your whole head."

My father, who had been listening attentively, started
to laugh.

"My dear Dumont," he said. "I don't want to be a wet blanket, but after all this rattling away about your precious society, aren't you afraid it might put you to the awful punishment designed for those who talk too much?"

Dumont, the pallor of fatigue standing out on his great pumpkin cheeks and around his tiny eyes, also laughed.

"Monsieur le Consul, I wouldn't mind betting you already knew I belonged to the Blue Band. It's an open secret. My friend the chief of the French police in Shanghai, the man who put me on to the organization, is not just a scoundrel, he's a real cop who knows his work. When I come into his office he gives me a wink and a glass of whiskey. He gives me a dig in the ribs to show he's laughing at me, but keeps a straight face in spite of himself. He greets me in a way that shows we understand one another, and his seriousness always ends in a joke. 'I swear you get yellower every day. Liver? Or the yellow blood you've drunk? But don't go turning yellow on *me!*' And then we chat like pals, laughing and understanding one another between the lines. He knows how far he can go to get things out of me, and I know how much to tell. Of course, after I've gone, he makes out a little card and adds it to his collection. Cops always file everything away. Occasionally he even produces a much vaguer sort of note for the consul general in Shanghai, who rephrases it for the use of the French agents in China. I'd be very surprised, Monsieur Bonnard, if you'd never read any official information about me and the Blue Band.

"Naturally Tu knows about all this. I tell him. In a way, that's what he took me on for. As you know, in China everything's devious. There's a strange trade in secrets here. You need to be able to sense them, seek them out, and know how to use them. You mustn't be clumsy in the way you handle them—you must use them to get hold of good bargains and maintain useful contacts. Otherwise, one word too many, a bit of careless talk, and you get your throat cut.

"It's been an education for me, the Blue Band. Of course, the minor people, the dogsbodies, those who merely carry out orders, it's in their interest to keep mum. But the big guns, the ones who've taken the blood oath, they manage to let the vague idea leak out that they're in the gang. It lends an aura to the respectable millionaires and eminent citizens and old duffers, a terrific importance which makes things easier both for their own schemes and those of the Band— they're always to some extent connected. It's all quite friendly. But in China friendship is often fatal. One day it's just a matter of being hand in glove, and the next it's a weapon those in the know make use of to twist each other or wipe each other out. In the Blue Band, as in every other league or gang or army in this blessed country, people are always either joining up with or denouncing one another. There's always something going on, even if it doesn't look like it. How many times, in Tu's 'drawing room', have I seen some wealthy chap trying to shake off some other rich man he was buttering up only the day before, and bawling, 'You've given away such and such a scheme formed by our sacred society—you're a traitor!' When that happens, Tu shuts his eyes to think and weigh up the pros and cons. It's very rare for him to open his eyes and give the signal or the word for death—except in the case of minor people. He just levies a tariff on the suspect tycoon's money. The whole thing's usually a put-up job he's organized himself, the idea being: 'So-and-so's been making too much; better skim some of the fat off.' Unlike your barbarian provincial war lords, Tu's a civilized man. Methods that are too brutal wouldn't go over at all well in Shanghai, where there are so many factors to take into account, where there are dozens of different aspects to every important Chinaman, and where the 'beloved brother' who's coughing up or making someone else cough up is also a respectable banker, a member of the chamber of commerce, the president of some charitable society, an official of the Kuomintang, a police informer, or I don't know what else. When it comes to big shots like that, things are taken care of by arrangement rather than torture. Anyway, Tu, through a mixture of secrecy and scandal, of silence and suggestion, runs the Blue Band marvelously efficiently. The only people he's ruthless with are those he suspects of being his rivals, and his real enemies. Even then everything is done with the utmost discretion; except when he thinks a certain amount of underground publicity would be good for discipline, he'll throw a scare into people and let them know he won't tolerate being really betrayed or cheated.

"He's complete master of the situation in Shanghai. Rubbing shoulders with him as I do, being his front man, seeing him there every day, all innocence, I've been staggered by his power. It's much greater than I imagined. And this unimaginable power is his true secret. One sign from him and everything in Shanghai can be brought to a standstill: the trams, the electric lights, the fans, the water in the taps and in the bathtubs. He has only to lift his little finger and there's a riot or a strike. The harbor deserted, the dockers nowhere to be seen, the boats just lying there idle. If he wants to, Tu can set the price of the main commodities, gold and silver, silk and rice. He creates public opinion among the people by 'advising' the journalists, and making them spread slander and insult. And if a Chinese millionaire really upsets him, he just gives the word and the fellow finds himself ruined: everybody abandons him—his debtors, his creditors, his employees, his friends, even his concubines. It's like a pack falling on the kill. But Tu's wisdom, the true explanation for his success, lies in the fact that he doesn't flaunt or overdo his power. He uses it to the hilt, but from behind the scenes, anonymously. All the same, the haughty consuls, even the smart white policemen, even the most illustrious British firms, know it is Tu and not they who is master of Shanghai.

"As for me, I'm Tu's emissary, his little messenger. My job is to go and drop a word in the ear of this or that European gentleman, to put forward such and such a proposition, start such and such a negotiation. My visiting card says 'Monsieur Dumont,' but what people read there is 'The Honorable Mr. Tu.' It was through this sort of interpretation that Mr. Johnson got hold of me. And don't go thinking that the admiring looks of the European gentlemen only mask their scorn, and that I suffer those tiny but terrible slights by which colonial society shows its contempt. At the worst, a few people whisper that I'm a bit coarse. That's a compliment. It means they think I'm a lively type. Of course the French consul general isn't likely to give me the Legion of Honor, at least not yet, but even that long streak of misery with his fixed grin sends for me whenever anything goes wrong —me and my pal the chief of police. We tell him what's what, and he jolly well attends to what we say. And one day when I heaved my guts up at the

Shanghai Club, not one Britisher stuck up his starchy red nose—the index of English indignation. I'd like to see them! I've never been blackballed by any of the clubs; on the contrary, I'm on the way to getting made secretary or treasurer, and will probably rise to president in the end. You know that sort of nonsense is the highest possible accolade in Shanghai. To put it in a nutshell, everyone there is my friend. And so, my dear French consul in Szechwan, you be my friend, too.

"Take the hand I offer you. You've all the more reason to do so because we stand on more common ground than you think. Do you know who is one of the most active leaders of the Blue Band? Now I can tell you something you don't know. I refer to the second son of Yüan Shih-kai."

This time the consul really was surprised by how much Dumont knew. For in the past he had made secret approaches to Yüan Shih-kai, as he had to Sun Yat-sen; they were the two opposite poles of Chinese politics at the beginning of the century.

Yüan Shih-kai was the man who so recently had held China in the palm of his hand, the one who, having betrayed both the ancient Empire and the new Republic, died in the grandiose dream of himself becoming the Son of Heaven. Just the same, he was a titanic figure. He was the China of the ages, of virtue and of order, adapted to capitalist exploitation. He was the tiger, the old military mandarin, the traditional overlord, the viceroy of the past, who had brought the art of deceit up to date. His life had been an epic of guile, pride, and systematic cruelty. Blood had run like a river. His was the art of ruling through lies and the lopping off of heads. He was a man of the old order improved by the dollar, the first Chinaman of

the old traditional society—which he wished to restore—who realized that the decrees of heaven needed
to be supplemented by guns, modern armies, and big
business. Foreigners believed in him and his practical
China emerging from whirling chaos. For three years,
from 1912 to 1915, Yüan Shih-kai was almost omni-
potent, deceiving Chinamen of all kinds and setting
up executioner's blocks everywhere. Day after day
in town after town he had hundreds of people decapitated. With gold he bought hundreds of con-
sciences. He flattered his enemies at sumptuous banquets which ended in the guests being poisoned or
otherwise murdered. But over and above all this the
worthy Yüan Shih-kai courteously received Europeans
important in the money world, the chiefs of the trusts
and consortiums and banks that ruled the world. They
came to discuss vast projects in which billions and billions were to be lent to him and which were to produce
incredible amounts of interest and dividends. The China of Yüan Shih-kai looked as if it was going to be one
solid gold mine—very different from what it became
afterward with the war lords, who were certainly worth
dealing with but produced comparatively little profit.
Under Yüan Shih-kai there would have been no place
for a beachcomber like Dumont. It was all on quite
a different scale then. Nothing but the biggest international finance, the bigwigs of money and politics, people trained from father to son to milk the whole world,
an upper crust of discreet respectable gentlemen, capable of anything, masters of everything, all in on the
kill of Yüan Shih-kai's eminently desirable China.

Among them was a Frenchman. He had a curly
mustache and the look of a polite middle-aged Apollo,
toned down by learning and reserve. His exquisite correctness was counterbalanced by the keenness of his

eye. He had all the habits of a good education, the bedside manner of a doctor. He was mildness itself, with a smile like a leather binding, like a bumper, like a shield against anything disagreeable. His serenity was the legacy of a family that was famous under the Third Republic, a family whose great men were buried in the Pantheon, a family devoted to philosophical progress as it was understood under the Third Republic. He himself was a shark. His contribution to human progress was the founding in Shanghai of a French bank designed to exploit Yüan Shih-kai's China. The old Chinese dragon and the bourgeois republican aristocrat were friends. The republic in this case was that of business. In Paris his clan was active and activating: the Chamber of Deputies, the Senate, politics, the Freemasons, the stock exchange, and the dynasties, noble or otherwise, that ruled the age. All these were behind the man who was to put obstacles in the way of the other French establishment in Asia, the one that had been set up in, did business in, and exploited Indochina. It was the beginning of a fight to the death.

The consul knew Dumont was going to start in on the subject of the bank in Shanghai, and sure enough he did.

"That's a fight you got drawn into in spite of yourself, my dear consul. For the Shanghai banker is the brother of your protector—the influential diplomat who got you into the Quai d'Orsay in return for the flowers you used to bring his mistress when they were flying their kite together—in Shanghai."

This touched the consul in a sensitive spot. He was like a hooked fish. The whole of him shrank and contracted. Nothing was left but fluttering and grimaces.

Usually, when his vanity was hurt, he just froze. But this time the shock was so great he quivered and trembled all over. It took him some time to find a suitable attitude to adopt, to retreat behind his pince-nez and mustache. He'd gone quite green. His face was fixed in an attempt at a smile that looked like pasted-on cardboard. He had plenty to be furious about. His own wife had thrown this story of the flowers at him only a few days before, and now this swine of a Dumont was flinging it at him again! The consul was as rancorous as an elephant when he was hit on the raw.

At last, having mastered his feelings and hidden his resentment, he put on an expression of false joviality, as if he were highly amused.

"Colonial life," he declared sententiously, "is always a matter of just a handful of people. Always the same faces at the same social events. It would be an utterly dull life if it weren't for gossip. Everybody is hounded by various tales that everyone else repeats and that he knows nothing about. Apparently I'm well supplied. I'd say it was the price of success. It's true I had a humble start in life. I'm a self-made man, and proud of it. But that story about the flowers is a lot of bunk—"

"It may well be, Monsieur le Consul," said Dumont, beaming with magnanimity. "It's repeated everywhere, as a joke, to pass the time. You have to amuse yourself somehow.

"But what isn't nonsense is that since the tragic death of poor Yüan Shih-kai, the French bank in Shanghai has been in bad shape. No more juicy alms for the asking. All the great hopes vanished. Things are so bad that your benefactor in the Ministry of Foreign Affairs is trying desperately to fill the breach. He's told all his consuls in China to help his brother's

business in any way they can. I'm quite sure of my
facts—I've seen a copy of one of the letters. And of
course you've had one, Monsieur Bonnard. And it
would be very ungrateful of you to take no notice of
it. Ungrateful and unwise.

"Yüan Shih-kai's son, my 'brother' in the Blue
Band, has bestowed on your protector's brother the
same friendship as his father. The two see each other
often. They have important interests in common. I
think you now see better where your duty lies."

My father had become a statue of republican dignity. Nothing moved but his white teeth, bright as
ever, chiseling out his final comments.

"My dear Dumont, I am just a servant of France.
The man you call my benefactor has always set me an
example of the purest and most inflexible patriotism.
He has written to me himself to say how painful it is
for him to have to intervene in this affair—people are
bound to attribute it to the lowest possible motives
and accuse him of nepotism, as you have just done.
But he managed to overcome his delicacy and scruples
with the reflection that he was responsible for the
influence of our country in this part of the world, and
could not honorably allow the firm that lies at the
foundation of French interests in China to collapse.
He came to his decision not in order to help his
brother, but despite the fact that his brother was involved."

Dumont pursed his lips and gave a little whistle of
ironic admiration.

"Noble sentiments sound good, Monsieur le Consul.
But what interests me is opium. I must have it, and
only you can get it for me. In the position we're in,
we might as well tell each other the whole truth.
The real truth.

"Without you the Yunnanese won't play. They're

out of their minds with pride. They remember that they brought about Yüan Shih-kai's death, by rising up in 1915 and leading the whole of China in rebellion against the old dragon when he seized the imperial scepter. They still regard themselves as the saviors of the Republic. And they hate the Blue Band because of my 'brother,' Yüan Shih-kai's second son.

"It's true that the Blue Band has infected a few Yunnanese generals and colonels—it initiated them, made them take the blood oath. But we don't know who they'll betray when the time comes—the Blue Band or the Yunnanese.

"What's certain is that the Yunnanese, whose armies 'liberated' Szechwan and Kwangtung in 1915, are now hard pressed in both those provinces, and that makes them furious. The marshal in Chengtu is an enemy of Tu, of Yüan Shih-kai's son, and of the Blue Band.

"Straighten that out, Monsieur le Consul. If necessary, promise these hotheads arms from Indochina. Talk to them about your railroad, which will guarantee their supplies. I don't see any reason why not. On the contrary."

There was a click. It was my father's jaws snapping shut.

"How do you mean?"

"I like to be blunt in business, Monsieur le Consul. One good turn deserves another. I'm broad-minded. I like your ideas. I could help you at the same time I help myself.

"Tu wants his opium. He'll get it. I know lots of people, the best kind of people, and I've as many connections in Saigon as in Shanghai. The French bank in Shanghai is really doing very badly, and is in danger of going broke. And then your protector in Paris would have a scandal on his hands. Now,

I'm on the best of terms with the bank that operates in Indochina. That's a sound affair—grasping and greedy and ruthless, but with the right touch of imagination. In fact, there's nothing it isn't ready to gobble up. And I know all the people in the government there, from those martinets of civil service officials to the half-breed policemen. I could do a lot for you there. As a matter of fact, I'll even see to it that the sending of French arms to the Yunnanese remains a mystery operation that doesn't rub off on anyone, not on the Indochinese authorities at one end, and especially not on you, Monsieur le Consul, at the other. That way, everything will go off smoothly, no trouble. But without me it'll take ages, something's bound to go wrong, and above all it'll come out, and you'll risk your skin. The Szechwanese wouldn't hesitate to murder you and your family the minute they knew. But if I'm in it there's no fear of any mistake or leak. It'll be a first-rate job. Leave it to me and I'll save your life."

My father sniggered, determined not to let himself be taken in, though he'd had a sudden vision of himself as a bloodstained corpse.

"But won't these arms suddenly disappear, like the ones you sent to the Yunnanese up the Yangtze, which reappeared in the hands of their enemies? Because of that I was besieged in the consulate by the marshal's troops. He was very angry, and I'm not surprised. That's all you've done for me up till now."

Dumont's stubby arms beat the stifling air like the blades of a fan trying to turn against impossible odds —an image of discouragement at the consul's stodginess. But his eyes gleamed with satisfaction. They were the eyes of a man who was getting his own way.

"That was nothing. A little consignment of no importance whatever. You don't understand business, Monsieur le Consul. The situation is different now—another kettle of fish entirely. What! I try to see your point of view, we think up a terrific scheme together, and then you don't trust me? My aim is to get the Indochinese government in on this affair of yours, and to make a packet there, too. So there can be no question of cheating them or deceiving you or burning my own fingers. And don't you forget that I'm perfectly capable, if it's in my interest, and it is, of playing several games at once without losing track of any of them."

"Yes, well, it certainly does look like a case of double-dealing. But what's your boss, Mr. Tu, going to say, not to mention your partner, His Majesty's loyal subject Mr. Johnson? You could lose your shirt, and find yourself bankrupt yet again. Or rather be reduced to the deplorable state of a corpse, as you were promising me I should be if I didn't accept your good offices."

Dumont beamed. His face was like an expanding eggplant.

"Don't worry about that. Old Johnson is one hundred percent British—toasts the crown and is fanatical about the government's policy. But he's got his own views, the views of a gentleman of experience, on this matter. His patriotism consists in helping to enrich England by enriching one of its most devoted subjects—himself—as much as he can. Everything is grist for his mill. So he relies on me. We've already made quite a bit out of supplies to the Szechwanese, as you know. But he's not the sort of person to turn his nose up at French guns for the Yunnanese, provided of course that it's profitable. Fat lot he cares if the En-

glish consul in Chengtu doesn't like it. I promise you
my old Johnson will be all right. And by the way, you
were greatly mistaken in thinking that the arrival
in Chengtu of young Johnson, and then the rest of the
Johnson gang, was at all to the liking of your British
colleague. He suspects something. You needn't have
gone to the trouble of having a row with him on your
birthday. I wasn't here then, but the story got to
Shanghai, and they split their sides over it at the
Sporting Club."

My father gave a wry smile. His face was shrinking,
his eyes staring into space, into nothingness, at the
ceiling, where there was no impudent Dumont. This
time his vexation had taken a different form. It wasn't
humiliation but offense—he'd taken offense. At last
he let his glance rest sourly on Dumont's fat bulk.

"Don't try to kid me, Dumont. The English, even if
they get their fingers caught, always manage in the
end to lead you up the garden path, for the greater
glory of Albion. They've been informed about you.
And don't forget I'm on my guard, too. No doubt
about it, Dumont—you've gone and upset the whole
of the Chengtu diplomatic corps."

"That's not saying much. In this hole it only
amounts to two or three little consuls who fancy
they're important. I don't mean you, Monsieur le
Consul. And anyway, Their Excellencies are quite
wrong. Once I, Dumont, have given my word—"

"But where does Tu come into all your schemes
and your square dancing?"

"Tu doesn't care about all that as long as he gets
his opium. He doesn't mind if I make a bit of profit
for myself—I always give him his share. He's smart.
He admires the arrangement by which I equip the
Szechwanese from Shanghai and the Yunnanese from

Indochina, and give him all the opium. He's above petty resentments; he's first and foremost a great politician. That's why he doesn't even want the Yunnanese to be routed completely—he needs them to contain the Szechwanese and prevent their war lords from overrunning the province. Because if those ruffians won, they wouldn't lose any time in demanding exorbitant prices for the 'black mud.' You have to divide them—buy some of them, do away with others. Very complicated. So you see I'm given a free hand."

Then came a heartfelt cry from my father.

"And what about my railroad in all that chaos you intend to create?"

"Pray for it. It may be given to you. But get a move on."

"What?"

"Go to it. Get on with it. And stop beating about the bush with me. Listen! For you, out of friendship for you, my dear consul, I'm going to bamboozle my 'brother' Tu a bit, just hoodwink him nicely, tactfully. Suppose that in the near future some French arms turn up in Chengtu—not a few old blunderbusses, but good stuff, and plenty of it, a huge stock. And suppose some fresh troops show up here, too, some of the regiments belonging to Tang Kiao, the chief of the Yunnanese, who's stayed behind in Yunnan, in his own town of Yunnanfu, and who turns a deaf ear to all the cries of distress from his marshals and generals fighting far away, here in Szechwan and in Canton? He's a clever old crook, the fat Tang Kiao, and wouldn't at all mind if the Yunnanese armies in Szechwan, who are playing a game of their own, got a good thrashing, or even got knocked out once and for all. It would get rid of the opposition, especially that of your friend the marshal of Chengtu.

If that worthy warrior managed to carve up the Szechwanese, mightn't he be tempted to go home to Yunnanfu with his victorious expeditionary army? It would be a quick return trip, just long enough to take over from Tang Kiao, who would wind up skewered or boiled or toasted. It's a very likely theory, and one Tang Kiao will certainly have thought of. He's a pal of mine, and I've done several little deals with him in tin and, I need hardly add, in Yunnan opium."

The consul's spirits plummeted again and he was once more obliged to assume an attitude of airy superiority—he had a whole collection of them, for he was a man who hated to be taken by surprise but often was. Especially that evening; the wretched Dumont was amusing himself by leading him on and playing cat and mouse with him. But this wasn't the time to put him in his place. So the consul manifested all the signs of good humor, putting as much joviality as he could into his smile and voice, and gaily waving away the smoke of his cigarette with a hand wearing a massive gold-initialed signet ring, which looked like another consular seal.

"My dear Dumont, what do you take me for? I knew all that. I assure you you're not telling me anything new."

Dumont swept my father's pretenses aside with a wave of his red-tipped cigar, and said with a mocking guffaw:

"Come on now! Admit I've got you in a corner, Monsieur le Consul. I've come to put the finishing touch on the opium operation here in Chengtu. It's been all over and done with as far as Yunnan is concerned for a long time. The opium from Yunnan passes through Haiphong and goes direct to Tu in

Shanghai. But Yunnan produces much less than Szechwan."

"Doesn't the French state monopoly in Indochina object? That's not the way for you to get in with the government there."

"I leave the state monopoly enough to keep its own pot boiling. You have to see that everyone's happy. That and a few envelopes I slip to some of the senior French officials—"

"Do you actually dare to suggest—"

"Of course, Monsieur le Consul. Apart from you—and you'll admit I haven't even tried to grease your palm—every man has his price. Even the civil service officials who put on such a show of virtue and wear their white uniforms as though butter wouldn't melt in their mouth. Nothing amuses me more than thawing one of those gentry out. He'll always start by putting on airs, with his rank and his dignity and his professional integrity, but he ends up by holding out his sensitive hand, and even counting the notes. I can quote you names and figures if you like."

As he did so, the consul pretended to be overwhelmed. He slumped down in his chair in the amorphous state he always fell into when he was in a fix. Then, as always, armed with the invincible courage he always managed to fabricate for himself in the worst disaster, he rose up again inch by inch ready to confront adversity, this time in the shape of Dumont and his litany of corruption. It was one of his acts, a way of showing he was tough, a well-worked-out little trick for putting himself in a good light. Usually it made people laugh. Afterward, as they left his office or the reception at which they'd seen it, they said to one another, "Did you see old Bonnard's latest? There's nothing he won't do to wriggle out of a spot. At least he's one person who's not afraid of looking ridiculous."

It was plain that Dumont knew all about Bonnard and his tricks. So he just let him preen and patch himself up without provoking him. For if anyone showed that he wasn't taken in by these little devices, the consul was capable of turning downright nasty. And if one wanted to manipulate him it was better not to antagonize him too much. It wasn't all that easy to manipulate him. One of Albert Bonnard's strengths, as Dumont himself had admitted, was that he wasn't classed as "corruptible." That was an important word, a key word in the colonialist world, and the first that was mentioned when people were discussing someone. "He was," or, in the rare negative form, "He wasn't." If one *was*, it immediately gave others a hold over one, though it didn't really stand in the way of promotion. But Albert Bonnard was honest, largely out of vanity—the fact of being a consul had really gone to his head. And also he was a coward. Beneath his façade of integrity he in fact envied other people their vices. He was a scandalmonger, always flattering people in public and running them down in private, or at least putting on a reserved expression suggesting there was a lot he could tell about the person under discussion if he chose. His indignation about Dumont and his accusations were completely assumed. All he really thought was that it must be damned uncomfortable and dangerous for a civil servant to be bought by someone like Monsieur Dumont. That wasn't his situation, thank God. He then made one last effort to defend the honor of the servants of France in the eyes of this swine. He thought he'd hit on a man who was the very quintessence of integrity—apart from himself, of course.

"But the director of the state monopoly in Indo-china is a man extremely strict about morals, a man absolutely above suspicion. He caused me endless trouble about my last delivery of Szechwan opium because a few grams were missing. He all but accused me of theft. There was report after report, and a correspondence that lasted six months. But I must say he made an extremely favorable impression on me. A great administrator. An empire builder."

Dumont's face was transformed into a flushed, drunken, obscene gargoyle.

"You're a sucker, that's what you are. You wouldn't have had any of that trouble if you'd let him take his commission. Do you know what the big Chinese merchants he deals with call him? 'The Honorable Mr. Ten Percent.' He's the most rapacious devil in existence. I've had trouble with him myself. The swine will never lower his rates, even for me."

A wave of anger swept over Dumont at the memory of his own difficulties with the individual the consul had so inopportunely selected for praise. But his ire evaporated and was succeeded by an expression of bland authority.

"But there's no danger of your having any bother with this lamentable fellow in the future. You won't have to deal with him any more because, thanks to me, all the opium from Szechwan will just go gently to Shanghai down the Blue River."

Dumont was not making fun of the consul now. He was giving him orders. His voice was tough, and the sentences were fired out like cannonballs. His eyes were two more red dots above the waning tip of his cigar. He tossed the butt into a champagne bucket.

"To get back to the subject. Tang Kiao. He's strong. The way he makes your marshal in Chengtu hang on his words, and the amount he makes him cough up! At present the marshal's like a little boy, begging and imploring in every way he can think of, sending messenger after messenger to Tang Kiao with attempts to soften him: 'We are at the end of our tether. We shall all be wiped out if you don't send arms and troops, and that will be the end of Yunnan's great crusade for the glory of China.' This is music to Tang Kiao's ears. He sends back the reply: 'My only thought is how to help you. I am getting thin and can't sleep at night because of it. I grieve for you. But before I can help you I must recruit soldiers, and train and equip them, and alas, my treasury is empty. So send me some money.' He demands enormous sums. That's why the marshal is squeezing Szechwan dry, and why the Szechwanese are arming more and more men to try and make mincemeat of him. But every month a caravan of mules laden with taels by the sackful travels under escort to Yunnanfu. Of course Tang Kiao puts all the money in a safe place under his own name—a bank in Hong Kong, where British law and order reign. He's so cautious he regards even Shanghai as dangerous. He keeps making sacred promises to the marshal, but he still never sends him so much as a single trooper or a blunderbuss. He just waits patiently for the downfall of the idiot who's making his fortune for him."

Dumont was brimming with complacency. He was half the fairground bruiser, half the club shark; part bovine, part foxy. But most of all he was the successful crook who could allow himself to demonstrate the ins and outs of an ingenious racket to a sucker, his victim. He was doing it for pleasure, and also to make it clear to his prey, the consul, that he must do as he was told. Albert tried to go on looking impassive, but succeeded only in looking like a baby owl. with his pince-nez poised motionless and vigilant on his beak. He neither moved nor spoke. He scarcely breathed. This and his affected attitude of stiffness and indifference were his last attempt at defending himself in the trap he was in. It was nonexistence—not yet defeat, but a way of not admitting it.

Dumont returned to the charge, this time with a cordiality as subtle as a blacksmith's bellows.

"Come on, Monsieur le Consul, don't try to be clever. Admit I've been putting you through it. And I still haven't come to the best part yet. Wait till you hear it—it'll floor you. So hang on to your chair, my dear diplomat."

The consul opened his mouth. His lips were thin, and he spoke in a cold, bored, impersonal, colorless voice. As if all Dumont's schemings didn't concern or affect him. As if he were trying hard not to fall asleep.

"My dear Dumont, I should be very surprised if you could tell me anything I don't know about Tang Kiao or the marshal or the Yunnanese. Your so-called revelations were all in my last report to the Quai d'Orsay. I wasn't born yesterday either, you know. I know how to keep myself informed. And there's another thing. I should like to point out that I haven't accepted any of your propositions, which I regret to say bear a certain resemblance to blackmail. I could complain to my superiors about your lack of courtesy—"

"Now, Monsieur le Consul, you really do wound me. Just remember one thing. Without me and my good graces, not one weapon sent by the French from Indochina would ever reach Chengtu and your protégé the marshal. Poof! It would all vanish into thin

air as if it had never been heard of, I promise you
that. The business of that delivery up the Yangtze
would be nothing beside it. And I wouldn't even
have to get involved. It would happen all by itself."

"Very interesting, my dear Dumont. Explain why."

"Tang Kiao would simply snap up this miraculous
windfall as it passed through Yunnanfu. Easy as pie.
Unless, of course, I persuaded him otherwise."

"I don't think we shall need you to give Tang
Kiao good advice. We have plenty of ways of bringing
pressure to bear on him. Yunnan is a backwater, its
only link with the outside world is through Indochina, thanks to the railroad that I should like to extend as far as here. We've only got to block the railroad to bring Tang Kiao to his knees and paralyze
the whole of Yunnan province. And we mustn't forget
that he's a great friend of France."

At that, Dumont started to fidget like a rhinoceros
with St. Vitus's dance. He shook with merriment,
cheeks, arms and legs dividing up into separate sau-
sages that flew about, ponderous and agile at the
same time. The broken veins and blotches of indigestion on his sweaty face gleamed like so many additional vulgar eyes. He thundered out spasms of laughter, fits which rang out like inextinguishable fanfares.
His chair creaked as if in an earthquake, his belly
directing operations, inflating, deflating, and rein-
flating with hilarity, his navel the epicenter. After a
few minutes this cataclysm started to alarm Dumont's
disciple, the lanky, silent character who in the course
of the evening had become so tenuous that he seemed
to have vanished into the air, which was thick enough
to cut with a knife. For a long time he'd been almost
invisible in a room that was like an enormous ash-
tray with only Dumont and my father in it, both

flickering like a couple of only too live cigarette ends. But now the fellow took on substance again and was reincarnated in the form of a vigilant stooge with the audacity to say respectfully:

"Keep calm, Dumont. Think of your heart or it'll start acting up again."

"Shut up, idiot, imbecile, asshole. I don't pay you to stick your nose in. Scram."

He slunk out under the elaborately indifferent eyes of the houseboys, who stood about like tall, empty shrouds, apparently neither seeing nor hearing, but gliding forward like shadows whenever another bottle of champagne or box of cigars was needed. They were omnipresent China, looking on serenely as the barbarians fought over the spoils of their country. But who among the Europeans they waited on gave a thought to what they were thinking?

Dumont suddenly calmed down.

"I'm in the pink of health," he said. "Forty years in China, and I've got a heart like steel and a constitution like a rock. You can't hope for better than that."

A cynical smile passed over the French consul's face. All the time Dumont had been disporting himself, he had remained chilly and patient, his eyes half closed with contempt, his head drooping wearily, his fingers tapping the table to denote how slowly the time was passing.

"But, my dear Dumont, we Europeans know all there is to know about one another, as you yourself have pointed out. It comes back to me now that I've heard people talking about a little attack you had in Shanghai. That being so, it's very unwise, as your friend says, for you to get as excited as you did just now. And between you and me, what did I say that was so funny? I confess I don't know."

"You've as good as given me a pint of new blood. So now, Monsieur le Consul, don't make yourself out to be stupider than you really are, with your silly arguments. People say you're a specialist, an expert, a connoisseur of the Chinese. Have you ever known one of them to get an idea into his head and not manage to achieve what he wants, unless he's thwarted by someone who's more cunning than he is? And with all respect, you don't mean to say you're smarter than Tang Kiao? He's a subtle Chink if ever there was one. If he decides the marshal of Chengtu is not going to have the arms from Indochina, your protégé will just have to whistle for them, I can tell you. And even if the French bring to bear the pressures you mentioned and stop him from helping himself to the goods directly in Yunnanfu, he'll get hold of them afterward, when they're on their way by caravan to Chengtu. There are dozens of ways he can do it. The convoy could be attacked by hordes of mysterious bandits. It could be ambushed by thousands of men pretending to be Szechwanese, or even by a real Szechwanese regiment. Nothing could be easier than for Tang Kiao to negotiate on the side without his marshal knowing it and come to a little arrangement with some Szechwanese group—for instance, that of General Mad Monk or General Little Weasel. A proper agreement, with various stipulations and a clause about the division of the spoils—in other words, the famous arms from Indochina, most of which would go quietly back to Yunnanfu and our friend Tang Kiao. Now tell me, Monsieur le Consul, who would have gotten the worst of it if that had happened—he or you? You, never mind the means of persuasion that you were boasting of and that made me laugh so much. Oh, dear, I'm still holding my sides!"

Dumont conscientiously thumped his ribs. The consul's face grew longer and longer.

"And even what I've just outlined is only one possibility. There are others that would be much more vexatious. For example, some important French public figure could be kidnapped. You, or better still, your son. And of course the condition on which the unknown kidnappers would restore the child safe and sound would be the handing over of the lot, the whole caboodle bearing the famous trademarks of Hotchkiss, Saint-Étienne, and Le Creusot. And who would dream of blaming Tang Kiao, far away from these deplorable events, in Yunnanfu? Especially as you may be sure he'd drown you in crocodile tears and turgid messages of heartrending sorrow; he'd stagger you with the sternness of the orders he'd send to the marshal of Chengtu, saying he was guilty at the very least of negligence, and telling him he would have to pay for the child's life with his own. The works, in fact. And it would all end in tortuous parleys with heaven knows whom, in which you'd give your precious arms to the Szechwanese, and they'd redirect the agreed proportion to Tang Kiao. And perhaps your kid would emerge in one piece. Or perhaps—"

Albert Bonnard rose to his feet, slender and upright. He was no longer a consul, whose job was discretion. He was suddenly metamorphosed into a representative of another institution of the state—the austere realm of the Law. His attitude was that of a public prosecuor. But there was nothing ostentatious about it, no trace of emotion, whether of anger of disgust. Just sternness. He was the sword of Justice. He'd thrown away his mustache and his pince-nez, his pretty little face and all his personal paraphernalia, and become morally naked in order to hold the sacred balance. There were no longer any mannerisms or even any expression. The greatness of the role he had to play made him impersonal. In the name of France, and in a voice that tried to be as curt and cutting as the guillotine, he accused Dumont of treason. He might have been in court.

"Monsieur Dumont," he said, "I have no alternative but to accuse you of threatening with murder an official of France and his family. I shall refer the matter to whom it may concern. You have quite clearly uttered words signifying that you would have me or my son kidnapped if I would not agree to your propositions. You have everything set up already. It is quite obvious to me that your tool in this plot will be your employee Mr. Cheng."

Dumont, all wind and flatulence, had also gotten to his feet. He did so with difficulty but with determination, piling each part of him up until the whole was almost vertical. This accomplished, he started to shout himself hoarse. His mouth was a spout in the middle of the porous masses of flesh, and from it came vociferations that completely drowned out what Albert Bonnard was saying.

"Don't talk nonsense, Monsieur le Consul. I don't mind you having your little fit of hysterics. But as for my meaning you any harm—you must be joking. All I meant to show you was that you must be careful with Tang Kiao. He's a dangerous brute. Very dangerous."

The consul's lips were moving faster and faster, as though they were just moving for the sake of moving and merely swallowing air. Beneath them his chin wobbled in sympathy. But the crescendo was useless, the effort vain, for you couldn't hear a sound he was uttering. Finally, overwhelmed by the vast flow of eructations pouring out of Dumont, the consul stopped trying to get a word in edgewise. Uncertain what to do, he trotted up and down by the table, his hands clasped behind his back and his face pale, sad and drawn. Dumont kept on bellowing.

"But I'm delivering Tang Kiao over to you bound hand and foot, gentle as a lamb and good as gold. That was the pleasant surprise I was going to give you just now, the nice little present from nasty old Dumont. But you wouldn't listen, you as good as told me to go and jump in the lake. So I took umbrage a bit, I got a bit cross. And I led you a way up the garden path. But still, let's be clear about it: all the disagreeable things I told you are true enough, and would be staring you in the face if I weren't here.

"But I am here. And I have Tang Kiao in my power. Because, let me tell you once and for all, Tang Kiao's my 'little brother,' the junior who owes me obedience. He belongs to the Blue Band, too, and in no uncertain manner. I myself initiated him, two or three years ago in Yunnanfu. I made him go through all the rigmarole I'd gone through with Tu. Imagine the terrible Tang Kiao kneeling in front of me in his shirt. The whole works—swords, interrogation, the City of Willows, the delicious kampé made of our intermingled blood, and finally the great oath. Ever since then, Tang Kiao has had to obey the laws of the Blue Band, and above all mine. For I was the master of ceremonies, and that makes me his master."

The consul, who had been pacing to and fro by the table more and more slowly and listlessly, now stopped as if exhausted, as if there were no more point to it. Slowly he perched on the edge of his chair, with cramped and grudging movements and a mortified expression. He knew he was beaten. But even when there was no hope left, he asked a question and raised a difficulty, just as a matter of form.

"You contradict yourself, Dumont. Didn't you tell me just now that the Blue Band had never really succeeded in infiltrating the Yunnanese?"

Dumont, realizing that he'd won, flopped back into his chair with a sort of plop—a triumphant collapse. He was like a jelly that had been about to boil over, but was now cooling again and becoming quiet and solid, a mass that filled his chair and overflowed onto the table, shoving aside crockery and bottles. Then, like a stranded walrus Dumont began, though cautiously, to enjoy his victory.

"Just now, Monsieur le Consul, I didn't tell you everything. You don't put all your cards on the table at once. You save your aces, my dear diplomat, just as I did. And what I was keeping up my sleeve was Tang Kiao."

A series of minor tremors rippled through the general mass of his self-satisfaction.

"There are two different kinds of Yunnanese. The ones here, those with the marshal, those hard-pressed conquerors you want to help out, are poor specimens, visionaries, ideologists, crazy fellows who set out in 1915 to seize all China in the name of great ideas. And as I've told you, they're living on ideas still, even though they behave like brutes and pirates here in Szechwan. That kind—your friends—can't stand the Blue Band. But it's a different story in Yunnanfu, with Tang Kiao, who no longer believes in harebrained notions. He's a realist. He's all for what's solid and tangible and sensible. It's because of his sound business sense that he became my friend, and Tu's. Between us we've got a splendid network stretching from Yunnanfu to Indochina and Canton, Hong

Kong and Shanghai. I'm the one who advises Tang
Kiao on his little investments. That'll show you how
much he trusts me."

Dumont licked his fat chops greedily with his fat
tongue. Then, with the randy expression of a bawd,
he swore:

"If I tell Tang Kiao to let your arms from Indochina through without touching them, he won't lay
a finger on them. No matter how many there are. I
promise you he won't let himself be tempted. Besides,
to be on the safe side I'll just slip a word in his ear
to the effect that if he did take the stuff and the
Szechwanese made mincemeat of the marshal and his
troops, there wouldn't be any more caravans of taels
arriving in Yunnanfu."

The consul saw the flaw in what Dumont had been
saying.

"You can't be as sure of Tang Kiao as you pretend
if you have to dangle the taels under his nose."

Dumont was tired, and exploded in a last outburst
of virulence, like a horse trader certain of his victim.

"Come, Monsieur le Consul, that's enough fuss. I'll
see to everything. All you have to do is get the official
papers from Paris and Hanoi so that we can get the
arms. And see that it doesn't cost a penny, not even a
'token sum' or any nonesense of that kind. And no
niggling. Quantity is what we want. And I give you
my word I'll deliver the goods to the marshal in
Chengtu less than a month after they leave the arsenal
in Indochina. And not so much as a screw will be
missing. And instead of being chopped to pieces by
the Szechwanese himself, the marshal can cut them up
in slices if he likes."

Dumont was overflowing with generosity, like a
great toad whose mouth brought forth flowers and
pearls.

"I always make a good job of anything I do. I can give your marshal an extra leg up by sowing discord among the Szechwanese. I've only got to give a few instructions to Mr. Cheng, whose true value you don't seem to appreciate. The Szechwanese are ruffians; it's easy to stir up one against the other over a deal or a contract— anything where dough's concerned. All you have to do is arrange for one of them to think the other guys have done better out of it than he has. Then they grab each other by the hair and the guts and the balls, and all because of nothing there's poison and bayonets and bullets flying. It's incredible how jealous these savages are. Mr. Cheng will have made them all crazy with rage among themselves just in time for the marshal to get his arms and fall on them and bump them off down to the last man. Will that satisfy you, Monsieur le Consul?"

Dumont beamed like the sun, all the blemishes on his face joining together in one huge expanse of warmth, a conglomeration of devotion, a burning bush of innocence.

"Tonight, Monsieur le Consul, I've no doubt you wish Dumont to the devil. And then I suppose Madame, your wife, is at you about me all day—I know very well she can't stand me. But I'm above your whims and fancies. I take no notice, I bear no malice, because I know you better than you know yourself. You want to succeed, and in a big way. The 'diplomatic corps' they're always dinning into us is like a farmyard full of wet hens, a coterie of gentlemen entirely concerned with cultivating such aristocratic vices as profit, chat, expressionless faces, and reports that don't give anything away. Above all they don't want to know. They're so careful they keep their lips and their other orifices sealed. But you're a man, a gambler, and a daring one, too. You don't know it

yet, but you need me, you won't be able to manage
without me. I won't let you down, my dear Albert.
And you'll see—we'll be just like that! As soon as you
realize how capable I am, you'll swear by me. We
have great ambitions in common. Arms and muni-
tions, they're a cinch, you'll see. The railroad will be a
different kettle of fish, with our banks being awkward
and all our Yunnanese, who're bound to wind up
one day at one another's throats. So you'll see—to
sort out all these financiers and Chinks, not to mention the English and the rest, you'll be very glad to
have old Dumont on your side. We'll get you your
railroad, by God!"

Under this avalanche of friendship the consul
crouched like a pygmy under the monsoon—puny,
surly, his head, arms, and legs all drawn in to protect himself from the deluge. Finally, when the hail of
words and the shower of splutterings stopped, he began to emerge like a tortoise from its shell. He looked
unhurt, neither overwhelmed nor enthusiastic—only
rather chilled, like someone just in from the storm. In
fact, as he came to, he was hiding behind a semblance
of polite neutrality—a bad sign with him, but Dumont didn't notice.

"That's all very well, Dumont. But let's get things
clear. What do you want of me here and now?"

"I want you to go and pay the marshal and his
stooge Mr. Lu a discreet little visit. And while you're
there, make sure not only that they hand over all the
Szechwan opium to Tu, but that they promise not
to raise the price no matter what happens. Even after
we've helped them beat the Szechwanese."

The consul was quite mild now. His face was calm
again, and his features had returned to their normal
place. With the shadow of a smile, like a good little

boy, he sighed rather than said the words Dumont
expected.

"Very well. I'll go and see the marshal and his adviser and try to persuade them."

Dumont brought his fist down on the table with a
bang.

"No joking. I want certainties."

The consul now put on honeyed tones, all obliging-
ness and obedience.

"You will be satisfied. Quite satisfied."

Dumont took in enormous gulps of air. He seemed
to be swallowing the room, the house, the whole world,
like a giant, a Titan, a god. He was full, crimson, a
hot-air balloon in nirvana. Calmly jubilant, he started
to expatiate on his own wisdom and philosophy to
the French consul, who drooped as he listened.

"That's how I succeed in business, my dear Albert.
I get my teeth into a thing, I chew it up, and I
swallow it. I eat all I can, I take my profit where I
find it, shove it all down till I burst my waistband!
The amount I can stow away! Fortunately I have a
digestion like an ostrich. You have to take care of
yourself, and not be shy about it, and get a move
on. There're still a few years left to be got out of this
place. But not more, whatever a lot of fools may say.
So you have to make the best of them. Myself, I mean
to be a real millionaire, and have plenty of my own
dough put by outside China when the day of reckon-
ing comes. For let me tell you, things are going to
come unstuck, and China will get its own back on
foreigners: China never gives anything away; you
have to tear it from her. And that's what I'm doing,
thanks to Tu and Tang Kiao and Cheng. But even
they—my partners, my accomplices, my 'brothers'—
are just bastards who hate me and would like to spit

in my face and make me give it all back, the way they'd like to do to all Europeans. When the day comes that China really blows up, it'll be better for us to be elsewhere.

"Don't look so pale, Monsieur le Consul. I hope you don't think the Chinese like you. That would be too absurd. But cheer up. The great Chinese revolution isn't going to take place tomorrow. There'll be some floundering about first. There's plenty of time. You'll get out of it all right, my ambitious friend. You'll make France great in these out-of-the-way parts of China, my friend the patriot, for you're a real Frenchman, a good one, not a bastard like me, a shyster who nevertheless does our country a hundred times more service than some figurehead diplomat or governor. I don't mean you, far from it, but sometimes deep down I'm very upset by certain insults and acts of ingratitude. People don't believe it, but I'm sensitive. . . . But I don't snivel about myself. Let's talk about you, my friend. You don't mind if I call you 'my friend,' do you? You'll achieve great things for the tricolor in these rubbishy provinces, among these rotten savages of Chinks, thanks to opium, arms, and the railroad. You've got a unique opportunity. You'll make your mark, you'll be one of the bigwigs, a gentleman whose origins everyone wll have forgotten. And if everything falls to pieces here, you'll already have nipped off to some nice civilized post elsewhere, so what will you care? Believe me, you'll rise fast if you're clever about it—you'll shinny right up the greasy pole and get yourself made consul general, minister plenipotentiary, ambassador—why not? On condition, to begin with, that you don't act stupid with me. Because it's expensive, my dear friend, to think you can play the fool with Dumont. Before you know where you are you're reduced to ribbons, torn to shreds, no use to anyone."

Dumont, having said all he had to say, yawned fit to dislocate his jaw. You could see right down his gullet, as red and sticky inside as out, all gurgling and rumbling and subsiding again like the interior of a boiler. Then he gave a start, opened his eyes, and blinked blearily through a pink rheum.

"Your champagne was sour, Monsieur le Consul. It's turned my stomach. I'm going to hit the hay."

To rise, Dumont braced his fat stumps of arms on the table as levels for his inert legs and paunch. As he did so his face passed from the animal to the vegetable: it turned the color of a red cabbage—he looked as if he was about to have a fit of apoplexy. Then instead of dragging his body off the chair, he dragged the cloth off the table. There was a cascade of glasses, plates, ashtrays, and other objects, accompanied by the smashing of crockery and the sound of various liquids spilling. The consul looked on with indifference, not stirring from his place. The houseboys nipped smartly forward and caught the huge figure of Dumont, handling it as if it were weightless, a mere bubble. The operation took only a few seconds, and while it was going on, Dumont's head flopped to and fro. Once on his feet, he began to vomit at regular intervals, while uttering rhythmical rationalizations.

"It's your champagne, Monsieur le Consul. Terrible stuff—make even a missionary heave his heart up."

Hanging between two boys like a great shapeless lump, he staggered off, his heavy thuds contrasting with the airy tread of the men supporting him. He stumbled, and swore like a bargeman. At last the consul was left master of the field. Like Napoleon at

Austerlitz, he gazed long over the scene of the fray,
looking at the sullied remains with ironic satisfaction.
He put his hands behind his back and raised his
head to get a better view of the carnage. Then a little
wave passed over the victor's proud countenance,
made him shut his eyes in voluptuous delight and give
himself up to his dreams.

PART
FOUR

Around the consulate the darkness was black as pitch. It was two o'clock in the morning. The dining room was strewn with the relics of the orgy, during which the white men had exchanged insults and the amenities of blackmail. The slanting eyes of the servants were like glowworms. They looked at my father, now alone in the room, pale with cold sweat and weary triumph, lit jerkily by the flickering electricity. The only sound was the irregular purr of the generator. Monsieur le Consul, under all those hidden glances, withdrew, but not to go to bed, not to rejoin my mother and go to sleep. He moved along lightly instead of with his usual deliberately firm step denoting the virile, precise, methodical person he tried to pass for during the day. He stole like a thief toward the drawing room, and a divan by which stood a big head of Buddha on a pedestal, wearing the happy smile of ambiguity and compromise. Everyone knew what was going to happen.

On certain evenings, when my father had stayed late in his office working away at letters or a report, fanatically adding dashes and exclamation marks to give his missive added force, or when he had lingered willingly or otherwise at table with the gentlemen, exchanging colonial jokes and gossip, sometimes in the midst of these pleasantries manipulating the harsher undertones of a business argument, as he had done this evening with Dumont—then, when Anne Marie had long since gotten tired and gone to her room and so couldn't take him by surprise (she was completely indifferent anyway, as far as he was concerned), instead of retiring to the marital couch, he would go and lie down on the divan, without a sound or a word or an order, to calm himself, idealize himself, taste happiness. Always susceptible to flattery and vanity, which normally ringed his face like quivering open wounds, when he was tired and his nerves were on edge, his imagination sick and hurt and humiliated, he would give himself up to the Great Peace, the Manna of Consolation. He was not a drug addict, but sometimes he had a terrible need for illusions, a need to be what he was not, to reach the goal that eluded him. He long for the delights of the imagination. Then everything became like a shadow show. The staff knew what they had to do: they all stayed hidden in their corners, patiently and curiously watching. It felt like emptiness and solitude, but there were people everywhere. Only one approached my father, and he was scarcely a presence, more a stir of the air. This was his favorite servant, the head houseboy, who crouched at my father's feet with his instruments. The lights went out and were replaced by gleams and shadows and scents. My father lay there waiting, trembling a little. The head boy was like the slender curve of a painted roof, from which everything falls away, leaving nothing but the almost insubstantial ridge reaching into the horizon. Everything vanished with him, even his body, and especially his aquiline skull. The frontal bones narrowed into nothingness, his neck was just a bridge between the evanescent head and a gaunt trunk which tapered off into sticklike legs disappearing in the distance. He had a gift for feeling nothing, for being impervious to all the mannerisms and twitches and gripings and sighs and peevishness and pains and groans and japes of Monsieur le Consul. Although he seemed to be always disappearing or absent, in fact he was always there, to serve as a kind of human cuspidor for my father. In this almost inorganic role he knew how to anticipate all his master's wishes, desires, and needs. The consul's sensitiveness, or rather hypersensitiveness, expressed itself in constant gymnastics. He needed to be understood in advance, to have his wants divined, to be made much of. This should have been Anne Marie's job, but she declined it with mockery and steely contempt. So it was the head boy, always bowing and fluid, who guessed his secret wishes, whether they concerned a choice of underpants or undershirts, or the need for a sleeping pill, a laxative, or a drink. Thanks to him, my father was waited upon hand and foot without having to give any orders. All his whims and fads were gratified without his even noticing the existence of this factotum who got only enough attention for the consul to be able to bawl him out, feeling highly ill used, for the very small errors he managed to discover. On such occasions the head boy offered no protest, but assumed the sad, apologetic, apprehensive attitude of someone who has done wrong, thus enabling his master to renew his remonstrances and finally obtain relief. Anne Marie said the head boy did just as he liked with my father, and that he even, through whispers and scraps of sentences, acted as his informer, denouncing the household, the town, and even herself. But that evening the head boy took care not to obtrude at all. It was no time for the ordinary play-acting in which my father needed his servant's sympathy so badly. All he needed now was the servant's skill, to enable him to take off on his own toward greater heights of satisfaction.

The consul sprawled there, jerking with impatience and shrilling at the servant to hurry up. The man was like a little laboring insect, an ant or a bug; all that could be seen of him were his hands. They had the precision of a torturer's hands on flesh, a convent girl's hands on her embroidery, an alchemist's hands mixing his potions. They were marvelous Chinese hands, so thin and sinewy they seemed more like metal wires than assemblages of bone, and appeared to exist by themselves, apart from the rest of the body, like independent engines eternally at work. They were diligent machines, perfect mechanisms; only an occasional twitch of the skin would show they had any feeling. In the cone of light cast by the lamp presiding over the opium rites, all that was visible were the eyes of the Buddha, the pale, drawn face of my father, and the skillful hands of the servant, which, with the aid of a scraper and little tools like needles and knives, transformed a drop of "divine mud" into a little round pellet already slightly cooked. The rapid gestures, the almost imperceptible sounds, the wafting scents, went steadily on. Soon the moment would come when the boy, having put the pellet in the tiny bowl of the pipe, offered my father the stem. My father sat up slowly, like a blind man, his eyes closed, his mouth searching, then finding. Then he drew in an enormous, avid breath. He looked wild, distant, unfeeling, except for a sort of fixed, petrified concentration, with underlying sounds of swallowing, gasping, slavering. He sat in a strange, uncomfortable position, making a frenzied effort to absorb the smoke, while at the other end of the pipe the pellet spluttered in the flame of the lamp and from the air being drawn through it. For the servant was there directing the operation, seeing that the bowl of the pipe was turned toward the flame and that the stem was in my father's mouth. The Chinaman presided over all this like an insubstantial spirit, a subtle elf, while my father seemed to be a buffalo or some other heavy beast gone mad or possessed. Still sitting up on the divan, his flushed face strangely fixed, still gulping down air as he swallowed the smoke and filled his lungs frantically so as to profit from the whole of the pellet, my father, unlike the peaceful Chinese addicts, who themselves dissolved in wreaths of smoke, seemed more solid than usual. He produced blasts, expectorations, heavy silences ending in grunts and scrapings. Meanwhile his pupils grew smaller, a kind of voluptuous pleasure spread over his face, and when at last the pellet was finished he fell back with his eyes still shut, shaken by a little cough. Monsieur le Consul appeared to be asleep, lying nice and straight, snoring a little. But he wasn't really asleep. He sat up again like a robot just when the next pipe was ready, rising like a big lizard to seize the jade mouthpiece as if it were an insect, a bird, or a dream dragon. Each time he went through the same antics and to the same trouble, more adroitly perhaps as he went on, with fewer strange noises and less stiffness, adopting more easily the positions that best facilitated his holy communion with the opium.

Time went by, and nothing changed beneath the helmeted gaze of the Buddha; the indefatigable fingers ground and kneaded the drug and at regular intervals presented the doses of ecstasy to my father's lips. The miracle was performed to a mathematical rhythm. The consul of France lost some of his heaviness, tossed about less, and started to look like a rubber sack, a drifting toy, a living corpse. Gradually he came to wear a smile of bliss. At last he opened his eyes a little, but he couldn't see, he just flickered his eyes at the boy to tell him, "Faster, faster." By the time he reached the fourth or fifth pellet he was seized with more urgency, a desire for more, more and better. The boy's fingers accelerated, and my father, even before he'd finished a pellet, opened his mouth and gulped down air like a stranded fish. Then he filled himself again with smoke, and was swept away on a tide of bliss.

He cleansed and purified himself, wrote in his head the story of his own superiority. Normally, without opium, he hadn't much imagination except about trifles: maneuverings, the art of flattering and being flattered, being a tyrant and a consul and Albert Bonnard, while remaining a servile petty bourgeois. His life had been one long assiduity, ceaseless, impecunious, undistinguished, full of humiliations sometimes swallowed and sometimes not, a preoccupation with importance, that which he attributed to himself and that with which he tried to butter up his superiors. Despite his flushes of vainglory, all this had left him with an open wound in his heart. When he was in a certain state of over-excitement and fatigue, like tonight, opium saved him. Time and reality no longer existed. The only thing left was thought, which he could manipulate as he pleased, unfurling it to infinity amid the sweet and spicy fumes. Albert Bonnard in all his glory, with an entry on him in the encyclopedia: "Albert Bonnard, French diplomat who brought the railroad from Tonkin to Szechwan, and

extended French influence over a large part of China."
There on his divan, still up to his neck in bargaining,
in mud, and in blood, in a medieval Chengtu where
nothing was settled and danger lurked everywhere,
he let his pipes bear him off into a crazy but logical
delirium in which he saw his triumph celebrated, his
railroad brought into being. He was fêted, famous,
recognized all over the civilized world, by eternal
France, by the governor general of Indochina and
his entourage, by the priests, the bankers, Tang Kiao,
and all the other Chinese. His epic didn't change
either people or the world; it gave him pleasure to
represent them as they were, with their meannesses
and little virtues, in all their farcicalness. For the
consul, that was what life was like, this comedy of
little creatures, little flies, this cesspool, with all the
calculation and rottenness that were the foundations
of patriotism; that was all he understood, all he knew
—sumptuous paltriness against a background of Oriental cruelty. But there in his opiate dream he could
select from his experience, his past, his future. He
could make the puppets do as he pleased and cast
himself as the super-puppet who made all the others
skip about. He took his marionettes from the upper
crust, the corridors of power and money, there where
he had to crawl and where he now transformed himself into the master, mingling, as in reality, the great
interests of colonialism and the music hall of life,
imagining all that was most sordid, stupid, naïve,
harsh, and cruel. Oh, he didn't stint himself, the
consul, on his couch—choosing as his actors the important people he had met or glimpsed, who existed,
but so far above him, like the governor general and
his wife and the Indochina officials who had once
despised him. Now, thanks to the smoke, he held them

in the palm of his hand. He was cleverer than all of them.

The hours went by. My father, still lying on his divan, kept on putting out his lips like a blind man for his tenth, his fifteenth pipe. But while he sucked away, his brain had been set loose. The Chengtu train whistled, the train of his triumph! His cheeks grew hollow, he was neat, handsome, insubstantial, more and more like a well-laid-out corpse, the corpse of a good Frenchman. He wasn't asleep, he wasn't dead, he was telling himself the consoling story of what his railroad would be like. What a godsend opium was, to be able to help a poor harassed, threatened consul to happiness! Flying from one cloud of smoke to another, my father built his mausoleum, his monument, his cathedral, his masterpiece.

"Not all that wretch of a Dumont says is stupid. He knows what's what. He saw right away that I was someone who could do great things in Szechwan. And he settled on me at once like a fly on rich dung. He's as good as a Chinaman—he can pick over piles of excrement and reeking rackets and come out with gold galore. But as he showed me—that fat tomcat ringing his bells—why shouldn't an honest man like me, behaving honestly, come out of all this intriguing, where I'm risking my balls for love of France, with the rank of consul general or minister plenipotentiary? I would have earned it. And why shouldn't I do even better, if ever the first train from Hanoi comes rolling into Chengtu blowing its whistle and pulling up in clouds of steam and a clatter of pistons? I can see it now, swathed in banners and shields, bringing the most distinguished people in full uniform—perhaps a minister from Paris, but anyway the governor general of Indochina and his entourage, and crowds of generals and admirals, important residents and lots of aides-de-camp. Probably the Quai d'Orsay will be represented by my beloved protector, who will congratulate me with his gray eyes and his long straight nose, without raising his voice too much or making too many gestures, but letting some insignificant phrase drop from beneath his mustache, as he usually does when he's pleased. He's not one to show his feelings. But he mustn't go and break his neck first by getting himself mixed up with his brother's bank—the foul Dumont kept turning the knife in that wound. Perhaps there'll be some famous journalists—probably even Albert Londres himself. There'll be a whole article on me in *L'Illustration*, and who knows, maybe my photo on the cover. Some important mandarin will represent the emperor of Annam, some ancient valetudinarian with hardly any hair left, who will splutter servilities through his few loose teeth. Not to mention all the bedizened Chinamen from Yunnanfu, with a forest of ready-made smiles concealing impenetrable thoughts. First among them will be Tang Kiao, unless by then he's been supplanted by some Yunnanese ruffian who's lopped off that great head, expressive as a billiard ball, and who'll take his place very worthily, as if nothing had happened. In short, for me, because of me, nothing but the highest society, the cream of the French Republic, the French Empire and its satellites. Ah, but I was forgetting, and this is very important, the ladies of these gentlemen, for some of them will have wanted to come, and they'll have had special creations made for the journey, as if for flying or riding, and flowered dresses for the ball, for I shall give a ball at the consulate, and I shall open it with the wife of the

governor general, who they say is much too young and
pretty for him. . . . There'll be all the luggage and
boxes full of decorations to give to the natives. I
myself should get the insignia of the Legion of
Honor. . . ."

The head boy vanished, no longer existed, was only
some distant object. A bittersweetness swallowed up
the movements, the noises, the whole alchemy of
preparation, which nevertheless continued. My father
had crossed the bar, and was drifting in another world.

"But before all that I shall ride a couple of hundred
kilometers on horseback to meet the train. I shall halt,
dismount, and bow solemnly to each excellency and
timidly kiss the hand of each excellency's wife. My
modesty will produce the best possible effect. Especially as it will be a triumphal journey all the way.
The line will be guarded by sentries with bayonets
shining as brightly as the new rails; Tang Kiao's guard
of honor will be posted among the VIPs' sleeping cars,
their guns at the ready at each window and door, and
there will be other soldiers with machine guns on
the tenders and the roofs of the coaches. All this
martial display will be organized by Tang Kiao, partly
as a precaution but mostly as a matter of 'face'—his
own and that of the distinguished foreign guests. But I
only hope nothing will go wrong—that there won't
be bullets flying or anything else troublesome. But
that's hardly likely. Tang Kiao, having gotten his fill,
isn't one to join the party if there's the slightest risk to
his own skin. On the contrary, to add spice to the
situation I might tell the bigwigs, the top Europeans,
that in his zeal Tang Kiao has had his troops comb
all the mountains along the line, and there have been

some battles, and a couple of hundred bandits killed or executed. No, that's a bad idea! It would just throw a scare into all those famous people comfortably installed on their nice soft cushions—they'd get cold feet every time the engine went through a pass or a gorge. And stories about brigands decapitated in their honor wouldn't seem in very good taste to these civilized ladies and gentlemen visiting Szechwan as if it were some sort of exotic park. No, what these worthy official tourists would like is to have the whole population flocking there to see them—the benevolent wrinkled faces of the old folk in the front row, next to the ruddy countenances of the girls carrying yokes. There'll be a crowd like that at every station, expressing its joy with huge banners and unicorn dances and the whole bag of tricks, and a genuine scholar with rattling bones who coughs as he reads a scroll praising the generosity of France and the paternal goodness of Tang Kiao. The only person who'll be taken in will be the governor general, that white-bearded veteran of radical socialism with his Southern accent, who doesn't even know what goes on in the deltas and jungles of the model colony he's been parked in to get him out of France. The people from Indochina, especially the civil servants in the governor general's entourage, will have no illusions about the spontaneity of the public's feelings. Tang Kiao's method of producing them is the same they've been using for a long time in Tonkin and Cochin China for anything and everything—the opening of a market, an inspection by some old fogy, even the collection of taxes. But these gentry won't utter a peep, even when some lady from France twitters, 'All these poor Chinese—how affectionately they look at us! Like faithful hounds! The way they've been

slandered, all those tales about their cruelty, all those
horror stories!' Actually, on such occasions, the plebs
look dull and stupefied, even if the day before or the
day before that they've been pried out of their mud
villages and brought at bayonet point to the huts that
serve as stations, in order to show their enthusiasm
when the time comes. The people's eyes are staring,
dim, popping out of their heads, their eyes don't
believe their eyes as they gaze at the fire dragon with
its terrible head gasping out sparks and smoke, its
round teeth growing out downward and chewing up
the elements, the earth, the mountains, the rivers, the
fields. The fire dragon has a long body, too, resembling a steel snake, flying over the ground like the
wind on its little round legs. The people think the
fabulous creature has been tamed and serves as a
steed to the terrible, dangerous men who lurk inside
it, barbarians given to infernal magic, and the insatiable Tang Kiao. And the people, while they wonder,
also tremble with fear at the thought that henceforward Tang Kiao, astride this monstrous beast, can
turn up with an army at any minute to fall on them
and extort still more money, down to the last cent
and the last pound of rice. And so, for the moment,
the people in their apprehension acclaim Tang Kiao,
do all they can to swell their acclamations. Tang
Kiao sometimes shows his dog face at the window,
through the bullet-proof glass he insisted on having
installed. He knows very well that if the people got
hold of him they'd enjoy tearing him to bits with
their bare hands, and he acts accordingly. But the
governor general of Indochina swallows everything.
At the sight of so much enthusiasm he feels obliged
from time to time to hoist up his corporation and
greet the populace with little waves of the hand to

thank them for their warm welcome. In short, you might say everything's right on schedule.

"The big moment will be the arrival in Chengtu at the real station, the big station I'll have had built: a glass roof, switches, sidings, platforms, and buffers. And the ceremony—my God! The place, just finished, will be more impressive than the Grand Palais or a pavilion at the Great Exhibition. It will be groaning with flags and pennants and big banners painted with huge letters; there'll be a sea of French tricolors and a sacred wood of potted plants. And presiding over it all, suspended in the air, will be a full-length photograph of Tang Kiao, and beside it a full-length photograph of me, with the legend: 'To our bene-factors, who have brought the balmy breeze of progress to Szechwan—Tang Kiao and Albert Bonnard, fathers of the railroad which has crossed the mountains and leaped over the clouds to link Szechwan to the modern world.' In the station, all ready, will be everyone in Chengtu who wears a uniform or bears a sword, includ-ing a lot of war lords all dolled up and waiting with a certain amount of apprehension—some of them will never have seen a train before. In this novel situation they won't know what to do, until a little French engineer tells them where to stand to welcome Tang Kiao as he gets out of his compartment. Standing proudly alone a couple of paces in front of the group is the marshal, his face expressionless so as to conceal his thoughts, for he is not sure, having been practically independent in Szechwan up till now, that he's all that pleased to welcome his boss, Tang Kiao, who henceforward can keep dropping in from Yunnanfu whenever he feels like it. All the more reason for seeing that everything goes smoothly. So he'll have ordered the civilian dignitaries, a great crowd of whom are gathered in the background, to wear frock coats, this highly civilized garb being the only one worthy of ushering in modern times in the shape of the new railroad. But as only the diplomats in Chengtu have such a thing as a frock coat, all the previous month Chinamen will have been coming to my office to beg for the loan of mine for a few hours, just long enough to have it copied by a member of the guild of master tailors. And he will have copied it exactly, without one alteration or modification, as if every Chinaman in Chengtu was exactly the same size as me. This will produce a rather comical effect at the station, with all the old boys crushed together on the bit of platform allotted to them like a lot of yellow dolls, some in striped pants that are far too big for them, others splitting at the seams, and one trying to hide his naked behind. But apart from this it will all be very solemn. Around the dignitaries, all on their best behavior and silent out of protocol and patience, a whole regiment will be stationed, half reassuring and half threatening: the cats' eyes of the soldiers in the ranks, the almost closed slits of the motionless officers, the ritual language of the bayonets at vigilant ease. A little way off is a great mass of curves, tubes, bulges, pipes, and gleaming metal: the big brass band. But for the moment everyone is waiting.

"Then come asthmatic grunts, enormous blasts, clankings, splutterings, the final expectorations. The train appears, advances a little, then comes to a halt between the platforms. In the station a thousand hitherto motionless Chinamen, with the chief dignitaries acting as figureheads, start to jerk about like puppets and sway to and fro like falling tops. This is to signify their admiration. In China this must never be expressed by unbridled emotion, which is considered dangerous and unseemly, but by a compulsory imitation of the real thing—deliberate, ordered, conventional, rhythmical, and collective—a ritual which when properly performed produces an extraordinary impression of intensity and even genuineness. The sudden galvanizing of all these salutations shows that the sacramental moment is at hand when Szechwan is going to touch in the flesh its conqueror and possessor —Tang Kiao, who has just been brought here like a parcel thanks to my railroad. A few oppressive seconds, then one of the doors opens and Tang Kiao appears before his subjects, unwieldy, his face a danger signal, his cylindrical body so heavily done up he looks as if he's wearing an iron corset, his eyes lifeless. Everything about him is terrifyingly dull and heavy, no expression emanates from him at all except when he raises his cap and a few rolls of flesh twitch on his sandpapered skull. Tang Kiao explores each of the three steps down to the platform with his foot, then drops hulkingly down them one at a time. As he starts this lengthy operation, the station seems about to explode with groans and howls: the brass band, and the officers giving orders to their men. When Tang Kiao arrives on the platform there is the gleam of a sword before him—the slim marshal has unsheathed it and twirled it about in homage to his leader. Then the other war lords welcome him with bared swords in token of their vassalage. Tang Kiao is somewhat uneasy at this array of cutting edges so close to him and in such hands. He gives a sign, and is covered by a wall of swords—safe ones this time, at least in theory, belonging to the soldiers of his bodyguard. After this he doesn't take one step except inside this sheath of steel—bayonets, pikes, and so on. The worthy governor general, when he finally emerges from his coach, is rather taken aback and rubs his eyes at what he sees: while martial music blares out, he is confronted with Tang Kiao and his mobile armor, the war lords following him like pickets, a row of sentries presenting arms so close together that their swords form one silver streak, here the gleam of machine guns, and there a lot of strangely dressed Chinamen bobbing and bowing as if they were performing gymnastics. When I go over to the governor general, who's still goggling, I start to introduce the yellow excellencies, civil and military: one bows to the other, the other bows back, they both bow again, like whirligigs. On every side, nothing but bows and bayonets. At this point I give the boss of Indochina a dig in the ribs and mutter, the '*Marseillaise*.' For that's what the army band is playing. In fact you'd need to be as well trained as I am to be able to recognize our national anthem in the versions offered by the military band of Chengtu. The one performed on the day the railway is opened is particularly egregious. 'Are you sure?' asks the governor general. 'Yes, Your Excellency.' So we stand at attention. Tang Kiao, some ten yards away, stops, stiffens, and gives a showy military salute. At once the war lords follow suit; so do the ordinary officers; the troops present arms. The civilians wonder what's the matter, and finally realize they ought to stop bobbing politely and stand up straight. These are moments of glory for France and for me. When the last notes have died away. Tang Kiao summons the governor general under his metal arch and shakes hands with him over and over again, saying, 'France has shown itself a great friend to me. Please convey my gratitude to the French government.' He also gives me a ceremonial embrace.

I have the impression Tang Kiao rather forgot the governor general in the preoccupation of his arrival: the marshal might have been waiting for him at the head of rebellious troops, ready to betray him. These fears dispelled, Tang Kiao makes up for his neglect by inviting the governor general to a symbolic tea party in the stationmaster's office. We find all the French delegation there, including the ladies, and they all sip from fine porcelain cups under the benevolent eye of Tang Kiao. I disappear for a few moments. It is my duty to go and congratulate the two worthy Frenchmen who got the train here—the driver and the stoker. I find them in overalls, two veterans of the colonies and the Indochina railway. 'I'm the French consul in Chengtu,' I say to them. 'Was it a difficult journey.'

" 'We had to keep our eyes open—some of the bridges weren't any too solid. Some of the contractors didn't overexert themselves.'

" 'Your names will go down in history as the two pioneers who drove the first French train beyond the Blue River and right into the heart of Szechwan.'

" 'Well . . .'

" 'I'm going to ask them to give you a decoration. You deserve it. The Labor Medal, and the Dragon of Annam.'

" 'Thanks. We'd rather have a bonus.'

"I leave these simple heroes, and in the now half-empty station have the pleasure of meeting the English consul, who looks as if he had jaundice. There wasn't any 'God Save the King' for him, and now all the Trade from Szechwan will go out through Haiphong. A Chinaman in a uniform worthy of a war lord is puffing strenuously into a whistle and getting it to produce an occasional blast. He's the stationmaster,

and he's already seen stations at Hankow and Shanghai. He's the eldest son of an important merchant,
appointed to this elevated and demanding position
after his honorable father paid the marshal enough
money to prove his scion's merits. To get off to a
worthy start in his new job, the young man has had
the grand costume made and the grand office built.
In the latter, Tang Kiao is busy honoring with some
familiarity, almost tête-à-tête and with the official
unction that passes for intimacy, the governor general
and his suite. So it came about that the stationmaster,
driven out of his lair, is attempting to recover lost
face by producing these ear-splitting blasts up and
down the platform, as if they could actually cause the
trains to go! Fortunately the real work will be done
by a French engineer, who on my instructions will
keep out of sight. That's China. It's beginning to take
possession. The first Chinese dirt has already mysteriously appeared here and there in the building in the
form of smells, spit, and deposits of excrement, small
or large. The latter makes a mess, and can only be the
work of coarse uneducated people with no sense of
economy—like the soldiers.

"It's a triumphal entry into Chengtu, for the station
is surrounded by a seething mass of people, a tempest
of tangled arms and eyes and heads. An incredible
conglomeration. The crowd is much larger than Tang
Kiao intended, than he ordered to be there. The
innumerable people are crazed with the Chinese passion of curiosity, all mad to see the iron beast, the
locomotive, and its children, the railway coaches.
There's almost a riot. Tang Kiao frowns and gives a
sign. A regiment charges, thousands of soldiers lay
about them like robots with the butts of their rifles,
hitting at random among the fleeing mob. In a few

minutes the place is cleared, no one left, not even a casualty lying on the ground. Tang Kiao is delighted and turns to the governor general.

" 'If the people's enthusiasm gets too great, it can be dangerous. It was for you I got rid of them all, so that you could make a peaceful entry into Chengtu.'

"And sure enough it is through deserted streets that our long procession makes its way to the consulate. At one point the governor general whispered to me:

" 'Tang Kiao is too kind. It wasn't necessary. All those people beaten because of me. It's a queer way of starting my visit.'

"I reassured the worthy fellow.

" 'It wasn't really for you; it was for his own sake he had the crowd dispersed rather roughly. He doesn't like crowds, especially in Chengtu. As a matter of fact, he's just ordered everyone to keep away when he goes into the town with his soldiers. Notice he didn't let them use their bayonets. That was certainly out of regard for you and your feelings.' "

There was an unbearably long pause. When the time came for the twentieth pellet of opium, the head boy's hand wasn't ready to hold it out to my father's lips. This was because the consul, in his bliss, had accelerated his pace, as if he himself were the boiler of a locomotive that needed more fuel to go faster. A growl, and all was right again. The consul drifted on.

"Afterward the governor general was delighted: ten days of sumptuous and ingenious celebrations! Perhaps Tang Kiao overdid the martial displays a little. Reviews, parades, torchlight tattoos, cavalry charges, artillery fire, wave after wave of infantry creeping forward, then hurling themselves yelling into the attack. The dust, the heat! But when the governor general got a bit bored, Tang Kiao came up to him beaming and said:

" 'Those guns are French—excellent weapons, the best in the world. I have my armies drilled in the French style. But despite their efforts, they've still got a long way to go. But if you would vouchsafe your invaluable criticism, we could correct and improve ourselves.'

"Sly old devil.

"Then comes the round of feasting—meals consisting of a hundred dishes, a thousand guests seated at little tables, thousands of servants, an army of soldiers with torches, bowls light as butterfly wings, food disturbingly outlandish. The governor general and his wife are very worried over the curious consistency of the contents of little bowls full of soft, viscous, crunchy, unidentifiable objects. The first incident occurs when Tang Kiao, using his own chopsticks, those he puts in his own mouth, suddenly stretches out his great arm and descends like a locust on various dishes, choosing the tastiest morsels to offer with a courteous inclination of the head to his neighbor in her flounced gown—the wife of the governor general. She, instead of appreciating this supreme condescension at its true worth, gives a shriek like some parvenu maidservant. Where on earth did her gouty excellency of a husband find her, that cheap stuck-up piece that he now drags around with him as an official *grande dame?* Anyhow, with a supercilious expression and a voice acid with anger, she turns to Tang Kiao and says straight out: 'I'd like a fork, please. A clean one.' Tang Kiao, instead of taking offense, as any less knowledgeable war lord would have done, very graciously has one brought. The brute even laid in a supply of European tableware anticipating just this sort of contretemps! His own city of Yunnanfu has long been linked by rail to Indochina, and he's seen loads of Europeans, especially French people, arriving from Hanoi and other towns in the colonies—big shots and nobodies, but all puffed up with colonialist vanity. He knows them inside out, with their fusses, their fads, their pretensions, their little games, and their wives who are even worse—sluts with a high idea of themselves or imperious old bags, all affected pains in the neck. Tang Kiao has gotten used to them, learned to make use of them. And during this trip to Chengtu, with all those excellencies and all those interests at stake, he doesn't want anything to go wrong. He's like a mother, eyes everywhere, looking out for squalls, especially wanting to prevent too many toasts, for it's obvious the governor general has trouble with his liver and something wrong with his innards, and his pale face is running with sweat. The governor general, although he behaves very correctly, unlike his shrew of a wife, hardly touches any of the food that's paraded under his nose for hour after hour, some of which almost makes him retch. Tang Kiao doesn't force him to stuff himself, as is normally the duty of a host, with encouragement, proverbs, saws, and maxims.

"The small quantity ingurgitated by the important couple from Indochina is made up for later on by the quality of the official eloquence, the solemnity of the phrases, the nobility of the sentiments exchanged. The governor general, who made his way up among the cassoulets and election banquets of the South of France, where after having had a good blowout you start doling out the rhetoric, finds himself in good form for a speech at the end of this exotic and to him poisonous repast. What a flow of words sweeping majestically along the railroad of friendship! And all in celebration of its contribution to the happiness of the Chinese, not mentioning the fact that, for a start, some tens of thousands of coolies died like cattle building just the new stretch from Yunnanfu to Chengtu. Tang Kiao replies in the brief but forceful manner befitting a soldier. Finally, I myself make a somewhat emotional little speech—there are almost tears in my eyes. Tang Kiao himself gives the signal for the applause. The handshakes last an hour—the Chinese keep clasping and shaking and unclasping and reshaking hands as if this gesture, which represents a new conquest of China, ought also to represent an idea of eternity.

"For it's important to Tang Kiao to be on the right side of the governor general. The governor's a good sort, but getting on, with a permanent thirst, blinking eyes, a belly, indigestion, always a bit scruffy, especially around the chin, always tired, and still in love with his wife, which is not good for his health at his age. You can see he's been used to being one of the VIPs, showered with honors, for ages—one of those ugly, jovial, solemnly vulgar old gents who make up the life of the victorious Third Republic, with all the absurdity and especially the virtues that implies: honesty, dignity, a touch of the old fox in the farmyard of politics, but also a cast-iron knowledge of men and of power, a tearful, quavering, happiness-for-the-people aspect concealing the malicious phrase, the harsh order, the devastating paragraph. Beneath his soft carapace he has a sense of authority and of France, for his nibs is a Jacobin, a patriot, and pitiless when it comes to the interests of the country—a real old radical socialist. But unfortunately, with time, his virtues have fallen to the distaff side, and he's not much more than a weary old elephant, touchy about his little comforts and vanities. He lives in a semi-inertia, a lazy cynicism, not believing in anything much any more, not wanting to take on anything, adapting himself to mediocrity, with just an occasional interval of lucidity or will power when someone treads on his toes. He has brought to perfection the art of ruling without doing anything, surly when he's in a bad temper, jovial enough when things go well, sometimes unexpectedly letting drop some ironical observation that makes people think but isn't carried any farther. In short, he's a typical, prematurely senile, republican proconsul, with traces of his former glory but no more great ambitions. But what I've found out is that his better half, the impudent, impertinent, preposterous little woman, has ambition and to spare on his behalf. She's determined to hoist them to the top of the greasy pole by the scruff of the neck, the seat of the trousers, or the goatee. She drags the potbellied codger around in her wake, always egging him on."

An odor grips the atmosphere, a bittersweet smell that spreads through the air, making it almost solid. It swirls everywhere, creeping even into the throats of the servants crouched watching in the dark. One of them coughs. The sound echoes inside Albert's skull like the stroke of a gong. He starts and grumbles, on the point of awakening. But the head boy makes haste to present him with a fresh pellet, and he is off again in his dream.

"My ball at the consulate was a terrific success! I must admit Anne Marie arranged the garden with exquisite taste, with paper lanterns floating over the flowers and shrubs and buffets, and over a dance floor set up beneath the pomegranate trees. The orchestra was a sort of gypsy ensemble from the chief nightclub in Hanoi. I had them brought in the van of the inaugural train—a pretty penny that cost me! The governor general's wife, all titivated and swathed like a nymph —which only made her look like a tart—and with two handsome young men in tow she'd taken care to have appointed and brought along as aides-de-camp, nearly fell down in a faint when Tang Kiao, heavy and solemn and done up like a clown in decorations and boots, bowed before her—a difficult operation because of his shape—and asked if he might have the honor of the first waltz. This time the governor said to his wife, loud enough for other people to hear, 'Accept—I insist,' to which the charming creature replied, 'I'll get you for this.' Meanwhile, as soon as 'The Blue Danube' began to flow through the Szechwanese night, Tang Kiao, his powerful mask far above such little accidents, seized the lady in his muscular arms without deigning to notice the face she was making. The fact was that it was a terrible bore for him, too, but he considered this heroic deed a duty, a privilege due to himself, and a patriotic gesture of both diplomatic and international importance—a consecration of the alliance between Yunnan and Szechwan on the one hand and France and Indochina on the other, an alliance already sealed by the railroad. As a matter of fact, the war lord, his gravity carefully preserved, had never yet performed any Western dance, even at the biggest consular galas and parties in Yunnanfu. That gives some idea of the importance of this event, and the historical significance of Tang Kiao's capers. With his sword flapping between his legs, and holding at arm's length his half-wit of a partner, who had passed from reluctance to acting the fool, and now giggled and laughed, with glances intended to bring the rest of the party into it, Tang Kiao waltzed as if on a parade ground: one, two, one martial step forward, one, two, one martial step backward, four each of these figures to the minute, twenty military movements over a distance about one yard long as the crow flies. When it was over he dipped the top part of his body forward to thank the lady, who was left standing high and dry, and burst out in a peal of nervous laughter. Then he dipped in front of Anne Marie, to invite her. She had just been dancing with the governor general, who, as I had hoped and planned, had opened the ball with her. The governor general, old dodderer that he was, still jigged up and down with springs and sweeps and gallops and all the romantic circlings of the beer-drinking student and gay dog he used to be at his provincial university long ago, so that he ended up panting and doubled over with exhaustion, then collapsed into a chair, saying he was past it. Anne Marie, who had been perfect with the old boy trying to act young, was equally so with the war lord when he started his clumsy gyrations all over again with her. She seems to have a gift for being above absurdity, with that sweet, indulgent, yet ironical half-smile which in some mysterious way is in but not of what surrounds her. After his two exploits, Tang Kiao considered his duty done and withdrew in strength. His stooges, in full regalia, who stood like posts silently watching him as he went through his choreographic maneuvers, now lined up behind him to make their exit with a step modeled on that of the Legion. There's French influence for you! As a matter of fact, I'd had a tune based on the 'Consular March' written for my nightclub orchestra, who all had ravaged faces like confirmed night birds, and I'd gotten Tang Kiao to listen to it a couple of days before: he'd decided it was to be the new Yunnan-Szechwan national anthem. So of course on the night of the ball I signaled my musicians to play it as soon as I saw Tang Kiao getting ready to leave. At the first notes, while he was still saying goodbye, his terrible face lit up with a really satisfied smile, and he went off proud as a peacock to those glorious sounds. As soon as he'd been gotten rid of, the evening really began. People danced their feet off, though there was a scarcity of ladies. Anne Marie made a great hit, despite her distant manner and her way of being there and not there at the same time. She was the perfect society hostess, a charming and agreeable young woman with a gift for conversation and seemly pleasures, yet still a mystery. I wanted to dance with her, too, and she didn't object. But as soon as I took hold of her, she pushed me away and said, 'You're holding me too tight.' The governor general's wife, who doesn't miss anything, dragged me off, laughing. 'You must have been quite a lad when you were a bachelor. But now I don't suppose you have much fun.' There was no holding her down. She was jerking and staggering around merrily, half tight, calling out to the men. The governor general, appalled and fearful of a domestic row, talked about his election campaigns and pretended not to hear his wife, who brandished a glass of champagne and sang the 'Barcarolle' from *The Tales of Hoffman,* adapting the words to make them refer to China. The civil servants stood protectively around her, solid as the Great Wall of China, even if they did think she was an old fool.

"To tell the truth, I don't really like these fellows.

The more correct they are toward me, the stiffer their attitude and the more supercilious their smiles. They think it's something wonderful to have conquered a tiny place like Indochina. They took down their noses at the French in China—they think they're too frivolous, not really sound and respectable, and don't understand Asia as well as the Indochinese hands do. And all because they haven't managed to get control of the whole of China and establish proper colonial law and order there. I'd like to see how they'd have made out with my war lords, and yet they practically try to tell me what's what. They did thaw a bit, though, on the night of the ball, and one of them, the governor general's chief private secretary, even paid me a few compliments for the first time. 'Nice work, this railway, my dear consul. And a very good party.' I know these people inside out. I used to be more or less in their power when I was a young man in Tonkin.

"Indochina is their machine, a precision mechanism in which not one screw must be allowed to come loose. They think it's the cat's whiskers, thanks to their flawless administration: one informer for every ten inhabitants, one cop for every hundred, a handful of tame mandarins to lick their nice smooth asses and eat the common people alive, and a few obedient princes, including an emperor at Hué that they have to keep changing in order to find a good one—in other words, an idiot. They keep a few regiments of marines, and a prison at Poulo Condore in case of trouble, but there isn't very much. As they say, their own natives are not really likely to act up; they know the score, and they're not the belligerent type, even though they're sly and you have to keep your eye on them. There's no question of upsetting the perfect clock-

work of the order of peace and prosperity by admitting
non-Europeans into the Indochinese civil service, not
even the young Westernized types who've done brilliantly in their French examinations. They could
never really understand loyalty to the state. On the
contrary, these Annamite intellectuals are the most
dangerous of all, and the only thing to do with them
is to turn them into clerks and pay them less than a
drunken illiterate European foreman in the Public
Works Department. That's the system, and the civil
servants are always moiling away to make tiny im-
provements in it, to keep themselves on top, and
underneath, the happy and grateful masses. In this
way they've made themselves into a superior caste,
touchy as porcupines, with a curt and suspicious self-
satisfaction, and a sort of irritated stickling for formally that's half provincial and half colonial, a cross between Honfleur and Hanoi. Their wives are typical
white women, most of them ugly as sin, some the cook-
general type, others middle-class and sharp-nosed, but
all very conscious of their own importance and careful
to make the proper distinctions. These people entertain one another within their little closed world, but
according to the complexities of hierarchy; their dinner parties are deadly boring. The gentlemen talk
about nothing but work, and the ladies about nothing
but the morals of the ladies not present. And this even
if their own morals are not beyond reproach, as is frequently the case in the colonies. Only one rule is binding on wives, which is that they should not stray outside the proper circles and compromise themselves with
inferiors. That they might do so with non-Europeans
is too horrible even to think of.

"The civil servants will never forgive the governor
general, who has lucid intervals, for such nasty cracks

as: 'Still waters, if you ask me, those natives of yours! If there aren't some changes, the Annamites are going to wind up cutting the Frenchmen's throats. I shall have gone by then. But you won't, and you'll see.' Of course there aren't any reforms, but the white colony seethes with rage after such 'indecent' remarks. Fortunately the most obvious, immediate, and tangible indecency is embodied in the governor general's flighty wife. To revenge itself on the heretical husband, the whole of white Indochina keeps its eye on his spouse, and there's a flood of gossip in respectable houses, clubs, and cocktail parties, overflowing into dinner parties and receptions until it fills the whole of social life with a typhoon which is quiet only in its eye, its center, the area occupied by the governor general himself. His wife, far from behaving better because of this outcry on the part of all the nice people of Indochina, only gets into worse scrapes, to show her defiance. Her sleeping around has become the great 'affair' in Saigon and Hanoi, the great preoccupation of the Defense of Political and Economic Colonialism. So it comes to me automatically in the luggage of the governor general and his wife. And so it happens that my railroad, my career, my future, are all suddenly linked to the virtue, or lack of virtue, of this little lady. At about two in the morning I have a feeling that my ball is going bad.

"The governor general, having expatiated on his memories of the good old days, has fallen asleep, snoring a little, his mouth opening and shutting at random, his jowls emitting grunts and streaks of salivia. His head is resting on the back of a cane chair, and every so often it straightens up as if he were about to regain consciousness, then falls back again drowsily. I sense an uneasy feeling in the people around him.

The orchestra, with sunken eyes and haggard masklike faces, play listlessly, with an exaggerated professional emptiness, as if the evening were all but over; only one or two couples are still dancing. The members of the civil and military staffs stand about in attitudes of elaborate casualness, trying to make themselves as small as possible. Their 'ladies' are there right enough, most of them seated—all dressed up and bejeweled and becorseted, not speaking, but with faces watchful as owls and blinking eyes straining to see what's going on in the dark. Suddenly the governor general raises his head and wakes up, looks around him blearily, and growls, 'Where's my wife? I can't see her anywhere.' And that's why everyone is waiting with bated breath, that's the secret that's paralyzing all this distinguished company. The little tramp disappeared into the consulate gardens half an hour ago. I didn't dare send Anne Marie to look for her, for fear of what she'd find. But by a miracle, just as her august husband emerges from his snooze and sees she isn't there, she pops up from behind a hedge with an innocent ripple of laughter. 'Oh,' she says, 'I had a headache. Perhaps I had too much to drink. I went for a stroll by the pond Madame Bonnard showed me this afternoon. I'm feeling much better now.' The governor general looks grumpy and unconvinced. No one mentions that all the time the lady was recovering from the vapors his favorite aide-de-camp was also missing. But this time the husband, who usually swallows everything like a good sugar daddy, gets into a temper. 'You might have told me,' he says. 'You make me look ridiculous. I'm going to send you home on the first boat and get a divorce.' At that moment, a tall fellow from the English consulate collapses in front of the buffet, stewed to the gills, and lies there like a log with his nose bleeding. A broken glass falls from his hand. But thanks to the providential Englishman, the domestic row is cut short: all the guests busy themselves with him.

"I hesitated for a long time before asking the English to the party, but I couldn't do otherwise. And they came, despite the fact that my train sticks in their throats and in every other part of them. But although the railroad transfixes them with pain and rage, there is no trace of this on their faces. When the train arrived at the station they looked a bit put out, but since then they've recovered themselves. So along they came draped with decorations, their ladies in lace fronts—more British than ever, charming and suave, paying due respect to the governor general and especially his moll, as if she were a princess, and congratulating me in the most friendly fashion. 'My dear Albert, we're so happy for you.' And to make it quite plain that they are completely unaffected, they throw themselves heart and soul into the party, whirling about, drinking, and joking. And that's how their colleague came to fall, a victim to duty, overzealously carefree in the service of His Majesty. The ladies swarm around him and wipe his face with handkerchiefs and damp napkins, and he soon comes to. His first words are heroic: 'More champagne.'

"Now, as if inspired, the governor general's lady starts to clap her hands and chortle. 'That's what I call a man. Let's dance a farandole to him.' And panting and pawing the ground, her eyes blazing and her body burning, her hair streaming and her dress trailing, she drags her husband's surly sixteen stone out of their chair as if she were the leader of an army. The governor general, as if irresistibly drawn to her despite his bulk, lets himself be dragged, and even flings his free arm out toward his private secretary. The latter obeys, and soon all are caught up in the dance. The governor general's wife heads the saraband, which includes austere gentlemen and reserved ladies who pretend to find it amusing; the English, as rowdy as schoolboys; and Anne Marie and myself. A long chain of high society, of people in uniform and evening dress, of bodies all done up. A transformation scene of compulsory gaiety, with the governor general following his wife and giving the lead, swinging his hips, shaking his belly, the life and soul of the party. The orchestra sounds the charge, Madame dances and sings and whispers to her husband, 'You know I love you, Pettikins.' They make up. It turns out to be a magnificent evening after all, worthy in every way of my railroad. A success. Anne Marie is the only one who never brightened up. She behaved very well, but she remained as impassive as the Mona Lisa.

"The days that follow are also a success. The atmosphere that has been built up remains propitious, and the shrewd Tang Kiao realizes that after all the official to-do my troop of distinguished guests could do with a holiday. So he lets me show the governor and his party around Chengtu. I'd already concocted a program, knowing that a purely state visit like this has only one object, and that is the pleasures of tourism. In short, for my illustrious joy-riders, my railroad is a sort of Colonial Exhibition. So there's great excitement on the first day set aside for seeing the town and its surroundings. The men are wearing sun helmets and the ladies are all in tropical dress, with big hats and veils. Like middle-aged kids. The governor general is very jovial and tries to show off his knowledge of the East by asking me intelligent questions. 'Binding women's feet is supposed to stimulate sen-

suality, isn't it? The subtlety of these Chinese! What
won't they think of!' But before I can answer, his
wife replies, 'Well, darling, if it's to stimulate sensu-
ality, you wouldn't need to do so much binding with
me, would you?' Then she turns to me and says,
'Albert, dear, what have you got to show us that's
nice and spicy?' In the town she flits about like a
dragonfly, in a crazy mood, determined to make use
of her liberty, knowing the ladies and gentlemen
present will take note of every eccentricity to regale
Indochinese society with when they get back. So she
piles it on. But pending their return to Hanoi to
recount 'the latest' about her exploits in China, the
senior civil servants condescend to be good-humored,
with just a trace of testiness, and their spouses do
their best to be agreeable. We set off modestly on foot,
followed by a string of saddled but riderless horses
and empty sedan chairs, ready at a sign, to scoop up
their lord- and ladyships. All around us are servants,
interpreters, mafus, and coolies in consulate livery;
a few soldiers sent by Tang Kiao head the procession
and bring up the rear. Their number is carefully calculated: enough to show consideration for our importance and 'face,' but not enough to spoil that feeling
of playing hooky so strangely congenial to Europeans.
A hundred in front and a hundred behind, and for
once their bayonets don't look threatening, and even
they themselves are grinning—by order, of course. But
they have nothing to do, for the crowds stand back
as they watch the comic spectacle we present: all these
Europeans and their dames, more of them than have
ever been seen in Chengtu before, disporting themselves
like schoolchildren. But no one swarms up close to
us. Perhaps Tang Kiao has given instructions.

"The farther we go, the more I feel the influence of

Tang Kiao, invisible to the governor and his entourage but very visible to me. He's presented us with a different Chengtu, transformed, scrubbed, and shining like a new penny. One colonial lady even says, 'How disappointing! It's hardly any more picturesque than the native quarter in Hanoi. Where are the famous beggars?' It occurs to me that while we were busy with our galas, Tang Kiao, with his well-known efficiency, was getting his thugs to round up any poor wretches who might offend the eyes of the governor general and his wife and create a bad impression of Chengtu. I fear Tang Kiao may have taken advantage of this opportunity to rid himself once and for all of these unfortunates, by having them shot by the thousand outside the city, beside graves they dug with their own hands and into which they fell as corpses, thus giving their executioners as little work as possible and costing no more than the price of the bullets. But on making inquiries I find I am mistaken in this hypothesis. I wasn't allowing for Tang Kiao's genius: he used a much simpler method, one that didn't cost anything, and even brought in some profit. In his wisdom he merely sent some emissaries among the people concerned, telling them to get out of the city while the barbarians were there, and that they could come back afterward and resume their usual charming occupations. This order was meekly, even gratefully, obeyed: his majesty the king of the beggars, after consulting with his government, decided to levy a special collection among his subjects, and gave Tang Kiao a large sum of money to thank him for his kindness.

"So Tang Kiao managed to avoid incidents. He knew that although these human rejects were a blot on the city, the other inhabitants wouldn't have taken

kindly to seeing them slaughtered, for they were also
a part of Chengtu's soul, a genuine social class, an
age-old institution, almost an adornment—though one
not to be seen by the noble guests brought here by
the railroad. What amazes me the most is that the
other carrion, those with no legs on which to take
themselves off, those who are nothing but lumps of
ordure, precious tanks of excrement, spreading streams
of pestilence, ragged remains of flesh and bone, unnamable substances, horrible liquids, reeking matter—
all these have vanished, too. Chengtu had spruced
itself up, had a great spring cleaning, and made the
acquaintance of hygiene for the first time in all its
centuries of history. But how? Tang Kiao must have
given strict orders to bring about this result. Isn't dirt
a part of morality, and cleanliness a bee in the bonnet
of the barbarians? Again I make inquiries. And I'm
told that all the morning, while we were still sleeping
off the ball at the French consulate, the whole population had been galvanized into action. Armed patrols appeared at dawn in every street and alley, with bayonets
fixed and revolvers aimed, and told the people of
Chengtu what Tang Kiao wanted: 'Anyone who two
hours from now hasn't cleaned the street in front of
his house, and taken away any dirt or unseemly
rubbish lying there, will get two hundred strokes.
Anyone showing reluctance or serious negligence will
be shot on the very spot he has failed to clean properly.' There was no arguing with the soldiers, not even
to save such sacred merchandise as the tubs of human
excrement, which on Tang Kiao's instructions were
specifically classified as 'unseemly.' The attitude of
the troops was so firm that with the aid of a few
bayonets they got the whole population working like
a swarm of ants attacking a bone, as an old Chinese

expression puts it. In two hours, as laid down, the town looked as if it had been disinfected, despite the lack of water and tools. From naked children of three to centenarian grandmothers in rags, everyone worked like mad, with whole streets of bent backs and people passing things from hand to hand. But one thing I don't understand. What did the diligent population do with all the rubbish they collected from the streets? Where did they put all that putrid stuff? It was because there was nowhere else for it to go that the streets had always been its natural receptacle. I think the answer is this: by an ingenious device fully worthy of the locals' intelligence, when doomed to sanitation they offered hospitality inside their own houses and hovels, where they themselves crowded to live and eat and sleep, to the rubbish hidden at the behest of the formidable Tang Kiao. And when the time comes and the governor general and his entourage have finally gone, they'll put it back where it was before, in the streets, together with what has accumulated meanwhile. This domestication of 'unseemly' objects is the best possible tactic in this difficulty, especially as it's also the best way of saving all the valuable dung that will fertilize next season's harvests.

"So that's how Chengtu has been made so neat, and even not too nauseating, which is very surprising when you think that every house is really a chamber pot and rubbish dump. But the governor general doesn't know this, nor do all the important people loafing in his train. I'm standing by, attentive but discreet, not too absent but not too assertive, to tell him about Chengtu. His wife, too, who's not all that feather-brained and is probably quite good on material trifles, she says to me with some acumen, 'It doesn't

stink as much as all that—not even a whiff of crap.
And I'd soaked handkerchiefs in lavender water to
stop my nose when it started to smell of burst sewer.
But I'm told there aren't any sewers. So how do these
Chinese of yours manage to do their business without
stinking the place up?" The governor's preoccupations
are of a more lofty order. 'My friend,' he says to me,
'what strikes me is how down in the mouth the natives look as I go by. In Indochina the people give
me a much warmer welcome—absolutely resounding.
I'm seriously beginning to wonder if the citizens of
Chengtu don't really like me, despite the benefits of
my railroad. What can I have done to make them like
this?' I'm counting ten before answering, when I'm
saved by the first show of enthusiasm, just as we leave
the working-class area to enter the shopping streets.
At the top of the street of the apothecaries we pass under a triumphal arch decked with leaves and erected in
our honor by the apothecaries themselves. On both
sides of the paved street the most eminent leaders of
the medical guild, noble old gentlemen in antique
dress, fold their hands and bow slowly and solemnly
to the ground. The whole alley where medicines are
sold is aflame with welcoming banners: as a supreme
touch of consideration there are lots of French flags.
Firecrackers start to sputter like sparks of joy. The
governor's heart is uplifted in a trice. 'My dear consul,
please tell these good people that I thank them with
all my heart, in the name of France. Tell them how
touched I am, congratulate them. . . .' I translate
this emotion in much less moving terms, so as not
to look like an idiot before these conscripted Chinks.
But deep down inside it's to Tang Kiao, who thinks
of everything, that I address my thanks.

"Our expedition becomes really splendid when we

enter, still in the same formation, with soldiers fore and aft, the main streets where luxury goods are sold, the local equivalents of the Rue de la Paix and the Rue Saint-Honoré; these have made Chengtu famous throughout China. The streets of silk, of jade, of jewels, of treasures, of silver, of yellow gold, of porcelain, the ancient street of bronze, the streets of antique prints, of royal garments, of sacred seals, of prayer wheels, of furs from the Roof of the World, of beneficent Buddhas. Everywhere there are triumphal arches, bowing lines of rich old gentlemen, banners. Our ladies and gentlemen, especially the first, become unrecognizable as they are suddenly seized with passion: their well-bred faces assume the expressions of looters or of housewives at a sale. They set out on the great curio hunt—'curio' is a nasty word invented by the Europeans in Shanghai to denote all the Chinese marvels they covet and pretend to despise. But there's no hypocrisy about it in Chengtu. It's just a mad rush, with frantic wives dragging husbands uneasy about their wallets into shops that look like empty holes but are very capacious inside. The Chinese merchants, without even speaking, their features equally mute and their movements so agile and subtle they seem motionless, draw out of unlocked lacquer boxes, with hands soft as caresses, objects that they bring lovingly to the light, and into the vulgar sight of all these people. It's an almost voluptuous ceremony, which I know very well, and its effect is to spur the ladies on to greater excess than before. They can hardly keep still, they're almost in a frenzy. The governor general's wife leads the charge. She has decorated her little head with a tiara of kingfishers' feathers, greenest of greens, absolutely smooth, green as night, as a deep lake, the green of tragic sternness and fatal beauty, the green of princesses who must die. But the governor general's wife only looks like a shopgirl on the spree. She plunges her hands in heaps of rings, bracelets, and necklaces set with amber and turquoise, some heavy as chains, others fine threads of silver or gold. Without fear she winds around her neck a snake of red gold which completely obliterates her bosom, and hangs her fingers with magic rings engraved with skeletons. In the midst of all this she gurgles with delight, 'I've always been mad about jewelry.' The governor general shakes his head, resigned. The other ladies, wives of civil servants, are more sensible and parsimonious, and they are interested mostly in the brocades, already imagining the dresses they'll have made back in Hanoi by a cheap half-breed dressmaker, or examine drapes that would look nice in their best drawing room. The husbands tend to prefer distinguished antiques, some terra-cotta or funerary statue, trying to tell its period and pronouncing it solemnly to be a Tang or a Ming. The governor general doesn't say anything, except, after an hour, 'How much?' It's left to me to conduct the negotiations. So I gird up my loins for the great pretense of bargaining, at which, I must admit, I'm pretty good. But to my great surprise the owner of the most famous shop, a fat, slippery old devil who reminds me of a bullfrog, answers in a voice as quiet as the rustle of his padded robe, distantly, as if he's thinking about something else: "I should not wish to bother such illustrious visitors over a few trifles; their coming to my unworthy shop is priceless in itself. We can settle mere financial questions tomorrow or the next day, or next week, or any time.' This makes me suspect a trap—that I'll be charged exorbitant prices when I come to settle accounts for my whole little party. But it's not that, as I see when I insist almost rudely on paying here and now, and he remains invincibly serene. He doesn't want to be paid at all. Then I understand: Tang Kiao has told him that he'll pay himself, or in other words he won't hand over a penny. Such is Tang Kiao's generosity, a secret generosity that costs him nothing, because it's the merchant himself who'll get the worst of it. What's more, he'll pay for it with his life—or more likely with an enormous amount of taels—if he plays any tricks. That's why the merchant, a typical Chinese knowing he's in trouble and not wanting to make it worse, looks almost happy while we skin him. As a matter of fact, I'm in trouble, too. What if I were to tell the governor general about these Chinese subtleties that in the end make us thieves? Would he understand? And if he got angry and insisted on paying for everything then and there, it would be disastrous—unseemly behavior, a great insult to Tang Kiao, who's been so kind to us. Thinking it all over, I decide to say nothing. Moreover, the governor, flapping from his noble countenance the flies that have had the impudence to survive Tang Kiao's hygiene campaign, has had enough. He wants to go home. To get it over quickly, he sets up his own generosity against that of Tang Kiao, all unbeknown to him. 'My dear consul,' he says, 'I consider these purcheses as part of the official expenses involved in my inaugural visit to Chengtu. Give the bill to me, or send it to me in Hanoi. I'll send you the money out of my entertainment allowance or the contingency fund.'

"When the ladies, and their husbands, too, realize that the bill's going to be footed by graft, they raid the neighboring shops as well. The honorable merchants welcome them with exquisite smiles and let them help themselves. Their places are sacked. Then, when they've taken on all they can, the ladies and gentlemen, collapsing under the marvels they've collected, the chief private secretary heaving a perfume brazier along like a coolie, all go and unload into the empty sedan chairs, which now become the equivalent of trucks. We return home like a victorious army, laden with the spoils of the town. When we get to the consulate the chief private secretary, who's in charge of delicate financial matters, gives me instructions about how to draw up the bill. I know the instructions are superfluous because I'll never send the bill. I'll sort things out with Tang Kiao."

My father remained stretched out on the couch. The darkness all about him had gone still. The murmur of Chengtu, a murmur of life that never stopped, had almost died away. You had to guess at the sounds of the Chinese city. The silence drew Monsieur le Consul out of his imaginary odyssey. He felt alone. But opening his eyes, with a sort of cloudy lucidity he saw the head boy there, not doing anything any more, just waiting for orders. It was really time for Albert Bonnard to go to bed. But he signaled the servant to go on. He wanted to be happier still, to reach a delirium of make-believe. He drew in the smoke until the dream returned, wilder than ever.

"Next day it's the picnic, an absolutely indispensable element in the organization of a governor general's official visit. The place I've chosen is a little agate-colored lake among wild but pleasant mountains with steep and flowery slopes; there's a wood with a pagoda where we can shelter if there's a storm. It's here that all the French people in Chengtu—always the same group: my wife and I, the medicos, sometimes a priest —go for picnics when there aren't too many brigands or soldiers about. The houseboys are sent on in advance to get everything ready—the crockery and knives and forks, the camping equipment, the bedding, the chairs, the various dainties. It's all very free and easy. I'm no longer the consul, we drink the wine as it comes out of the bottle, we sing songs, sometimes we dress up. We get ourselves up as Chinese, in long robes, and one day one of the doctors dressed as a 'little flower,' really artistic it was, with tennis balls for breasts, though they were much too big for those of a Chinese woman. Anne Marie wears a queerish smile when that kind of thing happens. People think I'm very amusing. After our nap we pay a little visit to the monks; we slip them a coin or two, and they welcome us as friends. All very simple.

"But in honor of the governor general we really clear the decks for action, and a whole caravan sets out from Chengtu. This time the ladies and the older gentlemen go in chairs, with a hundred or so porters taking turns carrying them, shouting and grimacing as if they weighed a ton. The governor general is perched in a magnificent litter especially sent for him by Tang Kiao. I'm on horseback, keeping an eye on everything, giving orders, trying to get them all to move. Those younger civil servants who have chosen to ride hang on to their saddles, for the little Chinese horses are extremely mettlesome. One great bean pole whose feet touch the ground manages only by using his legs as props. Anne Marie, who didn't want to be shut up in a chair like the other ladies, is riding sidesaddle, watching me. 'Don't be such a busybody, Albert,' she murmurs. But in fact my efforts serve to introduce a bit of order into all this chaos of men and beasts, all these Chinamen, coolies, mafus, and porters, pushing and shoving and insulting one another in their usual manner, so that the Europeans, whether in the chairs or on horseback, look like corks bobbing about on a stormy yellow sea. But at ten in the morning the column, after several false starts and various confused and inexplicable agitations, actually moves off, with incredible energy, smoothness, and regularity. All is well. Tang Kiao hasn't been stingy about security for the governor general: there are five hundred soldiers in front and five hundred behind, and machine guns carried on mules. Enough to inspire a healthy respect. The previous evening, twenty house-boys and cooks set out proudly to form a gastronomic advance guard—the pick of the Chinese turnspits under the illustrious direction of Mr. Pu, head chef at the consulate, his face like a corrugated sphere, a prince of domestics who never loses his head, never shows any feeling, and is always perfect. He considers himself the great master of Western tastes and will no longer take orders from Anne Marie; all she's allowed to do is suggest a menu each day. If she says one word too much he is very annoyed; his loss of 'face' shows itself in the fact that he still looks like a round balloon, but one weighted with unexpressed indignation. He's been having the time of his life since the governor general arrived in Cheng-tu. His great triumph was to set off yesterday evening to prepare the rustic banquet, riding in a litter, like a lord ruling over a host of servants walking on foot, and accompanied by a colossal larder borne by coolies. His importance is increased even more by the fact that he's going to be dealing with mysterious foodstuffs from the ends of the earth: the choicest products of France, which impress people and give those who offer them a lift up the social scale (at least among people in the colonial service, who regard local food as cheap and second rate, even when it's of excellent quality and well prepared). So today there'll be a veritable culinary revolution, with fat pullets from Bresse, soles from the Channel, salt-meadow lamb, and Cavaillon melons. All this stuff from the Paris markets on which Mr. Pu is to exercise his skill is yet another benefit derived from my railroad, which has continued to work well throughout the last few days. Thus, thanks to my trains, the day of the diplomatic bag up the Yangtze is over; apart from documents, it could only be used for canned stuff, because of the length and uncertainties of the journey, and canned food is bad for the intestines in the long run—dries them up. From now on we shall be able to eat fresh food; it will make a great difference to life in general, and specifically to the picnic. So everything is there ready and waiting, and our procession moves steadily forward toward a first-class blowout, worthy of Maxim's—a Maxim's in the mountains of Szechwan, graced by the governor general of Indochina. . . .

"All is well. Our caravan, at first very strung out because of the narrowness of the Chengtu streets, passes under the great west gate, where I notice there are no heads exposed in cages, or any of the other bloody trophies usually to be seen there. Tang Kiao really has thought of everything. Then we set out in great style along a paved road, where we make rapid progress. The soldiers in front clear a way for us by shoving aside into the muddy rice fields the ceaseless stream of humanity we encounter—peasant women with yokes, men with barrows, porters, beasts of burden. Animals, people, the loads they are carrying, all collapse into the water without even daring to protest.

I sense that the worthy governor general is rather shocked by this zeal, and I ride forward to the officer in charge to try to get him to moderate it. But despite my repeated explanations, I come up against an obstinately unmoving face, the face of a soldier bound by discipline. He's a colonel, and he thinks I'm not showing a proper appreciation of his ardor. He's offended, the discussion works up into an argument, and I think it best to withdraw, putting the best face on it I can. But what am I to tell the governor? As chance would have it, at about this moment, as if they'd spread the word among them, the people on the road all start to take their own precautions, and stand aside for us to pass—true, they're standing up to the waist in slush, but it's all organized; they don't get hit, and their burdens don't get spoiled. And so a whole crowd, drenched, mere shapes covered with earth and slime, watch us go by in our splendor. I take the opportunity to whisper to the governor general: 'It wouldn't have been correct according to Chinese etiquette for someone as august as yourself to be incommoded by the common people as he went by. But I've persuaded the escort provided by Tang Kiao—part of his own guard of honor—to be more gentle from now on.' The governor is pleased. But he soon has other things to think about. Our party now leaves the road and goes along narrow dikes— thin outcrops of earth rising out of the realm of water, the lumps of floating turf, the black mud, the reeking expanses of green rice shoots stretching as far as the eye can see, interspersed with water-lily leaves. Even these thin films of solidity, on which the procession itself thins out to a file some two kilometers long, are oozing and waterlogged, and almost as uncertain as the besieging sheets of water they cut across.

Before long there's a terrible mix-up, the horses' hoofs
and the porters' feet all intermingling, slipping and
sliding and spinning around, but all righting themselves in time, the animals whinnying and the coolies
laughing. Meanwhile they have inflicted awful tilts
and tremors and dizzy spells on some European lady
or gentleman, who feels quite isolated in the sedan
chair or the saddle, as the case may be, and can
already see himself or herself ignominiously pitched
into the watery kingdom. But it's really an artificial
disorder and an artificial danger, for both the Chinese
and their animals have a prodigious sense of balance
and extraordinary strength. Perhaps they're amusing
themselves a little at the expense of these 'barbarians'
stuck up there in their pride like Buddhas in their
shrines. More probably their maneuvers are merely
intended to bring out the difficulty of their work, so
that in due course they can ask for a few more pennies.
But to a foreigner unused to these gymnastics, it's
terrifying. The white faces of the Europeans have
gone even whiter, with the exception of that of the
governor general's wife, who looks as if she's enjoying
herself on a gondola at a fair. But her husband,
crouching inside his splendid red box—red is the
imperial color—is in a cold sweat. The Chinese colonel
casually signals some of his soldiers to come, with their
bayonets, to the rescue of the Europeans. Their
appearance instantly restores absolute calm among
the porters, coolies, mafus, and even the animals.
They go on again in a rhythm so smooth and regular
that the bearers' legs seem like pistons. It's like a
human train. But it's at this moment that an accident
occurs. A chair overturns, and a smart young European lady pitches headfirst into the rice paddy, where
she remains struggling with her face in the mud and

her behind in the air, arms and legs flailing like a
frog in a vain effort to free herself. The other ladies
and gentlemen alight from their various means of
transportation to form a rescue party. The gentlemen,
after getting the poor thing out of her embarrassing
situation, turn their backs and form a cordon around
her to protect her modesty. This is all the more
necessary as it would be very shocking, even in its
political implications, for any Chink to catch a
glimpse of the flesh of a white woman, especially that
of a 'civil servant's lady.' Inside the enclosure, Anne
Marie and two or three other matrons clean up the
victim, who isn't hurt but looks like a Negress. She
doesn't make a fuss while the other ladies scrape off
several pounds of nauseating mud, for she's only the
wife of a very junior official. In fact, her husband
manages to come up to her and whisper, 'Whatever
you do, don't complain and upset the governor general.' Finally she puts on some underwear and a dress
Anne Marie has brought along in case of accidents,
and gives a heroic smile. Again all is in perfect order.
Again the ladies and gentlemen take their places in
the air, and the coolies take their places on the ground
below them. The column moves off again.

"What wouldn't the governor general give now
to be driving along in Indochina in his official car
on one of the fine colonial highways constructed by
French genius through swamps and mountains! After
having confronted the realm of Neptune, where he
risked no more than a dousing, he faces death and
the abyss if his bearers make the slightest false step.
The caravan is now going along a mountain track.
Before that the path went peacefully through a forest;
not impenetrable jungle—that doesn't extend right
into the heart of Szechwan—but a sort of natural

cathedral. A gentle slope is covered with regular columns, trunks like pillars supporting a roof. A hundred feet above the earth stretches a smooth expanse of leaves, below which is an odoriferous emptiness, a sort of holy space, a semidarkness full of glossy bushes and the bright red globes of flowers. But once this natural sanctuary is left behind, the real China suddenly reveals itself, dangerous even in its texture. Earth like risen dough—cracked, fissured, pustular. It, too, is splendid—but terrifying. Mountains like suddenly frozen breakers; like great crazy balloons; like wild beasts about to leap, with horns and teeth and claws; mountains slit with wounds; mountains like smooth and endless precipices, with just a few oozing patches of vegetation. Mountains made in the image of the Dragon Empire, full of mystery and contradiction. A jumble of dream and nightmare. Here steely granite, there funereal sandstone, somewhere else limestone that is porous, cracked, crumbling, honeycombed with caves—more like ruins than mountains. There is every color, too, from blood red to ebony black, either in patches or in streaks. Overhead, raveling clouds. No valleys, but everywhere gulfs, deep and narrow clefts, lacerations with depths you cannot see but rivers whose low murmurs you can hear. Here the path we follow is no more than a notch in the side of a cliff, which it climbs in crazy zigzags. The gravely path just affords room for the porters' feet, but scarcely enough for the sedan chairs carefully balanced with their burdens of ladies and gentlemen; at the bends in the path, on one side they scrape against the side of the mountain and on the other they overhang the canyon. The porters are strangely tense: as they climb, they utter regular raucous rattles, a kind of hereditary breathing. On their foreheads a vein stands out, indicating the concentration and thought necessary for each step, to choose where and how to pause safely for a fraction of a second until the next foothold has been selected among the bristling rocks, the sliding heaps of scree, the crumbling patches ready to subside. The coolies' eyes are fixed and staring as they pick their way along. The animals, too, are solemn, making the same sort of calculations. There is silence throughout the whole caravan as it climbs smoothly. It's so long, though, that it has to twist and turn to follow the meanderings of the path around outcrops and indentations in the face of the cliff. The only sounds are the grunts of the porters and the brief orders of the foremen telling them when to change shifts. An impressive silence reigns: now and then, when a hoof or a foot stumbles, you can hear a stone go hurtling and ricocheting down the mountainside, to be swallowed up soundlessly in the depths. Every time this happens the governor general trembles, as do all the other Europeans whether on horseback or in chairs; they picture themselves pitched into the abyss. As a matter of fact, there is no danger at all, so used are the horny-footed coolies to this sort of thing—to negotiating mountains and chasms carrying enormous loads along faint tracks worn by millions and millions of other feet before them. My fellows are young and stuffed with rice; they could carry the governor general as if he were a straw from one end of China to the other. I wouldn't have endangered the rest of my career if there'd been the slightest risk of the governor general or one of his followers ending up in a thousand pieces at the foot of a precipice. I myself have traveled about so much in China that this is a very ordinary little climb. I must admit, though, that this isn't the governor general's view: in the end he's so frightened he abandons himself to his fate and shuts his eyes so as not to see it coming.

"At last we get to the top, a kind of bare plateau, a flat expanse polished by the rain and the wind. I announce that my lake isn't far now, and my picknickers take courage. But they collapse again a bit farther on when the caravan stops at a break in the surface of the earth, a narrow shadowy cleft whose depth is indicated only by a froth of white foam far below. The one way over this awful crevasse is across a bridge about a hundred yards long and made of vines; it curves right down in the middle and sways in the slightest breeze. There's no handrail, and once you're on it it creaks and trembles and gives. But despite the way it looks there's no danger, unless the vines have rotted. Yesterday I told Mr. Pu to check. But did he do it? I'd better have an inspection made here and now. I call out for the caravan to stop, and order an examination. All my Chinks, soldiers and servants alike, pull a face at the prospect of this extra work. They are peculiar people: usually they'll do anything to live, to survive, but often, out of laziness, they'll gamble with existence. They'd rather risk their lives than bother with what might be unnecessary effort. They have a very curious sense of economy. As a result they'll use a thing until it wears right out, especially if it's public property; nothing is mended until it actually breaks, and then it's replaced. If somebody gets killed, it's just too bad.

"But of course I can't afford to lose my governor general like that. While the whole long line of Chinamen crouch down, as if about to relieve themselves, in an attitude of mocking expectation, like a paralyzed caterpillar with its bristles stroked the wrong way, the governor general, a vexed bigwig remembering his own importance, remarks to me irritably, 'What's the matter? Deplorable organization, Monsieur le Consul. Where on earth have you dragged me to? This sort of thing is very bad for my health.' His civil staff stand around him, their expressions reinforcing what as yet, in their worthy chief, is only peevishness. I stammer, 'It's nothing, sir—just a small precaution,' and start to prod my Chinks. The colonel gives very martial orders to his men to check the safety of the bridge. But what confidence can one have in soldiers who, apart from their skill with the bayonet, are laziness personified? So I summon the foreman of my coolies, and spur them on with the promise of an extra tip. From the start they've racked their brains and tried every possible way of obtaining an addition to the little gift they always get anyway at the end of the day. My promise transforms them, fills them with enthusiasm. They rush to work as fast as they can, examining with animal intensity every inch of the span which hangs there like a narrow, worm-eaten old hammock. They sound the fibers with eyes, feet, and hands, stopping at the least doubt and dangling in space to check the top, the underneath, the sides, and to strengthen or tie up the weak parts with bits of wood and reed and string. Finally the head boy bows to me, with his hands on his heart to show he is telling the truth, and says we can cross. 'My dear consul,' barks the haggard governor general, who would like to retreat, 'you do realize the responsibility. . . .' But I stick to my guns. 'I have complete trust in what the head boy says. Besides, we can't go back now without losing "face" vis-à-vis all Chengtu and the whole of Szechwan.' 'Oh, well, in that case . . .' His Excellency obeys the call of duty, but doesn't seem too well disposed toward me for seeming to gamble his life on the word of a Chinese domestic. How could I make him understand that a gamble depending on the guarantee of a conscientious head servant spurred on by the prospect of reward is the only kind of gamble that's absolutely safe in China? Anyhow, during this aside, the column has re-formed, set itself in motion again, and begun to absorb and swallow and get the better of the passageway in question. In front, the soldiers run and caper about like monkeys as they go across, no doubt to mock us and our alarms and precautions. Next over the jiggling contraption of vines goes the heavy equipment—horses led by their mafus, empty chairs, and all the usual impedimenta of Europeans. All passes across quite easily and without trouble, as if the bridge were not merely suspended over empty space. Lastly comes the string of ladies and gentlemen in single file, about thirty of them, all moving stiffly like clockwork toys, with expressionless faces and clenched teeth, trying to look calm and brave. The ladies are quite stoical. Only the governor's lady doesn't have to make an effort—she's enjoying herself hugely. The governor, propped up in front by me and behind by the chief private secretary, totters forward like an ancient doll, his eyes cast upward, with only enough strength to groan, 'Never again, never again!' Suddenly he stops as if the machinery's broken down, and refuses to budge. What on earth am I to do? If he just stays like that he'll fall. Then his wife sings out to him like a camp follower, 'Come on, Pettikins, show what kind of man you are!' This marital admonition has a wonderfully tonic effect on the governor, who completes the crossing with his dignity restored.

"After that we're on terra firma again, but this time with a marvelous view. Here is my lake, an expanse of

dark and limpid water without a ripple, clasped in
the smooth and majestic embrace of reassuring hills—
mountains not strange or forbidding in shape, but
like great tame beasts with sides that bid you welcome.
Forests, brooks, the springing of scent and sap, perfect
peace, life—even if Mr. Pu and his men are at first
the only living creatures in sight. But they must have
been working like ten thousand devils. Their hell
consists of flaming ovens roasting huge masses of
meat, which have attracted the little monks from the
nearby monastery with their bowls. Mr. Pu chases
them away when we arrive, and stands before us—the
governor, the ladies, and me—with a mixture of the
humblest respect and justifiable pride, in the immaculate white robe of the high priest of good fare. In a
cradle of greenery at the foot of a slope that climbs
gently but interminably up to where its peak wreathes
itself in a halo of thin clouds, Mr. Pu has spread his
banquet where the gentle slope enters the waves of the
lake. The edges of the water shine blindingly white
with quartz and crystal hewn by nature into oblongs
and other geometrical shapes. On a flat part of the
bank Mr. Pu has made a clearing among the clumps
of rhododendron and beds of wild lilies, and in the
center of this stands the table, for which Mr. Pu
has brought the finest linen, the most delicate china,
and the heaviest silver plate the French consulate
affords. He promised Anne Marie, who is very fond
and proud of all these things, that he would supervise
the porters so fiercely that nothing would get broken,
and nothing has. He has even set out the place cards
exactly according to my instructions, without any
mistakes. These little cards are very important to Mr.
Pu. While the governor and the ladies and gentlemen
seat themselves according to the rules of etiquette, our

soldiers and coolies spread out in groups, some mounting guard while others light fires to cook the rice, which they stir with their bayonets. The landscape is transformed into a camp devoted to gastronomy, ranging from the sumptuous offerings of Mr. Pu to the forage provided for the mules. Every stomach prepares to be filled, every nostril enjoys delicious whiffs. The yellow faces are solemn at the prospect, for I've done things handsomely, and given both the colonel and the foreman of the coolies enough to improve their men's rations by the honest purchase of suckling pigs in the hamlets we passed through; the inhabitants had expected looting, and were most relieved to be able to trade instead. Now there's a general uproar—the shrieks of pigs being slaughtered. But this is music, joy, to Chinese ears. I am surrounded by China in a state of bliss. Everything is perfect.

"Everything except the banquet. As soon as we arrive, the governor general collapses on his chair like a pricked balloon. Has he fainted? It might offend him if I ask our doctor from Chengtu, who I made sure was with us, to examine him. I look for guidance toward the governor general's staff, but they are careful to give no sign of any opinion. At last the governor's lady pats him on the cheek, and these caresses bring him back to life. But he doesn't utter a word; just flops there red in the face and breathing with difficulty. And when a governor general doesn't talk, no one likes to try and make conversation around him. The duly arranged ladies and gentlemen pointedly remain silent. Even the governor's lady herself doesn't chatter. I decide heroically to adopt a playful tone and tell a few little anecdotes about China that I personally find rather funny. But they fall flat, and the governor finally speaks and says, 'I've had China,

up to the eyebrows.' There's a heavy silence. Under
Mr. Pu's watchful eye, the boys follow each other in
constant procession bearing the dishes he's prepared,
skillful examples of Western cuisine. But alas, all the
rare delicacies brought from Paris to Chengtu thanks
to my railroad are failures. The pullets from Bresse
taste like cardboard, the salt-meadow lamb isn't fresh,
and the Channel soles are half rotten. 'Pah!' says the
governor at the first mouthful, and spits it out onto
his plate. Anne Marie is pale with embarrassment.
What finally helps to save the situation are those
two pillars of the colonies, Camembert and Beaujolais.
For wherever there are Frenchmen, even in the wildest
and most distant part of the Celestial Empire, even
in a jungle or a desert, they always manage to get these
two things sent to them, and they lavish all kinds of
imagination on the providential and almost miraculous consignments. My compatriots in China claim,
often with justification, that they get on better than
the other Europeans with the Chinese. But you ought
to see them with one of these mysteriously transported
parcels of cheeses and bottles! The leers, the appetite,
the jubilation, the flood of opinions, judgments, com-
parisons, memories, and longings—and the display of
technical knowledge! The erudition! For them it's the
profoundest form of intellectualism. At the Sporting
Club in Shanghai they spend more time expatiating
on Camembert and its varieties and peculiarities than
on any other subject, even including sex and money.
And its appearance now at this depressing lakeside
picnic serves, together with a little red vino, to revive
somewhat the living-dead company. And yet this
cheap, rather grainy wine is far inferior to the famous
vintages that have gone before, served with the appropriate ceremony. But those sacred nectars, which cost

me as much as if they'd been liquid gold, were left lying in all those dozens of glasses, the guests saying disapprovingly that they didn't travel well, while this rough red wine of mine is swilled down in gulps. The governor general brightens up as he swigs it to wash down the Camembert, which itself flows pretty freely, oozing out of its boxes in nauseating putrefaction. It's a stench worthy even of China, but even China with all its stinks hasn't come across this one before, and the waiters have to make an effort not to turn up their noses with disgust. It must be admitted that my cheese is definitely ripe! But all is jollity now, with people making the old jokes tried and tested all over Asia, wherever Frenchmen meet for a blowout. The governor general wittily observes that if he used a Camembert as a litter he could go back to Chengtu without the slightest risk of attack. The thought of the return journey, with all the supposed difficulties, which he can already see again in his mind's eye, haunts him. But he laughs, good-natured now rather than irritable, and as if to give himself courage in advance, guzzles glass after glass of Beaujolais and sinks his teeth into the Camembert. His lady, who so far has been sitting beside me like a good little girl, now wears an excited grin which suggests she's about to try one of her tricks. I'm not mistaken; she starts to lisp and cluck like a hen: 'Poor little consul, your picnic hasn't exactly been a riot, has it? Not your fault, but dull! A lot of stuffed dummies. Just like with the President of the Republic or the Emperor of Annam, the old boy, when my husband keeps dinning into me hours beforehand that I mustn't open my mouth. Not that he has such interesting things to say. But those deaf-mutes don't give you a Camembert like this one, so nice and gooey, like cream. It reminds me of something—puts ideas in my head.' These sibylline words are greeted with complete silence. Not in the least embarrassed, she continues to wriggle about, and goes on: 'I'm fed up with sitting still. I'm going to stretch my legs. Go for a little stroll to walk my lunch off.' Whereupon she gets up with a rustle of skirts and goes off gaily, wiggling her hips, toward the nearest bushes, signaling her favorite aide-de-camp to accompany her. Her husband is in no condition to object; his original exhaustion has passed, but been succeeded, with the aid of the Beaujolais, by a restorative slumber, and he is snoring with his head on the table, a happy expression on his face. But the lady and her gallant have scarcely gone ten steps when about forty soldiers, arms at the ready, start up from behind a bush and begin to follow her at a respectful distance. 'What's this?' she bawls. 'Am I a prisoner?' I put on an air of cautious regret and explain that it has nothing to do with me—it must be the Chinese colonel looking out for himself, for if anything happened to her, with all the bandits there may be about . . . She's furious. But I pretend not to understand, and instead of begging and praying and wilting under her displeasure, I just say, 'Why don't we go and see the pagoda? To make up for your missing your little stroll? It's very unusual and pretty.' She replies just as curtly. 'Some entertainment. You know what you can do with your pagoda. Tonkin's lousy with rotten old Buddhas. I can't stand the sight of them.' But I go on touting the pagoda in my smoothest manner. 'You won't regret going to see it, Madame. It's a very famous monastery, and lots of pilgrims who visit it in despair come away rejoicing. It's got a giant statue of Buddha made of red gold; its navel is an emerald as big as a saucer. And anyone afflicted in mind or body who rubs himself against that stone is said to be cured immediately. The place is a kind of Lourdes without the waters.' 'You won't catch me that way. Monsieur le Consul,' she answers. 'I'm in the pink of health physically, and as for loose screws—keep it! You and your Lourdes for Chinks! But perhaps you have a reason for being so enthusiastic? Perhaps the Buddha's naval cured you of some unmentionable disease? I can just see you rubbing your poor thingamabob on the famous emerald. . . .' The slut laughs her head off, until the governor stops her by saying, 'Don't talk like that, my dear—you'll make me angry. Please forgive her, my dear consul. She's fond of a joke, but she doesn't mean any harm.' I just go on reciting my learned catalogue. 'And there's a staggering representation of hell, the most fantastic ever imagined—the hell of ten thousand tortures. In a dim room lit with torches you find yourself face to face with a fresco twenty yards long— a nightmare showing people of every age and sex being tortured in colors and relief, and in incredible detail. All seething and trickling and swarming and oozing from limbs chopped off or burned, with orgies of meticulous gestures, in dazzling colors, especially the blood which is spurting everywhere. The torturers hacking up the human flesh, using innumerable different instruments, have the peaceful faces of conscientious workmen plying their trade. Something you ought to see, believe me. And you'll discover there are a lot more positions for torture than there are for love. It also tells you a good deal about the Chinese mentality—in Europe, despite the efforts of our ancestors, we've never reached such levels of invention in atrocity. But the pious monks of the temple surpassed themselves in this picture of Gehenna, trying to demonstrate in no uncertain fashion what's in store for the faithful if they don't observe the law of Buddha, especially as regards generosity toward the servants of God.' 'Thanks very much,'' says the governor's wife. 'So I'm supposed to fork out for these idolators so as not to roast in their hell. But I'm already provided with a hell, and the one my fine priests promise me for nothing is quite enough. And what's more, I don't happen to be mad or perverted, and all the nasty things you suggest I should get an eyeful of don't tempt me, even if it makes your voice tremble just to describe them. Torture, always torture—that's all you ever mention in your entertainments. No, thanks very much—you can keep that sort of pleasure.' Then another soothing intervention from the governor general: 'Darling, don't be so disagreeable to Monsieur le Consul, who's going to so much trouble to amuse us and show us China. Don't be cross with her, my dear fellow. She's a bit sharp sometimes, but she means well.' I remain impassive. I know I'll hook the whore in the end; I've got a plan. I've worked out something that can't fail. So I go on quite calmly with my exposition. 'The monks are especially famous for a certain strange, almost inexplicable power, which they guard very jealously—a power much stronger than that attributed to the Third Eye. Nothing is easier, if you ask politely, than for them to reveal your whole future.' 'Spare me that,' says the governor's lady, attempting to cover her temptation with hostility. 'As you may imagine, ever since I've been in Indochina I've tried plenty of these nutty fortunetellers, male and female, with their powders and straws and bits of intestine and other offal, and their grass that turns to dust, and their ridiculous prayers, incantations as they call them, as if I had a thousand husbands all snoring away at once. And their dreary dances in honor of the spirits—enough to frighten away the Holy Ghost himself. I've even tried magicians, all yellower than nature made them and thin as rakes. And all these prophets aren't worth a damn. Not one of them is as good as my concierge on the Rue des Abbesses in Paris. When I was a little milliner working for myself in Montmartre, she consulted her crystal ball and her tarot cards and told me I was going to marry an elderly gentleman, but that he would be kind and have medals—in other words, Pettikins!'

"But I, scenting victory, go on mildly but obstinately. 'I think I can say without boasting, Madame, that this time you won't be disappointed. These monks really have what I don't hesitate to call a supernatural gift. They don't just tell or foretell your fate—they make it rise up before you visibly, like photographs of the future. Astonishing!' The governor's lady still pretends not to be interested, but in fact she's well and truly caught. 'You mean to say I can see what I shall be like five or ten years from now? Not widowed, I hope, or too middle-aged. I can tell you now, I'll shut my eyes if these monks of yours conjure me up as a shaky little old woman—I'll refuse to recognize myself. I want to see myself still young and desirable. Well, consul, I don't believe in your magic, but I'm willing to try it.' So I get my own way at last, as I usually do—especially with the ladies.

"It's only about a quarter of a mile away, but the governor general goes in his chair, while the rest of the company walk, like conscientious tourists. Halfway there we come to the start of a path leading to the temple, a royal way made of great regular stones carefully fitted together, venerable slabs all alike and very hard, but each polished and even hollowed in the middle by the feet of worshiping crowds. But today the road is deserted, as if the faithful had been driven away to make room for us. As we advance we are guarded on either side of the giant roadway by beasts of granite—lions, phoenixes, unicorns, and even elephants, posted as sentinels of piety. And in addition to this divine protection, we have of course that of our soldiers following behind. But whereas they usually chatter like magpies, here on the Avenue of Heavenly Peace they are silent, as if they felt their presence to be sacrilegious. The way leads up a gentle slope and in among the foliage of age-old tutelary trees, mossy and beneficent, forming an inner enclosure. The sacred wood, like the increasing number of sculptured animals, shows we are approaching the pagoda. As I march gaily along, I tell myself that this time the monks are going to pull out all the stops. I know these tonsured rascals: if they don't manage to fleece rich pilgrims completely with their divine tricks and religious mumbo-jumbo, they have them captured afterward and stripped of what's left by bandits who are their accomplices or in their pay. But I know that for my guests the rogues are going to put on a big show, the works. In their case I haven't relied on Tang Kiao to inspire them with enthusiasm, for without plenty of good hard cash this mob wouldn't put themselves out even if the chief war lord threatened them with punishment and torture. They're the only people in Szechwan who don't give a damn for the terrible Tang Kiao, who regard him as a blustering old blimp, a moth-eaten and impotent bully. The general run of monks, monkesses, and monklets in their saffron-yellow robes, the color of humility, with their naked skulls bearing the sacred brand, are regarded by the people as greedy criminals, hardly better than soldiers, whether they grow fat in monasteries or roam the roads strewing blessings and holding out the avid hand of poverty. But the monks of this large and powerful temple, although they are worse charlatans, thieves, liars, brigands, lechers, and criminals than their despised brethren, are venerated by the people as saints, reincarnations of Buddha, living gods. Probably they're merely smarter than the ordinary workers in the faith. Be that as it may, the swine enjoy the respect and admiration of the Szechwanese to almost the same degree as their famous competitors in Ho Mi Chang, the mountain of fifty-six temples, marked with the footprint of Buddha. Even without the aid of a divine foot, my own monks would have only to utter a few well-calculated prophecies to raise the inhabitants of Chengtu and the rest of the province against Tang Kiao. So he takes good care not to interfere with them or their interests. In front of the five-story porch, where statues of martial spirits with square beards, curved halberds, and red masks forbid any emanations of evil to enter the pagoda, our own soldiers stop and fall to the ground in attitudes not of prostration but of rest and readiness, carefully languid and relaxed —the Chinese technique of economizing physical effort. They let us enter alone, through a round hole like a hoop. I notice with justifiable satisfaction that the monks have taken the necessary measures to provide our governor general with their rarest attentions, a really exceptional service. The reason everything is thus set up is that this morning I sent my head boy here, and after a polite but close discussion of fees he gave them the number of taels required for the big welcome and the whole ceremony.

"After the first, there are two other entrances. The pagoda is surrounded by a series of walls, magic fortifications guarded by a garrison of good-luck sym-

bols, mostly winged monsters, wooden giants, rigid
gods whose glance can slay the wicked. At last, where
the trees thin out and you feel you are almost at the
top of the hill, there beyond the branches, just below
the summit, is the glitter of arcs and arches painted
in indefinable colors. The curves are the roofs of
temples, each span uptilted toward the sky. More
spirits, more stone guardians, more steles, another
door—and then we are amazed by the beauty of the
bizarre, at once attracted and repelled by the harmonious chaos spread before us. A great sea of flagstones,
huge cold courtyards, broad steps flanked by dragons,
and then *it*. At the same time a bristling and a flat-
tening, holes, turrets, pointed pavilions, and lastly
the pagodas themselves, all in a kind of delirium.
They seem to exist only as cascades of tiles, as roof
upon roof overlapping, outsoaring, mingling, joining,
struggling, heavy yet about to take wing. Heaps of
roofs both cowering and leaping, like superimposed
carapaces of some crawling creature stretching out
pinions to fly. Roofs like the spine, the coils, the
scales and legs of a dragon. In the middle is the
biggest pagoda, the pagoda of Harmony, from which
emanates a strange quietness, and which itself emanates from the world of fantasy, the animal and metaphysical anguish of humanity. Its peace is the inexhaustible seething that is China, the abyss of horrors
and treasures, the ceaseless movement of thought
straying among dreams, chimeras, fears, desires, and
curving in the brutal precision of calculations and
arguments designed to assuage passion by victory. All
that is contained in this place full of reptilian and
fantastic forms. But there is also the other, deeper,
truer peace, that of the sincere believers, the peace
which Buddha preaches: the attempt to renounce all

the tumults of this wicked world, to vanish from the
tragic scene of the living and enter, through wisdom
and virtue, into disinterestedness, disintegration, the
void, the nirvana where nothing exists any more. For
the only happiness that is possible is no longer to be,
in any form whatever, in any present, past, or future.
Sanctity, authenticity, ever more perfect and demanding, consists in the withering away of the self, complete non-existence, non-being in a non-universe, dis-
appearance from the cycle of globes, things, lives, and
eternities. That is liberation and the path of virtue
which my monks claim to follow, these wily inmates
of a crooked monastery where there is a bit of everything, from images of human voluptousness to a glimmer of the serenity of Buddha.

"The governor general has alighted. Behind him,
in an awkward group, we are just going up the top
steps when we are engulfed in a sort of apocalypse, a
monotonous storm—the monks' orchestra, a ceaseless
hum broken by sudden noises. I recognize the banging
of gongs, the dull beat of steel drums, great hollow
cylinders producing long groans that seem to fill space,
terrifying curdled sounds coming from giant horns,
the remains of legendary beasts that used to haunt the
heights of the Himalayas. Above all is the moan
emitted by the ecclesiastical trumpets, simple thin
tubes about seven or eight feet long, which the player
has to blow into with might and main. From some
way off in a belfry, a hundred or a thousand little bells
moved by the air, the wind, or a breath let fall a crystal
shower of sounds. Then the whole racket suddenly
ceases. We are in the sanctuary, in front of the famous
giant Buddha with healing powers. As a matter of
fact, instead of looking at the miraculous navel, I am
more drawn by the almost imperceptible smile, a mere

thought of a smile—not a smile of kindness or love
or charity, merely detachment. At his feet, adoring,
are a hundred monks in the lotus position, in long
robes, a hundred big bare branded skulls oscillating
to and fro, a hundred clerical heads all banging themselves on the ground at the end of their swayings and
prostrations, a hundred mouths singing a plainchant,
the words tumbling from bad teeth and empty gums
in a solemn purr in which certain intonations constantly return. The monks are arranged according to
age. In front are the infinitely old, though they are
still capable of taking part in this choral and gymnas-
tic liturgy. They go at it for all they're worth, bending
backward and forward rhythmically, most of them
telling strings of large beads with their mummified
fingers. But these human leftovers, worn-out robbers,
have taken on, merely through their physical deteri-
oration, a resemblance to ascetics approaching their
ultimate end and fulfillment in nirvana. So long as
these 'elders' can go on rocking to and fro and making
noises they are of some use to the monastery, which
continues to feed them so that it can exhibit them
in public as models of sanctity. The reason these
wrecks bestir themselves so energetically is that they
know that when the day comes when they're no longer
good for anything, their younger 'brothers' will decide to let them attain the blessed void by means of
inanition. Behind these old crocks are the all-powerful
masters of the monastery, a few monks of about fifty
or sixty, those who have been the wiliest and strongest
and most slippery during their holy careers. Sharks.
But to look at they're the best of men, just in their
prime, compensating for brimming health and excess
fat with a sacerdotal cope and the supreme gravity of
their round faces. Usually, each of these slow gestures

and rare words, each movement and each sound emitted as they devote themselves to meditation on great truths, has its price. How often have I seen them haggling. But today they vie with one another in offering us this holy office free of charge. Next come the young ones, tonsured and branded, robed, still thin and sharp as knives, consumed by ambition and capable of anything. Then come younger ones still, and lastly the boys, charming little creatures with almond eyes who minister to every need and to the needs of everyone. For the monks of the temple are careful to abstain from women for fear of gossip and rumors that might harm their reputation and incidentally their prosperity. What they lust after is money rather than flesh. So the little boys serve the purpose. . . .

"After half an hour, when the ladies and gentlemen show signs of impatience, all lips are abruptly sealed and the swaying stops, and we are left alone with the indifferent Buddha, the monks having filed away in procession—it is almost as if they had flown—into the inner sanctuary. Then suddenly from amid the dark of the incense a belly materializes before us—a paunch surmounted by a sweetly smiling face, the superior of the famous monastery himself. With affected humility and tortuous unction, but with amusement and artfulness lurking beneath the surface, he murmurs: 'We pray His Excellency the governor general to excuse us, but when he deigned to enter this humble place, fit for the common people crushed by the wheel of life who come here in search of hope, my brother penitents and I were overwhelmed by the extraordinary honor. We ask the governor's forgiveness for having rendered thanks to Buddha, and even for having offered up to him our most powerful prayers. May he pardon our audacity, himself so well known

for his perfection that he has no need of our miserable
supplications to the Lord Buddha, especially as he is
already the beloved of the Lord Jesus. But we thought
it best that when a human being is charged with great
responsibilities he should have all the gods with him.
That was our intention.' As he was saying all this, his
face steeped in the balm of gravity, the rolls of fat on
his obscene skull shook like a tête de veau served hot
and without parsley. He's laughing up his sleeve at
us, this prelate of renunciation; he takes us for fools,
having already taken all those taels. But when I
translate the pious message, the governor can only
stammer, 'It's quite true, there's some good in all
religions. Tell him I am grateful and that since his
invocations to Buddha I feel much better already.'
His lady starts to giggle. 'Come off it, sainted governor.
Aren't you forgetting you're a Mason, with the triangle
and leather apron and all? Keeping me standing
around for half an hour just to watch all this mumbo-
jumbo. I had to take my shoes off, and all for nothing
—not one prayer for me! Come on now, consul, ask
the old fool if he can show me the apartment we're
going to live in, my husband and me, when we've
finished with China, Indochina, Asia, and all these
places full of wogs and louts and snobs.' When I ask
him, the superior nods his head gently, as if it were
the easiest thing in the world.

"We follow the saintly man into the monastery,
through room after dim gray room, past hundreds,
thousands of Buddhas, a whole divine population sitting in state, looking down, soothing, terrifying. Some
of them are standing, but most are seated, gold, copper,
or bronze, on plinths or altars. Some are in an ecstasy
of meditation, others are above all a belly, a monstrous
projecting belly, talking and laughing, a mass of well-

fed tripe culminating in a navel like a winking eye. Side by side with icy sublimity is the profligacy of good living. And all around are armies of sub-Buddhas, wise or beneficent goddesses, Kwan-yins of fertility, haloed Bodhisattvas resting on lotuses, holy old men stooped over their sticks on the quest for truth. There are lewd creatures, too, voluptuously shaped divinities ensnaring the beholder with their naked breasts, writhing legs, and innocent eyes. Sometimes they copulate with terrible monsters who have rows of bestial heads and thousands of arms, and lift them up on their sexual organs or crush them with their bodies. Sometimes black gods, with or without a woman, dance among bones, trampling their victims under their innumerable feet, holding in their equally innumerable hands revolting remains, torn flesh, serpents, flames. It's pandemonium where everything is intermingled, nature human and divine, animal and diabolical. The ballet of life.

"In one room I can see eyes above me: they are shriveled and purulent, but they belong to men. Can this be some form of levitation? Around the almost closed eyes I can discern matter—old and stagnant skin enclosing bones, a skeleton and a scrap of flesh. Bodies lying suspended above us in the air. The governor general is taken aback and rubs his eyes as if to drive away a sight so incompatible with reason, science, and the Rights of Man. His wife grabs hold of me with all the energy of fear, clinging tight and screaming bloody murder. I reassure her and all the rest of the party by explaining that it's only hermits in bamboo cages hanging from ropes attached to the rafters. A very common practice in monasteries. I admit that this kind of ascetic is pretty repulsive—they're so emaciated and stunted. These specimens are naked except for a bit of cloth around the middle, but they don't seem to be suffering in the slightest, and don't even deign to notice that we're there. The superior calls my attention to them with sanctimonious pride. 'They are two of my monks who are acquiring a great deal of merit for our monastery. Our ordinary penances are not enough for them. In order to escape more quickly from the illusions and appearances of life, they have chosen to atrophy, to destroy their carnel vestures by enclosing themselves in these cages, from which they will emerge only after fulfillment, when they are freed by death, which is their goal, their hope, and their reward, especially if it brings them the great nirvana out of which one is never reborn again. While awaiting death they are happy, removed from sordid realities, immune from the senses and from pain, not needing to speak or eat, swallowing nothing but a little air and a drop of water that is brought them once a month. They are beyond prayer, deep in the great meditation where they never bat an eyelid or move a finger. They can remain like this for years, objects of veneration to the crowds who come to see them but whom they do not see.' The superior is obviously highly delighted with his moribund monks. This time the governor's wife is not just the little lady you can't get a rise out of. She rushes right in, feeling gut pity for the two wretched-looking prisoners. 'What!' she cries, appalled. 'Do you mean to say these poor devils never get a morsel to eat? And they don't pass out? If I miss a single meal myself—' But I cut short her good intentions with a touch of condescension, as one who knows. 'Don't trouble yourself, Madame. I'm quite sure that when there aren't any pilgrims around the worthy superior lets them have a bit of rice—not too much, of course, so that they stay thin and in proper

condition to make the faithful pity them and loosen
their purse strings. That's the whole object of the
exercise. These poor saints are profitable, so they have
to be kept going, but not too well. Of course at this
rate they're bound to end up dying properly one day.
Then the monastery organizes around their remains—
a few odd kilos piously taken from their death boxes—
a series of elaborate ceremonies which attract masses
of people: the right kind of people, people ready to
cough up. As a matter of fact, it's as corpses that these
ascetics bring in the most money. After that, the
finances of the monastery require that they be replaced
as soon as possible. So the superior nominates succes-
sors from among the other monks, who fight like
fiends to escape this glorious but unenviable fate. He
makes his choice from among those who have incurred
his displeasure—sly ones who've tried to cheat him or
clumsy ones who don't know how to fleece a customer
properly. The selection gives rise to much intrigue,
but those chosen, once well beaten and drugged and
starved, make very good saints there in their cages.'
'But how horrible,' moans the governor's wife, almost
fainting. 'Let's get out of here before I'm sick. And
I'm not the sort of woman who pukes easily. Tell your
monks I thought they seemed very much like our own
worthy priests!' I wasn't going to let her get away with
being snooty to me and my monks. 'This is China,
Madame,' I said. 'And these excellent monks have an
even more impressive trick up their sleeves—religious
suicide by fire, the great resource when things go badly
and the money stops rolling in. When the people's
faith gets too lukewarm, the monks heat it up, about
once a year, with a pyre on which some holy man
burns himself alive. The superior has it announced
everywhere that one of his monks who's in a particular

hurry to reach nirvana is going to be immolated in the great hall of the monastery. On the appointed day the people come in crowds, women and children included. All the monks in an official body pray before the great Buddha, at whose feet a man with a crown on his head is enthroned on a neat heap of logs. He sits in the same position as the lord Buddha, his legs folded under him and his head held high, but very much alive, with eyes open, calm, quiet, serene, splendid in his yellow robe and venerable with his tonsure. He is in a state of supreme indifference. The sacred trumpets of the temple sound—the moment has come. When the wood is kindled and flames climb and flicker upward to become a lacy mass, a scarlet heart, an enclosing shell, the saint remains unaltered in his detachment—not a sign is to be seen on his face. It is as if he felt nothing. And yet the smell of burned flesh, bitter, cloying, and acid all at once, fills the nostrils, ears, and mouth. The last time it happened I was there—I'd come for a nice little picnic the French were having. I saw the blaze reach the man, just licking at him at first, then seizing hold of the feet and attacking one limb after another until the whole body was a brand. Finally the head suddenly caught and became a jet of red, the eyes bursting, the flesh melting, all disappearing in the flames. When they died down, big heavy whorls of black smoke rose out of the waning pyre—a heap of paling embers, changing from ocher to gray. Then the saint reappeared, lying on the embers, a sullied crumbling skeleton already disintegrated, the skull rolled aside, and the shins, ribs, and shoulder blades lying there like absurd trifles. A monk with an iron rod broke open the brain pan. A few more minutes' cooking, and what remained of the bones melted away. Then the prostrate monks began to intone the great hymn of glorification, and the crowd fell on the still burning cinders and rubbed them over their faces. But the superior ordered them to retire, and had the remains gathered up and put in an urn. Then two monks dipped their hands into the urn, brought forth handfuls of ashes, and scattered these relics over the faithful. I was intrigued. I wondered how the monks had prepared the saint to play his part so perfectly. Our doctor, the one who's with us today, passed me some inside information. Apparently it's a method that's well known in all the best monasteries. The victim is prepared by being given a potion made of opium and potent Indian herbs, which puts him into a trance or state of hypnosis so that he can feel nothing and is bound to appear completely serene. To make assurance double sure, they break all the bones they can—including the arms and legs—without actually killing him. Then they swaddle him in a tight bamboo corset which is hidden by his robe and holds him up in the required position—that of the Buddha. And to make sure he holds his head up nice and straight, they make a hole in the skin at the back of his neck and insert a rod. After all these careful preparations, all they have to do is put him on the pyre. The illusion of voluntary sacrifice is complete.'

"But this time I've gone too far. By the time I've finished, the governor general looks disgusted and all his party is disgruntled. My hard sell of the monks hasn't worked. They wanted Oriental mystery, magic, the supernatural, and all I've given them is revolting fakery. There is general disappointment, and the little governor's wife, quite recovered from her previous emotion and with her feet planted more solidly than ever on the ground, turns on me. 'Monsieur le Consul,' she says, 'you are pulling my leg. How can I be expected to believe in your monks' predictions now that I know they're only charlatans? The whole thing's a cheat. You've brought me to this horrible place for nothing.'

"It was at this point that my wife intervened. Usually Anne Marie, tall and slim and graceful, looks like a lily bending slightly backward with the weight of her chignon. She speaks in the manner of her native Anjou, in a slight drawl, very gentle but clear. This streamlike smoothness is often very intimidating. The few simple sentences she contributes to a conversation carry more weight than all my speeches and witticisms. I am well aware of the strange force that emanates from her in spite of herself. When she does allow herself to speak at length, she employs a language that is easy, poetic, fascinating, colorful, enchanting. You never know what she's really thinking, but it's silly of me to worry—in public she is always absolutely as she should be: she saves her nasty cracks for when we're alone. In her own way she's always ready to come to my rescue when necessary. And she can really tell a story very well when she puts her mind to it.

"'Because of having to pit himself against the Chinese,' she says, 'Albert has got into the habit of thinking of them, and representing them, as absolute scoundrels. But they're not as simple as that, even in their complications. For example, that story of the burned monk is much stranger than he told you. It happened exactly a year ago, during the famine. The sun scorched the sky, the sky scorched the earth till it was like a dried-up orange peel, cracked, hard, brown, nothing but dust. All over the countryside people were dying, having sought in vain for bark or herbs to eat. Chengtu had closed its gates to keep out the hordes

of starving people, though they were too weak to do
any harm. But in the city there were stores of grain,
and the war lords ate with a clear conscience because
they were the protectors of the people. The soldiers
ate because they were the defenders of the people. The
rich ate because they had gold and were the fathers of
the people. At the consulate I'd given orders that only
canned goods were to be used, though the servants
considered this unworthy of our dignity. Of course
there were more corpses than usual in the streets, but
they weighed hardly anything and were dry and
healthy, not disgusting as during the floods, with all
the water and germs and swollen bellies. Naturally all
the ecclesiastics were busy trying to call down rain.
The monks in the pagodas used prayer wheels. The
Christians held processions led by gaunt images of
Christ, looking as if he, too, were starving. But every
day the sun was redder, the sky more blue and pitiless,
the earth more bare. And then a ray of hope began
to spread among the people of Chengtu: in this famous
monastery whose prodigies never failed, a saint was
going to burn himself so that the fire that consumed
him might extinguish the fire of heaven. A miracle
was guaranteed. On the appointed day, thousands of
believers managed to get out of the closed city to witness the act of salvation. And Albert and I, and the
doctors, and in fact all the little French colony, were
curious, and on the excuse of going for a picnic, set
out for the temple. Across the naked country we
went, the country of the dead: lying singly or in
groups among empty mud huts or on the hard ground
were things like little bent sticks, dead bodies, shrunk-
en, not offensive, cleanly picked skeletons. Vultures
swooped down to do the picking. The wretched folk
who'd come from no one knew where, from every-

where, and who like us were going to the sacrifice, were not dangerous either. They were resigned. Why, in the midst of disaster, are crowds in China sometimes gentle and meek, sometimes wild and angry? Who knows. These human tatters dragged themselves toward the monastery like a mass of bones moving, a forest of bones. They didn't beg, they didn't speak— they were using all their strength to walk. We passed many of them and finally arrived safely at our little lake, where Mr. Pu had gotten the usual meal ready for us. But at the picnic place we were surrounded by a ring of people, mostly children. Mr. Pu chased them away with a severe reprimand: "Aren't you ashamed to bother these honorable lords and friends of China, you worms and sons of ten generations of bitches?" They took themselves off without a murmur. Faced with all those empty stomachs, I didn't want to touch any food, but Mr. Pu, full of indignation and with an unheard-of audacity, which he allowed himself only because he knew he was right, pointed out that by abstaining I would lose "face." The duty of a person of my importance was to eat my fill when the dregs of society ate nothing and starved. The sound of music from the pagoda announced that the propitiatory sacrifice was about to begin. I couldn't bring myself to go. But Albert had a sandwich and went with the doctor. He was back an hour later, very gay at what he'd seen. "Rain! They'll be waiting for it till the cows come home, those idiot yokels," he said. He told me how it was all a put-up job, just as he explained it to you, and it's probably true. But he'd hardly finished giving us all the technical details and his comments on the monks' dishonesty, when we were enveloped in clouds. They swept down from the tops of the mountains and settled in the hollows and

depressions. In the middle of the afternoon we'd
been plunged into damp and spongy night, full of
frightening gusts—a heavy darkness lit up with storms
and so red it was as if all nature had been transformed
into a pyre with the lightning for the flames. And then
the rain started to pour down. Mr. Pu and his worthy
acolytes told us we should pack up and leave as fast
as we could, furious torrents would soon come streaming down the mountainside and might wash us into
the lake, which had started to rise and toss angrily.
With the peals of thunder, the howling of the squalls,
the beating of the waves, and the pounding rain, it was
like the end of the world. You could hardly see your
hand before your face. Still, we set off, groping our
way miserably upwards, afraid of being buried in a
landslide. The horses were frightened and lashed out,
and the mafus had to use all their strength to keep
them from bolting. Albert and I dismounted and
went on foot. At last we reached the flat, bare plateau.
There was no longer any danger of being swept away
by a landslide or a sudden torrent, but we were now
exposed to the elements—wind and rain and lightning.
We were walking through clouds, which clung to us
like wet clothes or sheets. But we pressed on until we
got to the ravine with the bridge of vines over it.
The hugely swollen river covered in swirling foam
filled the cleft in the rock almost to the brim. On
either side, thousands of small streams fell, rushed,
and cascaded into the narrow ravine. The bridge,
though still secured at either end, swung in the air,
groaning dismally in every fiber. Mr. Pu, looking
grave, consulted earnestly with the head boys and
mafus and told us we ought to cross over at once, as
the bridge might break or be swept away at any moment. If we waited and the bridge went, we'd be

marooned on the wrong side. We followed Mr. Pu's orders and crossed with our hearts in our mouth. It was like being on a drifting boat, tossing as if on waves of water and wind. At every step we were lifted up by the immense forces of nature trying to tear us from our fragile support, which instead of curving downward as usual, flew upward like a kite. But over it we went: in China bravery is sometimes the only choice. And we were right to have done as Mr. Pu told us, for not half an hour later the bridge snapped, drowning a hundred or so people who'd come to see the suicide that was to call down rain. They got more than they'd bargained for. So I think these monks, whether they're dishonest or not, have certain very extraordinary powers, at least as far as meteorology is concerned. In fact, I'm afraid of them. I'm sure they have strange powers, whether for good or evil, natural or supernatural, scientific or magical.'

"All the party are obviously impressed with what Anne Marie has said, and prefer her sense of mystery, fantastic as it is, to my too realistic skepticism. So to recapture their attention, I treat them to a few more lofty and even philosophical reflections. 'The Chinese are strange brutes. You never know about them. It's the most difficult thing in the world to distinguish their wickedness from mysticism: they're capable of the noblest and most exalted feelings as well as the others. Good and evil, which are always extreme, with them have exactly identical features, like twin brothers. So it's not impossible that these monks, who have a reputation for being revolting tricksters, also have a certain odor of sanctity and some magic or even metaphysical knowledge. Haven't I already praised their powers of divination? Everything is possible, even that the burnt monk was a volunteer and that his

sacrifice moved heaven, which immediately watered
the earth. But I don't think so, even though I don't
understand it.' I've hardly completed this when I
am greeted with a peal of laughter, turkey-like gob-
blings, and a concerto of squawks. It's the wife of the
governor general. With eyes gleaming like searchlights
and her nose ferreting about like a corkscrew, she
screeches at me, 'Well, anyhow, Monsieur le Consul,
your monks are real pigs.'

"This is because we have just entered the gallery
of hell, the room violently bedaubed with all kinds of
tortures. It's so realistic that the governor general
moans, 'I don't want to look—it'll make me ill.' His
wife is completely icy and indifferent as regards most
of the tortures—the dissections, the quarterings, the
burnings, the cuttings up, the scaldings, the skinnings,
the impalings, the various perforations with hooks or
red-hot irons. She is unmoved by the groups of males
and females intermingled, wretchedly yet tragically
naked, who in their abjectness are like ghosts or
clumsy swellings or piteous fleshless gnomes; yet they
have completely retained, pushed to its very extreme,
the human power to suffer, the ultimate greatness here
turned to mockery. The governor's wife is unperturbed
by these masses of bodies tangled together in the
grotesque attitudes of their torment; most of them
are no longer even whole bodies, but just exist in the
form of a torso or head or pair of buttocks or legs,
the rest having disappeared under the knife or in the
flames, into pots or pans, or into the coils or jaws of
all sorts of monsters, some huge, some tiny, with
scales, wings, fins, crests, fangs, and stings—terrible
and magnificent hydras breathing fire, sinister birds
tearing out intestines with their beaks and claws, and
above all noisome creatures of the night, reptiles, vam-

pires, rats, insects that swallow and suck and sting
and tear all that comes within their reach. The governor's wife, left cold by everything else, is madly excited by just one panel—the one that shows the punishment for lust (the damned are arranged in categories,
according to the nature of their sin). The penalties
for pride and avarice do not interest her, but she
goes almost crazy at the sight of the expiations inflicted
on the lecherous: this is because the representations
are mainly concerned with the unruly members themselves, the sexual organs, shown in frenziedly obscene
forms of martyrdom. It almost takes her breath away,
but at last she manages to hiss, 'This is terrific.' She
stands rooted to the spot in front of the incongruous
shapes that seem to emerge from some sea or jungle:
cavities like opened oysters, projections like trunks,
and all being devoured by something dark and shapeless and seething. At first this confused mass seems to
be vegetable or mineral, like polyps, sponges, seaweeds,
or coral reefs, but it is really erotic flesh, sullied and
mutilated, being torn to pieces by nightmare flora
and fauna: masses of precisely delineated vaginas and
phalluses attached to mere scraps of women or men,
but difficult to recognize because of the universe of
torturers swarming over them. Gaping female orifices
have trees growing out of them, with poisonous flowers
and sharp thorns; or are full of writhing serpents,
some of which thrust their heads outside to bite, while
others plunge into the entrails and leave only their
tails visible; or serve as caldrons for boiling oil or
molten lead, braziers for heating pincers to tear at the
breasts, the skin, and the eyes of the woman herself
and of the rest. Other orifices, lengthened with claw
or cutlass, occupy the whole body, and evil spirits
with animal heads fish out the organs, starting with

heart and liver, and feast on them. In others again, devils, beasts, and monsters trample in a concert of claws and membranes and beaks, hovering above and then driving in enormous darts, some like pikes, some like swords, some like clubs bristling with barbs and nails which tear out all the innards, some like bundles of lashes that reduce them to bloody pulp. Into others, infernal gods with a hundred arms plunge their hundred members, members of fire, poisoned members emitting seed that corrodes and burns and pierces holes through all the body. Orifices penetrated in every imaginable way—by diligent and terrible ants, by giant dogs that are the symbol of shame and infamy, by tigers and dragons that copulate with fantastic hairy organs that are fatal. Orifices that are muck heaps or cemeteries, where living skeletons throw dead bones, pestilential carrion full of diabolical voices shrieking, and full of germs and purulence contaminating all the flesh and covering it with wounds like slavering mouths, with craters of all colors like a putrefied rainbow, and swellings that disintegrate in outpourings of pus. Ordinary orifices on which junior officials of hell, assiduous little clerks with minute heads like indifferent pins, engage themselves like robots on routine operations: compressing them between grills like flattened bits of meat, throwing in various ingredients, the whole larder of punishment— burning coals, slimy toads, blades and sickles, some of them ingeniously arranged in the form of machinery to cut from within, knots of sharp-sided metal, a satanic imitation of the human intertwinings the adulteresses were once too fond of. There are steel phalluses introduced like real ones, in every possible way, but as instruments of vengeance; some like the organs of lecherous old men who have paid for favors

—these resemble burettes pouring out incandescent gold; others like phenomenal erections of requited lovers, but thick as beams and hot as hell. Around all these the upper parts of the women have disappeared, and they are reduced to spread legs, sprawling in postures which might once have been those of pleasure but are now those of suffering. When a body remains fairly whole, it is so that it may be impaled through every orifice, made a pincushion with dozens of rods on every side. No form of depravity has been left out, and each has its special treatment. The creature of dream, princess or courtesan, who would manipulate herself with her delicate fingers is now clawed with a nail of iron. The sodomite is pierced by a brace and bit. There is even a newly delivered mother whose child, the fruit of adultery or incest, is speared with a trident and thrown into a pot where imps make soup out of human giblets. Everything is inexorably punished. Sometimes a sinning couple is made to copulate eternally, so that their organs are galled with use to blood and fire. When the guilty parties are many, men and women are all spitted together on a thread, a writhing string like those on which the Chinese peasants take small fish or birds to market. Sometimes the thread on which they're strung is some reptilian beast, a cold and sinuous dragon, served by a cloud of black butterflies, which cluster around the victims and feed on their eyes and sexual organs. There is also a kind of transparent tapeworm whose white skin is covered with thousands of hard protuberances, teeth or phalluses, on which hang masses of men and women, dying devoured or raped. The huge worm moves along with its load like bacilli caught on innumerable barbs which may be sucking mouths or devouring penises—probably both. In general, just as

the vaginas are open, gaping and empty, so they can
be filled with dreadful things and beings, so, with the
same frenzy, the men's penises are crushed, destroyed,
annihilated, and by means of the same beings and
things. The governor's wife howls with delight at this
universal castration, all these phalluses, some in erec-
tion and some not, thrusting up from mutilated bodies
to be themselves exterminated: the demolition of
virility, making mincemeat of the supreme pride
which with all its attributes still springs from the
groins of men reduced to nothing but torsos, limbless
men at the mercy of the powers of darkness. In the
field of torture, the harvest is a great harvest of pricks.
There are all sorts and kinds—old, ugly, shriveled bits
of skin, and splendid ones aspiring to the sky. The
demons, the army of ancillary monsters which haunt
the minds of the Chinese, are reveling in a sort of
abattoir. Sometimes their pleasure takes the form of
a brutal dismantling, a delight in wielding tooth or
saber to create eunuchs dying in a state of humiliation.
'Look'—the governor's wife chuckles—'how that imp
slices up that prick, like slicing a sausage at a delica-
tessen.' The splendor of the slicing steel . . . But sometimes the process is slow and careful, vivisection accompanied with all the apparatus of torture and all the
symbols of evil. And still all these winged and crawling
swarms, vying with the male organ and bent on destroying it by swallowing it and tearing it to pieces.
In the empty belly of a man, in place of his entrails,
a cobra uncoils and strikes at the phallus, to swallow
it, to tear it. Everywhere a frenzy of emasculation.
Some of the visions are simple, some complicated, like
those showing men impaled, with the stake coming
out of mouths filled with some unnamable matter,
some white dung or motionless worm or solidified pus,

while below, their sexual organs, already torn in several pieces, are being plaited into thongs by bats. The governor's lady splits her sides and says. 'Marvelous! Nothing left. All put out of business. I know some blokes who'd look pale if they could see this. My word . . .' And the bitch looks around at all the gentlemen of the party, including me but not her husband, with a meaningful laugh. The men, the usual colonial types, dummies of official dignity, pretend not to notice what's amusing her so much. I go up to her and whisper, 'So you don't like men? You'd like to see them rendered harmless?' She chokes with indignation. 'What do you take me for, Monsieur le Consul? Do I look as if I don't know a good thing when I see it? Men—handsome, well-built ones—I've always thrived on them, I've lived for them. If they were all castrated I'd go into a convent. But if it happened to a few of those prigs who flatter my husband and run me down, I'd be glad to light a candle to the Virgin Mary or even Buddha. No, my dear Albert, this hell of yours makes me angry, but I can't help it, it excites me, too.' She might be Chinese, for both men and women in this country always need a good deal of cruelty and artifice in love, including bound feet and the rest. It strikes me that the monks are very clever, the way they pretend to make people disgusted with the flesh by this display of tortures, whereas in fact they inflame the visitors' imaginations. It must bring the monks loads of money, this damnation which inspires desire, this brothel where pleasure is mingled with atrocity, perversity, and cerebral abandon.

"It isn't only torture that interests the natives, but also superstition—the Chinese are eaten up wih superstition. They will do anything to get on the right side of gods and demons, to get them to commit crimes. In

the trade with the formidable and mysterious emanations of ether, atmosphere, sky, the abyss, paradise,
hell, and tombs, the chief figures are the soothsayers,
with their specialists in good and evil, ready for anything. Though there is a lot of competition in this
field, my monks here, as I've told the governor's wife,
have a reputation for being outstanding. The temple
is a sort of prediction factory. It is empty today because of us, but usually there are the same feverish
crowds as in the gambling dens, with, instead of the
subacid singsong of the girls calling out the numbers,
the monotonous voices of the monks telling fortunes.
They have made divination into a kind of lottery. The
customer draws from a wooden Buddha a sacred card
with a prophetic inscription which the officiating
monk reads; if some calamity is announced, the
monk undertakes, for an additional consideration, to
ward it off with a prayer. The thing that brings in
the most money of all is the 'tribunal of truth,' at
which the plaintiff consigns the person he has a grudge
against to ghosts and devils. For this form of pious
murder, which apparently never fails, a simple offering
is all that is necessary.

"But for persons of our importance, and thanks to
my judicious greasing of palms, the superior, as saintly
and rubicund as ever, has laid on the Big Show, the
supreme magic which abolishes the passing of time
and conjures up past, present, and future through a
brief illusion by means of which each of us can, if he
wishes, see, in the elements of his life suddenly materialized before him, the essential truth about himself,
what he has been and what he will be. It's a frightening thought, and I'm very curious, for although at the
Camembert stage of our colonialist picnic I plugged
these Oriental prodigies to the governor's wife, I've

never actually witnessed them, I suppose because of an apprehension I didn't like to admit to myself. Now, when the mystery is about to be performed, my interest is mixed with dread. But I try not to show it, for it is absolutely necessary that I retain control over our party—they, too, are uneasy and suspicious. The governor general, though still tottering, scatters raucous grunts and furtive looks, as if he were being drawn into something disgraceful. He's probably wondering if it's in accordance with the dignity of a proconsul, the big chief of Indochina, to take part in this sort of thing. Behind him the civil servants and their ladies are disapproving, and march along as stiffly as if they were on stilts. But Anne Marie, serene as ever, like some white goddess of the tropics, walks on smoothly and gracefully while the governor's lady presses forward with her little sharp nose and her ferrety eyes, all excited and without any hesitation. She absolutely must know. But what? So on she hurries, even when the unctuous superior, torch in hand, leads us into a dark tubelike stairway leading down into the depths under the pagoda. We are in the catacombs, which are followed by narrow tunnels and cavities hewn out of bare earth. A labyrinth, a secret universe, forbidden and threatening. Deeper and deeper we go into the stuffy atmosphere, the heavy clammy cold, with water oozing down the walls and ceilings and a stifling odor of death and decay. Then the flickering light from the superior's torch spreads out more widely to reveal a big cave. A charnel house. An open pit is full of tons of bare bones that look as if they had been denuded by time or scraped clean with a knife before being thrown there. You can distinguish skulls, shin bones, whole skeletons. The superior, waving his torch around over the sinister hollow so that we can see better, suavely explains: 'This is where we put the remains of our dead monks, both those who have attained nirvana and those who must be reborn again in some form or other. We have been throwing their remains here for centuries: this is called the Pile of Great Humility. But have no fear—no spirits emanate from them, no devils to throw themselves on you. There is no danger, because of the holiness of the dead and the power of our exorcisms.' All around, in niches in the walls, are urns, which the superior complacently tells us contain the ashes of his predecessors, the venerable heads of the pagoda who have succeeded one another ever since it was founded over a thousand years ago. 'I have had my own urn prepared, and soon I shall be there, a handful of dust. For like all the superiors here before me, I know the day, the hour, and the moment when I shall go to the Realm of the Yellow Fountains. A few months from now I shall be freed from illusions and appearances.'

"Fifty yards farther on we come to a large and splendid room. This is the hall of divination. It's as if you had to pass through death in order to get to predictions about life. The superior points out a monk with a body like a heron and a head like a falcon, with deep-set yellow eyes close on either side of a nose like a beak. All you notice is these sunken eyes in the narrow, harsh, withdrawn face, its look fixed and phosphorescent. When this strange figure bows to him, the superior tells us: 'This man has the power to see into time, for he is beyond it. Several times in recent centuries he has been placed on the Pile of Great Humility. Each time he was born again in a different body, nearer to an animal, because of his impurity. But in the course of these transmogrifications, which brought him ever closer to the brute beast, since he could not free himself from matter he learned to penetrate its secrets, and this with the aid of a perhaps diabolical force, master of what disappears and reappears in evil, of what is decomposed and recomposed in pain. We shut up this maleficent monk here, beyond the room of the dead, so that he should not defile the place where they try to merit annihilation or at least good reincarnations. He can, with the help of his infernal protectors, escape from the wheel of existences and project himself into the cycle of time. Let whoever among you dares to do so ask this monk to make him experience now something of his past, present, or future. And then that daring person will see.' In a word, it was a challenge, and I was in a nice fix. I inwardly cursed the superior, whether he was going to pull the wool over our eyes or really expose us to black magic. For despite my European skepticism, I have lived too long in the neighborhood of Tibet, where there are so many lurid stories on the subject, not to believe in their devilish tricks and be afraid of them.

"And is this monk here really a man, or partly a bird of prey? I can't help wondering, as I look at the pupils of his eyes, the jutting cartilage of the nose, and the hands that are almost claws. I must be going out of my mind. Everyone in our party has gone pale. The governor general, sweating profusely, says, 'It's a hoax—just a hoax. Very bad taste.' But the man like a falcon gives a sort of shriek: 'Who wants to see himself as he has been or will be?' I translate. There is dead silence, and then our own charming little bird stands up to the human carnivore and says, stamping her foot, 'I do, I do! I want to know. I'm not frightened. Be my interpreter, please, consul!'

"Suddenly three Buddhas emerge from the shadows,

as if lit by electricity. What's this? There's no electricity here. The three Buddhas are all in a row, exactly the same as one another, of medium size, sitting
meditating and indifferent, very ordinary Buddhas except that they are black with soot and hatred, and instead of sitting on lotus flowers they are sitting on
skulls. Moreover, each of them holds a vertical panel
covered with chased silver—an ancient Chinese mirror, reflector of images. At this moment the bird-man
swoops down on our ruffled little parakeet, the governor's lady, stands looking at her coldly, and tells her
in a toneless voice: 'These are the gods I serve. On the
left is the Buddha of the past, who will show you
what you have been, for you do not know, any more
than any other human being, the things you have
really committed. In the middle is the Buddha of the
present, who will show you what you are, for you do
not know, any more than any other human being,
what you are really doing. On the right is the Buddha
of the future, who will show you what you will be, for
you do not know, any more than any other human being, what you will become, though it is already accomplished in the immutability of time. You, like
every other human being, are in an impenetrable fog
as regards your past, present, and future, though the
three are really all one. But my masters can bring you
out of the mist of uncertainty. First say, though, of
which of the three Buddhas you first wish to ask the
truth.' Scarcely have I finished translating this than the
obstinate, wearing voice of the irrepressible governor's
wife rings out: 'The Buddha of the future. The Buddhas of the past and present can just have a rest. I'm
not an idiot—I don't need them to tell me anything
about myself. But I'd give a lot to see now what I'll be
doing in a few years' time—say five years. For that I'd

consult as many old Buddhas as you like—I'd sell my
soul to the devil.' This produces a murmur from the
rest of the party and a remonstrance from the governor:
'You must be crazy!' But I am enjoying myself. I know
all about the lady. She winds her husband round her little finger, working away at him either in the privacy
of the bedchamber or by means of crudely outspoken
remarks in public, just like the pert maid in a comedy. That's why everyone in Hanoi hates and slanders
her so. But little she cares. When she gets her husband
back to Paris, she may be able to make a Herriot out
of him, perhaps president of the Chamber of Deputies. Provided that between now and then he doesn't
kick the bucket or go completely senile! And that's
why now, in the gloomy bowels of the pagoda, a
stone's throw from the charnel house and right in
front of the three infernal Buddhas, she's ready to
do the will of the bird-man, to find out.

"It all happens very quickly. I wonder whether the
sorcerer isn't wearing a mask, his face is so stony. The
features look as if they were carved out of smooth
wood. He seems neither all man nor all beast, but both
at once. He stands over the governor's wife like a vul-
ture over its prey, stretches out his arms, and starts to
utter not the soothing incantation of the monks that
induces oblivion, but shrill whistles, long and weird,
sounds not of this world but like demons calling to
each other through space. He is no doubt invoking
the spirits. After a minute or so, the monk consecrated
to evil stops and asks in an absolutely neutral and
lifeless voice: 'Are you ready? For the winds of the
other world are at hand. You are about to feel them.'
He puts into her left hand a sort of little bag made
of some cold material, like human skin, framed with
bones. Suddenly the governor's wife cries, 'There's

something moving inside! It's alive! I'm frightened!'
And indeed the rubbish inside the amulet, magic
carrion and excrement, no doubt, is moving. She is
almost fainting, but the accursed monk takes her by
the shoulder. 'Have no fear,' he says. 'Respect the
divinities which have come to you. Now that they have
taken possession of your body, they will be quiet and
put themselves at your service. Take this lamp in
your right hand—it is your entity, the permanence
of your being throughout time, outside time.' Madame bravely takes hold of this object, a heart-shaped
cone of dark-colored resins. Then the bird-man falls
back as if almost detached from the earth. He gazes
at her as if to take possession of her, out of hard,
stony eyes that get larger and larger until one sees
nothing but them, like immense stars. Beneath their
gaze the cone suddenly sputters into blinding light,
and it is as if the governor's wife becomes disincarnate,
disappears, ceases to exist. But the strange lamp she
is holding suspended in the air casts a beam of light
which falls on the silver mirror of the Buddha of the
future. And the ancient metal starts to stir, to move,
to fill with patches of color which join together and
mingle to form a whole. It grows clearer, steadier, it
is full of people and things, as at the cinema. I seem
to recognize houses, a part of Paris, some kind of military parade. And suddenly, in the midst of the crowd,
in the flesh, all alive and kicking, the governor's wife,
in full evening dress. The governor, stupefied, has
scarcely time to shout, 'Darling, darling, what's happened to you, where are you? I'm coming!' when
everything is as it was before, as if nothing at all had
occurred. The governor's wife is there among us, just
the same as ever, and I'd think it was all an illusion
if it weren't that she looks so radiant, tranfigured, like

a haloed saint. Panting with excitement, she tells her
worthy husband of her happiness. He doesn't understand a word. Half stunned and half agitated, he rolls
his globular eyes and whirls his stubby arms to get
hold of his ecstatic and excited darling, to protect
and embrace and clasp her to him. 'Pettikins, Pettikins, it was the Elysée Palace, I swear it! I recognized the gate and the courtyard and the porch and
the guards with drawn swords! And the salons and the
tapestries and the chandeliers and the footmen! And
the people, all the upper crust. I can't have been mistaken; you've taken me there five or six times. Every
time you lectured me so much beforehand that I didn't
open my mouth, even when the President smiled and
said polite things to me. But this time you were the
President, with the ribbon across your chest—majestic,
handsome, kind, neat, a magnificent Pettikins receiving the greetings of the official bodies and the
diplomatic corps. You were making a marvelous little
speech. And I was the President's wife, with a dress
as prim and proper as anything, but lovely! I was so
pretty and poised, so respected. I swear I'm not crazy,
Pettikins—I really was there!' At this moment there is
the sound of an imperfectly suppressed laugh from
one of the ladies or gentlemen of the governor general's entourage. Pettikins, all red and embarrassed
and not knowing what to think, manages to say, 'I
can't believe all that. They were teasing you. But for
a moment I thought you weren't there any more, and
I had a horrible fright. Where were you? Did anyone
take you away? Did anyone hurt you?' 'No, Pettikins
—I've told you. I was at the Elysée Palace. It happened quite simply and gently, naturally and without
any shock. For a few seconds I must have been in the
future. But now I know you are going to be President

of the Republic, and I'm going to be first lady.'
Various coughs and throat-clearings from those present. Pettikins hangs his head as if he felt embarrassed
and ridiculous, the grand master of a Masonic lodge
seeing his spouse transformed into a sort of Lourdes
visionary. But there is no way of keeping her quiet;
she's embarked on her golden legend. 'You'll see, Pettikins—we'll make a marvelous couple at the Elysée.
The whole of France will love us. You won't let yourself go any more—you won't have a throat like a wine
cellar, or an upset stomach. No more disgusting jackets
on which people can read your menu. No more waking
up in the morning with heartrending groans. No more
grumpiness and bad moods and depressions, or letting
people do anything they like with you for the sake of
peace and quiet. You'll work. You'll take care of your
appearance.. You'll study your files. You'll listen to
what visitors say. When you meet the people you'll be
dignified and gracious, you'll be eloquent, and you'll
find phrases that touch the masses and bring tears
to their eyes. I'll be at your side, just as I should be,
a real lady I swear you won't have anything to reproach me for. . . .' The governor's wife's marital
harangue is made all the more comic by the fact that,
as she blathers on, the room loses absolutely all its
mystery. It is now quite an ordinary place, with some
rather grubby Buddhas and some little oil lamps
struggling against malodorous and dirty shadows. The
magician, the bird-man, now looks to me nothing
more than a scraggy, silly old monk with puffy eyelids,
whose only resemblance to a falcon is an abnormality
of the skull which makes it completely flat—more like
that of a duck. I suddenly suspect it may be all my
fault—I may unwittingly have been responsible for
the governor's wife's misadventure. I must have given

the monks too much money, and they've gone too far trying to earn it. The superior stands beside me, fat, content, and smooth, as if he had really given us our money's worth. I won't get anything out of it all. And I'll never know if it was magic or not, if it was a spell, hypnotism, or mass hallucination produced by a carefully calculated buildup which upset people's nerves and imaginations.

"As a matter of fact, this sort of phenomenon is one of the chief subjects of dinner conversations among the Europeans in Chengtu. Everyone contributes his own anecdote, some tale to make the listeners' hair stand on end. When I think of what they usually say, and of all that's been seen in the lamaseries and monasteries of Szechwan and Tibet, what's happened today seems very small-time. I've heard of levitation, thought transference, visions across space and time, not to mention murder by remote control, apparitions, armies of corpses on the march, graveyards turned into diabolical fairs where dead bodies are brought and sold for magic, orgies of shrieking skulls and flesh and bones, gatherings of infernal spirits paying homage to their king, accompanied by their courtiers—dragons and monsters. It's not only the people who live here and have taken on local color who believe all these tales. It's also the visitors, the silk people working for firms in Lyons, the perfume representatives who venture as far as the Roof of the World in search of musk, that disgusting and evil-smelling secretion of animal glands or bladders from which are derived the exquisite scents of the Rue de la Paix. To tell the truth, I'm not very pleased when guests at the consulate introduce this subject. For my clamorous compatriots, always ready to squabble and know best about everything by the time we get to the dessert stage, become

really apoplectic on this topic, some claiming it's all
trickery and others insisting there's something in it.
I usually refrain from giving an opinion. And now
I've gone and forgotten my usual prudence, and by
exposing the governor general's ladylove to ridicule,
if not to actual danger, I've made a real blunder. For
there's no doubt about it—in a few days all Hanoi
will be having a good laugh over her misadventures,
and especially over her naïve prophecies. And they'll
probably think I'm an accomplice in it all, and a
charlatan. Even before that happens, the governor
general may be very angry with me.

"Meanwhile we beat a hasty retreat. We emerge
from the catacombs and depart from the pagoda,
where as a last gesture the monks all bang their heads
on the ground in front of the great Buddha, by way of
farewell. Most certainly, I was too generous with them.
We collect first our soldiers, then our coolies, bearers,
and mafus, all belching away from having stuffed
themselves all afternoon. As the caravan prepares to
start off, the governor general administers a mild re-
proof: 'I'm sure you meant well, but you were taking
risks. And with my own wife at stake. It's true she
was all for it, but still . . .' But his wife draws me
aside and reassures me. 'Don't you worry, I'll talk to
my husband and straighten it all out. I thought your
monks were terrific. I still believe in it. The Elysée
and all that.' She looks at me out of the corner of her
eye. You know, Albert, I like you. If I'd met you
before, we might have got together and had a good
time. But now, with that Anne Marie of yours watching you so closely . . . I bet you don't have much
fun.' I'm flattered, but I retort, 'I imagine you keep
your husband on a pretty tight rein, too.' Whereupon
she draws herself up and fells me with: 'But *I* love *my*

husband.' And she leaves me as angry as a turkey cock, for I'm sure her hint that Anne Marie doesn't love me is quite wrong. She does love me, even if she doesn't show her feelings much. Meanwhile the procession moves on back toward Chengtu. The return journey goes without a hitch. The governor doesn't even complain about the difficult parts; it's as if he were sustained by some inner contentment—perhaps he, too, sees himself at the Elysée. Anyway, he's smiling all over his face, and when we finally get back to the consulate he behaves with magnificent generosity. He hands over a large number of taels for the colonel in charge of the soldiers to divide up among his men. I can just imagine the split! He also gives a large sum to the head servants, for them, too, to share out. But here things don't go so well, of course. The governor has scarcely gotten inside the house, where as usual he flops into a chair, before there's an uproar outside, practically a riot, with all the coolies and mafus and porters yelling that they've been robbed, and shouting at the tops of their voices at Mr. Pu and other dignitaries. Mr. Pu, attacked on all sides and buried under a hail of arms and fists, bawls as loud as all his assailants put together, and doesn't yield an inch. In the end I have to intervene to restore order."

An element of uncertainty had entered the room. The darkness was less dense, bearing within itself a corruption or cancer of the shadows, and auguring a first streak of light. It was less a sign than a feeling, and it affected the consul himself. He stretched in his sleep, woke a little, looked at his watch. It was four in the morning. The head boy was still at his feet like a set of knucklebones. All the objects in the room flickered with a light that didn't yet exist. Outside in the yard

the fowls were beginning to stir and scratch about.
The town, too, was coming to life with an almost
imperceptible but unmistakable movement. The consul was again struck by the idea of going to his room.
But would he actually go? He preferred to end his
night of glory with the governor general and his wife.
He took a vindictive pleasure in projecting his own
vulgarity, which Anne Marie never stopped reminding
him of, onto this superior couple, especially the impossible wife.

"Only two days left before the official visit of the
governor general of Indochina to Szechwan is over.
More vexations for me. To begin with, the bishop's
hanging around, and it's certain he has some request
to make. I'm not very fond of this rough, unkempt,
arrogant fellow with coal-black eyes, a fanatic, always
in a state of irritation. He comes into my office, hesitating and awkward. 'I'd like to see the governor general, Monsieur le Consul.' 'But you've already seen
him, Monseigneur.' 'I need to speak to him again. It's
a matter of great importance for the future of Christianity in the province.' I suspect he wants to ask for
money for his mission, which, heaven knows, isn't
exactly poor; and I get ready to snub him. But it isn't
that. After beating about the bush for a while, the
bishop finally says, 'Monsieur le Consul, before I meet
the governor there's something I'd like to ask you
about him—something rather delicate, I admit. But
you're a good Christian, and that gives me confidence.'
This is an unexpected compliment, for my faith is
very lukewarm. It shows he's trying to prepare the
ground. 'Well, Monsieur le Consul, what I'd like you
to tell me is whether, as I've heard, the governor is a
Freemason and an enemy of Christ.' This *is* a surprise.
I count ten before answering. 'I really don't know,

Monseigneur. It's possible; I can't say more than that. But in any case I can assure you he's as well disposed as he can be toward the Church, and protects it energetically in Tonkin and Indochina.' 'Thank God. You take a great load off my mind. I'll pray for him before I ask him to help me.' An Our Father emerges from his hairy throat. When he's done I ask, 'What do you want the governor general to do?' 'I want him to speak to the Pope. To make a row. As you know, the Chinese, even those who have been baptized and are members of our flock, need to be kept under firm control, otherwise Satan gets hold of them again. Well, believe it or not, the apostolic nuncio in China, an Italian, wants to establish a Chinese clergy, with priests, bishops, and archbishops, to take our place. Can you imagine it? The devil must have put him up to such a thing. At the most you can make Chinese Christians into sacristans or vergers or catechists. But to ordain them and make priests and bishops of them would be to undermine and destroy all the holy work of evangelization for which in Szechwan alone so many missionaries have suffered persecution, martyrdom, and death. The governor general must remember that France is the official protector of the faith in Asia, and must warn the Pope of this mortal danger.' I play the innocent. 'But how could the governor transmit your request to the Pope? The church and the state are separate from one another in France.' The bishop sweeps this argument aside with a swish of his beard. 'The missionaries are the best and most useful sons of France in the East. We do more for French influence than all the bankers and businessmen put together, and saving your presence, all the consuls. The governor will see what I mean.' And sure enough, confronted by the rugged prelate with his grim and fiery eye, aggressive but self-conscious, tangled up in his Breton seminarist's vocabulary, the governor assumes the character of a glib official who, despite being a layman and of so elevated a rank, is very sympathetic toward that noble institution so important for France and for mankind as a whole: religion. So he is all good nature —prodigal with words, gestures, and eyewash. His sidelong looks betray his vast inner amusement as he puts the mad priest off. 'Monseigneur, I have often heard the same fears expressed in Tonkin and Indochina by many French missionaries, holy men, soldiers of God, and as you have pointed out, thorough patriots. I understand your anxiety, although I'm not sure you're right about where the interest of the Church and of France really lies. But you know I have no authority and no means of addressing His Holiness directly. And you know the peculiar situation between France and the Vatican—we don't even have diplomatic representation there. Still, I'll make it my business, through the discreet unofficial contacts that still exist, to bring your problems to the attention of St. Peter's successor.' An excellent demonstration of pigeonholing, and the silly fool of a bishop is very pleased with it. So much so that he draws back his thick lips to reveal his black stumps of teeth, which he never brushes, in a gracious though malodorous grin redolent of recent meals, and says grandly, 'Tomorrow in Chengtu Cathedral we shall celebrate high mass for the redemption of your sins and your complete success in the eminent duties to which God has called you.' 'I thank you, Monseigneur, on behalf both of myself and of France. Of course my wife and I will be present at the holy office, and this will enable me to see how the Church flourishes in Szechwan under your dispensation.' Then the bishop blesses us, withdraws, and rides off on his mule. The governor laughs.

"The cathedral is a pagoda with curved roofs decorated with figures of St. George slaying dragons, a
symbol of the victory of the believers over the infidels.
Inside it's crammed with religious objects, innumerable Virgins of all sorts, with and without Holy
Child—immaculate, haloed, in glory, lamenting, weeping at the foot of the cross, or being carried up to
heaven by flights of angels. There are crucifixes, stations of the cross, a whole jumble of Bleeding Hearts,
banners of St. Joan, pictures of the Holy Family, side
chapels devoted to the favorite saints of foreign missions, representations of the grotto at Lourdes, and
collection boxes. The main altar, in the center, is
monumental—enormous, solid, with all the trimmings: lace cloths, candelabra, flowers, a tabernacle
full of consecrated wafers, and beside it a flickering
flame signifying the presence of God. And in the
cathedral are the crowds, the humblest of the people
of Asia. For the priests rarely convert rich and influential Chinese—these have their own methods of protecting themselves against the perils of existence.
Those who adopt the true faith are the poor, the
suffering, the oppressed, those in want. These find in
the Church not so much holiness as powerfully organized help, the sort of thing the Chinese understand
and appreciate, a kind of 'protective society' which,
under the sign of the cross, sells its protection mainly
for earthly and immediate purposes. Heaven is just
an extra. For the Chinese, the Church is a guarantee
of a better life in this harsh and dangerous world, of
escape from hunger and misfortune, and so of probably not dying too soon, not arriving too quickly in
the Christian heaven, whatever felicities it offers. I
know very well—only too well!—that the priests fight
for their flocks like tigers against the war lords, the
soldiers, the bandits, the judges, the other Chinese,

and against disasters of every kind. For the safety and
prosperity of their converts they enter into the most
dubious and complicated intrigues and chicaneries,
and into endless quarrels which bring them in contact
with all sorts of people. Holy persistency! And yet
they're partial and unfair, and don't shrink from pious
fraud and threats, or even from bearing false witness
to support one of their congregation in court against
one or more infidels. They're always insisting that I
should protest and run hither and thither, wearing
myself to a shadow demanding redress, compensation,
guarantees, the exemplary punishment of criminals:
floggings, tortures, decapitations. They want me to
get the authorities to admit negligence or guilt, to
make apologies or denials or proclamations on behalf
of the religion of Jesus. If I listened to them I'd always
be in my litter, on a crusade against some war lord,
some head of a merchant guild, some judge in his
solemn but wretched court, or the representative of
some band of brigands. But that sort of expedition is
always useless. It always ends in a typical Chinese
conversation with some character whose face is smooth
but whose expression is absolutely grim; who denies
everything, professes himself insulted, and blackmails
me. When I come back empty-handed the missionaries
are furious, and I've got a splitting headache. They're
insatiable, these priests! The truth of the matter is
that their Church is a gang in competition with the
innumerable other gangs, but a very powerful one,
which it's better not to interfere with, and one whose
members manage to live in peace and even to prosper.
The only trouble is that the converts know the other
Chinese hate them and look on them as traitors. But
even this hostility works for the greater glory of God,
for the Chinese Christians, the rice-bowl Christians,

confronted with the execration of their fellow countrymen, go the whole hog. To save 'face', they pretend
they're motivated by grace and not by interest, and
indulge in all the rituals of piety. Above all they
cling to the priests as if they were life belts or saviors.
In return for their protection and the material advantages that protection entails, the priests exact blind
obedience and complete submission, demanding demonstrations of devotion no longer attempted even in
France itself. So their converts are more Catholic than
the Catholics, for when the Chinese play a game they
play all out. Their life is bound up in the feasts of
the Church, splendid processions, elaborate liturgy,
pious vocabulary, confession, which includes not only
avowal of one's own sins but the denunciation of
others, severe penances, fasts, and sacraments. Their
days are filled with banners, monstrances, genuflections, acts of contrition, ecstasies, novenas, signs of the
cross, Gregorian chant and dog Latin, and mass after
mass after mass. They are unspeakably deferential
toward their white pastors, because they depend body
and soul on the suspicious looks or irritable words
they let fall. By dint of all their piety, the converts are
no longer quite Chinese. They are 'good' Chinamen,
the only ones who don't hate the 'foreign devils,' the
only ones who've really been emotionally corrupted
by them.

"All this by way of explaining that our high mass at
Chengtu, thanks to the yellow faces rapt with adora-
tion, is one of primitive fervor, the depths of sacred
mystery, the very word of God. The governor general
and his wife are installed in the front row in sumptuous red chairs with armrests. Around them, on
ordinary chairs, are Anne Marie and myself and the
ladies and gentlemen of the governor's suite. We form,

to tell the truth, a little island of the profane in the anonymous flood of Chinese, who pray and go through the rest of the ritual with desperate intensity, kneeling, standing, and crossing themselves as one man. They hold big missals and move their lips in prayer, intone the Gregorian chants to the accompaniment of the organ, drowning the music with a vast snuffling. All faces are grave, all eyes intent, bony hands tell rosaries, and here and there old ladies like convulsionaries crouch and babble. There are clenched fingers, muttering lips, heads banging on the hard ground—supplication everywhere. It is like a vision of the Middle Ages. Yet again I am astonished at how the Chinese, who by nature are so anarchical, individualistic, and selfish, can, once they are caught up in a 'system,' become crazily conformist, vying with one another in perpetual zeal and invention. Certainly the masters of the Christian 'system' have tightened all the screws and taken every possible precaution: they leave nothing to chance, and keep the closest possible watch. The bishop himself is officiating at the altar, looking like Judas or one of the thieves with his hairy face. But he is surrounded by little yellow cherubs, masters of cruet, censer, and sprinkler, little clockwork toys taking part in the sacred ballet and squealing out the responses in their shrill voices. Standing out above the natives bent in prayer are the heads of the young priests and old nuns in charge of the congregation, watching everyone's exact degree of enthusiasm and taking note of any deficiency. The army of Christ is divided up into battalions according to age and sex. All one bay is occupied by orphan girls in blue-and-white uniforms, real daughters of Mary, graceful, diligent, gentle, and of exemplary goodness. The tallest are in front and the smaller ones behind, and among them are some very young Chinese nuns, freshly blown, little flowers in winged coifs who were once waifs, naked and dying, but were picked out of the gutter and fed by God, and then consecrated to His service. Their faces with their fine, round, delicate, almond features seem expressive of happiness, unless it is the Chinese form of resignation, smiling acceptance of the inevitable, of superior force. The force that snatched them away from death and gave them to God is there, vigilant, in the form of those female dragons, the mother superiors. They come from the remotest corners of France, little peasants with fresh complexions and ruddy cheeks, to be the scullions of God. The priests are His mandarins, but the nuns are their underlings, left to slave at relieving poverty, want, hunger, dreadful diseases, and ordinary death, until as a result of fighting against horror and treachery year after year they turn into these old women with haggard, yellow, furrowed faces, eyes of steel, and shriveled flesh. They are poor, harsh, expressionless saints, possessing goodness without tenderness, ruthlessly vigilant and strict in the service of virtue, which for them is represented by the daily ignominy of caring for the wretched dying: old men or newborn infants, all abandoned by proud pagan China. Their reward is the contempt of the Chinese, who accuse them of gathering in souls when they are dying and defenseless. And the discipline they impose in order to keep alive and in the path of the Lord the bodies and hearts of the few human rejects they have saved from physical destruction! Prayer, toil in hospital and workroom, graces and embroidery, all in exchange for a spoonful of rice. Such are the sublime and dreadful nuns, poor wrinkled weather-beaten old women, innocent yet terribly experienced, struggling in the mocking immensity that is China, never giving up, always dying in harness, some rapidly, others so **toughened** that they die of old age. But all behave so humbly toward white men, not only the priests but also the few other Europeans in Chengtu, especially myself, and are always hanging around us, hoping for some help. So today, for the governor general's high mass, they have turned out with their entire contingent of invalids, little yellow sisters, maidens, babes, and nurslings, all clean and orderly and well behaved, with the intense, almost abnormal goodness the Chinese show when they believe or pretend to believe. This goodness is also to be seen in the seams and patches of faces belonging to the handful of aged men and women from the old people's home run by the nuns. The same goodness is grave and radiant on the young faces of hundreds of little orphans. For apart from their Catholic lepers, the nuns have brought all their flock to the service, perhaps partly out of innocent vanity, partly out of pious self-interest, in the hope that the governor general will notice their hard work and be moved to make some grandiose donation beside which the alms extracted from my wife and myself will appear mere trifles. Not far away is another, very different flock. This is made up of young priestlings fresh from France, still raw recruits, their faces stiff with faith, in charge of boys between ten and fifteen, the sons of Christian families whose fathers have set up fee-paying schools. It's considered a sin for a Christian couple not to send their sons there, to learn the catechism by heart by repeating it in chorus from morning till night, just as pagans learn the precepts of Confucius. This teaching, which presents no difficulties because there is never any unruliness or disorder or naughtiness among the pupils, only the intense Chinese desire to become a scholar—even of Christ—is entrusted to the 'shortbeards,' the young men of the missions, rugged as flint, ignorant but pure. This is only their first task. They have a long way to go before they become like the old priests, who, though they remain inflexible as far as dogma is concerned, have through the habit of conversion, preaching, command, and domination acquired the look of merry, companionable old boys who know a thing or two, saintly perhaps, but so amenable they are capable of anything for the greater profit of God and of themselves. The piety of these old boys stands out as frisky and humorous among the rest of the congregation, which is made up mostly of family clans, and whole groups of converts, living together in one street or village. These have come to the cathedral with their patriarchs, their old men and women, their Christian husbands and wives, and their baptized brats. They have come armed with medals, images of saints, all the apparatus of prayer. Each community belongs to one of the worthy old French priests, who knows everything about it, everybody's secrets, and is their head. Many of the priests run several such communities, and there they are among the flock they have ordered to come and attend the bishop's mass for the governor general, recognizing their own during the ceremony, winking at them, passing among them and being greeted with signs of reverence and respect. All around them hands are pressed together and lips murmur, 'God bless you, Father.' These thousands of Chinese are all done up in their best, and yet each man and woman is dressed in a hundred or a thousand faded scraps that look worn out or even verminous. But the Sanctus, the hymns, and the incense drive away misery. And a strange kind of mimicry emerges. The missionaries have come to look like elderly Chinese patricians, and the Chinamen have taken on the air of pious, sancti-

monious members of a European confraternity. As for
the old Chinese women, even those with only one eye
or no teeth or goiter, those who have nostrils but no
noses, those who have warts like great mushrooms
growing out of their flesh, those who dribble and have
a perpetual nervous giggle, all the old women de-
formed by their lives as coolies, slaves, laborers, bearers
of dung and of children—all these have caught perfectly the affectations of the old hens in some rich parish
in France. These wretched matrons are happy to have
survived in spite of all, and for them Christ and the
priest are good masters, the first god and the first man
ever to have bothered with them.

"There are no important Chinamen here today except one general in uniform, and his presence is due
to the thoughtfulness of Tang Kiao, who unearthed
a Christian among his thugs and promoted him to
one of the highest ranks so that he could represent the
war lord at mass. The fellow in question, who has
pointed teeth and a face like a mouse, has been placed
beside the governor general, who is ignorant of the
fact that he's an ex-brigand of very evil habits. Since
his conversion he's been careful to spare mission
property, and the priests protect him, refer to him
affectionately as the 'good thief,' admit him to confession and holy communion, and even pray for his salvation. Anyway, he's very familiar with the etiquette of
mass, and the governor general, who is out of practice, despite an earlier initiation in Tonkin, follows
him, getting up and sitting down when he does.

"A potbellied priest goes up into the pulpit to sing
the praises of the Church, God, the Virgin Mary,
France, China, the governor general, and even Marshal
Tang Kiao. There are organs, hymns, signs of the
cross, everything possible to delight the Chinese. God's

joy, God's suffering, Christ crucified. The boor of a bishop, with his black oakum beard, stands before the tabernacle, his eyes dark and wild, holding out the chalice, bringing the ritual to a climax and saying in his hollow voice: 'This is my body, this is my blood . . .' The yellow congregation is plunged into silence during the mystery of God made man, God given to man to eat—to the Chinaman, the coolie, the orphan. The governor general, who doesn't go in much for mysticism, takes refuge in a dignified attitude at once benevolent and republican. But all around him there is ecstasy. On one side the good thief beats his medal-hung breast, and on the other the governor general's wife kneels imploringly, a typical lady throwing herself on the mercy of God, a respectable adulteress wallowing in remorse, a Magdalene dressed up for repentance in a modest dark dress and a black hat with a veil. Meanwhile a sort of fanfare is heard, half Gregorian and half military, and all the Chinese start to move forward like an army. In perfect order, square after square, officered by the nuns and the priests, they advance toward the altar, faces rigid with concentration, dead with the hope of life, countenances full of compunction, solemnity, and inner contemplation, countenances from which all physical want has disappeared. Hundreds, thousands of them file by interminably, a step at a time, waiting patiently, kneeling in batches of twenty or thirty on the steps of the choir, all simultaneously opening their mouths wide to receive on their tongues the host, God, which the bishop, like some indefatigable Titan, thrusts down their throats by the shovelful. For apart from the babies, all the Chinese take communion. Suddenly the governor's wife rolls her eyes and whispers to me, 'I can't resist. I'm going to have a mouthful of God, too'—just as if she were going to make love to the Lord. And up she gets and goes. Nothing daunts her, neither the yellow crowd parting to make way for her at the divine banquet, nor his grace the bishop, who, when he sees her at his feet with her head stretched out and her mouth open in welcome, stops for a few seconds and holds up the little wafer in triumph—the heavenly disk destined for her, her share of God. Then slowly he lowers it, and with his big hands, dirty as ever, deposits it with ostentatious gentleness between her teeth. A glorious moment, well worth a slight waiving of principle. For the boor of a bishop, like all the missionaries, is very severe and inflexible with any doubtful Chinese candidates for communion, interrogating them, ticking them off, and refusing them the eucharist if they have not prepared themselves for it by long exercise and worthy effort, and if they are not in a proper state of confession, penitence, fasting, and grace. But when a governor's lady, the wife of a notorious unbeliever, demonstrates her appetite for God and makes splendid display of her devotion before all Christian Szechwan, it wouldn't be right to put difficulties in her path. God moves in a mysterious way. She returns all small and humble, head bent, eyes half shut, hands folded, like an irreproachable maiden. She kneels again beside me and says in my ear, 'Done. Nothing to it. But my husband won't be pleased at my making up to the priests. What will his brothers in the Grand Lodge have to say to him! But I can't help it. I'm a Catholic. And anyway, what a lark!' And indeed her husband is glaring furiously. I wonder what to do to avert a row. Finally I realize that the only thing is to compound the felony. I sign discreetly but imperatively to Anne Marie to go to the altar, too. Usually she takes com-

munion only at Easter, for although she comes from
Ancenis, the most backward and clerical town in
France, she's as tepid and indifferent about religion
as about many other things that she doesn't consider
distinguished. She looks down on the Lord, as I sometimes think she does on me. And in her opinion the
missionaries in Chengtu are deplorably vulgar, mere
louts of the Lord who don't even wash their hands
before giving the sacrament. She doesn't like kneeling
in front of them, especially the bishop, and having her
tongue messed about with by their fingers. For her,
communion as practiced in Chengtu is a rather dirty
way of eating. But today she realizes from my manner
that it's a question of her duty as the consul's wife. So
she rises to her feet, still in the most natural manner,
with the gentle but lofty way she has when she means
to do things properly even though she hates it, if it's
part of her responsibility as the wife of Albert Bonnard, representative of France in Szechwan. She ac-
cepts God from the paws of the bishop, her face as
beautiful and calm as a madonna, and just slightly
tilted back with the weight of her chignon. She opens
her lips just as little as necessary. Her whole attitude
is perfectly correct, but this seemliness is peculiar
and hard to interpret: you don't know whether it
conceals boredom, scorn, or a very faint faith. Anyway, she's started the ball rolling. All the wives in the
governor's suite go and take communion, too, like the
good Catholics they are, while their husbands abstain
loftily like the Freemason governor, around whom
they remain in a group like a lay island. The Chinese
general, the good bandit beloved of the priests but
sent by Tang Kiao, is very embarrassed, torn between
his great piety and the necessities of diplomatic correctness. Finally he abandons God and sides like the

others with the governor general. All is for the best, thanks to the division of labor by which the ladies give themselves to God in darkest China, while the gentlemen remain implicitly faithful to the radical-socialist Republic.

"At last the high mass is over. The priests chase out the Chinese Christians double quick, as they serve no further useful purpose for the moment. But in the square in front of the cathedral they have arranged in ranks the orphan boys and girls and the schoolchildren, who stand frantically waving French and Chinese flags. The governor looks grumpy and is in a hurry to be off. But the old French nuns cluster around their heroine, his wife. Their shriveled faces are suddenly full of emotion, their eyes are misty with feeling, ecstasy has smoothed their wrinkles, and they are so carried away with irresistible boldness that they actually address this fine lady. They babble awkwardly and incomprehensibly, in broken words and unfinished sentences, stammering and overcome by the shyness characteristic of their calling, used to scorn, ill-usage, obeying orders, remaining silent, being humiliated. At last the mother superior manages to speak. A large Roman nose is all that remains of her aristocratic breeding; the rest of her face is just a colorless membrane, a worn-out frame. And she says to the governor's wife, 'Madame, you are a saint. What an edifying example you have set here in stubbornly pagan Szechwan. We know you yourself are won over to the cause of God. But we shall pray that you may be helped to bring your noble husband nearer to the Lord, and that he may take pity on the suffering and struggling Church in China. . . .' The priests are embarrassed and clear their throats to try to make her stop. The governor general, who has heard her little speech, comes over and tears his wife away. But the mother superior runs after her and holds out a little parcel in her skinny hand. The governor drags his wife off, but the mother superior still hurries after them with her present, begging, 'Madame, it's a table-cloth our orphans made for you. Please accept it.' The governor's wife takes it, examines it, and says, 'It's very pretty. I like nice linen. . . .' The perceptive Anne Marie notes that it's just an ordinary cloth, not the sort of drawn-thread virtuosity that requires years of work from a hundred girls slaving away in the work-room of a convent for years, from morning to night, day after day, with time out only for eating and pray-ing. Anne Marie reflects no doubt that the nuns, de-spite their compliments to the governor's wife, haven't broken the bank for her. Meanwhile the governor has been telling his better half off good and proper. Then he turns toward me with a sigh of reproach. 'If I'd thought I was going to run into trouble with the Church in China. . . . You should have warned me, Monsieur le Consul. These missionaries are crazy.' But his wife is in seventh heaven, so to speak. She gives me a hearty slap on the shoulder. 'You get better and better, Mon-sieur le Consul. A few days ago, at the pagoda, you made me the wife of the President of the Republic. And today at church you send me to heaven with a halo. You're spoiling me, Monsieur le Consul.'

"That's the end of the priests. And it will soon be the end of the official visit. I'm counting the hours. It's more than time for the thing to end, for while the governor's wife is in the pink of health, like a hen parrot who's never had such a good time in her life, and is almost beginning to love-peck me, the governor himself looks more and more like a moldy cod, or rather a lamprey. His face and stomach are swollen,

he's crotchety and peevish, lethargic, completely done
in. At the consulate he pants his bad breath on me:
'At my age and in my position, I didn't come to China
to open an Oriental fair. I came for the railroad.
Enough of this nonsense. Let's get down to brass
tacks.' "

The advancing day was already getting lighter. It crept
farther and farther into the room and reached the
consul's face: tousled and worn, almost deathlike. It
was the painful moment when the consul, who up till
now had been reveling in his own importance, would
find himself confronted with the real masters of the
railroad and of life: the people with the money. Even
under the opium he realized that if he wanted to
crown his fantasies and make his dream come true he
would have to foot the bill.

'The governor's going to be pleased, for the train,
which is working very efficiently, has just brought to
Chengtu some extremely austere gentlemen who certainly wouldn't have gone out of their way for official
ceremonies or mere exhibitions of local culture.
They're here for the money: how much will the railroad bring in? As a matter of fact, one of them has
been with the governor general throughout his visit,
but this character, the only person in the party who
isn't a civil servant, has up till now been so discreet
and colorless he's been practically forgotten. He's a
small, thin fellow with rather jerky gestures and a
gaunt, almost cadaverous head rather like a pope's
nose, with no special features except red eyes, a ruddy
skin, and a mustache that looks like tinder about to
burst into flame. He's very quiet, is clothed in the
usual colonial sun helmet and linen suit, has the

humble courtesy of a minor clerk, and wears an expression of modest attentiveness. You wouldn't think he could hurt a fly. But I've been keeping my eye on him: I know only too well he's one of those punylooking little Frenchmen who are really made of cast iron. He's the man who built the Chengtu railroad, the director of the railway company. Jungles, mountains, rocks, epidemics, coolies dying wholesale—all these are nothing to him. When he comes to a deserted work site, where the undergrowth has already covered up the yellow corpses of the workers killed by some disease, he just fumes and says, 'Clear up this mess,' and has sulfur strewn on the bodies, or rather what remains of them and their excreta after armies of ants and other creatures have been at them. At the most he makes the sign of the cross when he sees a dead white man, some wretched foreman, for these brutes can die, too. Sometimes it's even an engineer, some naïve young graduate, victim of the empire builders' dream, or a broken, burnt-out, hopeless old ruin in whom the remains of some technical knowledge had survived alcohol and dissipation. Colonial enterprises such as public works and plantations look very nice eventually in reports and speeches, but to begin with they are graveyards. The boss, the little chap who built my railroad, is not interested in horrors or fine feelings or anything useless. He sees things from the practical point of view. He faces up to everything, manages everything, despite the fact that he's consumed with malaria and dysentery. He gets the better of his exhaustion. He's shaped like a pin—a skull balanced with difficulty on a body thin as wire. But his innate obstinacy overcomes all obstacles, those presented by men and those presented by nature, which is like some shifting vegetable and mineral tempest, a black and

green and unreliable chaos. Every year he thrusts his
rails farther into unknown regions, where, apart from
a few miserable settlements on some peak or in some
depression, the only ordinary inhabitants are primitives or outlaws. But this little man, always absolutely
clean and always absolutely inflexible, goes on looping
his line over abysses, making bridges like spiderwebs
over canyons, tunneling like a mole through the
crumbling mountains. He is always irreproachable, a
model chief engineer with his surveys and embankments and explosives. His yellow men are recruited
by force and dig away like ants; his European employees are wild beasts ravaged by cirrhosis and madness;
his caravans of mules transport heavy equipment over
the wildest of paths; his daily statistics—very rough—
are of the numbers likely to die; his doctors are adventurers without qualifications or drugs; his hospitals
are morgues, and his cemeteries, patches of roughly
cleared jungle with a common pit for the natives and
a semblance of graves for the Europeans. Despite everything, he always keeps his accounts strictly up to date,
to the last penny and with exemplary honesty. To him,
money is sacred. And it was part of his plan, within
his budget, to continue the line and eventually bring
it to Chengtu. This financial correctness is the only
thing he prides himself on.

"That's the sort of person he is—phenomenally
lacking in feeling and imagination. He possesses all
the ordinary, average virtues of a typical Frenchman.
He's a composite of the good pupil, the successful
examination candidate, the paterfamilias, the respectful employee, the efficient executive, but in him these
respectable qualities, this devotion to established val-
ues, this respect for hard work, are all carried to a level
so extreme, so impenetrable and sacrosanct, that they

verge on the fantastic. I know the type well. French colonial history is full of them. After good and loyal service they usually end up as submanagers of the firm in which they started at the bottom of the ladder. They are given decorations, and die in France in their seventies, regretted by their families and wept over by their children. There's generally an announcement in *Le Figaro,* a scraggy widow in black, daughters-in-law in veils, and sons with degrees in engineering, looking sad and dignified, slightly more modern than their father, wearing crepe bands on their sleeves. These people's lives end quietly. Who'd ever guess how harsh they have been in the past? But my fellow here in Chengtu is still in his prime. His modesty is so deep and sincere that he's surprised if anyone compliments him on his work. When I thanked him, with many eulogies, for having brought my railroad right to Chengtu for me, he coughed and blushed and looked away, awkward and embarrassed, like a half-wit or someone at his first communion. 'I didn't do anything, Monsieur le Consul,' he stammered. 'I only carried out the orders of the board. Now they—they're really great men, men of experience. . . .' So all he's done, all those years beset by danger and horror and corpses in the jungle, which is a combination prison and battlefield, all that—the miracle of the railroad—he offers up in homage to his bosses, the distant big shots who 'guided' him by means of angry telegrams exclaiming at delays and expense and anything unexpected. All he knows are the revered names of high finance—people who deny ordinary, vulgar reality and express themselves only through files and balance sheets and profits. The civilization of dividends.

"I'm scared of this little fellow. For at bottom he doesn't care a straw about France, even though he's a good patriot and lost a son or two at Verdun. Despite his shy politeness toward me, I know I'm of no importance to him, any more than the governor general is. He'd be perfectly capable of turning on us one day, emerging suddenly from his timidity and patronizing us, shouting at us, making scenes, issuing ultimatums. I sense that he's worried and uneasy beneath his clerklike airs; he's getting more and more nervous, and nearly chokes every time he opens his mouth. Fortunately he keeps himself under control. The most he's done is whisper once to me, enigmatically, 'What will my superiors say? They're not going to be pleased.' He's like a little shrimp or a frog, but all ready to explode. Something's worrying him. Those figures, of course, the first on the profitability of the line. He's got a grocer's mentality about his great work. He goes about clutching a briefcase containing a sort of ledger, with a wide column for the liabilities—all the outlays and investments—and another, much narrower, for the assets. For the railway hasn't gotten off to a very good start; it looks as if it may even be a disaster. The freight cars travel empty, while the holds of the Yangtze steamers are fuller than ever. In the ports of the upper Yangtze the coolies crowd around them, with their chafed backs, to unload the goods from Shanghai and to load in their place the finest products of Szechwan—sacks of rice, bales of cotton, teas, silks. Not to mention the opium, which also travels by that route. It's clear that the taipans of Shanghai have reacted. They've lowered the charges on their boats, and sent their compradors to the big Chinese merchants in Chungking and Chengtu with lots of promises in exchange for devious arrangements. All the railway company gets are claims from the families of people killed by the trains, for the blasted Chinese use the track as if it were a road, and go along it with asses and mules, paying not the slightest attention to the whistle of the engine. They don't even step aside. And others go gaily into the tunnels and get themselves run over in the darkness. And every time the elder brothers and self-styled widows claim fantastic amounts of compensation, stirring up the crowds, pestering the magistrates, and stopping the trains with hysterical shrieks. One furious crowd out in the wilds even started to lynch the French engineer who brought the first train to Chengtu—the one I congratulated. He's still in hospital, and he's told how, with some soldiers just looking on and doing nothing, a whole mob clambered up and grabbed him out of the locomotive, then threw him on the ground in front of the remains of someone who appeared to have been cut in half by a wheel. He'd never have gotten out of it alive if he hadn't sworn that the company would pay a thousand taels in compensation—a thousand times more than a Chink is worth, dead or alive. In other words, they've discovered a new racket. Of course this deplorable state of affairs, all the various troubles, are the result of a deliberate conspiracy. The hand of Albion is mixed up in it. The worst of it is that Tang Kiao, that good friend of the French, doesn't do a thing. And heaven knows he can make himself felt when he wants to! But for the moment he, too, doesn't care.

"Confronted with these catastrophic results, the little Frenchman controls himself, but he's getting thin and turning all colors of the rainbow. The only reason he doesn't explode is that he's waiting. He's been restraining himself heroically until his masters arrive in Chengtu—his revered bosses, the big bankers. Now that they're here, they take it very well, smiling faintly like people with hardly a care in the world, used to making their own interests prevail, but gently, inexorably, without any trouble or fuss. There are three of them. One does the dirty work, a sort of slug made not of jelly but of rubber, reddish in color, who draws himself up and down like a window or a guillotine, making faces and uttering strange croaks. The second is the retired cavalry officer type, carrying a flavor of the riding academy and show jumping, of the aristocracy and horse manure. With his bowlegs and his belligerent nose, this human heron is a sort of private secretary who, thanks to his long shanks, can lift even the dirtiest business out of the mud and manage to present it on a salver of rigid respectability, half social and half military. The third man is the 'Boss.' He has a big round face, pink and amiable, rather like a knuckle of ham. His eyes are pale, set against those healthy prosperous cheeks, his hair well brushed if slightly faded, his skin highly polished, redolent of a lengthy toilet and eau de Cologne. In a word, he is the incarnation of Faubourg Saint-Germain elegance, a sort of peasant prince. He has a perfect way of turning up, appearing, making his presence felt—heavily light. A perfect way of shaking the hands of the gentlemen and kissing those of the ladies. There's a sort of sterling weight about him generally, both physical and moral. He has a good body with no paunch, but aristocratically well covered and solid, and a discreet suggestion of powerful muscles kept in trim by a judicious balance of whiskey and gymnastics. A good companion, a good talker, outspoken but polite, bold, with a touch of gallantry, always ready with an understanding smile on a face of genial reserve, highly sociable, good at starting off an animated conversation with a good-humored word, or quietly waiting for someone else to make a witty remark before urbanely expanding the subject. And all these pleasing arts without ever putting himself forward or saying anything especially important or funny or out of the way—just a sound way of expressing himself, and prudence. Nevertheless, you are always like a cat on hot bricks with him, for it's clear nothing escapes him: he sees everything, weighs it and, in his own way, reacts. You keep having the feeling that with all his skill at banality, he's planting signs and warnings and ultimatums. His language is a kind of mysterious code made up of a thousand tiny nuances corresponding to the secret notes he's always giving out. Sometimes there's a flicker of the eyelids: the iris is round, with an uncertain gleam in it, but it clears rapidly, innocently, leaving everything misty and vague and well-bred, while at the same time everything is registered in his mind, sharp as a scythe. If anyone presses him on a specific point he resorts to a deliberately naïve and rustic irony, a foolishness nicely calculated to show his own intelligence and the stupidity of the person who's bothering him. If the other still doesn't catch on, our man's voice grows honeyed, with an acid and dangerous sweetness. But it takes exceptional circumstances to make those pink lips utter one of his devastating phrases, curt and precise as a bite. On the whole you'd take him for the nicest, most easygoing and charming chap in the world. What I wonder is how his complexion can still be so fresh and clear after living all those years in Saigon, which is like an oven. Everyone else in the colonies bears the stigmata—streaks, speckles, sweat, too much fat or not enough, cirrhosis, swellings, discharges, or desiccations. But not him. He's always as fresh as paint, a bourgeois on the fringes of the nobility, a patrician of the Jockey Club who looks as if he'd never left France and Paris society. It's as though the fans in Indochina, instead of making him go hot and cold and suffer the flushes and tremblings of fever together with all the other drawbacks they inflict on everyone else, have only wafted him and his porcelain puss to the miraculous seventh heaven and eternal spring of finance. He is completely unmarked by colonial life, and yet he's the biggest—and most respected—shark in the French empire. He's the enemy of my protector in Shanghai. How's he going to treat me? What makes me even more scared is that he and his pals have a gruesome reputation. They're called 'the executioners.' They've systematically exploited Indochina, but legally, respectably, with the blessing of the Indochinese government and civil service. They have only to lower the net and haul in the fish. They are as nice as can be when times are prosperous, when rice and rubber from Cochin China are booming, when Saigon is festive with its brave pioneers, its worthy 'old hands,' its fine French colonials half crazy with piasters and schemes and champagne and bragging and taxi girls—crazy to clear the forest and set up plantations, discover mines. A real spree. In this bear garden our friends the bankers give credit to all comers, anyone who wants to take a risk, anyone setting up a business, likely or unlikely, sound or unsound, honest or crooked. People's imaginations run riot—they all want to go one better, they all want to do something, anything. Only the bankers keep a cool head: their safes are full of IOUs, clearly set out in the proper legal forms, in terms that are severe but not usurious. Then all the bankers have to do is wait. For they know the economics of the tropics. They know that upsurges are followed by depressions, that after breath-taking rises markets can collapse with tragic suddenness. Eventually there comes the moment of despair, ruin, suicide, with Saigon a dead city, and hard-pressed debtors imploring the bank to give them a bit longer to repay. The banks have the best will in the world; so have the bankers. But they are terribly sorry, they have no alternative but to say no, for they have to think of their shareholders, and they have to be strict in order to avoid going bankrupt themselves. It's a very enjoyable strictness, which enables the bank to take payment in kind, and to rake in the goods, property, and land of all the many defaulters, all the suckers who borrowed and slaved and achieved something, who thought they were succeeding and then suddenly found themselves penniless, cleaned out, without anything left. And all done in the correctest possible manner, with the proper legal forms. The bank is like a great octopus.

"I must admit that, confronted with this group of bankers, I'm frightened. What a trio—the executioner, the killer with the bloated face; the straight-laced window dresser who lends a good appearance to murder; and the Brain, the Mastermind, the one who thinks up and directs the crimes, and pockets the winnings for the greater glory of the bank. Of course it's only economic murder—there's no blood, except sometimes when a few desperate victims take refuge through suicide in another world, where there aren't any bankers. A slight hitch in the system. But in fact butchery by piaster or latex or paddy fields is just as cruel as slaughter by the sword. Only in this case it's done cleanly. Whereas in other French colonies it's a shambles and a muddle, with cheating and small-time tricks and feeble fraud, the native getting a kick in the behind and the customs clerk and petty civil servant ruling the roost, Indochina is grandiosely pure.

Pure with the lofty purity of big money in the abstract, dominating and governing everything but never appearing in the open, except to pay the clerks and to grease the occasional palm. In this intangible and implacable universe reign my three lords of money, colder than the English in Shanghai, more devious than the big Chinese and the tiny Annamites, cleverer psychologists than the Jesuits, knowing everything, exploiting everything; perfect cash registers. Click, and a transaction is completed. They're not content with cleaning out the country. They're not content to speculate on all the currencies and stock exchanges in Asia: a tip, a few telegrams, a few maneuvers, and they make an enormous bundle every time. But they are formidable because despite what they really do, they are not adventurers. They are fundamentally respectable, professionals from the best families, who've passed the highest examinations and been trained in the best ministries. Everything they do is secret, mysterious, leaves no evidence, and yet they always have the relevant documents up to date and open to inspection, irreproachable. Woe to anyone who suspects them or gets in their way or tries to trip them up. For they are sacrosanct—respectable monsters in their offices by day, men of the world in the evening, the real masters of Indochina at all times. But their highest trump is that they are not just money merchants. They don't confine themselves to speculation, to the financing of businesses, trading channels, imports and exports, 'schemes.' They are also creators. They really create Indochina, the Indochina of wealth, with forests of rubber trees, canals and dikes multiplying the rice harvests, new cities, factories where the workers get hardly any wages, ports full of cargo ships, roads and railways. The trick it to make other people put up the capital—the ordinary Europeans, who are later crushed, or the Indochinese government, with which they come to an arrangement. Provided it's a paying proposition. In other words, it will go hard with me if my Chengtu 'line' is losing money.

"There's a formidable session in my office. I'm surrounded by solemn faces—serious, stiff, grave, preoccupied with money. It starts off badly, with the little Frenchman, the insignificant but terrible engineer, giving an account of things. He grunts away like someone with constipation trying to relieve himself, misfortunes and accusations pouring out of his pursed lips in a rapid, halting whine. The governor general gives me a disagreeable look: the old boy resents having trouble, and he's getting ready to be angry, working up a masterly bad temper, one really worthy of the governor general. He's breathing heavily already, his veins are standing out, he'll have a stroke if he doesn't watch out. I must say the faces of his subordinates, naturally cold and pale, are no more enticing. On the contrary. As for the bankers' faces as they listen, you'd think it was the Last Judgment! The Elastic Man grins and works his jaws like an eager sword swallower. The Blimp sits at attention, ready to give the firing squad its orders. The Boss rubs his hands voluptuously like some Genghis Khan of finance getting ready to slaughter everyone, beginning with me. I feel lost, done for, reduced to a jelly. But suddenly the head banker, instead of dealing me the finishing blow, makes an O with his lips and says, 'Tut tut tut,' like a little boy playing with his trains. It's a signal to stop the little Frenchman, who's exhausted and breathless, but keeps spitting out wretched little moans of accusation. It isn't on me that the thunderbolt falls. 'That'll do,' says the great financier to his little man.

'You're getting far too worked up. You'll make yourself ill if you go on like that.' And he decks his face
with a happy smile, broad, winning, contagious. He
radiates satisfaction, stroking his fingers coolly, non-
chalantly, serious and easy at the same time, and raises
his head slightly before addressing, slowly and genially
this time, the noble assembly, who are completely
taken by surprise. 'Your Excellency, gentlemen,' he
says. 'What did you expect? The situation is exactly
as I predicted. It was certain that our friend Tang
Kiao would only be biding his time. He wants to get
some more out of this project than he's gotten already,
this great friend of ours. He's greedy. But we'll make
him see reason. Only, Your Excellency, you'll have to
make another little sacrifice. It's up to Indochina to
satisfy Tang Kiao—Indochina is the party chiefly concerned in the Szechwan line. I and my bank have done
all we can. More than we can, in fact. Out of pure
patriotism. But it can't go on like that.'

"The afternoon session takes place in Tang Kiao's
yamen. A very muted occasion. Scarcely a bugle in our
honor. Not from lack of respect, but out of discretion:
in China, too, money is dealt with in silence. We all
crowd into a little dark room like a safe, about a
round, marble-topped table. You'd think it was a
conspiracy. The big moment has come. The faces stand
out in sudden, tragic relief, though for nearly an hour
they remain wrapped in the wadding of politeness.
The higher the stake, the longer and more unendur-
able are the hors d'oeuvres of insignificance. Tang
Kiao, not dressed in any special way, inquires minutely
after the governor general's health, repeating the same
question a hundred times. His rhinocerous muzzle
clouds over with emotion as the governor general
complains of how tired he is and in particular of the

pains in his innards. Finally Tang Kiao murmurs a
few words to Mr. Siu, who withdraws. Siu embodies
the civil element in Tang Kiao's entourage. So he's
adopted a startling, flamboyant, 'super-Peking' personality, with swallow-tailed coat, patent leather shoes,
starched shirt, and bow tie—an aggressively pacific
symphony in black and white. The most astonishing
part of his getup is a massive, shiny top hat, which fits
exactly on the almost equally heavy and solemn cylin-
der of his skull. Mr. Siu is young, not yet forty, with
a skin so smooth and tightly drawn over a burgeoning
layer of fat that there's hardly any room for his tiny
features on that lumpish, self-satisfied baby face. He's
so swollen in his vanity that you can hardly tell he's
got two eyes, two ears, a nose, and a mouth. But he
can see and hear 'schemes' all right, and understand
them better than any old monkey or shark of an older
Chinaman. He's the one Tang Kiao has most confidence in, and he's appointed him head of his 'Yunnan-
Szechwan government.' Siu is of course a Yunnanese.
He's trying to get Tang Kiao to declare a state independent of China, which would be a semiprotectorate
of the French, provided they were willing to pay
enough. But would they really cough up? There is no
doubt that this is what is in Tang Kiao's mind today.
For Siu is the only person he's chosen to partner him
in the game against all of us. He's given Siu the job
of selling his, Tang Kiao's, wares to the French, of
making them part with a few more millions for the
railroad. To pull the wool over our eyes, Siu has first
been sent by his master to get a miracuous potion to
soothe the governor general's intestines. He returns
with a bottle cut from an agate, protected by a dragon
carved in the veins of the stone. It contains some
murky liquid. Siu, looking odder and more like a fat

boy than ever, waves his chubby little hands to bestow the Chinese elixir on the governor, whose rear end, on his own testimony, is damper than it should be.

"Then the real contest begins. I don't say anything. As a matter of fact, everyone looks asleep, but that only shows how intent they really are. Heads nod. Tang Kiao, listening to the Frenchmen, wags his pate steadily to and fro the way a coolie crouching on the ground wags his behind. Mr. Siu, eyes shut, looks as if he hasn't any eyes at all. The governor general is probably the only one who's genuinely asleep. But it's up to him to speak. He grouses to Tang Kiao about how disappointed he is. Why doesn't Tang Kiao see to it, as he undertook to do, that the trains are full? At this point inspiration forsakes the governor general, and when his boss dries up, the chief private secretary can contain himself no longer. He yaps like a mongrel —a typical French official outraged by the inefficiency of the natives. He goes for Tang Kiao as if he were a mere Annamite mandarin. European rage. One hears the words 'incompetence,' 'inadequacy,' 'negligence,' 'dishonesty,' 'laziness,' 'disloyalty,' slackness.' A typical colonialist bawling out. Tang Kiao, instead of playing the proud war lord and being angry, bows his head, beats his breast, adopts the attitudes of humility and remorse. His formidable figure all crumpled and bent, he murmurs tonelessly, 'I am greatly to blame. I didn't manage to take the necessary steps to show the people of Szechwan how useful the railroad would be to them. I feel very guilty.' At this point the banker from Indochina, the money lord, stirs loftily, worried and embarrassed. The discussion has taken the worst possible turn: Tang Kiao's mildness is going to cost a pretty penny. His acceptance of the insults of that fool of a secretary, his actual systematic exaggeration of them, his self-criticism and surrender of 'face,' may just be a bit of dangerous playacting, a trap. It looks like a trick. Anything is possible. Or else suddenly, after making all these gestures of good will, Tang Kiao may pretend he can no longer contain himself and burst into a fit of fury which can only be assuaged with money. More probably, in order to prevent any actual outburst, to avoid having him pass from tearful grimaces to open threats, he'll have to be muffled with bank notes and gold pieces. And, of course, fat Siu is standing by to direct operations. Then the banker, in his frankest manner, frankness being his strong suit, takes the lead. He even bows to Tang Kiao with a mixture of respect and complicity. 'Lord Tang Kiao,' he says, 'has set us an example of magnanimity by taking all the blame upon himself. But he is by no means responsible for our setbacks; he did all he could. It is we ourselves who have made the great mistake of underestimating the English—they're the ones responsible for this mess. They've done all they can to throw a monkey wrench into the works. Now, instead of squabbling foolishly among ourselves, we ought to join with our friend Lord Tang Kiao to find the answer and take the necessary measures.'

"Despite these words, Tang Kiao seems to have reverted to his former apathy. Now is the moment for Mr. Siu, a great baby in a tall hat, to play his first card. This is the 'opening,' the crucial moment in negotiations with the Chinese, a moment which it always takes hours to reach. For this purpose Mr. Siu, his face slightly relaxed, his eyes open, a smile precise as arithmetic spread across the little features, uses the jargon of the 'Westernized' Chinese, as ridiculous as his attire. He makes a little speech: 'Allow me, despite my unworthiness, to state my point of view. I once studied economics in the greatest universities of Europe and America. I learned that it was very difficult to alter established trade currents. It takes great changes to do that. In the present situation the building of the railroad is not enough. It's necessary to create modern industry at the same time. That's what my master Tang Kiao thinks. If the French made it possible for him to set up big factories in Szechwan, they would naturally be oriented toward Indochina, which would have the benefit of all the provincial trade.' There is an enormous growl. It comes from Tang Kiao. The veins stand out on his wall-like brow, his eyes gleam with desire, his mouth is cannibal in its voracity. His concupiscence is unleashed in a sort of sacred fury, almost apoplexy. 'What I want,' he belches, 'is an arms factory to make my own guns. Then I can crush my enemies and increase my power at the same time that I benefit my French friends. I also want machines to make my own steel and electricity. I want—' The horrified governor general attempts in vain to stop him by stammering, 'My august friend, your suggestions are very interesting. Fascinating. But they raise important problems, especially from the financial point of view. As you know, the Indochinese budget . . . It will have to be very carefully looked into. . . .' But the appeals to reason made by the governor, anxious about his piasters, are lost in a general delirious hullabaloo. The banker, in ecstasies, has clutched Tang Kiao by the sleeve and is smirking up at the giant—eyes, hands, and lips all flying, his imperious and arrogant self-control for once forgotten. 'Lord Tang Kiao is right,' he cries. 'As a matter of fact, I had similar projects in mind myself. France's duty, its mission, is to industrialize Szechwan. I can guarantee there won't be any problem about investment: the prospects are so good, with all those raw materials, all those men! The best thing would be to form some Franco-Szechwanese companies under the aegis of General Tang Kiao and a few important merchants in Chengtu, and let them begin with the basic activities.' I can see what he's after, artful wretch, slavering away already over future dividends and profits. Of course Tang Kiao isn't going to get his arms factory or his blast furnaces—heavy industry is too much bother, too much of a commitment, doesn't produce easy profits. No need to tell him this now; he can be consoled in due course with cash and a few old pieces of artillery. In any case, old Tang Kiao is going to have to be fattened up like a pig. But what does it matter? If the affair's properly handled it will bring in a hundred or two hundred percent profit every year, at least. And they've already had experience with how to do it in Tonkin. What's needed is a few cement factories, some factories for mass-producing textiles, especially cotton, a few silk factories, coal mines and power stations, and various establishments for producing things like salt, opium, cigarettes, possibly beer, alcohol, and iceboxes. In short, the idea is to take a society that's still in the Middle Ages and load it with a whole lot of modern comforts. Not luxury. Just goods produced on the spot with local materials by proletarianized and underpaid coolies and women and girls, and then let loose on people who get to like them, become used to them. There's no need for expensive, delicate, or complicated machinery—just a minimum, a lot of boilers and taps and cables and cogwheels, motors and pistons and generators. But first and foremost, what you have to make use of are the hands, backs, muscles, and fingers of the poor wretches, men and women, who are shut up in sheds with a few traditional Chinese tools and some rudimentary equipment imported from France. What with famines and floods and all the rest, you can get as much labor as you want from the hovels in the country and the towns alike—peasants, beggars, orphans, vagabonds, runaway concubines, abandoned children, coolies, sampan men, all kinds of waifs who only have to be disciplined and trained. It costs practically nothing. Two or three energetic Europeans to every factory, and a few dozen Chinese foremen with sticks—that's enough to manage the workers. Two or three cents a day for wages so that they can afford a bowl of rice and not die of starvation—and that's already a great advance on the period before industrialization, when the people's daily problem was precisely that. Social progress at the cheapest possible price. Planks to sleep on, forty or fifty people to a hut, that's quite enough. No need for medicine and all those frills—the vitality of the Chinese is well known. If anyone dies you just cart the body away and replace him. It's a fine sight, the people of Asia engaged in industry. For the mines, a winch and a drill, and thousands of human ants bury themselves underground with their spades and their little baskets to bring out the ore. In the textile industry it's the women, in front of all those whirring looms. The silk factories are like ovens; for sixteen or eighteen hours a day, little girls with their neat fingers empty the cocoons by dipping them in bowls of boiling water. A few little carts and above all plenty of men can carry the loads and the finished goods. Work, work, work. But the Chinese are liable to rebel: they have to be kept in check. You have to track down the Red agitators trained in Shanghai. To do that you need to be in league with Tang Kiao and the other Chinese big shots, the merchants of Chengtu. It's better to have them with you and on your side, as the taipans are beginning to find out. They established firms in Shanghai that were out-and-out British and white, employing Chinese only as minor compradors. This policy is now causing them serious trouble, in both Shanghai and Canton. Szechwan is too remote to have been corrupted yet, but there's not much time. It could be terrific for a while, with a hundred million Szechwanese to be transformed into consumers, customers. But the creation of this new market will destroy the old society and all the traditional social structure. It will break the guilds and the old trades, ruin the artisans and the watermen, deliver the land over to the nouveaux riches, to the lords of the land and their allies—the big merchants who have caught on and converted to the new ways, and who'll suddenly grab everything. Modernization will also be a massacre. It can bring troubles, wars, revolution, ineradicable hatred. So the thing to do is make as much money as you can as quickly as you can, get your outlay back in three or four years. After that everything you make is clear profit. The game is certainly worth the candle. Investment capital can easily be found in Indochina, France, China, the bank, high finance, the big companies. A whole lot of little companies can be formed with registered offices in Chengtu, Yunnanfu, or Hanoi. But all the same it would be best to get the guarantee of the Indochinese government in case things went wrong sooner than expected. . . .

"I can see all these thoughts running through the banker's skull. And I can feel them spreading out, filling the air, and taking possession of everyone else. All is joy, happiness, enthusiasm, the beginning of a new era. They're already discussing how to set about it. Tang Kiao tells the governor general that he urgently needs a loan in order to strengthen his hold over the army, which enables him to control Szechwan, the kingpin of the whole scheme. After some reluctance and hesitation, the governor general mutters something that sounds like a promise. At least, that's how Tang Kiao takes it. His whole face is immediately wreathed in bliss, contentment, friendliness. He declares that from tomorrow on, all the trains will be full. He'll see to it himself, take the necessary steps, persuade his friends the merchants to do as they ought. He even gives thought to the details. He tells us of one very sound decision. To counteract the vexatious Szechwanese craze for getting squashed to a pulp in the tunnels, the railway company will pay a lump sum of a hundred sapeks for every victim—in other words, so little that it will discourage people from resorting to this shameless form of extortion. Everyone laughs. Tepid champagne is produced. The euphoria increases. Only the governor general looks a bit harassed. When we leave, Tang Kiao's face beams on us like the full moon, a great big moon full of inward hilarity. As for the money lord, the banker: having congratulated Tang Kiao, he now congratulates himself, casting self-satisfied glances around him. His dogsbodies quiver with delicious greed. But the governor general's wrinkles are still full of worry, and just before we get to the consulate on the way home he tells me straight, 'I'm going to have to pay dearly for you and your railway, Monsieur le Consul.' I reassure him: in matters of finance he has only to leave everything to his administrators in the civil service. They take a particular pride in monetary matters. Every year, they produce for Indochina, as for all the other territories that go to make up the union, a budget that's a marvel of accounting, always balanced to the last piaster. They're not the sort of people to spoil these masterpieces by uncalled-for generosity: this caution is their way of respecting the success, the civilization, and the achievement of France. No, they know a trick worth two of that. The governor general has nothing to worry about. Keeping the budget as it should be does not prevent the administrators from seeing the need for banks and trusts, also indispensable instruments of colonialism. In Indochina patriotism, and everything that derives from it in the form of progress, peace, the people's welfare, and noble sentiments, is above all, in both the public and the private sector, a matter of money—big money. Everything is linked with everything else. So the administrators, who regard it as their duty after all to do their best for the financial powers that be, have a thousand tricks and subterranean methods, both indirect and efficient, to do this and not upset the official figures. The figures are always in order in Indochina, at least at the level that matters: that of the administration and the financial big shots. Once again, the governor general needn't worry. Since the railroad and the Chengtu factories appear to interest the big moneybags so much, the administrators will do the best they can for them in the name of the highest interests of empire.

"My speech reassures the governor general. Moreover, he's caught up in and excited by the last festivities, the festivities of departure. Everything has worked out, and it's time to go back to Hanoi. But before that there are still some wild parties ahead—the final celebrations, even more sumptuous than those that greeted his arrival, swimming in all the potions and juices and sauces of Friendship, now swelled into a warm flood, a cataplasm. It's to be seen in the folds and creases, the little eyes, the fat jowls, the shaven cheeks

and the thick lips of Tang Kiao. It pours out of all
the Chinese. There are tons of friendship, enough and
to spare, in their toasts, their salutations, their bowings
and scrapings, their thoughtfulness, their considerate-
ness, their hopes and wishes and vows and promises, in
every speech, every sentence, every pore of their skin
and stitch of their uniforms, every tooth and every
whisker. It's in the sleeves of the big merchants, the
plumes of the generals, the bugles and bayonets of the
soldiers. The sublime flower of Franco-Szechwanese
friendship blooms for the eternal welfare of both
peoples. What a flow! And then there's the ceremony
of the presents. The governor general takes out all the
decorations he's brought with him in his baggage—a
whole bazaar of medals and sashes ornamented with
moons, elephants, and suns made of artificial enamel
and artificial gold and silver, nice cheap colonial orders, very useful and very picturesque—and these he
hangs on the celestial breasts, mumbling the time-honored formula and handing over the certificates. 'In the
name of the French Republic,' he keeps bleating. It's
like handing out beads to savages, but this unworthy
thought doesn't occur to anyone. The governor general
goes so far as to kiss Tang Kiao in a manly fashion on
both cheeks. Tang Kiao is surprised at first, but after
a moment's hesitation bravely submits. Universal emotion. Tang Kiao's band plays the *Marseillaise*. The
ladies are present. The governor's wife, in a low-cut
dress, claps her hands. And that isn't all: the governor
general also has a surplus of Sèvres vases which he
hands out, the largest going to Tang Kiao, who probably reflects that it will make a good spittoon.

"But these are all trifles compared with the presents
the Chinese give in return. There's a deluge of sandalwood boxes with sliding lids containing all the trea-

sures of the Middle Kingdom. A cascade of jewels falls both on the ladies and on the gentlemen, precious stones, silks, terra cottas, bronzes thousands of years old, carved ivory. And they are all pieces much more precious and rare than any that the Europeans managed to snag for themselves in the shops when they first came to Chengtu. Only the finest materials, the most elaborate shapes, the most majestic splendors of China. Enough to fill a museum. Every important citizen of Chengtu has contributed without stint. There must be a very powerful interest at work to make these old Chinks part with such examples of the delicate workmanship they delight in and hand it over to ignorant 'barbarians.' Yes, but it's the future that's at stake. It shows how this business of factories and industrialization must have spread through the town and stirred people's imaginations. The Chinks vie with each other to show, through the magnificence of their offerings, their love for France and the French. In actual fact, what they are doing is compromising them morally, for in China anyone who gives, even humbly and without conditions or allusions, creates in those he gives to an obligation to show gratitude. And the rich men of Chengtu think that with their knickknacks they are building up a capital of gratitude with the governor, the administrators, and the bankers, payable ultimately in the form of millions, machinery, and dividends. Nothing is said. Everything is understood. To be on the safe side, the Chinese shower not only the governor with 'curios' but also his whole suite; the whole French colony is showered with little parcels, right down to the last dogsbody. Needless to say, the governor has no idea of these calculations and ulterior motives. 'People often make the Chinese out to be disagreeable, but they are very nice,' he observes.

Presents turn up everywhere—beside your plate at table, on the chairs, in the beds, accompanied by compliments written on rolls of red paper. Sometimes one of the Chinese, as a token of his own unworthiness, does not venture to send his gifts by messenger, and bribes the consulate servants, who take them in and leave them in the most unexpected places. It's rather like a treasure hunt. The governor's wife is in the seventh heaven, half greedy little girl, half old-clothes merchant who's found undreamed-of loot. For of course the Chinese are clever enough to overcome their scorn for women and make her the chief target of their generosity. She is submerged in boxes and cases, which she opens with her teeth and nails, not letting anyone else interfere, uttering caustic remarks, squealing, making faces. She has moments of ecstasy and others when she is suddenly quite cool again, a shop assistant counting up: 'That makes thirty jade necklaces, eighteen red-gold bracelets, ten agates . . .' and so it goes on. And then, thanks to Tang Kiao, comes the most sublime surprise of all. For the present offered by Tang Kiao, the most important of all the Chinese, the one who thinks of everything, is not 'chinoiserie,' however splendid. It's unanswerable, a knockout. It's come via Shanghai from the Rue de la Paix in Paris! A Western present, a super-Western present, a thing for a duchess, a millionairess, a great lady rolling in money or an insatiable cocotte: a velvet case containing a blue diamond rivière, ten stones in all, of the finest water, with flashing facets—the smallest seven or eight carats. The governor's wife swoons at the sight of it. Then she comes to, grabs the diamonds, kisses them, and weeps. 'Look, Pettikins, look! Oh, I'm so happy. . . .' But Pettikins, red in the face, scowls and says, 'You can't accept that. I'd be accused of selling Indochina.' Then she snarls like a wolf: 'Idiot! You won't get these diamonds away from me. I'd rather kill myself. Here they are and here they stay. I've earned them. Do you think it's much fun living with an old wretch like you, stingy into the bargain, you and your ridiculous principles! You couldn't even give me one little brilliant when we got married. His lordship wants to be respectable, he's thinking of himself, and I can go and jump in the lake. Well, this time I'm not having any.'

"I realize my hour is come. I venture to point out to the governor general: 'Your Excellency, it's impossible to send the necklace back to Tang Kiao. It would be a mortal insult, it would make him lose "face," it would jeopardize everything.' 'Very well. Monsieur le Consul—you can explain the situation to him.' 'Your Excellency, Tang Kiao will never understand. . . .' Of course what I say is true, but it also comes at the right moment. I ought to be given some credit for my attitude: Tang Kiao has only given Anne Marie a measly little solitaire, which confirms my reputation for integrity but doesn't take my importance sufficiently into account. For after all, the railroad and all these projects for industrialization are largely my doing. I am slightly annoyed, even though Anne Marie doesn't seem to care about the smallness of her jewel. She's smiling her strange smile. Anyhow, the governor gives in—not to his wife, but for reasons of state. It comes to the same thing. During the evening his wife, decked in her diamonds, takes me aside in the drawing room. 'Albert,' she says, 'I'll never forget what you've done for me. Thank you. But one good turn deserves another, as my husband says—he's fond of proverbs. So come to Tonkin, alone, and I'll repay you in kind.' I am perplexed. This is a dilemma. To refuse the

favors of such a woman is always dangerous, for she
might be angry and vindictive. But at the same time
it would be very risky to sleep with the governor
general's wife. It might go wrong and ruin my career.
In my embarrassment I mutter something inaudible.
But the governor's wife is a good sort: 'Well, Albert,
you're not very gallant. But I like you just the same.
Anyhow, if you're ever tempted . . . I know how to
show my gratitude.' Then off she goes laughing, and
Anne Marie swoops down on me, her eyes flashing,
her face grim. She starts to speak to me in a curt, severe
voice, but quietly so that no one can hear. 'I see what
you're up to. Of course, in one way it would be a
relief. You know I'm not very fond of that sort of
thing. But I advise you to give up the idea. I don't
want to be the laughingstock of Hanoi—poor little
Madame Bonnard. . . .' How strange she is, Anne
Marie. She always has to hide her tender feelings and
give me false reasons, whereas in fact she loves me;
she's jealous. Fortunately I know her detachment is
only assumed, I know there's affection underneath her
pride and her distant, inaccessible, queenly airs.

"Everything is going splendidly. Marvelously. Without undue vanity, I can be pleased with myself. Despite
a few unavoidable hitches, which I managed to sort
out with a tact and skill that do me credit, the governor general's trip to Szechwan has been a huge success. I can truthfully say as much in the long report
I'm going to write for the Ministry of Foreign Affairs—
it'll make my detractors and rivals at the Quai d'Orsay
go livid with rage. I can't but observe that all my
guests show me the greatest consideration, friendship
even; whenever they speak to me they're full of compliments. Even the chief private secretary, who cold-
shouldered me at first, has thawed. He calls me his

dear Albert, smiles at me like the Cheshire cat, and
even pats me on the shoulder. I'm rewarded for all the
trouble I've taken. I'm tired, couldn't be otherwise,
but all these fine people are going now; all I've got to
do is see them to the train. This is the final flurry. All
Chengtu is rounded up for the demonstrations of
enthusiasm, duly mingled with signs of regret at parting. It's all carried out in the grand manner. Tang
Kiao really does do things properly; he's an organizer
who in a few weeks has managed to impose a sense
of propriety on a people who at first were indifferent
and lacked order. Now that he's got the situation in
hand, he, too, is off. He's returning to Yunnanfu with
the governor general—he wants to escort him that far
himself. He's also taking with him an armored truck
with a couple of dozen enormous metal cases, like
coffins. The corpses are in fact the spoils of Szechwan
—all he's been able to rake in in the way of gold and
taels while he's been in Chengtu. He hasn't been
wasting his time! His iron guard surrounds his treasure with bayonets and machine guns. The spectacle
conjures up an unpleasant thought. What if Tang
Kiao took fright? What if he was afraid there might
be a military coup in Chengtu in which they'd cut his
fat throat? Supposing, once he had the loot, he just
cleared off to enjoy his ill-gotten gains in safety?
Perhaps, despite appearances, the situation is precari-
ous in Chengtu, and things might happen to throw
my railroad and factories into confusion. China! Nothing's ever certain here, nothing's ever gained for good
and all. But I stifle these thoughts so as not to spoil
the brilliant reputation I've established with the governor general, so as not to depress His Excellency as
he goes off in the happy certainty that thanks to me,
France has won a large part of China. The farewell

ceremonies at the station are a ballet even better organized than the arrival. Again the rhythmic, modulated,
well-timed pandemonium of fanfares, bows, 'Present
arms.' Everyone who's anybody in Chengtu is bending
low, all the Chinese falling over one another to pay
homage to Tang Kiao, as to a god. In the midst of all
this the little group of French is like a typical family
taking leave of one another: effusions, congratulations,
embraces, tears, kisses on both cheeks, handshakes,
final confidences, last-minute advice, ultimate prattle,
lachrymose promises to meet again, knowing smiles
and laughter. While the Chinese are as if hieratically
fixed in the rhythms of their salutations, while the
locomotive gets up steam, wheezing and panting, the
French, both those who are going and those who are
staying, are still vying with each other in affability
and friendship. Tang Kiao climbs into his coach with
suitable deliberation amid the thunder of bugles and
the lightning of bayonets. The governor general's
wife, still on terra firma, gets a big handkerchief out
of her bag and waves it in my face, by way of a last
joke. Suddenly her husband, who hasn't yet boarded
the train either, takes me by the shoulder and draws
me aside, literally melting with affection toward me.
He clasps me to his bosom, and at last manages to
say, 'Allow me to call you Albert, my dear consul. An
old man like me tends to be mistrustful, and all this
time I've been unobtrusively watching you. Well, you
have now won my esteem, and it's not often I say that
to anyone. You have shown me this strange China of
yours, and made me come to love it. The difficulties
you have overcome! But you've always managed to
get well out of them. And thanks to you, France is
established on the Yangtze Kiang!' His Excellency
stops to get his breath back, then continues to eulogize

me with an expression of sly authority: 'You know, the French administration is short of good servants, men who are disinterested, capable, patriotic. I tell you, the country needs you for still more important tasks. Sometimes people take me for an old fool, a nitwit—don't protest, my dear Albert: there *are* days when I'm a bit daft. However, I do count for something in France. I carry some weight, I have sound friends in the government, the Assembly, and the ministries, including the Ministry of Foreign Affairs. So you can count on me. You take my word for it, in a little while you'll be an ambassador—you're going to become a very great ambassador. . . .' "

PART
FIVE

Dawn. A pale light slid over the painted roofs, picking out golden dots here and there, slipping through the bamboo-paper windows, blotting out the chant, the glow, the domination of the opium lamp; lighthouse of imagination, reflector of illusion. The scene of the night gradually disintegrated. The Buddha's head and eyes no longer gleamed with approval, but were once again merely those of a "curio" in a consul's drawing room. The head boy still crouched on the floor, but his fingers had stopped working and were now inert like the cranks of a machine. The boy himself had shrunk to nothing, a useless object waiting for my father to revive enough to give orders, but at the ready, and with no signs of fatigue on his smooth skin or in his slanting eyes. Having nothing to do, he automatically began to tidy up his little tray and apparatus, arranging in rows the bowls of opium that had been emptied: my father had smoked at least fifty pipes. The almost imperceptible stir reached the consciousness of Monsieur le Consul, and he murmured faintly to his servant, "Don't make so much noise. That's right, put out the lamp . . . Open the doors, let in some air. It's stifling. God, my head. . . . Quiet, the slightest sound makes it split right open. Careful, you fool . . ." Though furtive, mute, and intangible

as a bat, the head boy still irritated the delicate nerves
of the consul of France, who, it was plain, was still all
at sea and in a foul temper. His eyes were two holes
black as coal, and his face, worn away like that of
certain weather-beaten old statues, was covered with
a little dark moss, the stubble of his beard. Monsieur le
Consul presented a rather dreadful appearance—he
who was always so spruce, never letting himself go,
shaving twice a day because of his vigorous beard, so
powerful and messy that if he touched Anne Marie's
cheek with his during the day she would say, "You're
all prickly!" Then my father would go and scrape at
his face and freshen up his skin with eau de Cologne:
he was always very dapper and distinguished. So it was
rare to see him as he appeared in this dawn—a wreck
revealed by daylight, with wrinkles, creases, dilated
pores and pupils, red eyes, his hair in a tousled mass,
and his chin bristling with black whiskers. The servants had stayed up all night with him, watching,
crouched down observing, and the state he was in did
not seem to surprise them. They were probably used
to it. Anyway, the secret army of servants held its
breath during the painful and uncertain moments of
daybreak during which Monsieur le Consul came to.
For he was always in a murderous temper, and woe
betide anyone he caught unawares. . . . It was the
monopoly, privilege, and last duty of the head boy to
deliver Albert of himself and help him return into
the world.

They all knew the rules of the game: Don't get
caught. They watched my father go through the range
of his usual grimaces as he resumed contact with reality. Not that he ever completely lost sight of it, for
even in his dreams he knew he was dreaming and stage-
managed his own dream is a sort of semilucidity. The

works . . . But now he was struck by the cool of the morning—unless it was fever—and his teeth were chattering. He was yellow as a quince. He was trembling all over, even in his words as he called to the head boy, "I don't want to catch pneumonia—give me my coat, quick!" For he'd taken it off for the opium session, and had boldly smoked in his shirtsleeves. The servant managed to lift the consul's arms one at a time and put on his jacket after much struggling—a respectful struggle against the insurmountable lassitude which had seized my father's body. When this operation was over, my father managed to get up off the couch, groaning and leaning on the head boy's shoulder. Where now were the comic but powerful gesticulations of the night, the rhythm of the drug, the jerks of the head and torso to seize the mouth of the pipe, Now it was the slow descent toward reality, with all the accompanying pain, stiffness, sighs. Suddenly a thought that struck him when the dream was fading returned. The shock made him suddenly stiffen.

"Dumont! But he'll really go and see the governor general of Indochina. He'll get around him and maneuver him and cook up something against me. As soon as he leaves Chengtu he'll rush to Hanoi. And from there, the swine, he'll certainly go to Yunnanfu to make a deal with Tang Kiao, to betray me. For him all those people are real and easily accessible, to be actually manipulated and negotiated with. He'll turn them into his playthings, make pawns of them. I can just see the respectful manner he'll put on for the governor general, and the air of friendly collusion he'll wear for Tang Kiao! The scoundrel will get them all tied up with his arguments and his tricks and his schemes. Yes, as soon as he leaves here, pretending to be my friend, he'll make for them one after the other, and pimp them and puzzle them and play me some lousy trick. Off he'll go from Chengtu when he's got all he wants out of me, kissing me and mauling me, and while he's going down the Yangtze to Shanghai, and from there by boat to Tonkin, and by train from Hanoi to Yunnanfu, I'll be stuck here with my heart in my mouth, away from everything, helpless, at his mercy, just having to wait for whatever mischief he chooses to perpetrate. . . ."

Meanwhile my father had put himself to rights. Thanks to the helpful dexterity of the head boy, he'd put on his bow tie and his very small, narrow, pointed patent leather shoes. That was one of the things he was proud of—the fineness and daintiness of his feet. But they were also very sensitive members, and every morning he could be heard complaining, sometimes feebly and sometimes furiously, when the head boy, for all his gentleness, hurt his extremities as he helped him put on his shoes. This particular dawn, the operation went off smoothly; the consul was preoccupied with other thoughts, cogitating fiercely and systematically working himself up against Dumont.

"And to think that just now, at dinner, the wretch had the audacity to blackmail me. Me, Albert Bonnard! He wants to make use of me to do his errands with the marshal of Chengtu and his Yunnanese. I'm to get him and his Blue Band the opium trade, or else. . . . And all that leading up to it with insinuations, threats, rolling eyes, and quivering stomachs—the pretense of sincerity, the putrid promises! Who the devil does he think he is?"

My father had sat down again on the edge of the sofa, his legs trailing on the floor. The dream had faded, leaving him face to face with things as they were when the day broke. Meanwhile Dumont must be asleep, hatching his plots, full of satisfaction and guile. The brute had him where he wanted him: *he* didn't need to console himself with imaginings and the delights of opium. He was snoozing away peacefully, perhaps with a happy smile. For him, opium was just tons and tons of profitable merchandise that he would soon be getting his hands on, big money, enough to fill his pockets and his bank accounts. What was more, he intended to make something out of everything—arms, the building of the railroad, all my father's patriotic and disinterested efforts. And to think that this crook had been able to go to sleep with such pleasant prospects. But it wasn't going to be like that. . . .

At this point, at the thought of Dumont snoring, my father felt quite sick. He grew tense, his features crumpled. Then he composed them again coldly, with a faint and bitter smile. He withdrew into himself; his face became completely impassive. The inside of his head was seething like a caldron. But from the outside he was more and more formal—like a sheet of icy metal. His head was a thin lozenge rising higher and higher as he stretched out his neck in the way he did when irked by a stiff collar—it was like the flat head of a cobra, coiled, furious, swaying ready to strike. Albert Bonnard often had this sort of attack, a concentration of rage and bitterness. But he differed from a snake in that the poison he secreted, vexation—and he had a gift for being vexed—was usually held back inside himself. He could mix with people for hours, days with his chin jutting, his head held stiffly, his eyes blank, his lips compressed, looking preoccupied— the image of a poor fellow transfixed by injustice but restraining himself—especially if the company included some important person who shouldn't be upset.

Sometimes he made the supreme effort, overcame his legitimate pain, and descended to be once again among people and part of this wicked world. Then he would wear the thin smile of a man who had mastered himself, and venture a jest or a gallantry. But deep inside he had been breathing vengeance, forging and tempering the resentment which would manifest itself later.

And so it was that day. After a period of being like a stuffed owl, my father took up his normal life and usual mannerisms. He spoke aloud to himself.

"Dumont's not going to get away with it. I'm going to prick that great windbag, deflate it, cut it into bits. Yes, but he mustn't suspect anything. I must set about it quietly. I must abandon the joys of anger for the pleasures of hypocrisy. I have a little plan. I must tell Anne Marie to be nicer to him. . . ."

My father, suddenly radiant although exhausted, prepared to rejoin the rest of the household. He got up from the couch, stood, walked almost unfalteringly. His shoes could be heard crunching on the ground as he went across the courtyard. They could be heard going up the wooden stairs to the master bedroom, where Anne Marie was asleep. All around him was nothingness and quiet. Everyone vanished: the head boy, who disappeared from the scene of his duties as a lizard slips back into its crack; the hidden others, who rose from their places of concealment in their white robes and went off peacefully like morning ghosts. Li, cheerful and insensible as a cucumber, came into my room, approached the bed to make sure I was asleep, rubbed her snub nose affectionately against mine, and then went away. I lay there watching, for my Chinese education had long ago turned me into a little spy. I saw everything, heard everything, and understood a good deal without ever showing anything. As well as being able to listen, I knew how to walk without making any noise. I listened to my father's footsteps, waited for two or three minutes after he'd joined Anne Marie, then, in the still-deserted consulate, among the faint noises from the waking city already beginning to stir busily, went to the door that led from my parents' room to my own. As I expected, they were quarreling. I could hear their voices through the wall, which was almost as thin as paper.

Poor Albert! Every time he stayed up till dawn like that, drinking, strutting about, arguing, or smoking, he was always seized afterward with a pressing desire to talk to Anne Marie, to "let down his hair," to serve up while they were still hot his confidences, clevernesses, boasts, and other exploits. Of course he didn't tell her everything. He would adopt an air of studied detachment in order to lie, and there was a special tinge of vanity in his voice when he detailed his astuteness and embroidered what he said with apt comments. But first it was necessary that his wife should hear him out. So now, to begin with, before launching into any floods of oratory, before getting undressed, he would try to wheedle her. The first difficulty was waking her. When he entered the room and saw her tall, fragile, sleeping form, slim as a wand between the sheets, with the slumbering features, the regularly breathing mouth, the coil of hair above her oval forehead, and the long lashes that lay over her eyes like curtains, he went through a series of antics to try to rouse her: coughs, sighs, shuffles, clumsy stumbling over furniture. When Anne Marie finally opened her eyes, raising herself slightly on the pillows, lifting up a face already vaguely irritated and alert, the soft skin beginning to crease into vexation, chin set and brown

eyes shining in anticipation of a fight, my father tried
to kiss her and say "I love you," just like someone on
a nineties postcard. He was incorrigible, for almost
every time he had been soundly snubbed. And so it
was that morning, and even more firmly than usual.
Anne Marie, in a harsh, jerky, almost rasping voice
quite unlike her usual soft murmur, cut short her
husband's amorous and consular efforts.

"Don't touch me," she said. "You want to what?
Get into bed and talk to me? But you stink of alcohol,
my dear, and even worse of opium. Go and sleep somewhere else."

"But, Anne Marie, I've got some very important
things to tell you. They couldn't be more important."

"They can wait a few hours. I know the sort of night
you've had. You showed off in front of Dumont, he
took you down a peg or two, you felt humiliated, so
you started to take opium. It wouldn't be so bad if you
really liked it. But the way you smoke is despicable—
just an insignificant man trying to make himself believe he's important. You only use your pipes to lull
your own weaknesses. How many—forty or fifty? Stay
with them if they make you feel like a genius. *I* can't.
So go away."

"And what about your obligations—"

"Don't be a cad on top of everything else. There's
no point in going into it all again. Don't give me your
turkey-cock look. I suppose that's what you did to
Dumont before he took you down. It won't work any
better with me than it did with him."

"Anne Marie—please . . ."

"And don't try to make me feel sorry for you. I'll
listen later—I promise. But for the moment, leave me
alone. Go to the other room—the bed's made up. And
no nonsense, if you don't mind—no moaning and

groaning and stamping and banging of doors. You always wake the boy up. By the way, did you see that he went to bed early?"

"That's your business."

And with this parting shot, Albert went off to the little room to which my mother often consigned him. As his place of exile was on the other side of my own room, I often saw him passing through in disgrace. Sometimes he was in a rage—fumed, broke things, stamped, left a wake of desolation behind him. But more often he withdrew like an insulted nobleman, haughtily, with a face as cold as marble that seemed to say: "You'll be sorry for this, my lady." Sometimes he sniveled a bit or even cried, snuffling and using his handkerchief. But usually it was a mixture of all these forms of expression.

Thus it was this morning. His face was like a sculpture of solemn anger, but its dignity was spoiled by twitches of resentment and an impulse to remain a little longer to try to awaken Anne Marie's interest, or to get the upper hand with some ingenious Parthian shot and then sweep out as victor instead of vanquished. But he couldn't pull it off: his imitation of a Roman emperor didn't impress her, his sarcastic darts fell useless before the armor of her indifference, and she rebuffed him with the tranquil calm of rooted disdain, absolutely established, and skillfully gauged. So what finally predominated in his face and behavior was an almost childish anger, a combination of slammed doors, tossed head, and loud repetition of what had been said before; also of dampness around the eyes, puffy eyelids, and a hangdog expression. Having set his countenance in folds at once stoical and pained, with a look of fixed melancholy that stared into the distance as though there were no walls, he left—or rather pretended to leave, until Anne Marie half sat up in bed, with the covers pulled around her by way of defense, her mood expressed in the twitching of her lips, lips ready to utter really venomous words, the kind that rankle for weeks and wound to the depths of the heart. Then, seized with fear, Albert decamped, before Anne Marie let fly like some horribly lucid Fury from a mouth like the crater of a volcano. Silent and white, still sitting up with only her head showing above the eiderdown, she pointed the direction in which he was to go: the direction of my room.

Needless to say, by the time he passed through my little kingdom I was already snug again between the sheets, my brown, regular face, slightly oval like Anne Marie's but with my father's big nose, resting on the white linen and breathing deeply and steadily like the good, ordinary little boy Albert believed me to be. For instance, he was sure I would do well at school and come out first in the exams, and every time the diplomatic bag arrived he would give me presents of things I didn't like and tell me to be well behaved and obedient and work hard. Often he would say in a maudlin voice that he was bleeding himself white for me and was going to get me a tutor. Meanwhile, because of him, one whole wall of my room was covered with books by Jules Verne and the Comtesse de Ségur, which I never read. The floor was occupied by an electric train, which my father had laboriously installed with the aid of the head boy, who did all the putting together although he had never seen a train in his life. When the first set of coaches went through a tunnel, my father beamed and said, "There—my little boy's little Szechwan railway. Perhaps one of these days he'll graduate first in his class at the Polytechnique. . . ." That had been several days ago. Since then, on the sly, I'd deliberately broken the rails and the switches and the locomotives. And on that very morning, as I lay pretending to be asleep, I thought to myself: Father's sure to trip over the rails, And then won't he let out a howl! It was a scene not to be missed, so I just opened my yellowish-bronze eyes—cat's eyes, as guests used to say, admiring me to please my parents. And there my father was, going toward his room and looking more like a little boy than I did myself. And it happened: he tripped over a piece of track, a station, got his feet entangled in the whole thing, and hopped about moaning, "Ow, ow, ow!" and massaging his toes. But instead of getting angry, he stopped and came across to me, bent over my ostensibly sleeping form, and kissed me on the forehead with his wet lips. "My son . . ." he said, at last having found an outlet for his tender feelings. I pretended to be unconscious of all this, to be deeper asleep than ever. And from the other side of the wall came the voice of Anne Marie: "Don't make use of the child to snivel over. Let him sleep." My father disappeared. I went back to sleep.

The morning sun, like a caldron of light in the pure clear sky, sent a slanting band of heat through my now open windows, a sort of hot crisp doughnut that I tried to take between my teeth. I woke up. And all Chengtu, with its flow of sounds, and with its smells, too, came to greet me! It was a time when the city was full of intense activity, like a gong resounding with all the footsteps, cries, all the forest of sounds, all the joys of being, eating, living. But in the foreground, against this continuous murmur, the voices of my parents, coming from their room, stood out. The voices were no longer quarreling. My mother, dressed

for the garden in a long sheath dress and carrying
secateurs had just come in from cutting flowers:
wreaths of wild and wreaths of gentle petals, flamboyant orchids, proud lilies, sweet and sad chrysanthe-
mums. And all the scents. With long hands like unbound hair, chignons of languorous and sensitive flesh,
Anne Marie arranged her harvest in vases, with the
assistance of Li. Her head was like an amphora covered with tresses, braids so heavy that they made her
lean her face to one side—a face full of perfect serenity,
inner tranquility, peaceful looks. Once again I, though
only a taciturn little boy, was rapt with admiration
of Anne Marie's grace, her sense of gesture and pose.
For the door was open and I had gone to her, to
cling to her and feel the softness of her cheeks, the
texture of her skin, the shining darkness of her hair,
the limpidity of her eyes. She stopped arranging the
vases in which she combined together so well the
terrible blooms that were tongues of fire or sinister
funnels or carnivorous maws, with those of ecstasy,
of consolation, of gentleness. And she took me in her
arms with the accurate nonchalance of a goddess.
She was composing a picture of mother and child—
a picture which contained nothing of sensual, devouring motherhood, merely a harmonious image in
which everything she thought too material or animal
or instinctive was sublimated to beauty and graceful-
ness; in which a most extreme, strict, and at the same
time elegant simplicity, coming from the heart, reduced behavior to a controlled, almost symbolic form.
After a few moments Anne Marie decided that our
communion—for that was what it was—had lasted
long enough, and that if it were prolonged it might
become commonplace, too natural. So she gave me a
little kiss—just brushed me with her lips—and quickly
withdrawing her arms from around my shoulders,

plunged them back among the flowers and said, "Run away and play, son. Li will dress you." "And what about me? Don't forget me!" said Albert, in a loud voice.

He was sitting jovially at table in a scarlet dressing gown with a tasseled belt, eating his breakfast, making sure his boiled eggs were properly done, the head boy standing ready behind him. There he was, not even looking washed out any more—cheerful, freshly shaved, almost exuberant in his multiple role of paterfamilias, husband, and father, not to mention consul. He was brimming over with prattle, confidences, jokes, tricks, and snatches of song; and Anne Marie seemed to accept it. Nothing would do but that he must snatch me up and put me on his knees to play ride-a-cockhorse, bouncing me up in the air and sticking his mustache in my eye. "Let him go out into the garden or the stable," said Anne Marie. "He'll enjoy himself better there." I don't know whether this was to rescue me or to get rid of me; perhaps both. But my father was well away and pleaded my cause: "Oh, no, Lulu won't be in our way. He doesn't understand what we say." And he got hold of me again and tossed me up to the ceiling, then ran around carrying me like a horse, trotting, galloping, whinnying. At last, exhausted by this outburst of paternity, he stopped and put me down. I squatted on the floor in the Chinese manner, pretending to look at a picture book, but in fact all ears.

Now as I look back on this scene as an adult I can see its real meaning. Then I was only a little spy watching my parents' drama, just guessing it might be my own drama, too. It was only years afterward that things became clear to me and took on the fullness and sharpness of meaning they have today.

Having finished his breakfast and sent the head boy away, my father started to lark about like a young man, humming a song about "the girls of La Rochelle" —which was where he came from. He never unbent to this extent except when in the highest good humor and really pleased with himself—and assuming Anne Marie was prepared to put up with such accesses of self-satisfaction. On that particular day, far from shutting him up, she looked at him out of the corner of her eye with a mischievous air that was imperceptibly mocking. She knew that every so often she had to play her role as muse, confessor, and counselor. It was her job. Rather than do it with a bad grace, she preferred to throw herself into the task conscientiously, at a moment of her own choosing, with a sort of friendship and complicity. But she did it in a way that puzzled and surprised my father, and demolished his arguments and pretensions, his caviling and complacency. Her method was destructive honesty, forceful frankness, and provoking commonsense. And as she assailed Albert with rough and cynical advice which left him in a muddle, she would shrug her shoulders as if to say: take it or leave it—it's all the same to me. It's not my business.

That day she was particularly kind to him, without any undercurrent of distaste. Her voice was suave, even gay, and there was a smile on her lips and in her words. Albert was purring already. But it wasn't hard to guess that this affability was not a very good omen for him. In the timbre of Anne Marie's voice you could sense sheathed claws that would tear the consul to bits before long. Directly or indirectly, she always made him pay dearly for her kindnesses and show of interest. But he was naïve and trusting. Above all, he couldn't do without her.

And so Anne Marie, her lips curled back—she had

long, flexible lips which she set in strange positions—
began with what was for her a charming attention.

"Well, my dear, you *are* in good form, considering
the night you had last night. Not even any tummy
aches! Well, then, what was it that was so important
that you had to disturb me when it was barely light?
What's bothering you?"

The consul, still in his dark-red wrap, stopped
playing the boyish husband and grew serious, unctuous, deliberate, concentrated, as became a consul. He
chose his words carefully, voicing them as if they were
written characters, with vocal curlicues corresponding
to dashes, commas, and periods. He was at once a grave
magistrate and a sort of choirboy at the mass of diplomacy. He opened his mouth, not wide like my mother
—just to a reasonable size. Then he produced a considered argument.

"My dear Anne Marie, I'm going to ask you to do
something for me that you may not find very agreeable.
But I do so only after carefully weighing the pros and
cons. And this is the conclusion I've come to: you have
to be much more easygoing with M. Dumont. In the
consulate you behave exactly as if he didn't exist. You
avoid him. And when you do actually encounter him
it's worse still. You look through him as if he were
invisible, and turn away. When he bows to you, you
don't even nod—all you do is stiffen your throat in a
way I know to be a sign of disgust. You withdraw your
hand calmly and methodically so that when he bends
to kiss it he meets with empty air. And by the time he's
straightened up again, which with his figure takes him
a few seconds, you've already turned your back. All
you'll say to him the whole day is 'Good morning' and
'Good evening.' The rest of the time you're just there,
not even supercilious, but distant, with your face like

that of some inaccessible madonna. Sometimes in his presence you give a couple of sniffs and shudder, as if he smelled nasty, as if he were no more than a whiff of bad air. And at table you don't speak, you don't smile, you just pick at two or three mouthfuls without listening to the conversation or paying any heed to M. Dumont, who half kills himself paying you compliments. Then, when the dessert has been served, after ostentatiously stifling your yawns, you withdraw without a word of apology. And when you've gone I'm left there embarrassed, trying to make excuses and invent explanations, though of course they don't hold water for a moment. All this is very mortifying for M. Dumont. And I must admit that—very politely, gallantly even—he's complained to me about your behavior. He's hurt."

Confronted by the consul's reproaches and requests, Anne Marie merely drew back her lips even further. Her teeth, rows of little shiny pearls which she brushed at least five or six times a day—it was even more of a mania with her than with Albert—were separated by a faintly trembling opening through which she breathed quickly and hoarsely. You could tell her throat was fluttering, though she didn't say a word—it was just that her panting breath became almost imperceptibly more rapid. On the surface, above the collar of her blouse, the tendons twitched like a sort of false Adam's apple that, as my father had said, appeared when she was excited. Her eyes were motionless in their great tapered sockets, but in them there were sparkling pinpoints—the sands of a kind of laughter. All these little agitations did not stop, but increased when my father fell silent and stood there like a post waiting for an answer that never came. Anne Marie left Albert to stew in his own juice. She felt like playing a practical joke that would teach him a lesson. But she had plenty of time.

Anne Marie's attitude to life and its little contingencies, the down-to-earth, ordinary side of her, the key to her moods, were to be seen around her mouth, which she used with versatility, making it widen or contract, grow larger or smaller, clamp shut like a lock, or open in any one of a thousand fleeting suggestions of meaning, hardening it sometimes to launch a thunderbolt through white and furious lips like layers of steel. Anne Marie's mouth was her strength and her weakness, her nature, the focal point of countless nerves that were in a way unfeeling and yet at the same time easily wounded, requiring a lofty vengeance which denied that Anne Marie could ever be touched by suffering or made to submit to it. That was how she would have liked to be—beyond the reach of Albert, of men, of people. But her mouth betrayed her, for on it one could read the alphabet of her feelings: her exasperation, her sensitivity, her implacability, her pitilessness, above all her scorn.

It was her stage, her theater, where she revealed herself through an incredible range of expressions, labial acrobatics which sometimes seemed to me incompatible with her undeniable dignity. There was one face which irritated me even when I was quite young, and that was the one that accompanied the meticulous manner in which she chewed her food. Masticating away with bulging cheeks and allowing plenty of time for the saliva to work, she made me think of a rather unappetizing old woman playing some alimentary fox trot on her few remaining stumps of teeth. Such a sacrilegious idea terrified me.

What was very strange was that Albert didn't notice the importance of Anne Marie's mouth, with its ebbs and flows, as an instrument of her personality. True, the center of his own being, the rallying point of all his emotions and states of mind, was in his nose and mustache, his eyes and all the whiskers and every possible kind of wrinkle around them. In the case of my father, his passions were always manifesting themselves in a jumble of mannerisms, a mess of mawkishness, a display of bragging, a bazaar of sorrows, a rostrum of susceptibilities, demands, complaisances, respects, considerations, submissions, resignations. His face was both the right side of the page and the obverse, showing all the artificialities and sincerities, all the airs: that of the trustworthy employee, that of the martyr, that of the master of ceremonies, that of the important official, that of the poor fellow who is misunderstood, that of the wily horse trader, that of the clever strategist, and that of the man who knows how to enjoy life despite all its mysteries and frustrations. A touch of the Pietà, a touch of the false coin of stoicism. My father's face was a distorting mask of his ego, an exhibition of his innards, feet, heart, liver, brain and intellect, bile and caprice, his blood and his corpuscles, his stools, his fevers, his amoebas, and so on. In all that, what was truth and what was lying, what was playacting and calculation and what real suffering? He had at least three dozen roles and performances and acts, always the same, all studied and played to elicit the right response: "He's a sly character!" "What a good fellow!" "The consul's a brave chap!" "An incorruptible servant of the state!" "He's really something!" And also: "What an excellent father!" "What an ill-used husband!" "What a marvelous host!" His performance was aimed at everyone, of every social class, whether he was treating one individual to a private lesson or dealing with people en masse. All that mattered was the result. The Chinese servants, seeing him rolling his eyes and in a foul temper, were supposed to realize they mustn't get in his way. The English had to see from his gaiety that they hadn't got the better of him and draw the appropriate conclusions. And even my mother, observing that he was wearing his sadness around his nose like a bandoleer, had somehow to be touched and brought to be nice to him.

As a matter of fact, it very seldom worked with her, and more often than not it was, on the contrary, catastrophic. For all Albert's manifestations, each of which Anne Marie knew by heart and would gnash her teeth at inwardly, were so many signs indicative of the character he was in the process of playing. So she could upset and confound him as she liked, by means ranging from a mere "Do be natural, Albert," to the twitching of her mouth. Albert floundered about, completely in the dark as to his wife's moods. He hadn't the faintest idea that her ordinary behavior, the aesthetic gentleness that enveloped her, was in itself an escape from and denial of him and all the pettinesses of existence. And even when some crisis made her lose this equanimity and she was gripped by fury and the need to hurt him, he didn't see the signs of the storm—those white lips drawn back from the red gums, the stiff cheeks, all those susceptibilities, all that sick soul. For the basic and only motivating power in Anne Marie was an exacerbated pride, a pure and absolute need that was almost monstrous. Such singlemindedness was obviously not within Albert's possibilities; the only things he knew about were the vanities that could be used in the service of compromise.

But that day Anne Marie didn't show repulsion,

deep offense, insurmountable disgust, or the icy rage
in which her whole being contracted in order to explode. Today she was indulgent toward Albert; she
promised herself she would only play with him like a
cat with a mouse. She found it rather amusing to cast
him in that role for while he was not a coward when
faced with a cobra, he shook like a jelly as soon as he
saw a mouse. He was so terrified he became aggressive.
What panic! Shrieks, howls. Albert either fled the
room or sought refuge on a table. An army of boys
rushed up with brooms and sticks to hunt down and
kill the little creature, while Albert, from his perch,
alternately encouraged and upbraided them, dancing
about with fright. All this lasted until they brought
him the eviscerated corpse of the guilty party, dangling
by the tail between the finger and thumb of whichever
servant had wrought justice on it. Then they had to
rush to rally around Albert and hold him up, for he
often fainted. What a strange man he was, Albert—so
sensitive he would almost expire at the sight of a
field mouse in his bedroom or a hair in his soup. The
tiniest whisker in his plate and it was clear the decks
for action. When the offending item had been removed with tweezers, and duly brandished as an object
of shame and execration, then there was a hunt to find
where it came from, inquiries to detect the person who
had dropped it, the appearance of the fat chief cook,
whose case was that it couldn't be him because he was
bald. A pitiful farce, which Anne Marie bore with
resignation because there wasn't anything else to do.
She merely lifted her head as if toward some other
horizon. But on the day we are speaking of she could
make Albert pay for those occasions on which he
hadn't even been aware of his absurdity and odious-
ness. The opportunity presented itself in the form of

his discomfiture the previous evening by Dumont. Anne Marie was not openly hostile; rather, she exulted inwardly. In her mind was the thought: I wouldn't mind betting he let Dumont wind him around his little finger.

A pleased smile showed she had come to a conclusion, though she had no intention of revealing it. Her silence forced Albert to resume his wretched speech, and to embroil himself even further in his request: "Couldn't you be nice to Dumont?"

The silence disconcerted Albert. He would have preferred anything else from Anne Marie—bad temper, insolence, defiance, refusal, any sort of denigration. But Anne Marie was not disagreeable or cross. She was merely mysterious. Which in fact was much more disturbing. . . .

Thirty seconds had gone by since Albert had finished his first paragraph and been silent. The two half-open mouths confronted one another—Anne Marie's thin lips, from which no sound issued, and the thicker, fleshy ones of my father, which the ladies described as sensual but which for the moment were out of commission, waiting for a reaction from Anne Marie, some indication of her mood which would enable him to resume his oratory with the arguments and considerations most likely to succeed. But nothing came. So he plunged into the unknown and started to speak again, trying what flattery might do.

"Darling, you're the most marvelous hostess in China. And I'm not the only one that says so. A lot of very important people here and in Shanghai and everywhere say there isn't another consul's wife to touch you. It's a well-known fact that by charm of manner alone you captivate all our guests and fill them at once with ease and with respect. Some even

say that without you my career wouldn't have made
such rapid progress, and that in the most honorable
way you have contributed a great deal to my advance-
ment. Mind you, I don't take offense at that assertion,
I admit there's some truth in it. I owe a lot to you. . . ."

The consul stopped for a moment to observe the
result of his eulogy. He felt that in actually admitting
Anne Marie's contribution to his consular successes he
was making a great concession. On the whole this was
a subject he disliked, and he not only avoided it
himself but also frowned crossly when he heard exaggerated reports of his wife's virtues, unless the accounts
made it quite clear that she was his pupil and it was
to him she owed her training. So today, by admitting
her skill, he was really making a gesture. But he got no
reward for it: still nothing happened. Anne Marie,
her eyes shining softly, just watched Albert getting
entangled in his own subtleties, like a fly in honey.
She was also thinking that the consul must have gotten
even faster and deeper into Dumont's clutches than she
had realized, for him to be appealing to her like this.

As she remained silent, Albert reduced his voice to
a thin treble touched with a tinge of hesitation. He
even decided to use an affectionate diminutive.

"Mimi," he said, "I really don't know why you're
so hard on Dumont. I'd even go so far as to say you
weren't absolutely correct, and that for once you didn't
perform your duty absolutely as you should have done.
You lost sight of the fact that you were the consul's
lady and therefore obliged to treat this gentleman
properly, since, even if you don't care for him, he is a
Frenchman, a compatriot, an important businessman,
and what's more our guest, under our protection and
that of the tricolor. Of course I don't ask that you
should actually like him. But there's a difference be-

tween that and cold-shouldering him as you do. . . . I must say it's a lapse, and one I haven't often seen you guilty of."

Instead of laughing, Anne Marie assumed a humble and repentant smile. When she spoke her voice was a murmur of contrition and confession. Albert ought to have been on his guard.

"You're right, my dear, as always," she said. "Though you are perhaps rather hard on me. I haven't actually ill-treated Monsieur Dumont—I've simply kept him rather at a distance. But as he's your friend now, I'll make an effort to be more agreeable. You might have warned me about the change."

Albert, embarrassed, coughed. His eyes narrowed and his voice grew affected, as was his habit for delicate explanations.

"My friend! That's going a bit far, Anne Marie. No, he isn't my friend. Let me explain. . . ."

He started to whisper. He cupped his hands around his mouth and spoke in a muffled voice as though through a bandage—as if Dumont or his spies were all around, listening. As he let out his secrets in this way, he grew more and more ecstatic. He wore a wide, satisfied, happy smile, so sure was he of being really remarkable, of having impressed Anne Marie with his diabolical subtlety.

"To tell you the truth, I'm out to get Dumont. And get him I shall, even if I have to wait months or years. It won't be easy, but one of these days I'm going to show that bloated, pernicious, stinking wretch who I am. You know what I'm like—once someone offends me I never forgive them. And last night Dumont was extremely disrespectful. I hate him. And that's the reason why I—and you, too, Anne Marie—must be particularly nice to him for the rest of his stay here:

so that the clown doesn't suspect. So it's the full treatment for him, the velvet glove, hail-fellow-well-met—and behind it all the sweet thought of revenge. I want him to wallow in enjoyment here, and never imagine what I'm storing up for him later."

And Albert put on a thin, assertive smile—a smile sufficient in itself, with all Albert's genius in it, a monstrance of his self-satisfaction. A knowing smile, a secret viaticum to be given only to the few, a word to the wise. Let Anne Marie be enlightened and admire, but let Dumont, blinded by self-congratulation, go on making the monumental error of taking Albert for a fool. Albert would break him. All was well.

And indeed Anne Marie did seem convinced. She was smiling, too, a luminous smile, her head thrown slightly back, her arms behind it arranging her hair, so that Albert had a full view, without any shadow of reticence, of her expression of delight and surprise. She was still speechless for a while, this time apparently with jubilation, her eyebrows, eyelids, nostrils, and lips slightly flickering. Then at last she spoke again, anxious to hear more detailed reasons for rejoicing. She wanted to know everything; she wanted him to dot the *i*'s and cross the *t*'s.

"But, Albert, how did Dumont manage to vex you? He can't hold a candle to you. He's so insignificant. If he was rude to you, the consul of France, why didn't you put him in his place right away? You never wanted to have him here, remember. Well, send him away then, instead of asking me to be nice to him. I really don't see it. . . . You want to do him in, and yet you treat him like a king. You grovel to him yourself, and now you ask me to lick his boots as well."

Now Albert began to sense danger. To counter it he adopted what she used to call, even in front of him, his calf's look. That is to say, he became graciously solemn. He was now playing the lecturer, the mentor, the expert, the artist and Metternich of Chengtu. His mustache was like a banner, each word was brought forth like a benediction. He was the superior being condescending to enlighten the ignorant. But in fact he was thinking and hesitating, and while selecting his argument, vocabulary, and intonations, he was already prey to a fear he would not acknowledge.

"My dear child," he said. "As I've often told you, diplomacy is a job that calls for the rarest and most skillful qualities. You have to know what's possible, you have to be able to make sacrifices. As you know, I've devoted my life and health, my strength and ability, to this project for the Chengtu railway. You know the terrific, apparently almost insurmountable, obstacles that I've come up against. Well, Dumont, despite his revolting demands and his totally tactless and ignorant way of making them, can in a way be useful to me in connection with the railroad. And that's what I found out last night in the course of our discussions, disagreeable and even disgusting as they were, God knows. The coarse fellow has plenty of worldly wisdom and a lot of experience in the countries we're dealing with. And he knows everyone in China and Indochina, and not through the back door. He offered me his services, and disagreeable as it may be, I didn't think I could refuse. A leopard can't change his spots. I'm a slave to duty, so what can I do but obey my conscience whatever the cost, even if it leads me into something that's dangerous, or liable to misinterpretation, or that may turn against me? What do I care? My first thought is for France. And anyway, to get my railroad I'd swallow any insults—I'd make a deal with the devil himself."

Anne Marie laughed, for the first time. It was like

an alarm signal, like the whistle of the nonexistent train. Perhaps it wasn't yet very loud, but it was enough to be dangerous—a delighted registering of my father's much-hoped-for and long-expected foolishness. She hadn't yet reached the stage of judgment, condemnation, scorn—before that she needed to find out more, all, to have the pleasure of making him admit his folly. It was a laugh in which the first mockery and the beginning of the inquisition mingled. Hardly had it died away before Anne Marie leaned forward excitedly, her face sharp and intent and poised like a drill. My father realized he was going to be found out, and, confronted with the predatory countenance of Anne Marie, he changed his attitude completely. He broke out in beads of anxiety about what was going to happen, for at last it had dawned on him that he'd given himself away with his bragging, that he'd stupidly delivered himself into Anne Marie's hands. So as always when he felt trapped, he turned into a great lump, a sort of soft blockhouse bristling with the guns of denial. In a few seconds he could generate, in his inner bastions, pound upon pound of pretense and pigheaded resistance. It was a physiological phenomenon that enabled him to pad and protect himself, to absorb shocks. Beset by her stricken and hostile fury, he was like some large boil that Anne Marie wanted to lance. How she would enjoy making the matter ooze out! But she had to be careful, so that instead of releasing just ordinary pus she would manage to reach that which Albert wanted above all to hide: the crushing, pitiable reality.

So it had come to a confrontation. A suddenly collapsed Albert, starchy even in his collapse, muttered wearily:

"That's not nice, Anne Marie. You haven't even

been listening. You're making fun of me just when I need support. . . ."

He made as if to go away, an unfortunate misunderstood husband. But of course he stayed. Anne Marie, realizing she had been going too fast, put on her sweetest smile, glowing with human warmth. There was a well-proved tactic: first, prick Albert to make him emerge from his padding of pretension. But if you struck too soon and too hard, he might take refuge in obstinacy, and then nothing could be gotten out of him. And the trouble it took to lure him back into the open! But this is what seemed to have happened now, and Anne Marie, seeing that she had gone about it the wrong way, tried to repair the damage in order to end up eventually with an Albert both malleable and punishable. So instead of raising the corners of her mouth and using them as a catapult, she lowered them to let out honeyed words.

"Don't misunderstand me, Albert," she said. "I'm a good wife, and very attached to you and your interests. But you behave as if I were still a little girl from the provinces. You insist on telling me all your business, yet at the same time, instead of treating me like a real woman, you act as if I were a sort of straw dummy, and allot me brilliant roles that have nothing to do with reality or with what actually happens. I just help you to show off and congratulate yourself, that's all. Your nonsense annoys me, I admit. I could be of better use to you, my dear Albert. I'm the only person in the world who can tell you the truth. But you turn up your nose at that. You use subterfuge with me the way you do with anyone else, and all you want is compliments. But you use subterfuge too much. You use it with the whole world, including Dumont, and I'm not sure that you don't mislead yourself with your complications. If you'll only be sincere with me, now, today, I'll give you all the help I can."

Albert looked sulky.

"It's not help I need so much as affection," he grumbled. "Affection is what would help me. But you never miss an opportunity for thinking the worst of me, as if I were a mere good-for-nothing."

My mother's smile included us all—my father in his hell-colored dressing gown, me still squatting on the floor. The Holy Family. Anne Marie was as radiant as some sacred statue, with her even voice and shapely cheeks from which flowed parallel streams of tenderness and femininity. It was an almost supernatural, mystic apparition, for the sun's rays, slanting into the room, embraced Anne Marie and seemed to bear her aloft.

This vision was enough to touch the consul. Although by nature voluptuous, a sensual character very dashing with the ladies, he was always moved spiritually by the beauty of the girl from Anjou who had become his wife, whenever she relented a little, or pretended to. The poor fellow was still irretrievably trapped in the lofty transports that had pierced him to the heart that day at the station at Ancenis, not many years ago. Anne Marie had not lost her charm for him, in spite of her coldness and disdain, despite the way she treated him as a parvenu. And the moment she consented to tolerate him a little, he was immediately caught up in that poetry of hers, which was like the poetry of her own native country and river.

She was forever the daughter of the river. The Loire —slow; fascinating; dangerously peaceful; full of haughty currents glittering smooth and cold; full of impassive eddies and terrible pride; untamed and never complaining; languid, fierce, and ardent. It is the river at once of treachery and the joy of living, sumptuous aristocracy, magical light, and perfect civilization. Anne Marie was like the river—a woman who could not be conquered, but who sometimes deigned to let herself be tamed a little, or at least appear to be. When that happened my father was transported with delight, and immediately showed a crude joviality which swiftly annoyed Anne Marie. But that day she controlled her annoyance, and Albert cheered up and became as merry as he had been at breakfast.

So now it was an Albert who was happy, relieved, exuberant, overjoyed. Everything in him expanded, not like a bag of ill humor but like a sea anemone, the features swelling and shining, the eyes damp, the lips wet, the voice rolling richly. Every pore opened, like lukewarm specks, very brown and rather sticky. He began to sing again, one of his favorite risqué pieces, which always made Anne Marie start nervously. But this time she repressed the shudder, and instantly resumed her smile. It wasn't that she was prudish. In her view, a real man was allowed to do anything, and it could be merely a sign of worth. But Albert!

Albert said, in a voice become somewhat thick and stumbling, "Times like this console me for everything, Anne Marie. They reinvigorate me. . . ." And in his strength he stood up, the tassels of his scarlet dressing gown flying, his beaming face black with dilated pupils and dark whiskers. He marched over to Anne Marie, put out his arms to clasp her to him, and thrust his thick lips forward with the intention of kissing her passionately on the mouth. Anne Marie, who had recoiled a step, let out a little strangled cry—not a rebuff, for she had herself under control, but rather the almost reluctant warning of an accessory: "Careful, Albert, you mustn't forget the child. . . ."

Once again I was innocently playing the part of the providential son for Anne Marie. I was used to it.

She often made use of me. It always had an irresistible effect on Albert—an infallible argument. He was stopped in his tracks as soon as she called attention to my presence. For Albert prided himself on being a good father, and he was embarrassed; he even blushed and shuffled his feet when it seemed that I, little Lulu, who was everywhere, might have seen him showing something resembling the beginnings of ardor. Anne Marie systematically used and abused this highly convenient correctness.

One day when I was playing in the courtyard at the English clergyman's, where we regularly went to have tea with his wife, I overheard my mother saying something in the drawing room to her worthy hostess, with her bulldog's face. She spoke in a flat, rapid voice.

"Albert's terrible—he revolts me. I don't like that sort of thing. Fortunately my son sleeps in the next room, and that stops Albert from losing control of himself and behaving badly. He's too normal—monstrously normal. No better than a brute. So much so that before we were married and there was no girl handy, he's supposed to have made do sometimes with one of the houseboys. Dreadful, isn't it?" "Shocking," was the placid comment of the English lady, a greasy round ball munching toast and marmalade, imperturbably manipulating a whole armory of knives and forks and spoons with her pudgy fingers, and rounding her lips to pop in each mouthful. "Shocking," she repeated even more majestically, dispensing the fruit of long experience and knowledge of the ways of the world. "But you know what men are. Take my husband. A clergyman, and at his age, with his paunch and his dog collar—but the things he gets up to still! Your Albert's not a bad fellow. Don't be too hard on him, even if he is a bit uncouth. But whatever you do, don't let your son get mixed up in it all. . . ." As a matter of fact, in spite of Li's caresses I didn't understand what went on between my parents. But already I had a feeling of repulsion when I saw a certain expression on my father's face, when he spoke to Anne Marie in a rapid, hollow, breathless voice. Sometimes I heard sounds coming from their room. No, I hated it when my father went near my mother.

So on that particular day I was very pleased that my father was suddenly turned into a pillar of salt, his panting nostrils petrified.

Albert, motionless, looked at Anne Marie out of eyes that were fixed, resentful black dots. She was swept with almost imperceptible shudders. Of relief. But instead of showing how triumphant she felt, she disguised her trembling and assumed a certain air of confusion, even disappointment. That was enough to make Albert, the good sort and easy dupe, assume the same pretenses, imitations of a disappointment that was shared. He changed completely, from bitter vexation to respectable, almost happy regret. But it wasn't difficult to see that Anne Marie was taking him in. It was all part of the same strategy that she had endangered a little while before by being too zealous, laughing too soon and too provocatively.

So now she was all sweetness and light, even though she didn't grant Albert anything concrete. But it was enough for the consul. Then she drew me to her like a shield, between the long white arms along which the veins flowed in blue transparencies. Again the group of mother and child. Albert, having fastened his somewhat disheveled dressing gown around him, clicked his face together, stood stiffly and comically at attention, then bent over double in a low Japanese bow. Solemn even in his undress and this ridiculous posture, he assumed his company voice, an artificial and velvety purr, to say to his own wife: "Allow me, dear madam, to bestow a respectful kiss upon your hand." Anne Marie, smiling, joined in this gallant but fundamentally sad pleasantry, and held out a hand, on which he imprinted, with a lot of fuss and to-do, an exhaustive imitation of official chivalry, his homage to inaccessible beauty. Having brought Albert well to heel, Anne Marie sent me back to my picture book on the floor—not too far, in case she should have further need of me.

After this courtly interlude it became clear that the time for serious political conversation had come. Anne Marie, still standing, very light, very graceful, took little steps around the room looking for the best places to put her vases, little boats filled with huge bouquets. Ostensibly occupied with this task, walking about, her eyes still, her fingers putting the last touches to the flowers before leaving them in their rare splendor, Anne Marie talked at the same time to Albert, in precise, not too emphatic phrases, in a neutral tone with a warm undercurrent of cordiality and friendliness. A few more vigorous words were sprinkled here and there. And so, without seeming to do so, graciously absorbed in other things, like a good wife, a good friend, a perfect consuless and a great lady, she came to the Gordian knot.

"My dear, I'm uneasy about that conversation you had with Dumont last night. I sent you away first thing this morning because I wanted to talk to you properly. Tell me what arrangements you came to with him. He promised certain things—so I gathered from what you said, and anyway I'm sure of it. Otherwise you wouldn't have asked me to be careful with him. I know you, Albert. . . . All right, you hate him

—but you're shaken, you're tempted, like a fish by bait or a dog by muck. Obviously you're not very pleased with yourself—you have a pretty good idea there's a hook hidden somewhere, or poison set, but you're weak and you can't resist temptation. Don't pull a face. You know my opinion's worth having. Tell me what it's all about."

Albert hung his head guiltily. He had the same pained, profound, stricken look he wore when he was constipated.

Anne Marie had stopped walking about the room and stood up straight beside my father, the shears in her hand, like a shining black crow, one of the birds that will sit endlessly in a tree waiting to swoop on its prey, some carrion lying on the ground. They perch there, black patches disdainful of the human agitation around them, with their eyes and beaks and fixed indifference, their sinister intentness, and their sudden flight toward their spoil in a heavy, funereal flapping of wings. Her glance was like theirs as they sit crouching motionless, watching, their eyes mad and bright with vigilance. A glance determined not to miss its opportunity. She stood like that for some while, not moving, yet seeming already to wheel around him in wide, menacing circles. But Albert was quite placid and quiet, resigned to telling all, cravenly relieved, and much more uneasy about the memory of Dumont than about the presence of Anne Marie.

"You know that this Szechwan railroad is more to me than my life, the most important thing in the world after you and the boy. Dumont was clever enough to get at me through that passion, by showing how useful he could be in that respect. Maybe he did get around me—I don't know. Anyway, he was very cunning, the swine. He laid his cards on the table one after the other with diabolical cleverness, so as to impress me with his influence, his wealth, his contacts, his power. And I was flabbergasted, because he's in cahoots with all the bigwigs in Asia—war lords, secret societies, English taipans, big bankers. I had to listen to four or five hours of his bragging. You can imagine what he was like: slimy, tipsy, ingratiating, blustering, an out-and-out crook and swindler. I assure you, I put up a fight. At first I wasn't all that impressed. He started by telling me things of no importance whatever. Things everyone knows anyway—that he was in the pay of the taipans, that he was always welcome at the French consulate general, that he was top dog at the Sporting Club, and even that he was the informer and accomplice of the famous chief of police in the French Concession. He rolled his eyes as he told me all this, and I thought to myself: talk away, you bastard. I wondered what he was getting at. But on he went. You know there are rumors that he belongs to the Blue Band? Well, I began to prick up my ears when Dumont, far from denying this, told me about it with great jubilation and with all the details: how he'd gone through the great initiation ceremony, how Mr. Tu had become his 'elder brother,' and how ever since then the power of the gang was at his disposal. All the time he was talking like this it was as if he had his arm around my neck, strangling me. . . ."

He gave a pale smile. Anne Marie, her overbright brown eyes resting on him with a distant expression, just said in a mathematically precise and regular voice:

"And this person, who admitted all these connections in order to blackmail you—you didn't have him thrown straight out of the consulate? I suppose you couldn't have, since you've just asked me to take particularly good care of him."

At that there was silence, complete and utter silence, a sort of heavy congealing of nature, despite the variations in the light and the scent of the flowers. But a strange, detached, immaterial smile spread over Anne Marie's face. The consul pulled himself together and began again with a sort of courageous weariness.

"Don't judge me too fast, Anne Marie. I could tell Dumont was dangerous. But I didn't know exactly what he was up to. I let him go on talking in order to find out more, so as to be able to decide what to do in the light of the real state of affairs. In my job one can't just act on impulse. . . ."

Now Anne Marie came down to earth again, with an indifferent look which didn't even leave room for scorn. It was as if she'd known Albert's character too well to have either the strength or the desire left to condemn him. As if she'd gone beyond severity. But for the sake of appearances her words were harsh:

"In other words, you didn't dare cut Dumont short. And all this verbiage frightened you so much that the only decent diplomatic course left to you was to let him kick you up the ass."

Albert was stupefied. His eyes went round with horror, horizontal lines formed on his forehead, and his hands made as if to ward something off.

"Anne Marie, whatever's the matter? What's come over you? I can't believe my ears. You, whom all the gentlemen in Asia acknowledge to be distinction personified . . . You, whom everyone admires for your refinement . . . How can you use such language? I don't seem to know you any more."

Anne Marie gave a tiny laugh, slightly sad, slightly hurt—a laugh that was not a challenge, but directed rather against herself.

"You're right, Albert. I really don't know what came

over me. I apologize, my poor Albert. Go on with what you were saying. If you could listen to Dumont most of the night, I ought to be able to listen to you most of the day."

Then another little laugh, though it was impossible to tell whether she was mocking Albert or herself. Anyhow, Albert took it as a sign that an armistice had been concluded. So after coughing methodically three or four times, as was his habit, to clear his throat and steady his voice, and after having warmed his brains up with some silent preparatory cogitations, he began to utter a flow of smooth, well-formed, and articulated sounds, his mouth going through all the proper motions of elocution, the whole gamut of opening and shutting, half-opening and half-shutting, in order to produce the words as they should be produced.

In fact, Albert addressed Anne Marie as if he were making an official report, as if she represented the France of the Quai d'Orsay, as if she were a senior official at the Ministry of Foreign Affairs. He made use on such occasions of a ponderous style in which, by brightening up the necessary prudence with a few modest academic flourishes, he tried to steer between Scylla and Charybdis, the two dangers that lay in wait for him not on the Yangtze but in the corridors of power in Paris. To the ministry, and particularly to the Asian Department, and above all to the personnel service, so crucial to him, where colonial officials' careers were recorded and perhaps advanced, he used with the regularity of the monsoon to send presents to everyone, including the secretaries, to make sure that they were well-disposed toward him. Just like the Chinese. He was well aware of all the ill-wishers, all the well-bred colleagues with their caustic politeness and acid culture, who were forever raking up intriguing stories against consul of the first class Albert Bonnard. So he always tried to balance his missives in such a way that they might avoid the two opposing perils they were in danger of encountering on arrival. One was that some stuck-up fellow well established in the hierarchy and his office and his various degeneracies might out of boredom throw his reports in the wastepaper basket, saying to some colleague as starchy as himself: "Why does Bonnard keep churning out reports? He hasn't got the faintest idea how to write. I'm not sure he's even got his secondary school degree." Or else the same person, or maybe someone else, might say, Albert having laid the heroism and local color on too thick, blowing his own trumpet to a ridiculous extent while at the same time shamelessly toadying to his superiors in Paris: "Poor old Bonnard! There he goes again, trying to make us think he saved the situation at the risk of his life! He certainly fancies himself! And then he ends up licking the minister's arse. His Chinese quill is a peacock's feather dipped in shit." So to avoid this sort of comment, Albert, when he wrote to the Quai, stuck to a mean that was almost the truth, if perhaps a trifle inflated. He was so used to this way of describing things that now, when he was giving his wife an oral account of what had happened, he quite naturally fell into the bureaucratic jargon—flat without being terse.

Anne Marie, who was accustomed to this eternal drivel, managed to look interested and even intrigued. She leaned forward to listen. She puckered her forehead to understand. She fluttered her eyelids at the outstanding phrases. Albert began to perk up. Completely forgetting the humiliation of having to confess, he listened to the sound of his own voice, taking off higher and higher into something resembling sarcasm, a volley of witticisms. He warmed up as he went along, though being careful not to take too many liberties with the truth: he knew Anne Marie wouldn't stand for that. He was in an excellent humor by the time he came to the undesirable French nationals who made things so difficult for him. Dumont, for instance.

"Just a great blubbery joker. But I didn't know at first yesterday evening whether it was blubber or boar —whether it was really serious. Well, it was—damn serious. But I didn't know where I was. You know the Chinese dish sweet and sour pork—well, Dumont was like that, a mixture of everything. He was lavish with promises. According to him, without him or someone like him I wouldn't get anywhere in Shanghai, let alone Hanoi. Only he could stir people up, get the governor general off his arse, and produce some action from the bankers, who've always got all the time in the world and if left to themselves run down perfectly good stuff until they can swallow it up for nothing. Yes, if Dumont didn't take a hand in it, I could wait for my railroad till the cows came home! But he would get everyone moving, including the civil servants. According to him he'd already bought off half of them in the course of one affair or another. Always a joke on his lips, but the joke became sinister whenever he laughed and said, 'It may be funny, but it's true.' And all the time, directly or indirectly, veiled or naked—threats. But the later it got, the more willing he was to arrange everything for me. I didn't know what to believe. I cursed him, but I kept saying to myself, 'Watch your step, Albert. Supposing it's true?' "

"You really believed it might be true?" said Anne Marie. "You really believed it?"

Albert was taken aback. He scratched his right ear. "Well . . ." he said, nonplussed.

He labored to find out and bring forth what he had really thought. It was a difficult task: in the last twenty-four hours he'd harbored as many contradictory truths as an onion has skins. He was all mixed up.

"To tell you the truth, Anne Marie, I can't really remember. I was harassed, like an animal at bay. He paralyzed me. And the way he poked his nose into everything. 'Let's be allies and work together,' he said. 'I'll make your railroad my business; with me, it's as good as built. Of course you'll have to wait a bit. But don't be impatient. You'll get your toy, and meanwhile you've got plenty to keep you occupied,' And to crown everything, he laughed at me for worrying about my friends the Yunnanese here. 'So the consul's pals are about to be massacred,' he said, 'and the consul would like to save them! He wants French Indochina to make them a present of a nice consignment of arms. But if he thinks Indochina's going to let the arms out of its clutches like that just to please him . . . Never mind, I'll get them for you. But on condition that you're nice to me and deal me in.' It was all getting very difficult, I admit."

Anne Marie didn't look straight at Albert. She looked askance as she would at a piece of old fish or some overripe fruit when Mr. Pu, the chief cook, despite his good and loyal services, occasionally succumbed to the temptation of trying to get the better of her. He knew he wouldn't pull it off, but he couldn't help trying, in the hope that sometime or another he might succeed. When my mother caught him at these tricks she would put her head on one side as she did now, looking not at Mr. Pu himself but at his defective wares. She would just stare at them until Mr. Pu, realizing he was beaten, exclaimed of his own accord, "But these eggplants aren't worthy of Madame, and neither is the carp." And so the matter would be settled with the utmost delicacy, Mr. Pu learning his lesson but not losing "face." So there was Anne Marie, looking at my father as if he were a piece of moldy meat. She managed to hold her head still, tilted forward and to one side, the eyes in that lovely undaunted face gradually reducing my father to the state of an unappetizing lump of gristle. But it wasn't as easy as with Mr. Pu. Once Albert was brought down to his proper value—garbage, by that long, oblique, and penetrating glance—Anne Marie uttered a few words, quite simple, not even aggressive. But nothing could have been better calculated to spark an explosion.

"But, my dear," she said, "you're in a panic about nothing. That was just ordinary commercial-traveler's blackmail. You *are* impressionable, my poor Albert."

This time Albert emerged from his submissiveness and bristled all over. His mustache stood on end, his teeth gleamed, and he threw up his hands in a gesture of exasperation and discouragement at such lack of understanding.

"Christ almighty!"

Anne Marie, smiling again—amused even—put a finger on her lips.

"Don't swear like that in front of the child. . . ."

Albert strode about the room, grinding his teeth, muttering rude words to which the resplendent tassels of his dressing gown kept time. But to answer Anne Marie he used a special voice—the organ tones, the plainchant, the deep, solemn, clear, harmoniously harsh voice of some Mounet-Sully. My father had frequented the theater when he was on leave, before he was married. He had been introduced to this famous actor once in Paris, and Mounet-Sully had asked,

"Young man, do you know of a Chinese tragedy with a good part for me as the emperor?"

Anyhow, my father now cried out majestically:

"But, Anne Marie, I'm not swearing. . . ."

"Don't get into a temper, Albert."

"I am *not* in a temper at all. Are you out of your mind?"

"Calm down, Albert, and go on with what you were saying."

"But you keep on interrupting. How do you expect me to have the heart to explain? You take every opportunity of belittling me."

My mother smiled. She had a complete range of smiles, with every kind of musical intensity from a single fragile note to a full choir. They were guides to her gay neurasthenia, her attractive condescension, with all its different shades of sweetness—tender, playful, distant, haughty, scornful; all its different shades of scorn—resigned, disdainful, vexed, angry; all its different shades of anger—cold, suppressed, mobile, aggressive, searing, shrill, flamboyant. Yes, Anne Marie's smiles, with their economy of effort and their modesty of attitude, reflected her solitary confrontation—always containing a certain amount of violence—with the world. For that perpetual faint smile, in all its different degrees and kinds, had something underlying it that was sweetly bitter and implacable. Anne Marie was really much more inexorable than Albert. He thought he dominated her, but in fact he was putty in her hands. Anne Marie was quite happy with this situation. She went on playing the part of the gracious lady, revered and admired by all and delighted to be so, but always hankering after the grandiose, after the superior people and rare sensations that she never encountered as Albert's wife—

though English "five o'clock tea" and Chinese torture were considerable compensations: she took great pleasure in proving to herself that nothing, not even horror, could shake her or make her give way. The rest of the time, her most frequent and most legible expression was one that said: Oh, it's not worth getting cross about—whether with reference to Albert or to anyone else. When she adopted that somewhat deceptive expression of disdain, which really had significance only for her and for me, I would describe her to myself as "mischievous," using the English word to denote a kind of controlled teasing which might mean anything or nothing—a cuff just as easily as a caress. The reason I used this word about her in my mind was that she herself, when she wanted to convey something precise and subtle, used to say it in English. Thus, when I started to be unruly and annoying, she used to say to me, in her most smoothly authoritative tones, "Don't be 'mischievous,' little Lulu."

But in fact she wore that particular expression most often with Albert, to make fun of him without his noticing. It was a kind of cruel indulgence that led the few people who perceived it to wonder what she had in store for him.

And that was the question bound to occur that day, when Albert hunched his shoulders indignantly as if weighed down by her unfairness to him, and she replied softly:

"Don't talk like that, Albert. You know very well I'm on your side. Tell me what Dumont did. . . ."

Albert wasn't really upset. He'd just behaved for a moment as if he was being victimized, putting on a mixture of anger and depression. But the object of all this was to make her feel sorry for him. What he really wanted was for her to perform the role he had meant for her—she was to admire him, and at the same time be full of compassion for the way Dumont had ill used him despite his fierce resistance.

"I'd like to have seen you in my shoes, my dear. Then we'd have seen how haughty you would have been—with him! Heavens, it makes me feel sick just to think of it. Excuse me, Anne Marie. . . ."

And he started to belch and hiccup in a rather disgusting manner. But Anne Marie was marvelous.

"I'll get you some soda. Unless you'd rather have aspirin. Poor thing, you're quite pale—you don't look at all well. Would you like me to send for one of the doctors at the institute?"

But my father straightened up and rejected with a virile, even heroic gesture illness or anything resembling it. He assumed the faint voice of the sufferer triumphing over his sufferings. Though his jowls were still drooping, he managed to fetch up from his innards not unseemly noises but noble words.

"No, no, Anne Marie—don't disturb the doctor, whatever you do. I'm better, I assure you—I feel fine. It was just a passing malaise. Just give me a drop of water and a couple of capsules. . . ."

Not the head boy but Anne Marie herself went to the white medicine chest that was always full of countless vials and bottles, as numerous as my father's maladies, imaginary or real. Sometimes he opened one of them in front of me, with a sad, almost funereal air.

"You see how I've ruined my health, my boy, in the service of France? I have to take all sorts of rubbish in order to keep my strength up. If I were ever to die, would you be sorry, Lulu? Would you mourn for your papa, who loved you so much? And would you think of him sometimes, afterward?"

Every time he did this I pretended to cry and Anne Marie told him off.

But that day it was a different game that was being played. Anne Marie, like a real nurse looking after a real patient, came back carefully carrying a glass of water on a supererogatory saucer, and took two capsules out of a bottle and handed them to Albert.

"There, these will do you good, my dear," she said encouragingly.

"Thank you, Anne Marie. I'm only taking them to please you. I don't really need them—I feel quite better."

He started to writhe about and make faces again, this time in his efforts to swallow the pills.

"Ugh, they're horribly bitter! Quick, some more water . . . Ugh. . . . That's done it."

When this operation was over, Anne Marie bent over Albert and asked:

"Well, what was it Dumont said that's upset you so much?"

"Don't let's exaggerate. I'm not dead yet, thank God. Don't look so worried—you're not going to be a widow for a while; you're going to have me on your hands for some time still. And I'll show friend Dumont . . ."

It was characteristic of the consul to chew over his preoccupations aloud, to bang away at them, go over and over them, changing from one register to another, from lamento to cocka-doodle-doo, or vice versa. He had to go through at least a dozen variations before he found the right note for his concerto. But this time Anne Marie was impatient, and decided to hurry him a bit—carefully, of course.

"Come to the point, Albert," she said.

"I am," he said. "This is what happened. That

swine of a Dumont saved up his dirtiest trick for last.
'Well, Monsieur le Consul,' he said, 'if you're so clever
—suppose you *are* a big boy and manage to get the
arms from Indochina all on your own. You can take
my word for it they'll never get to Chengtu without
the help of your humble servant. Old Tang Kiao
would grab them on the way. Do you follow me,
Monsieur le Consul?' Of course I followed him. His
lousy argument was clear as crystal. But I'd put on
my stiff expression, the one not even you, Anne Marie,
can interpret, and I said, 'So you enjoy the unique
privilege, Monsieur Dumont, of being able to make
Tang Kiao do exactly as you like! You can tell him not
to touch the arms, and he'll leave them alone! Don't
make me laugh!' But it was Dumont who laughed. He
fell on me like a big fat avalanche, and revealed in
honeyed words the secret in which his strength consisted—namely, that unknown to the Yunnanese, Tang
Kiao belonged to the Blue Band, and that it was he,
Dumont, who had initiated him into it."

Anne Marie, listening, seemed to have become transparent, as if her body vanished in the intensity of her
icy passion.

"So what? My dear Albert, do you mean to say that
for once you didn't shine in your role as French consul? Do you mean to say that you, who so much enjoy
sending in official reports, didn't tell Dumont that you
would of course pass on information about him and
his schemes to whom it might concern? Do you mean
to say you didn't tell him the relevant home truths?
What about your powers of persuasion? Didn't you
point out to him that France, whose representative
you are, has much more hold over Tang Kiao than
he has, in spite of his illicit trade and his gangs?
Haven't you told me again and again that without

French Indochina Tang Kiao is nothing—it's Indochina that keeps him going, Indochina that's bought him, more or less? And do you mean to say you didn't fling all this in the face of the horrible Dumont, after having dinned it all into *my* ears so often?"

My father buried his face in his hands, so that it was almost invisible. Then he slowly removed this scaffolding of support and protection to reveal a head bent forward, mournful, lonely, almost blind, with eyelids pressed close together as if to escape from the weight of the world and the sight of the universe. A deep sigh as from a bellows, slowly exhaled, was the sign that he was waking up and becoming conscious again. Slowly, too, he at last opened his eyes, blinking as if the light hurt them. When he spoke his voice was a plaintive rattle.

"Anne Marie, you ought at least to do me justice and admit I don't give up easily—I hang on like a mastiff. Even my enemies say Monsieur Bonnard's not to be intimidated. And yet Dumont made me back down. I admit it."

My father's eyes were sad, like a dog's.

"But the more I spoke like a consul, the more Dumont danced with delight. Choking with laughter and cigar smoke, he kept saying things like: 'Spare me the speeches. . . . You've had experience of China, and you know very well you really have to get a Chink into a corner to make him deal straightforwardly. If you think you've got Tang Kiao in the palm of your hand . . . ! I don't need to tell you that despite his protestations of eternal and infinite devotion to the cause of France, he'll play every kind of Oriental trick on you and leave you with nothing but your pocket handkerchief to cry into. You're lucky to be still alive! Tang Kiao could easily have you ambushed by brigands, irregulars—it's a trick as old as the Middle Kingdom itself. Even if your fine arms supplies do reach Yunnanfu, and even if they leave there again under escort for Chengtu and your friend the marshal, I bet you the marshal will never set eyes on them. And who will have captured them on the way? You'll never know. You'll be a complete laughingstock. And think of your pal the marshal of Chengtu, and how angry he'll be when no arms ever turn up. I wouldn't give much for your chances of survival in Chengtu. . . . And to think you could spare yourself all these little annoyances by working with me.' That's what Dumont told me, and I could see it wasn't just nonsense."

Anne Marie gave a sudden rapid shrug of the shoulders. The thinness around her collarbones brought out the whiteness of the skin, the tautness of the sinews, the blue of the veins. It was a sensitive area on her, rather gaunt, which quivered when she was really upset. This was a first reaction, a trembling of the flesh that was prelude to an explosion. But Anne Marie had not yet reached the stage where her voice went blank; now it was merely hoarse and rapid, with more mockery in it than thunderbolts.

"Now I understand everything, my dear Albert," she said. "I see why you smoked all that opium last night, why you woke me up, and why ever since this morning you've had your tail between your legs in spite of pretending to be so sprightly. You were ashamed, and you wanted me to console and praise and admire you. You kept beating about the bush, trying to make things appear in a favorable light. And to think I used to believe that professionally (because, as for the rest . . .) —that professionally you were a brave man, almost a hero. And now I find that you're a coward in that, too."

This accusation drove Albert wild. He champed his jaws, he showed the whites of his eyes, he was reduced to tatters. But he painfully picked up the pieces and, waving his hands, began a long mournful moan.

"That's not true, Anne Marie. It's completely untrue. You know it wasn't for myself that I was afraid— it was for you, and still more for the child."

Anne Marie was unmoved. A tendon stood out on her neck. In a rapid whisper, like that of a lady reducing some blunderer to silence, she cut my father short as if switching off a light.

"Shh. The child can hear you. You must be mad to talk about it in front of him."

I could tell I was going to be sent out of the room, and I wasn't pleased. I knew the routine. It was true that my mother made use of me as a defense against some of my father's importunities. But on the other hand, when there was some festivity or other at the consulate and my father, at table or in the drawing room, started to tell a rather risqué story or bloodthirsty anecdote, she immediately signed to my father to remember that I was present. She would gesture toward me with her chin, then look at Albert conspiratorially with her finger on her lips. My father would fall awkwardly silent, I would be sent away, and he'd go on with his story under the quizzical eye of his wife. But his heart wasn't in it any more, and the phrases didn't flow so smoothly. I'd never understood why Anne Marie took these precautions. I was already exposed to all the perils of China: when I went about the city with Li and my mafu they regaled me with every possible lewdness and atrocity. And my mother didn't worry about me then. So I concluded that at home she used me, one way or another, to thwart my father.

But clearly this wasn't the explanation that day. Anne Marie really didn't want me to hear my father say certain things. And she sent me out of the room almost at once, not in her usual way, but cuddling me first a little, and then speaking to me very gently.

"Off you go, now. Your father and I have things to say to each other that wouldn't interest you."

So I went, not in the direction of my bedroom, in case my parents should be suspicious, but toward the wooden stairs leading down into the courtyard. After I'd shut the door I made a great noise going down the steps, then came up again quietly and stood on the landing. I could hear their voices, and see them through a space between two planks in the wall.

What I saw was a sort of confused ballet, a scene from a Chinese opera in which the actors wore masks and confronted one another with conventional and tragic words and gestures. My father was the emperor, prey to misfortune and confession; my mother the princess carried away with lucid and ruthless passions. There was agitation, declamation, fury. This scene often recurred to my imagination, but it wasn't until a long while later that I could clothe it in flesh and blood, and understand what it was really about.

My parents faced each other, my father shifting awkwardly from one foot to the other, Anne Marie motionless. Even her lips scarcely moved when she asked him:

"Now tell me the truth. Is the child really in danger?"

My father wriggled.

"Well, yes and no. It's hard to say. But Dumont did rather obscurely refer to the possibility of his being kidnapped. Not by him—by Tang Kiao. Of course this was only a hypothesis, he said, but Tang Kiao would do anything to get what he wants— namely, the arms. The boy would be given back in exchange for their being handed over to the kidnappers. Of course Tang Kiao's hand would not appear in all this. It would be the usual devious Chinese trick, with the kidnappers in the pay of Tang Kiao, and Tang Kiao playing the saint while at the same time giving them orders. Yes, the child's life could be in danger. . . . Dumont went into all the details, but said it was only a supposition on his part and that in any case, if I went in with him nothing would happen, and he'd keep an eye open. . . ."

Anne Marie, far from being angry at these admissions, looked like one of those Chinese statuettes made of pure crystal. A solid, sourcelike translucence. As if she no longer had a body or organs, or anything material about her. Yet in this marvelous limpidity she burned, but with a flame so fine and pale that it could only be discerned as a white and blinding glow. But in reality it was a terrible fire in which she was tempering her arms.

In a perfectly ordinary voice and manner, just as if she were asking a perfectly ordinary question, she said:

"And you didn't kill Dumont on the spot?"

My father was so dumfounded that he couldn't even look astonished, and all he managed to answer was:

"No, no, Anne Marie, you don't mean that. A French consul can't go slaughtering a French citizen. . . ."

"In that case, didn't you hit him?"

Albert suddenly started to yell. Usually so careful about acoustics and echo and resonance, imagining hidden listeners everywhere and modulating his voice accordingly, expert at speaking furtively so as not to be overheard by snoopers, expert, too, at deliberately fulminating for the edification not only of his interlocutors but of everyone within earshot, he now bawled for all he was worth, without a thought for the consequences or for all the hidden ears that might be listening, including my own. He shouted so loudly that the padding he wrapped his words in when he used a lot of volume now became a sort of hiccup.

"No, Anne Marie. I thought of the child, and restrained myself."

Anne Marie answered very calmly, bringing out every syllable, like a schoolmistress pointing the moral of some small incident.

"You were quite right, Albert. One should never commit oneself. You acted very wisely, as a consul, as a gentleman, and as a father. You couldn't do otherwise, in the circumstances, than take the hand Dumont offered you. For all the reasons you've given, and above all to prevent the boy from being in danger. In short, you sacrificed yourself for him. I understand very well, Albert. . . ."

She put on an amused smile, just on one side of her mouth, and asked, gaily, innocently:

"So you made peace with Dumont, Albert, and you're in league with him under the most honorable conditions. With Dumont, your good fairy, who occasionally just threatens to murder your son. It doesn't matter if he picks up a few crumbs in the process. . . . That's it, isn't it?"

Albert, happy to have got off so lightly, adjusted his face and his dressing gown, and nodded repeatedly. And having recovered his spirits, he also opened his mouth again. But before he had time to give moved and solemn utterance, Anne Marie said winningly:

"But tell me, Albert—Monsieur Dumont certainly wouldn't have been content with just offering you his services, even if he makes money by them. That wouldn't be enough for him. He likes some immediate profit, all ready and waiting. Cash down is his motto. He didn't come to the back of beyond for nothing. So what does he want? What dishonorable service did he demand of you? Albert, you've agreed to do something for him. What is it?"

Albert, crestfallen, tugged at his mustache.

"What he's interested in is opium. The whole of the Szechwan harvest. He wants it for Mr. Tu and the Blue Band. And he knows very well he won't get any of it unless I put in a good word with the marshal of Chengtu and Mr. Lu."

"So you're going to pay them a discreet visit and persuade them to be nice to Monsieur Dumont."

"Yes. I don't want to. But I've said I would. There was no alternative. It will be disagreeable, but still . . ."

Anne Marie didn't look at all shocked. It was as if she'd accepted what her husband had said. But how could she, so shrewd and intelligent, have swallowed it? Even though she'd forced him to tell the truth, it was clear he was still holding something back. Albert, even when he collapsed, never gave in completely. And did he really know himself when he was being sincere? His son had served as an excuse, as if it was as a father that he'd capitulated to Dumont. But the fact of the matter was that Albert hadn't been able to resist the word "ambassador" which his fat friend had dangled in front of him. It was an irresistible bait. Often, to justify himself to Anne Marie, he used to say, "You don't realize—you're married to a future ambassador." But did she believe him? She had the gay, promising, rather seductive laugh of a dutiful and obedient wife who admires and delights in her husband. But Albert's cheek now twitched uneasily. For this laugh was a sign that Anne Marie had not been taken in: she was agreeing with him too much—far, far too much.

"That visit you promised to the marshal—you'll have to pay it, Albert. Pay it soon and bring it off properly. So that thanks to you Dumont gets his opium and is happy, and grateful to you. I'd like to see your friend happy. . . ."

The consul was pleased, but only tentatively, as if again wondering what his wife was up to. He decided to adopt the English tactic of "wait and see."

"As always, you're right in the end, darling," he said. "I'll go and see the marshal as soon as I can—but you know the Chinese and their confounded politeness and incurable suspicion. If I act too quickly they'll be surprised, and start to be mistrustful, and wriggle and reflect indefinitely, wondering if I'm setting a trap for them. But you can count on me to settle this unpleasant matter with all possible speed. For as you may imagine, there's only one thing I want: the same thing you do, and that's to say goodbye to Dumont, bag and baggage."

Anne Marie put her face coaxingly close to Albert's, so near as almost to rub her delicate nose against her spouse's proboscis.

"Hurry up, my dear. Why do you make so much fuss about the marshal? He'll let you have Dumont's opium as soon as you ask him. So why wait? Why stand on ceremony? While you're about it, why don't you discreetly make another little request? You could just slip in a word at the end of the conversation suggesting he might free you from Dumont once and for all. Since you want to be rid of him, you might as well do the job properly. . . ."

My father didn't understand, didn't want to understand, these enigmatic words. But he sensed that their meaning was stormy, and that was enough to make him adopt a state of alert. He drew arms, legs, body, and head all tightly together, and set a blinking eye at the top, on the defensive. What was Anne Marie cooking up for him?

"What do you mean, my dear?" he said in a strangled voice.

The caustic note was growing more and more dominant in Anne Marie's laugh. It was merry still, but ominous.

"Don't shut your ears, Albert! What I'm suggesting is just common sense. Why not pay Dumont back in his own coin, beat the idiot at his own game? He bullied you, didn't he, by conveying that whenever he liked he could have all three of us liquidated, courtesy of his dear and diligent friend Tang Kiao? Well, what's to stop you from saving our heads by asking your friend, the marshal of Chengtu, for Dumont's? I'm sure the marshal would be delighted to render you that little service. And you can be sure he'd perform it as skillfully as Tang Kiao would have dispatched us if the shoe were on the other foot. It would be a typical, inextricable Chinese affair, in which your hand wouldn't be seen at all and you'd be absolutely uncompromised. . . ."

The consul started. All his features moved a couple of centimeters upward, in a flabbergasted frown. Then they all fell back into place again, their ebb leaving behind a bantering smile which indicated that it was a joke, that his wife's words were not serious, it was just a typical case of a woman getting worked up and making a scene. So he laughed accordingly, punctuating his hilarity with great tossings of the chin.

"Ah, women, women! One never knows what you're

going to think up next. Don't be angry, Anne Marie, but I don't think you realize that what you're suggesting is murder. It's too funny. . . ."

Anne Marie was silent, and my father went on laughing, only the laughter grew more and more forced. But as his wife clearly didn't mean to give in, he was reduced to sticking to that same constrained mirth, as if he were dealing with a mere foolish and dangerous prank, which it was his duty to put a stop to by talking like a husband and a father, indulgently and understandingly.

"Anne Marie, you're getting too worked up. You mustn't take Dumont's tales literally. I ought never to have told you all that nonsense. Just leave it to me to sort it all out for the best. Dammit, I wasn't born yesterday. . . ."

But Albert's liveliness ended abruptly, as did his attempt to attribute Anne Marie's strange suggestion to female inconsistency, featherheadedness, childish imagination. The consul's sprightliness, his gift for minimizing, his little words for soothing, consoling, taking in hand, all came up against the stony visage of the consuless. She was quite motionless, her breathing regular, her skin glossy as a rice husk, her hair shining like a dark forest. Never had her beauty been more pure. But the nerves beneath the skin were filaments charged with fluids and waves. Albert trembled for himself. It was as if he feared that this state of intensity might affect his wife's reason, leaving her disheveled and demented. There were certain marks in the eyes, certain tremblings of the voice, certain twitches of the mouth—not the usual ones, but others she had no control over. Whenever that happened it lasted only a few seconds, but it was terrible. That day he feared an even worse attack—real madness. Everyone cited Anne Marie as a model of good health, even in her extremes of ice and fire. And yet . . .

On the other side of the wall, I was standing on my toes to get a good view through the crack. It was a bit too high up for me. But I managed to stay in this difficult position, breathing as quietly as I could so as not to give myself away.

It made me shudder to see my mother in that state, for I, even more than my father, guessed at some black abyss in Anne Marie. In the Chinese theater I'd seen a lady of sublime nobility and beauty, a bird of jade who triumphed over a terrible fate until something cracked and she began to speak strangely, awfully, like those who dwell in the Realm of the Eternal Shades.

That day, for the first time in my life, I, who was afraid of nothing, had a shock, a feeling of a descent into horror, the certainty that my mother was beginning to enter that same kingdom of darkness.

But for the moment Anne Marie was sane, even if she had a terrible fixed idea. She knew exactly what she wanted: she must make Albert—spineless, phrasemongering, muddleheaded, vain Albert—make him man enough to make the necessary decision without bothering about trifles like ordinary morality and immorality. She had to hound him down, for he was fighting back and taking refuge in the platitudes of bureaucratic, petty-bourgeois, and misogynous convention. She joined battle.

"My dear Albert, stop cackling like a gander. I'm not a goose any more. The girl from Ancenis whom you liked for her simplicity is dead—you destroyed her by bringing her, without scruple, to remotest China. Don't be surprised that I've changed. Don't complain. Anyway, it's better so. Instead, listen to my advice. It's worth having."

Albert, automatically putting on his pince-nez, looked at Anne Marie with an expression of incredulity. He stared at her for a few seconds, as if searching. He was trying to convince himself that the woman confronting him was really his own wife, Anne Marie. Once he was convinced he took off his glasses. His manicured fingers played with them as he spoke, his voice already tired.

"Anne Marie, you will never cease to astound me. It's naïve of me to think I'm safe from your surprises, which are not always pleasant ones. When things go well I seem to know you inside out, and mentally I award you good marks for almost everything, I barely admit you may have a few faults. And then suddenly, bang! You're so strange, as if you were a hundred miles away from me, unknown, unpredictable, behaving in a way that's incredible, almost monstrous. And when that happens you frighten me. . . . Tell me if you're serious, if you really want me to plot the death of someone who's a guest under our roof."

Anne Marie smiled like a young bride who has just ventured some little independent action she is pleased with.

"Of course, Albert. Don't think me unkind. It's necessary."

"But, Anne Marie, we can't do a thing like that to Dumont. . . ."

"Why not? Nothing easier."

She smiled again, but this time like one who knows, a visionary. One step deeper into this revenge, and for her it might be breakdown, the abyss, the descent into madness. But at the moment she was a monument of conviction, logic, and reason. As firm as a rock.

My father's only recourse was to play the philosopher, a man who has seen and understood much and who is no longer surprised by anything, even his wife. He gave a little grimace that was half affectionate and half ironical, and said, to see how the land lay:

"In other words, desperate ills call for desperate remedies?"

"Yes."

"In other words, Anne Marie, you've become the Lady Macbeth of Chengtu?"

A scornful sniff from Anne Marie.

"You're so well-read. I know you even got your secondary-school diploma."

"With distinction. But I was poor, and I had to give up my studies to earn my living. I'm a self-made man. . . ."

Anne Marie brushed aside these eternal repetitions with a little wave of the hand.

"That's enough. Tell me what you've decided to do about Dumont."

Albert, his face vague, drummed on the back of his chair, breathing in and out noisily through the mouth: he was thinking. To be able to think better, he got up and walked meditatively around the room, then sat down again hesitantly, as if still prey to indecision. He sat there like that for a while, puffing a little, his face rather sorrowful. He was really working out a plan to persuade Anne Marie to give up her idea. It was far-fetched, not altogether silly, but really a little too crude for his taste, too blunt. A blunt instrument was perhaps what she was thinking of! The idea would certainly take care of Dumont—but carrying it out was another matter, and Albert didn't feel at all up to that. On the other hand, he didn't want to argue with this wild Anne Marie and her demand for a corpse. What could have made her like this? he thought.

Bloodthirstiness? Revenge? A desire to punish vulgarity? Or just instinct, a sense that it was kill or be killed with Dumont? If so, it would be legitimate self-defense. But none of these explanations really fitted Anne Marie. How she'd come to be seized by this rage was a mystery. But he wasn't going to give in. He kept repeating to himself that Anne Marie wasn't going to wear the trousers.

But he was careful not to say it aloud. What was he to do? Try to cheat her? In the distant and even the recent past, almost all his attempts to fool her had been fiascos. This, Albert thought, was because he was too confident and his methods were too obvious. This time he had to be really clever, and he must start by discharging ballast. He would pretend to agree with her, and then, going into the details of how to carry out the plan, they would both discover all the technical obstacles in the way of speeding Dumont into another world. He'd do it so skillfully that Anne Marie herself would decide that Dumont must be allowed to live.

But all Albert's behavior was so artificial that now, as always, Anne Marie knew he was not being sincere. As a matter of fact, she didn't expect him to be. So she was ready again to meet all his dodges.

He began once more to walk about, but now with head held high, carefree, arms swinging, feet triumphant. He was acting the part of a man sure of himself, lively, young, even roguish.

"Anne Marie, do you know who I can see through the window? Your friend Dumont, walking up and down in the courtyard. He must be waiting for us to go in to lunch. It's half-past two already. We'll have to go down."

He laughed uproariously, as if at a good joke.

"He'd laugh on the other side of his face if he could hear what we've been saying. Can you imagine his expression if he knew what you'd been asking me to do for the last hour? What a priceless situation! And to think that a few minutes from now you'll be going up to him, all smiles because you're going to have his head. And he'll be wondering why you're being so nice to him. You women really are tough. If I were in your place I'd be embarrassed."

Anne Marie gave him a severe look.

"Don't joke, please, Albert. I don't find this matter at all amusing. It's just got to be settled, that's all."

But he went on laughing impishly. The consul was a boy again.

"As you know, the Chinese, and even more their wives, laugh like mad every time they have someone polished off. And you were saying just now how you'd been changed by this country, which according to you is terrifying but charming. It would seem that you're more Sinified than I am—you take yourself for another Empress Tsu Hsi, whereas I'm only a false, white-livered sort of Chinese. So you should be laughing your fill."

"This isn't the moment for joking."

This remark made Albert pass from gay to serious cheerfulness. He wanted to show Anne Marie that he had the matter thoroughly under control, and that she could leave it to him. He seemed to confide in her completely. If *that* didn't please her . . . It wasn't his fault that he had to approach the matter gradually.

"Darling. I don't quite know how to say it, but I'm rather bothered. After all, I am the French consul. But I admit I do agree with you about Dumont. Alive, he'll play us all sorts of horrible tricks. So I'll go and see what the marshal can do. I'll be very insistent. Even if I don't actually spell it out, he'll understand and act

accordingly. I'll go so far as to make quite unmistakable allusions. I'll say Dumont is an undesirable, and
what a good thing it would be if he disappeared.
That's the sort of thing I'll say; according to Chinese
custom it's as good as a straightforward proposition.
And I'll know the result at once. If the marshal is
silent, that means he refuses. But if he says something,
even something vague—for example, that Dumont is
a nuisance, a problem that will have to be dealt with
one day—that means he agrees. And he'll see to everything, and I can wash my hands of it. What do you
think of my little plan, Anne Marie?"

Albert adopted his finest pose, that of benefactor,
the one he used when he wrote a commendation on his
visiting card for So-and-so to take to So-and-so, when
he promised someone else that he'd praise him lavishly
in his next report, or when he undertook to support
somebody's candidacy for a certain post. If Albert was
moved by generosity, as did sometimes happen, to
reward a person who had really earned his favors by
buttering him up and flattering him, his gestures were
ample, his words caressing, his laugh lordly. But
mostly my father's gifts were so likely to be poisoned
that the beneficiary did all he possibly could to avoid
accepting them, knowing that the consul was really
doing himself a service. For example, if Albert offered
to introduce someone in a humble position to someone
highly placed, it was so that the former might tell the
latter certain things in Albert's favor which were too
delicate for Albert to make known directly. So when he
handed out his false-bottomed favors, he was like a
traveling salesman who rings doorbells, urging his
goods on the reluctant customer, and keeps murmuring, "You're too kind. . . . Really, you mustn't trouble.
. . . I'm quite embarrassed." But Albert would return
to the charge until the unfortunate recipient was

overwhelmed by his gifts. Arms, eyes, and smiles formed part of the attack; he was all velvet, kindness, and modesty, saying at regular intervals: "No, it's nothing, nothing at all. . . . There's no need to be grateful. . . . Don't be embarrassed or I'll be cross. . . ." This was the method he now adopted to try to lead Anne Marie up the garden path.

She, while fully taking in Albert's dishonesty, remained imperturbable for the moment, to see just how far her hypocrite of a husband would go.

"So you mean just to make veiled insinuations to the marshal? Do you think that will be enough?"

"As you know, that's the Chinese way of negotiating. With the yellow brothers one never calls a spade a spade. Everything is done by hints. And in a way, when the people concerned are really distinguished, it's a method not without its merits. Nothing is said openly, so if anyone refuses to do something, no one can be offended because there was no real proposal. In my opinion it shows great delicacy, when one's dealing with something rather risky, not to dot the i's. There are some good things about the Chinese. Can you see me, the French consul, asking the marshal to have Dumont's throat cut? It would be extremely rude, a very bad solecism, and he'd despise me and I'd lose all my influence with him. But what would be thought very subtle and courteous and, in short, worthy of me, would be to convey that if he did away with Dumont in some manner I don't even wish to know about, I'd secretly show my appreciation; and that despite my official protests and demands, and there would be plenty of those, I would see to it that he didn't suffer for it. And then it's in the bag."

Anne Marie bit her lower lip, a sign of irritation which she couldn't repress.

"What a fine speech, Albert. I ought to have remembered that you're absolutely impossible to fault on China. China can be blamed for everything. Don't smile in that self-satisfied way."

She went up close to him.

"And yet only a few months ago you were aghast at the coarseness of the marshal and his gray eminence, Mr. Lu. You're forgetting you told me how astonished you were. That skeleton of a Lu, without any of the polite trimmings you've just described with such approval, simply asked you bluntly to get him arms from Indochina. You more or less promised that you would. So you're in league with him. You don't have to handle them with kid gloves. All you have to do is tell them that a certain Dumont, who wants to dabble in a big arms deal, is a traitor and will mess the whole thing up. Their lives are at stake. If you tell them frankly that you wash your hands of whatever becomes of Dumont, who's been foolish enough to come to Chengtu, I'm quite sure they will do the necessary."

Albert rolled his eyes, looking for a way of escape. Drops of sweat stood out on his forehead.

"You go too far, Anne Marie. You're asking me to deliver over Dumont—a bastard perhaps, but a compatriot, a French citizen whom it's my duty to protect at all costs—on mere suspicion, mere supposition. And in the most reprehensible manner. If it were ever to come out . . . ! I'm risking everything—my career, my honor, even prison. I could be taken back to French territory and tried and sentenced like a criminal. . . ."

"Don't be so lily-livered!" Anne Marie cried. "You're revolting."

Albert twisted his head in all directions and began to whine:

"Can you see me in handcuffs, between two policemen? And what would become of you? Oh, the dis-grace!"

Anne Marie eyed Albert as if she had just seen through his game.

"You're overdoing it, Albert. Let's stop this wretched playacting. You're not quite as stupid as all that."

Albert, found out, put on his most wily expression and clenched his jaws.

"But, my dear, the danger is real. The marshal might calculate that it's to his advantage to denounce me to Tang Kiao, and get back into favor himself. On the other hand, if he bumps off Dumont he'll be risking his neck. Tang Kiao would never forgive him. So you see the marshal has plenty to think about. I must be careful, very careful."

They were now engaged in the ultimate round of their great debate—quiet, without irony, without anger, almost monotonous. A pitiless battle of wills.

Anne Marie plunged in.

"No quibbling, Albert. To impress you and get his opium, Dumont told you about Tang Kiao's wicked plans, in order, he said, to foil them. Dumont! He tries to make a fool of you, a bloody fool, and you believe him! But the marshal of Chengtu isn't as gullible as you are. With his clever yellow brain he knows, you may be sure, that with Dumont alive he'll never so much as see a machine gun. He knows all his men will be slaughtered if Dumont isn't killed. So don't you worry—the marshal will listen to you if you talk straight to him. So go on and let's finish with it!"

Albert protested with the utmost vehemence, raising his voice several notes and producing something between a roar and a bleat. To add to the force of his argument he kept thumping himself on the chest.

"You're not telling me anything I don't know. It

was I who first warned you against Dumont and told you about his machinations."

Without even appearing to hear him, she continued, nervously toneless, with incredible inner force. It seemed nothing could stop the flow.

"Dumont must be executed. Once he's dead, properly dead, everything can change. And without trouble. Without that evil genius, Tang Kiao will be in our hands. . . ."

Albert put on his subtle smile, the smile of an old fox who doesn't need to be taught any lessons, and offered the following well-furbished objection:

"Have you thought of everything? The least Tang Kiao could do if anything happens to Dumont is to suspect. He'll tell Europeans about his suspicions, the Indochinese government will get to hear about it, and a nice mess I'll be in then!"

"You'll have nothing to fear if you take the necessary precautions."

"What precautions, my dear Mimi? Tell me."

"Obviously, if Tang Kiao is allowed to, he'll make difficulties. But it's easy to make him see reason."

"Tell me your recipe for it."

"Tang Kiao has feathered his own nest in Yunnanfu without leaving anything for anyone else. And there must be plenty of faithful generals ready to slay him and take his place. All you'd need to do is give one of them some discreet encouragement. . . ."

Albert was jubilant.

"You're insatiable, Anne Marie. Dumont's corpse isn't enough for you. You have to have Tang Kiao's, too. You don't do things by halves."

He laughed at his own pleasantry. Anne Marie shrugged.

"There's no need to touch Tang Kiao. It's enough

just to frighten him. You have only to send a nice long telegram in cipher to your protector in the Foreign Ministry, asking him to send the necessary instructions to the French consul in Yunnanfu and to the Indochinese government. In Yunnanfu there are all the men and opportunities you can possibly need: Annamite spies, French adventurers, half-caste policemen all of them professionals quite capable of getting together with one of Tang Kiao's henchmen. And when he finds out that the French are sending one of his devoted vassals money and arms for a coup d'état, Tang Kiao won't let out a peep when he hears the sad news of Dumont's death."

Albert looked horrified.

"And what am I supposed to tell my protector at the ministry to set him against Tang Kiao? As soon as Dumont's dead, he's going to remember all that and suspect. Everyone will suspect."

"Not if you set about it the right way. Say you suspect Tang Kiao of being up to some dirty work, which will strike everyone as likely enough; say he's trying to get hold of the arms that are supposed to be going to the marshal of Chengtu. Anything . . . Later on no one will see any connection between your dispatches to Paris and what happens to Dumont. You're home free."

Albert's eyes were like saucers.

"So, my dear, you want me to cheat everyone, including France, whose representative I am? I'm not up to that. . . . And besides, you have to remember that China's a place where complicated affairs get so complicated that you never know how they're going to turn out."

He started to joke again.

"And can you see my colleague in Yunnanfu getting orders to act against Tang Kiao? The poor fellow would die of fright. He's the learned Cosinus from the School of Oriental Languages, a Sinologist, and a philosopher into the bargain. He married some little student in the Latin Quarter, some Polish Jewess as ugly as sin, with no neck or legs or hair, and fat as butter. The old girl believes in the Chinese, and tries to spread the gospel in the French Club in Yunnanfu. She's taken it into her head to teach the ladies of the French colony the folk dances of their yellow brothers and sisters. Meanwhile, back at the consulate, her husband, with his square beard and beady eyes, puts on a great big red mandarin's robe to perform a very peculiar ceremoney. He recites Chinese erotic poetry, very hot stuff, looking as solemn as a judge and drawing inspiration from rummaging in the posterior of a naked Chinese prostitute. Can you see that grotesque grappling with Tang Kiao?"

But Anne Marie was not to be dissuaded.

"Forget it. It's not important. There's no need for all that with Tang Kiao; I only suggested it to reassure you because you keep caviling and looking for excuses. Let's simplify the business. It will be better in the end. I tell you that once Dumont has been liquidated, Tang Kiao won't be able to do anything to you. The Chinese are true gamblers and know how to lose without showing it. Tang Kiao will probably just think you've been very smart, and draw the appropriate conclusions. You don't run any risk as long as you play your part properly in Chengtu."

"What part?"

"You know very well what part. The part of a good consul. You've only got to be yourself, the marvelous Albert Bonnard. Just be natural—conscientious, determined, full of dignity and grandeur and the rights of France, as usual."

"I really don't see . . ."

"Don't play the innocent. Of course you see. It'll be like this. . . . One fine day someone will come to the consulate in horror and wake you out of your siesta to tell you that Monsieur Dumont, who went into town after lunch to take part in some secret negotiation, has been carried off by armed men. The accounts will be confused and contradictory: some will talk of Szechwanese soldiers, some of other people, irregulars, bandits. Anyhow, up you will bound, and in your fury you'll gallop unannounced to the marshal's yamen, past the sentries, force your way in, and speak to him in a manner worthy of you. You'll tell him you hold him, as governor of the city, responsible for Monsieur Dumont's life. With a few well-calculated threats, you'll insist that he do everything in his power to get Dumont freed immediately. He must issue a proclamation saying how angry he is, announce huge rewards for informers, and terrible punishments for the criminals unless they repent and release their victim. You'll demand that he call on all the troops and police and spies in Chengtu and the whole province. You'll be so carried away that you'll speak to him in a way that makes him lose 'face,' and in his humiliation and rage he won't dare to suggest the only sensible solution, which is to wait until an emissary turns up somewhere to start negotiating the ransom. So the marshal will unleash his thugs, who'll spread terror through every alley and hovel, on the pretext that they're hunting for the culprits and trying to save Monsieur Dumont.

"The result will be that Dumont's body will be found, for the kidnappers, taking the view that the marshal hasn't played the game and has broken the rules of business, will have been obliged to kill Monsieur Dumont instead of using him as a pawn. Then

you'll make a great display of your grief, you'll look
all pale and wan, and the marshal will offer you the
massacre of a couple of hundred so-called kidnappers,
together with a few kilos of gold as compensation for
France and for the widow in Shanghai. I can just see
you, with your gravity, your decencies, your speeches,
including a funeral oration describing all Dumont's
virtues. The city will be in mourning. The marshal,
in white, will come and pay his respects to the corpse.
You'll receive the condolences of all the other consuls
and all the local dignitaries. You'll endure all the
compulsory lamentations, the lying in state with the
flesh and the flowers decaying together, the blessings
and masses of the priests, the prayers of the orphan
girls as they file past making the sign of the cross.
You'll argue in order to get a good strong coffin.
Lastly you'll preside over the departure for Shanghai
of what was once Dumont, carried by coolies, to be
laid to rest in the cemetery of the French Concession.
Perhaps as a last token of respect you will accompany
the remains for part of the journey. Then you'll come
back to Chengtu and write an exhaustive account to
the Quai d'Orsay, to remind them of your zealous
efforts—alas, vain—to save Dumont. And you'll conclude by expatiating on the huge amounts of compensation you've gotten out of the Chinese, which shows
how they fear and respect France, whose influence is
now greater than ever, thanks to you. And then everyone will forget all about Dumont."

Albert, who had listened in silence, tugging at his
mustache, put on his subtle smile again.

"What kind of fairy story is this?" he asked.

"It's not a fairy story. That's how it will have to be.
Then no one will notice anything. They may even
praise your magnanimity. They'll say: 'All the trouble

poor Albert Bonnard went to for Dumont! And he
hasn't had any reward for it. . . .' I'm sure you'll play
your part perfectly. Anyway, I'll be there beside you.
I shall enjoy it. We'll be the only Europeans who
know the truth."

Albert looked long and sadly at his ecstatic wife.

"You terrify me," he said.

In her frenzy, Anne Marie was ugly.

"If Dumont hadn't threatened the boy, I'd never
have demanded his death. But after that I don't feel
any remorse—I'd die of rage if he wasn't punished.
He absolutely must be killed."

Albert pensively lit a cigarette and, taking his time,
breathed out little puffs of smoke, which floated
away like haloes.

"Your plan isn't as good as you think. The marshal's
Yunnanese can be counted on to do their work properly. But the wretched playacting we'd have to go
through has several weak points. People would be
bound to say: 'Why was Bonnard in such a hurry?
Why all those frantic ultimatums to the marshal? If
he'd played for time and entered into negotiations
with the bandits, perhaps Dumont would be alive
today.' My behavior might seem very questionable,
and give people ideas."

"You know very well that when a man's kidnapped
in Chengtu, nothing you can do is right. If you negotiate with the kidnappers they send you bits of the victim to extort more money and you never get him back
alive. No, in the case of Dumont everyone will think
that by stirring up the Yunnanese and having a great
search made you've tried the only possible means of
saving him. No one will blame you for having staked
everything, even though it turned out badly."

Albert, impassive, went on blowing ever more perfect smoke rings.

"You have no experience of life. I bet you the British will suspect some dirty work at the crossroads. They weren't born yesterday."

"You know the English and how phlegmatic they are. If they don't have positive proof they won't say anything. And there won't be any proof."

"One of the people in their intelligence service will write a note about it. And then we'll probably see some gentlemen slightly more alert than their present consul arriving in Chengtu, and I shouldn't care for that at all."

"You must be dreaming, Albert. At the most, a few people might suspect the marshal and the Yunnanese, but you—never. They'll just say as usual: 'Another typical Chinese affair. What a country! But Dumont asked for it, fiddling around with the Chinks.' That will be his funeral oration."

"Talking of the Chinese, have you thought about the Blue Band? They'll certainly know everything. . . ."

"What about it, even if they did? The marshal has only to inform the honorable Mr. Tu of his intention to honor the agreement on opium recently concluded by the unfortunate Monsieur Dumont. Mr. Tu will soon get over it, especially as he won't have to pay a percentage to Dumont now."

Albert put a hand to his brow, as if he had one of the migraines that usually brought life in the consulate to a halt.

"If you've thought of everything, have you thought of the marshal? If I get him to murder Dumont I'll never have another moment's peace. Every time he looks at me I'll see a sarcastic gleam in his eye. It would be permanent blackmail."

"He needs you more than you need him, so you've nothing to fear. Anyway, what's one man killed to a

Chinese? Just a matter of business. And you're already in business with the marshal. You're already accomplices, whether Dumont is killed or not. Unless you give up everything, including the very idea of the railroad . . ."

A groan rose from my father's inmost depths.

"No, I must have the railroad. But my conscience . . . Dammit, I'm not a savage."

Anne Marie drew closer.

"After an hour, here you are, still shifty and feeble. Now make up your mind!"

But Albert wouldn't hurry. He inflicted on Anne Marie the torture of time. He was normal, too normal, at ease, relaxed, ordinary, fussy, as if nothing were happening of any great importance, as if Anne Marie weren't there keeping watch on him. He went and got a leather case from the bedside table and began the ritual of the cigar: an enormous cigar, with which he entered upon a series of operations. He tapped one end of it at some length, guillotined the other end with a silver cutter, then turned the Havana round and round in his fingers, warming it and just letting it catch the flame of a match before lighting it properly and putting it in his mouth. One minute, two, went by. Happy clouds of smoke poured from his lips, as from a hearth radiating peace. He was absorbed and content in this mild pleasure.

"Don't stand quite so near," he said. "You might get burned."

The cigar was the emblem of revolt. Although Albert chewed and sucked at it without any warlike signs, he was now in a state of unshakable resolve. He wasn't afraid any more; he was made of stone.

Half an inch of the cigar had been consumed, and Albert flicked off the ash. Then he held it smoking in his hand, at a distance, and settled down in his chair, seeking the most comfortable position. With a rather languid smile, his eyes gleaming with a slightly ambiguous mockery of Anne Marie, of himself, of everything, he at last began to speak. His voice was rather thick, he rolled his *r*'s, his tone was one of ultimate weariness—not exhaustion, but the liberation that comes when all possible concessions have been made and the only thing left to say is the truth.

"Anne Marie, you've worn me out; your scene has lasted so long. I admit you were right about me. It's true I was devious, that I tried to discourage you with cavils and tricks. I would have liked you to give up your plan of your own accord, without my having to say no. I know how sensitive you are—I didn't want to hurt you by a blunt refusal. I know your motives are not unworthy. They're even understandable, in a way. You may be right. But I'd rather die than do what you want me to do."

Anne Marie listened, motionless. Albert got all the mileage he could out of playing the reasonable man. He stopped speaking, sat up straighter to draw deeply on his Corona, then resumed, in the settled pose of one who is satiated.

"It might be wise to have Dumont killed. And as you've realized, I wouldn't really be running any risks. I'd just have to come to a satisfactory arrangement with the marshal, and then there'd be the farce that you've imagined so vividly. Yes, it would be as easy as falling off a log. Except that I'm not a murderer, and never will be. . . ."

The consul was a kind man. And yet his face was becoming distorted, as if unkindness was mustering and swelling inside his mouth. Slyly and sarcastically, as if he couldn't restrain himself any longer, he said:

"But you're a terror, Anne Marie. You really are. I never dreamed you had it in you. I don't mind telling you it makes me a bit jittery about my future. For if one day you felt I was in the way, I wonder, now that I know the rapidity of your methods, whether you wouldn't dispatch me as you want to dispatch poor Dumont. . . . I'm only joking, Anne Marie. . . . Anne Marie . . ."

He stammered the last words in vain, helpless before his wife, now in hysterics. She did not look noble, like a dealer of thunderbolts, a creature of fire, an exterminating angel. Nor was she like someone whose overstrained nerves have given way and whose mind is wandering. It was worse than that. All that was left of her was an animal, howling. Her face was just a hole emitting inarticulate cries. It was a nightmare. She grimaced like the subhuman madmen one often met, tied up in chains, in the streets of Chengtu. She remained standing, her arms flailing around her stiff body, simian, unconscious, uttering cries that rent the flesh, pierced the heart, carried through the walls. Sometimes she showed the whites of her eyes, jumped, laughed. It seemed interminable. It probably lasted a few minutes.

Albert, frightened, like a dumb beast struck by lightning, could only murmur, "Good God . . . what on earth's happening? What shall I do? That was all I needed. . . ." Then he screwed up his courage and tried to take Anne Marie in his arms, saying reproachfully:

"But what's the matter, darling? What's the matter? I didn't mean to upset you. Calm down now—I'm here. Be careful, calm down, people will hear you."

Anne Marie, coming to herself again at Albert's touch, said, hiccuping, "Don't touch me! Don't touch me!"

Albert, more and more worried and looking very upset, murmured gently, as one does to people who are ill, "No, I won't touch you. Pull yourself together, Anne Marie. I'm your husband, who loves you—Albert. . . ."

Her cries had stopped and she was sobbing, tears streaming down her cheeks. She was human again: but ghastly pale, sodden, her lips still twitching, her chin thrust out and jerking in time with her palpitating throat and trembling shoulders. Life returned, light came back into her eyes just as a ray of sunshine breaks through masses of dark clouds that have swallowed up the whole world. In place of the St. Vitus's dance that had twisted her features, her face wore a distant mildness close to a saving loss of consciousness. She moved like a sleepwalker, without faltering, over to her bed. She lay down, serene. She was very beautiful, with the beauty that belongs to survivors. She closed her eyes as if to sleep. Her breathing grew calmer; the lips, so terrible a short while before, when they were an outlet for madness, were at last relaxed. Her breathing grew quieter still; became silence. A few seconds went by. My father bent over her, rather anxious at this unnatural stillness. But a clear voice came from her: "I'm furious with myself. That a man like you should be able to get me into this state! But I promise you it will never happen again."

Albert was put out by this cryptic pronouncement. What Anne Marie meant was that by touching her he had restored her to reason. It was a reaction of disgust, not of love—a feeling of shame, of weakness, of inferiority to her husband, which had brought her out of her annihilation.

She sat up and dabbed at her face with a handkerchief to dry it. She asked for a brush. She began letting down her hair, which spread all around her, brushing it for a long while, and then putting it up again. It took some time to arrange. That done, she rose, tidied herself, and went over and looked at herself in the mirror. At last she registered the existence of Albert wandering around her, playing the saint, fussing about but not knowing what to do except whine: "Oh, Anne Marie, you did frighten me! What a shock! Do you feel all right now? I nearly had a stroke—I don't feel at all well." At last, his hand on his chest as if to ease the pain, with a doleful expression and puffing like a grampus, he collapsed into a chair.

Anne Marie had finished repairing the ravages to her looks and dress—except for her eyes, which were still rather red. She turned to Albert, and instead of making fun of him and his sufferings, she smiled, and said with the impenetrable calm of deep waters:

"Forgive me, my dear. You are more Albert Bonnard than I thought."

"What do you mean?" said Albert, suddenly uneasy.

"You really are the consul. And it's for you to paddle your own canoe among all these Chinese affairs. They don't concern me. From now on I shan't trouble you with feeble-minded feminine advice.

"You know your advice is very valuable to me. I need you."

"You must find out how to behave for yourself. I really believe you make a great mistake in not having Dumont gotten rid of. But don't worry, I shan't refer to it again. I wash my hands of it all."

"I can tell you're angry."

"Not at all. But I want to say one thing. I'm sure that in letting that man live, you're heading for disaster. Well, I'll go along with you. Out of pride. Because I want to be above all possible misfortune. I have a strange character: I can't bear to lower myself, to show that I can be hurt, that I can suffer or be afraid or sweat with anguish."

"So I can count on you? You're with me?"

"Yes. Again, out of pride. Fate has linked me to you. I'm your wife. I know my duties, and I'll perform them. And no matter what horrible things may happen, I'll never reproach you. Never. At the most, if ever all three of us find ourselves about to be executed, I'll say goodbye with the words 'A sad specimen.'"

"That's not kind, Anne Marie. So you don't feel any affection for me ... you despise me."

"Of course I'm very fond of you, Albert," she said wearily. "There, does that satisfy you? All right, get dressed then. Let's join friend Dumont. He must be tired of waiting for us. We're nearly an hour late for lunch."

Albert obediently put on his trousers all by himself, without even summoning the head boy. He got all tangled up. I could see his hairy legs from my hiding place. He was pensive.

Anne Marie gave a little laugh.

"Dumont will never know how much he owes you. Even my being nice to him. For I'm going to do as you say in everything, Albert. At the beginning of our conversation you asked me to be pleasanter to him. Well, he's going to be astonished by the transformation. He'll get my best attention. You know I can be charming when I like. ..."

Albert gave a start.

"But don't exaggerate. Don't go from one extreme to the other. He may start thinking who knows what."

Anne Marie laughed outright.

"You're never satisfied, Albert. Don't you trust me? You're wrong. I said I'd help you all I can. Look, I'll

even tie your tie, since you can't manage it yourself. . . ."

This was a rare and precious scene—unique. For the
first time in my knowledge, Anne Marie laid hands on
Albert to take care of him, coddle him, spoil him. Her
long hands were white against the male flesh of his
neck. He was purring. Blissful, he put his lips to her
temple. Anne Marie, instead of turning away, instead
of registering an expression of rather disgusted surprise, offered her face. All that agony for this . . . But
suddenly, as if that was enough, she said, "That'll do,
Albert. Put on your jacket and let's make haste to go
and woo Dumont."

I didn't care for this intimacy. I didn't like my father to approach my mother; to me it seemed a sort
of stain. Anne Marie had long distilled to me her
feeling of disgust for Albert. I didn't hate him, but
already I despised him as somebody vulgar. So all this
made me feel ill, and I didn't want to see or know
any more. Anyway, it was high time I left my observation post if I didn't want to be discovered by my
parents. I went down the stairs, a sturdy, silent, secretive child with a heavy heart. As I was walking across
the stones of the courtyard toward the dining room,
head down, deep in my thoughts, I knocked into something hot and flabby, hard and sticky—exactly like
the beast that devoured me at night in my nightmares.
I started away, but a hand grabbed me, a laugh engulfed me, I was confronted with the fat and mirthful
countenance of Dumont, all red from his shave and
apoplectic with health. He got hold of me and lifted
me up level with his face, his little hard sparkling
eyes. I was his prisoner. His fingers were digging into
my ribs, and the fleshy mouth asked me, with a good
humor that held a threat:

"Well, things got hot, did they?"

I looked at him as if I didn't understand.

"Come off it, you little rascal—it won't work with me. Don't you try it. You heard everything. You must have gotten a good earful! They sure went after each other!"

"Put me down, please. You're hurting me."

"You scamp. Suppose I told your father and mother you're a little spy, always watching them from behind doors. You'd get a jolly good licking! And they'd probably send you to boarding school in France, to try to improve your ways. That would put an end to your princely life here."

"You won't, will you, Monsieur Dumont?"

"No. But in return you'll have to tell me all you heard. If you're nice to me I'll give you whatever you want. Old Dumont's not a bad old chap, you know. And he likes intelligent children."

"I'd be glad to tell you all I know, Monsieur. But I don't know anything. I'm not old enough."

He looked at me with a vexed expression, his jowls puffed out and his eyes reddening. But he managed to keep his joviality.

"Try. Your mother shouted a lot. Why?"

"I don't know, Monsieur Dumont."

"You're lying. At least tell me if they mentioned me?"

"I don't think so, Monsieur Dumont."

He was furious. The veins stood out red on his face. I felt a pain. Dumont was yanking the lobe of my ear.

"Scamp! Don't think you'll get away with it. With me, everything has to be paid for."

At last he let me slither down his belly to the ground. When I'd gotten far enough away, I looked him straight in the eye and said:

"Monsieur Dumont, if you tell my parents I listened

to them, I'll tell them you hit me to make me tell what they said."

I hadn't been careful enough. Dumont already towered over me, a wicked look on his face. His paunch butted against me, and he lifted his hand as if to box my ears. But the gesture turned to a caress. He patted my forehead. For the consul and his wife had appeared at the top of the stairs and were coming down into the courtyard.

They looked like a regular married couple. No trace of their quarrel. Happy faces. Albert was dressed up, but not too formally, given the time of day and the fact that the laws of hospitality required an easy simplicity. He smelled of eau de Cologne, his part was straight, his tie tied to perfection. And above all, the smile of welcome was on his face—not all of it, half of it, as propriety dictated. Anne Marie, wearing a big piece of jade around her neck, was the lady— but no longer the one who held her head high and looked at Dumont as if he were invisible, a nothing, a void. Now her look granted him flesh and substance, granted him life. Her head just bent forward, still very slightly distant, she, too, smiled at Dumont.

He was quite disconcerted. In a moment, the bully who had been threatening me became the good-natured fat man overflowing with urbanity toward my parents and affection toward me. But he stood with round eyes, gazing at the transformed Anne Marie without knowing what to make of it.

"Please forgive us for being late," said Albert in his company voice. "We waited because we thought you would need to rest after your long journey."

"Dumont's always in top form, as you know, Monsieur le Consul," he rumbled.

Anne Marie, still with her secret smile, conquered,

conquering, a queen, slowly held her hand out to Dumont, as if, with majestic generosity, she were offering him the consecrated host. To take it he writhed, bent his belly, creased his fat. At last he managed to kiss her fingers, to lay his thick lips devoutly on them. She showed no repugnance, she looked on him benevolently, she even made it easy for him. When at last he'd straightened up again, she smothered him in waves of sweetness.

"I hope you have a pleasant stay in Chengtu, Monsieur Dumont. And as the Chinese say, may the thousand prosperities be with you."

Dumont preened himself.

"Madame, with your protection, everything will be perfect. You can count on the consul and me to get things moving. I promise you his railroad is as good as built."

"I know very little about my husband's affairs, Monsieur Dumont. But I think he'll be pleased. Thank you."

"It's I who thank you, Madame."

Dumont was jubilant, fatly solemn, delighted. But he was uneasy, too, wondering if it was the real thing. He tried to think of a gesture to crown this admirable scene of friendship and reconciliation. He started patting my head again, saying to Anne Marie in complimentary tones:

"You have a charming little boy. Very like you."

My father intervened.

"He's rather reserved. I'm worried about it."

Anne Marie drew me to her side, as if she sensed I needed consolation. Did she also realize I'd rather have her kill Dumont than submit to him?

They all went in to lunch. I went and found Li. Then I fetched my horse, was joined by my mafu,

who was waiting outside, and plunged with him into
Chengtu, as into oblivion.

On a bare, flat, desolate plain a few miles from
Chengtu stood a porcelain tower. It was thin and
graceful, a model of balance. Its only decorations were
a series of roofs one above the other, very small, like
little fins. Inside there was a winding staircase and
ten shelves covered with white bundles. They were
newborn infants. Pious families who didn't want to
abandon their offspring in the street came and left
them here, paying an attendant a few coins. The tower
was the deadhouse for useless infants. The sun beat
down and hundreds of black birds came to perform
the funeral toilet. The smell was awful. It was a charitable institution.

That tower really existed. I knew it as a child, and
I knew what it was for. It haunted my dreams. In my
sleep I would struggle vainly, unable to breathe, some
great bird of prey wheeling above me, ready to peck
out my eyes. I used to wake up shrieking.

Recent events at the consulate had weighed me
down, child that I was, as much as the monsoon, which
was about to break. Every night the porcelain tower
rose up in my dreams. I remember how one evening,
in the midst of my terror, I was wakened by a flash of
lightning. The sky had split open. A new monsoon
season had begun. The clouds over the city were like
bladders bursting and spewing forth their rain.

For weeks the heat had been terrible. It was the end
of the dry season, and the monsoon was gathering
without actually unleashing itself. The sky was an
immense gray ceiling of hanging clouds, with harbin-
gers of thunder and lightning; but the clouds still
hung. On the earth below, all was hot steam and

humidity, but no water. It was a world at once damp and dried up. Stifling. Human beings and plants alike were waiting for the deluge that did not come. Everything was at the end of its tether.

But that night there were zigzags of flame, cataracts, a quake that seemed like the end of the world. At the same time came liberation, the end of oppression. The disaster was also a blessing that would make life possible again, make the crops grow, save the people, even if whole populations perished in the floods and epidemics that accompanied the madness of the waters. It was as if, in China, everything good was accompanied by suffering.

From the consulate windows you could see Chengtu in the darkness, its thousands of higgledy-piggledy roofs; hear the sound of houses crumbling under the assault of lightning and gusts of wind. It was a rumbling cacophony of strange and terrifying noises from the bowels of nature. Huge claps of thunder, accompanied by dazzling streaks across the sky, made the consulate tremble. Albert Bonnard got up, complaining, "Impossible to get any sleep in this pandemonium."

It was then that I attained the age of reason. I thought of the privileged life I'd led, like some young nobleman. But without realizing it, throughout my childhood I was being educated in cruelty. I had been a voyeur of atrocity, but until then it had all gone pleasantly, slowly, as if sadism, indifference, and horror were natural and the very conditions of a life worth living. It had all taken place in the midst of Chinese gaiety, the formidable ability to enjoy oneself while others were dying. My real teachers were my beloved Li and the mafu who was a leper.

But during the last days, which I have just described, I had discovered sorrow. It seemed to me the consulate had been touched by corruption. Everything seemed horrible to me—the war lords, Dumont, China itself. Above all, for the first time in my life I had judged my parents. I had seen the foolish vanity of my father, my mother's mad pride. Both were like fetuses doomed to be destroyed. And I was shattered because I guessed that I was like them: I was not a real Chinese, but a moral bastard, a mongrel child who like them would be seduced by dangerous desires—greeds that included railroads, shady deals, and probably, in the end, disaster.